Praise for RALPH ELLISON's

Juneteenth

"*Juneteenth* is written with unmistakable Ellisonian zest, depth, and elegance. . . . The work holds together as a complete, aesthetically satisfying, and at times thrilling whole." —*The Atlantic Monthly*

"Ralph Ellison's generosity, humor and nimble language are, of course, on display in *Juneteenth*, but it is his vigorous intellect that rules the novel. A majestic narrative concept." —Toni Morrison

"[F]irst-rate Ellison, exploring race and America in dreamlike prose." —*The Wall Street Journal*

"A stunning achievement. . . . *Juneteenth* is a tour de force of un-tutored eloquence. Ellison sought no less than to create a Book of Blackness, a literary composition of the tradition at its most sublime and fundamental." —Henry Louis Gates, Jr., *Time*

"Ellison's writerly skills are awesome. He enables us to relive the as-tonishment of the first generation to experience the movies and re-animates the commonplace pleasures of a type of boyhood that may never come again. He recaptures the heated fervor of the revival tent so vividly that you feel yourself begin to sweat."

—*Houston Chronicle*

"Impressionistic, jazzy, and Faulknerian, assembled from stories in-side of stories, dreams, flights of memory, and bolts of rhetoric."

—*New York*

"For anyone who cares about American literature and the seemingly insolvable pain of race, *Juneteenth* is a must-read." —*USA Today*

"*Juneteenth* may be one of the most important books of the year, if not the decade. . . . An eloquent, intelligent, and worthwhile statement on race relations in the country during the twentieth century."
—*The Tampa Tribune-Times*

"Ellison stands as one of the exemplary writers of the century. . . . This painstakingly assembled edition keeps his genius visible."
—*Fort Worth Star-Telegram*

"Demanding, dense, and undeniably brilliant."
—*Rocky Mountain News*

"On display throughout the novel are Ellison's wit, his marvelous ear for language, and his sublime intellectual approach to the visceral issues eating at America's heart." —*The Star-Ledger*

"The fun of reading this book—and there is some fun on every page—comes from Ellison's familiarity with African-American folklore and literature." —*San Jose Mercury News*

"Ellison's signature preoccupations with language and the racial markings of American Identity stream through a beautifully written tale." —*The San Diego Union-Tribune*

"Ellison, both as a prose writer and literary thinker, was and is an American master." —*The Denver Post*

"Ellison's long-delayed second novel is a fitting testament to his talent." —*The Dallas Morning News*

"Thanks to the astute and dedicated editing of John Callahan, we have a book that can fairly be called Ralph Ellison's second masterpiece. *Juneteenth* is, quite simply, a great American novel."
—*The Oregonian*

RALPH ELLISON
Juneteenth

Ralph Ellison was born in Oklahoma City in 1914. He is the author of the novel *Invisible Man* (1952), winner of the National Book Award and one of the most important and influential American novels of the twentieth century, as well as numerous essays and short stories. He died in New York City in 1994.

John F. Callahan is Morgan S. Odell Professor of Humanities at Lewis and Clark College in Portland, Oregon. He is the editor of *Trading Twelves: The Selected Letters of Ralph Ellison and Albert Murray* and the Modern Library edition of *The Collected Essays of Ralph Ellison* and is literary executor of Ralph Ellison's estate.

Charles Johnson is the S. Wilson and Grace M. Pollock Emeritus Professor of English at the University of Washington. A MacArthur fellow, he is the author of twenty-five books, among them the novel *Middle Passage*, which received the 1990 National Book Award for fiction.

INTERNATIONAL

Juneteenth

A Novel

RALPH ELLISON

EDITED BY JOHN F. CALLAHAN

PREFACE BY CHARLES JOHNSON

VINTAGE INTERNATIONAL

Vintage Books

A Division of Penguin Random House LLC

New York

FIRST VINTAGE INTERNATIONAL EDITION, MAY 2021

Portions of *Juneteenth* were previously published in different form in *The New Yorker*, *The Noble Savage*, and *The Quarterly Review of Literature*.

Grateful acknowledgment is made to the following for permission to reprint previously published material:
Houghton Mifflin Harcourt Publishing Company and Faber and Faber Limited: Excerpt from "Little Gidding" from *Four Quartets* by T. S. Eliot. Copyright © 1942 by T. S. Eliot, renewed 1970 by Esme Valerie Eliot. Reprinted by permission of Houghton Mifflin Harcourt Publishing Company. All rights reserved. Rights throughout the world excluding the United States are controlled by Faber and Faber Limited. Reprinted by permission of Harcourt Brace & Company and Faber and Faber Limited.
Liveright Publishing Corporation: "The Hurricane" from *The Complete Poems of Hart Crane* by Hart Crane, edited by Marc Simon. Copyright © 1933, 1958, 1966 by Liveright Publishing Corporation. Copyright © 1986 by Marc Simon. Used by permission of Liveright Publishing Corporation.

The Library of Congress has cataloged the Random House edition as follows:
Names: Ellison, Ralph. Callahan, John F.
Title: Juneteenth : a novel / Ralph Ellison ; edited by John F. Callahan.
Description: 1st ed. | New York : Random House, © 1999.
Identifiers: LCCN 98044868
Subjects: LCSH: African American clergy—Fiction. | Passing (Identity) —Fiction. | African Americans—Fiction. | Race relations—Fiction. | Legislators—Fiction. | Southern States—Fiction. | GSAFD: Historical fiction.
Classification: LCC PS3555.L625 J86 1999 | DDC 813/.54—dc21
LC record available at https://lccn.loc.gov/98044868

Vintage International Trade Paperback ISBN: 978-0-593-31461-6
eBook ISBN: 978-0-307-79736-0

www.vintagebooks.com

Printed in the United States of America
10 9 8 7 6 5 4 3 2 1

To That Vanished Tribe into Which I Was Born:

The American Negroes

To Ida, the mother, who bore me,

And to Fanny, my wife, who bears with me—

And most graciously!

This is the use of memory:
For liberation—not less of love but expanding
Of love beyond desire, and so liberation
From the future as well as the past. Thus, love of a country
Begins as attachment to our own field of action
And comes to find that action of little importance
Though never indifferent. History may be servitude,
History may be freedom. See, now they vanish,
The faces and places, with the self which, as it could, loved them,
To become renewed, transfigured, in another pattern.

T. S. Eliot, "Little Gidding"

CONTENTS

PREFACE TO THE VINTAGE
INTERNATIONAL EDITION (2021)

"My God, you don't write out of your skin;
you write out of your imagination."

Ralph Ellison

On November 27, 1990, when my novel *Middle Passage* received the fiction prize at the fortieth anniversary of the National Book Awards, held in the Plaza Hotel in New York City, I used my time at the microphone to deliver a tribute to someone in the audience: Ralph Ellison. I was the first black man to receive that award in thirty-seven years. Ellison's wife, Fanny, nudged him to stand while I honored him, and he proudly did so. Afterward reporters were eager to ask him questions, and he said two things that I believe are of great importance then and now.

Just to me, he said, sotto voce, "I thought I had been forgotten."

That statement was astonishing. It said a great deal about the vagaries of literary fortunes, about the author of *Invisible Man* (as well as how he saw himself) and what had transpired in literary culture since 1953 when his first novel received the National Book Award. By any measure, that was a watershed moment in American literature. *Invisible Man* was shortlisted with Ernest Hemingway's classic novella *The*

Old Man and the Sea, which later that year received the Pulitzer Prize for Fiction. According to Arnold Rampersad's biography of Ellison, William Faulkner was in attendance and the judges were a roster of this country's distinguished literary scholars and critics: Saul Bellow, Martha Foley, Irving Howe, Howard Mumford Jones, and Alfred Kazin.

Although *Invisible Man* was not a bestselling novel at the time of its publication, its influence grew over the next decade as it ceased to be simply a novel and instead became an American cultural artifact. That status was cemented in the 1960s, when a panel of literary scholars selected *Invisible Man* as the best American novel published since World War II. But with fame there also came controversy, for the 1960s gave birth to the Black Arts Movement, the cultural wing of the Black Power movement. No doubt his magisterial novel inspired awe and gratitude, but it also inspired frustration, because it presented a challenge to many readers' simplistic formulas about race in America. In his 1952 review, writer John Oliver Killens said, "The Negro people need Ralph Ellison's *Invisible Man* like we need a hole in the head or a stab in the back. . . . It is a vicious distortion of Negro life." Equally critical was Amiri Baraka, who dismissed Ellison as a middle-class Negro for his insistence that mastery of literary craft must take priority over politics in a writer's apprenticeship. (The superb poet Robert Hayden and master painter Jacob Lawrence also suffered similar abuse.) For Ellison that apprenticeship included T. S. Eliot as well as Langston Hughes, Pound and Hemingway alongside Richard Wright, Gertrude Stein, and Dostoevsky together with the blues.

Today we see once more a debate over race and racism in America fought across the old battle lines, and we are challenged to reflect on the second illuminating statement Ellison made on that night in 1990, when answering a question from a reporter: "My

God," he said, "you don't write out of your skin; you write out of your imagination." Earlier in his writings, Ellison stated that "by a trick of fate (and our racial problems notwithstanding), the human imagination is integrative—and the same is true of the centrifugal force that inspirits the democratic process." This crucial insight positions Ellison within the intellectual tradition of integration, which aligns his thinking with that of the NAACP, W. E. B. Du Bois, Martin Luther King Jr., James Baldwin, the civil rights movement, and our first black president, Barack Obama. He understood the undeniable interpenetration of our lives—of all life—and how, to quote scholar Kwame Anthony Appiah in his book *In My Father's House*, "We are all already contaminated by each other."

In one of the delicious ironies of literary criticism, Larry Neal, one of the principle thinkers behind the Black Arts Movement (along with Baraka), first published an essay critical of *Invisible Man*. Later, in the interest of honesty, he rethought his position and published a second essay praising *Invisible Man* as a work that achieved all the goals of the Black Arts Movement. And indeed, *Invisible Man* not only achieved the goal of a robust celebration of black culture; it gracefully blended many literary genres and traditions—from Mark Twain to William Faulkner, from the slave narrative to the surrealistic Kafkaesque parable, from black folklore to Freud—and by doing so forced us to experience in the novel's very techniques and inventiveness the spirit of democracy, diversity, and literary inclusion.

As if this were not enough, Ellison gave our age a new metaphor for social alienation. His definition of *invisibility* is so common now, so much a part of the culture and language—like a coin handled by millions—that it is automatically invoked when we talk about the situation of black Americans and *any* social group we willingly refuse to see.

Can we say, then, that Ralph Ellison was both a black writer and a quintessentially American one? And that there is no contradiction in that? I believe we can. In yet another powerful statement, he sought to remind us that, "The thing that Americans have to learn over and over again is that they are individuals and have the responsibility of individual vision."

So despite his death on April 16, 1994, we are by no means finished with Ralph Ellison's literary legacy. Nor will he ever be forgotten for composing one of the greatest novels of the twentieth century. Like that first work, *Juneteenth* guarantees that we will be discussing his nonpareil achievements for as long as we care about literature that is multileveled, ambitious, challenging, and crafted in the spirit of Ellison's belief that "the understanding of art depends finally upon one's willingness to extend one's humanity."

We are indebted, of course, to John Callahan for conjuring this portion of Ellison's second, long-awaited novel from more than two thousand pages revised and rewritten over a period of forty-two years. Everywhere in *Juneteenth*, Ellison's decades-long distillation of craftsmanship and originality of thought are in evidence. His dedication for this ambitious work ("To That Vanished Tribe into Which I Was Born: The American Negroes") signals his project of honoring and exploring the lives of black Americans who, from the nation's founding to the 1950s, and despite the burden of racial oppression, embodied our republic's loftiest ideals.

In *Juneteenth*, that Vanished Tribe is represented by the Reverend Alonzo Hickman, who raises a (probably) white boy named Bliss in the hope that he will recognize the complexity of the American experience and "speak for our condition from inside the only acceptable mask. That he would embody our spirit in the councils of our enemies." But Bliss, a shapeshifter much like the mysterious character Rinehart in *Invisible Man*, turns his back on the black culture that nurtured him, transforming first into a filmmaker, then into a race-baiting senator named Adam Sunraider ("the most vehement enemy of their people in either house of Congress") who is shot by a black assassin (who in an all-too-American twist of fate, turns out to be his son) on the Senate floor.

Unraveling the mystery of Bliss's odyssey from child preacher to con man to racist politician, and of his own failure, becomes Rev. Hickman's obsession as he keeps a vigil by the mortally wounded Sunraider's deathbed. Unlike *Invisible Man*, that barn-burning bildungsroman that explodes forward from one chapter to the next, *Juneteenth* spirals downward ever deeper through layers of memory, history, philosophical reflection, and culture—and in doing so delivers the most dazzling, breathtakingly seductive writing we have witnessed in more than half a century.

Here, in dozens of fully imagined, deeply felt passages refined and polished to the level of poetry, readers will find an exuberant, democratic fusion of fictional styles and American voices and vernaculars; symphonically rendered scenes of Southern revivals that celebrate "Juneteenth," the day (June 19, 1865) that Union troops entered Texas; an astonishingly beautiful tribute to Abraham Lincoln offered with the acuity that only a member of the Vanished Tribe could write, because it reveals our fourteenth president to be "one of us, not only because he freed us to the extent that he could, but because he freed himself of that awful inherited pride they deny to us"; and Ellison's characteristic humor and irony, his delicious wordplay and punning as he broods deeply on philosophical questions such as reality vs. illusion, blindness vs. true seeing, and the fact that our lives are *already* more integrated than we usually dare to acknowledge ("There's always the mystery," he writes, "of the one in the many and the many in the one, the you in them and the them in you—ha!").

In a word, *Juneteenth* is the long-awaited work we need now to bolster our discourse on race, just as we need the singular voice and deeply humanistic vision of Ralph Waldo Ellison to remind us, as he does in this capacious novel, that "man at his best, when he's set in all the muck and confusion of life and continues to struggle for his ideals, is near sublime."

Charles Johnson
February 2021

INTRODUCTION

In his later years, after hours, if he had put in a good day at his desk, Ralph Ellison was known to chuckle at the parallel between the "crazy country" he loved and contended with and what in 1969 he called his "novel-in-progress (*very* long in progress)." Ellison's projected second novel was a glint in his eye as early as June of 1951, when he wrote Albert Murray that he was "trying to get going on my next book before this one [*Invisible Man*] is finished . . ." In April 1953 he told Murray of his "plan to scout the Southwest. I've got to get real mad again, and talk with the old folks a bit. I've got *one* Okla. book in me I do believe." By 1954 Ellison had begun to put pen to paper, and in April of 1955 he sent Murray a "working draft" of an episode. From then on, even as he wrote numerous essays, taught at half a dozen colleges, held the Albert Schweitzer Professorship in the Humanities at New York University, and, in the name of citizenship, did more than his duty on national boards and commissions, the second novel remained Ellison's hound of heaven (and hell) pursuing him "down the arches of the years," pursuing him "down the labyrinthine ways / Of [his] own mind" until the end of his life in 1994.

From 1955 to 1957 Ellison was at work on the second novel as a fellow at the American Academy in Rome. "It was in Rome during 1956," he told John Hersey, that he "conceived the basic situation, which had to do with a political assassination." Not too long afterward, in June of 1959, Ellison wrote Murray that "Bellow [with whom Ellison was sharing a house in Tivoli, New York, close to Bard College, where both men taught] has read book two and is to publish about fifty pages in a new mag which he is editing—THE NOBLE SAVAGE—of all things." Telling David Remnick of *The New Yorker* in 1994 that Ellison had "let me read a considerable portion of it—a couple of hundred pages, at least," Bellow remembered vividly that "all of it was marvelous stuff, easily on a level with *Invisible Man*." In a later reminiscence Bellow wrote, "In what he did, Ralph had no rivals. What he did no one else could do—a glorious piece of good fortune for a writer."

During the next five or six years Ellison published three more excerpts in literary quarterlies. Meanwhile, the contract for the book, dated August 17, 1965, stipulated delivery on September 1, 1967. In his own mind Ellison was moving toward completion in the summer and fall of 1967 as he revised the novel at his summer home outside Plainfield, a village in the Berkshires. Then, in the late afternoon of November 29, 1967, Ellison and his wife, Fanny, returned from shopping to find the house in flames. With regret in her voice, Mrs. Ellison recalled being restrained from approaching the burning house by volunteer firemen who had arrived too late. "I wish I'd been able to break the window and pull out Ralph's manuscript," she told me years later. "I knew right where it was."

The Plainfield fire has taken on the proportions of myth to such an extent that it is useful to revisit what Ellison had to say about it over the years. Ten days after the event, he wrote Charles Valentine that "the loss was particularly severe for me, as a section of my work-in-progress was destroyed with it." Later in the same letter Ellison outlined the task he saw before him: "Fortunately, much of my summer's work on the new novel is still in my mind and if my imagination can feed it I'll be all right, but I must work quickly." According to James Alan McPherson, Ellison told him in 1969 that the fire "destroyed a year's worth of revisions," but that "he is presently in the process of revising it again." In 1980 Ellison told a reporter from the *Daily Hampshire Gazette,* "I guess I've been able to put most of it back together." To David Remnick, just before his eightieth birthday in 1994, Ellison made perhaps his fullest public comment on the fire: "There was, of course, a traumatic event involved with the book. We lost a summer house and, with it, a good part of the novel. It wasn't the entire manuscript, but it was over three hundred and sixty pages. There was no copy."

By the time of McPherson's account, done with Ellison's blessing and collaboration in 1970, the second novel had begun to loom larger than a novel or a work-in-progress. "He has enough typed manuscripts to publish three novels," McPherson wrote, "but is worried over how the work will hold up as a total structure. He does not want to publish three separate books, but then he does not want to compromise on anything essential. 'If I find that it is better to make it a three-section book, to issue it in three volumes, I would do that as long as I thought that each volume had a compelling interest in itself,' " Ellison told McPherson. On and off for the rest of his life, Ellison continued to work on his mythic saga of race and identity, language and kinship in the American experience. Sometimes revising, sometimes reconceiving, sometimes writing entirely new passages into an oft-reworked scene, he accumulated some two thousand pages of typescripts and printouts by the time of his death. His last published excerpt from the novel, an offshoot from the main text titled "Backwacking: A Plea to the Senator," appeared in 1977. Although he continued to write and revise until a fatal illness struck him at the end of March 1994, just four weeks after his eightieth birthday, Ralph Ellison did not live to finish his forty-year work-in-progress.

Ellison left no instructions about his work except the wish, expressed to Mrs. Ellison and to me, that his books and papers be housed at the national library, the Library of Congress. A few days after his death, Mrs. Ellison walked me into his study, a room adjoining the living room still wreathed in a slight haze of cigar and pipe smoke. As if to protest his absence, the teeming bookshelves had erupted in chaos over his desk, chair, computer table, and copying machine, finally covering the floor like a blizzard of ash. Anyone else might have given up, but Fanny Ellison persevered in her effort to do the right thing by what her husband had left behind. She whetted my appetite by showing me stacks of printouts, scraps of notes, jottings on old newspapers and magazine subscription cards, and several neat boxes of computer disks. At her direction I removed several thick black binders of typescript going back to the early 1970s from the first of two long, rectangular black steel filing cabinets next to his desk. The other cabinet, I was to discover, contained folder after folder of earlier drafts painstakingly labeled according to character or episode.

"Beginning, middle, and end," Mrs. Ellison mused. "Does it have a beginning, middle, and end?"

The question can't be put any better than that, I thought. Many times I followed the twists and turns of Ellison's plot, and his characters' movements through space and time; traced and retraced their steps as they moved from Washington, D.C., south to Georgia and

Alabama, southwest to Oklahoma, back again to the nation's capital, and reached back with them from the novel's present moment of the mid-fifties to spots of time in the twenties and thirties and even farther to the first decade of the new century when the Oklahoma Territory emerged as a state. And always, Mrs. Ellison's question pursued me and brought me back to the task at hand, for it was always clear that at the center of Ellison's saga was the story of Reverend Hickman and Senator Sunraider, from the Senator's birth as Bliss to his death. To use an architectural metaphor, this was the true center of Ellison's great, unfinished house of fiction. And although he did not complete the wings of the edifice, their absence does not significantly mar the organic unity of the book we do have, *Juneteenth*.

Of all that Ellison wrote on his saga of an unfinished novel, *Juneteenth* is the narrative that best stands alone as a single, self-contained volume. Like a great river, perhaps the Mississippi, for Ellison "the great highway around which the integration of values and styles was taking place," *Juneteenth* draws from many uniquely African American (and American) tributaries: sermons, folktales, the blues, the dozens, the swing and velocity of jazz. Its form borrows from the antiphonal call-and-response pattern of the black church and the riffs and bass lines of jazz. Through its pages flow the influences of literary antecedents and ancestors, among them Twain and Faulkner, who, like Ellison, were men of the territory. Above all, perhaps, in this work Ellison converses with Faulkner. *Juneteenth* realizes Ellison's dream, articulated in "Brave Words for a Startling Occasion," his acceptance speech when he received the National Book Award for *Invisible Man* in 1953, of putting into a novel "the rich babel of idiomatic expression around me, a language full of imagery and rhetorical canniness."

Perhaps picking up where he left off in *Invisible Man,* Ellison is deliberately, provocatively approximate about historical time in *Juneteenth*. In both novels his strategy is one of connotation and infiltration as he seeks to open up associations and create symbolic significance for events in the narrative. Even as his writerly time extended far beyond the fifties, Ellison continued to locate the story "circa 1955." From the "time present" of the immediate action, he said, "the story goes back into earlier experiences too, even to some of the childhood experiences of Hickman, who is an elderly man in time present." From beginning to end, *Juneteenth,* like *Invisible Man,* tests Ellison's conviction that time's burden—its blessing and curse—is "a matter of the past being active in the present—or of the characters becoming aware of the manner in which the past acts on their present lives."

In the wake of *Invisible Man,* Ellison also dreamed of a fiction whose theme was the indivisibility of American experience and the American language as tested by two equal protagonists. In *Juneteenth* the two principals are the Reverend Alonzo Hickman, jazzman turned black Baptist minister, and Senator Adam Sunraider, a self-named, race-baiting politician, formerly Bliss, in Ellison's words, "a little boy of indefinite race who looks white and who, through a series of circumstances, comes to be reared by the Negro minister." In different ways expressive of radically different values and purposes, each possesses an "intellectual depth," complexity and eloquence *visible* from the inside out, and, therefore, heard on the lower frequencies Ellison had identified with democratic equality in *Invisible Man.* With a level of fidelity that is stunning, Ellison conveys the intricate inner rhythms of consciousness felt by Hickman and Bliss, alone and in profound relation to each other. "Sometimes," he explained in an introductory note to "Night-Talk," an excerpt published in 1969, the two men "actually converse, sometimes the dialogue is illusory and occurs in the isolation of their individual minds, but through it all it is antiphonal in form and an anguished attempt to arrive at the true shape and substance of a sundered past and its meaning."

The relationship between Hickman and Bliss revolves around mysteries of kinship and race. As a boy seeking his lost mother and unknown patrimony, Bliss runs away from Hickman and his black Baptist congregation, later reinvents himself in the guise of moviemaker and flimflam man, and ends up a race-baiting senator from a New England state. After decades of separation during which he keeps track of Bliss through a Negro American network of "chauffeurs and pullman porters and waiters, anybody who traveled in their work," Hickman hears ominous tidings of danger. He arrives in Washington with members of his congregation to warn his prodigal son but is allowed nowhere near the Senator; the closest he and his followers get are seats in the Senate gallery for one of Senator Sunraider's speeches. There, suddenly, Hickman's worst fear comes true: a young black man rises up in the gallery and shoots the Senator. Reeling from the impact of several bullets, Senator Sunraider loses control. " 'Lord,' he heard," his standard idiom giving way to African American vernacular, " 'LAWD, WHY HAST THOU . . .' " To his astonishment, the Senator recognizes Hickman's voice responding from above him: *"For Thou hast forsaken . . . me."* At the hospital he calls for Hickman, and only Hickman, to be brought to his bedside.

Throughout the unexpectedly resumed relationship between the two men, in Ellison's words, "time, conflicts of value, the desire of one to remember nothing and the tendency of the other to remember too much, have rendered communication between them difficult." But as the narrative progresses, Hickman's will to remember and the Senator's will to forget engender paradoxical shared and solitary acts of imagination. Hickman's fatherly preacher's presence and the blues tones of his voice stir the embers of the dying Senator's soul. Ellison enlists the reader as witness to unspoken and spoken acts of memory that revive Bliss's childhood as the little boy who looks white, talks black, and is accepted and loved by Hickman and the others in his black Baptist congregation and community. In his delirium the Senator becomes Bliss once again and remembers Hickman initiating him, the precocious little boy, into a preacher's ritual of death and resurrection in his traveling ministry. Hickman, too, Ellison reminds us, is a trickster; in his calling as preacher he sometimes sees himself as "God's own straight man." A master of religious performance, he is willing to let congregations of believers and potential believers think that Bliss, a white-skinned young apprentice preacher, rises from the dead in a closed coffin covered in white satin outfitted with a concealed breathing tube.

Memories of childhood alternate with the Senator's feverish, impressionistic recollections of life after his flight from Hickman—from *bliss,* he puts it in one of his reveries, with a mix of irony and remorse. Raised as something of a confidence man in the service of the Lord by Hickman, years later he puts the tricks of the trade to good use in his travels through the small towns of the Southwest, hoodwinking people by posing as a professional filmmaker. In the present moment of silent recollection with Hickman at his bedside, the Senator relives a brief, intense, love affair twenty-five or thirty years past with a lovely black and white and red young woman in an Oklahoma town. Their passionate interlude has mysterious, fateful, doubly fatal consequences that Bliss is only partially aware of, Hickman tries to puzzle out, and Ellison coaxes the reader to piece together.

At the climax of their interior journey, Hickman compels Bliss to confront more fully and honestly than he desires the long-buried memory of the Juneteenth night that sent him wandering the ends of the earth like a biblical outcast. Under Hickman's prodding, he comes to realize, with a psychic pain as searing as the physical pain of his wounds, that he is tragically outcast from his true American self, which, whatever the unrevealed particulars of his genetic heritage, is "somehow black." In the end, as he sinks into delirium and the fever dream of approaching death, the Senator hallucinates a succession of frightening, unforgiving, and vengeful black American figures, and reaches feebly for the consolation now offered only by Hickman, the spokesman and elder of "that vanished tribe," the "American Negroes" to whom Ellison dedicates his book.

And Hickman, whom Ellison, as early as 1959, admitted was taking over the book, may be his finest creation. Hickman is a provincial, but he is anything but a hick. He clings, as the Senator does in occasional moments of lyrical lucidity that part the stormy waters of his cynicism, to that selfsame American faith—the democratic vernacular creed of experience and experiment, diversity and tolerance, compassion and resilience. It is a complex faith founded on the contradictory and compromised optimism of the founders, founded on the experimental attitude of Ellison's namesake, Ralph Waldo Emerson, found in the tragicomic lyricism of the blues, and in American geography founded on what Huck Finn called "the territory." Of "the territory" in *Huck Finn*, Ellison told Jervis Anderson two centuries after the Declaration of Independence: "Well, it is Oklahoma he is talking about. Oklahoma was a dream world. And after Reconstruction had been betrayed, people—black and white—came to the territory. Out of the territory came the state of Oklahoma." For Ellison the geography, history, and human diversity of Oklahoma embodied the actual and potential if oft-denied richness of the country. From tragedy—the Trail of Tears in the 1830s for the Five Indian Nations and the betrayal of Reconstruction for African Americans in the 1880s—followed migration to a territory open to complex possibilities. Ellison's story of the territory is the story of ancestors who populated the small black towns of Oklahoma like that in Toni Morrison's *Paradise*, as well as ancestors like his parents, whose presence in at once segregated and integrated places like Oklahoma City gave the culture an original flavor of speech and music before, during, and after World War I.

Confirming Ellison's passion for history, Saul Bellow recalled Ellison emerging from the ballroom where he wrote in their shared, shabby mansion to mix "very strong martinis" in the kitchen and talk. "Ralph was much better at history than I could ever be, but it gradually became apparent that he was not merely talking about history but telling the story of his life, and tying it into American history." Bellow conveys the feel of Ellison satisfying personal and artistic urges as he paced off the familiar ground of his life: "He took pleasure in returning again and again to the story of his development not in order to revise or to gild it but to recover old feelings and also to consider and reconsider how he might find a way to write his story."

So it is with Ellison's novelistic chronicle, *Juneteenth*. In telling Hickman's story of the early days in Oklahoma, and Bliss's (a.k.a. Mister Movie-Man) sojourn there in the twenties, Ellison, as Bellow sensed, is imagining and telling his own story. In their different ways, Hickman and the Senator recapitulate the world Ellison grew up in and heard the old folks in Oklahoma tell about. As he remembers his former life as the young prodigy of Reverend "Daddy" Hickman, Bliss, now Senator Sunraider but still Bliss on the "lower frequencies," comes to grips with the fact that he is "also somehow black," as Ellison believed was the case for every single "true American." With Hickman at his bedside, Sunraider silently confesses: "Ah yes, yes; I loved him. Everyone did, deep down. Like a great, kindly, daddy bear along the streets, my hand lost in his huge paw."

Here Ellison's recurring theme of "our orphan's loneliness" and "the evasion of identity" is felt and told on the deepest frequencies of consciousness—its autobiographical impulse transmuted into art by bold acts of imagination.

In conception and execution, *Juneteenth* is multifarious, multifaceted, multifocused, multivoiced, multitoned. After hearing Ellison read from the novel in the summer of 1969, James Allan McPherson brooded for many years about what he had heard and slowly came to the conclusion that "in his novel Ellison was trying to solve the central problem of American literature. He was trying to find forms invested with enough familiarity to reinvent a much broader and much more diverse world for those who take their provisional identities from groups." Finally, McPherson added what might serve as a benediction for *Juneteenth*: "I think he was trying to *Negro-Americanize* the novel form, at the same time he was attempting to move beyond it."

So he was. In a long letter written in August 1959 Ellison tells Albert Murray of finding "interesting things in Hemingway and Fitzgerald"; in their work and in Stephen Crane's and Henry James's he discovered the Civil War looming like some partially acknowledged, terrifying family secret. Then and for the rest of his working life, Ellison found his imaginative, critical deep well of inspiration and interpretation in the Civil War, the end of slavery, and the subsequent tortuous, zigzag path toward liberation: "When you start lifting up that enormous stone, the Civil War, that's kept so much of the meaning of life in the North hidden, you begin to see that Mose is in the center of a junk pile as well as in the center of the cotton boll. All the boys who try to escape this are simply running from the problem of value—Which is why those old Negroes whom I'm trying to make Hickman represent are so confounding, they never left the old original briar patch. You can't understand Lincoln or Jefferson without confronting them." And in one of *Juneteenth*'s most moving and powerful scenes, the old minister, denied access to the Senator, leads his flock to the Lincoln Memorial for the purpose of moral and spiritual renewal. There, he strikes through the mask of Lincoln as national icon to the man and the president attempting to forge his own moral union as well as the nation's. In Hickman's vision Lincoln waged a civil war fought in the provinces of his mind and imagination as well as on what F. Scott Fitzgerald called "the dark fields of the republic"; his humanity lay in his flaws as well as his virtues.

" 'Ain't that him, Revern? Ain't that Father Abraham?' " one of the sisters asks from the steps of the monument, and "too full to speak," Hickman answers in a reverie that owes a double tithe—to James Joyce and to the sermons of the black church. *Yes,* he repeats over and over to himself as he imagines Lincoln just "resting awhile before pulling yourself together again to go and try to bind up all these wounds that have festered and run and stunk in this land ever since they turned you back into stone." Hickman's reverie occurs within a reverie, for he is actually at the bedside of the sleeping Senator, startled into renewed awareness of the dying man's fall from grace. In a single thought the old minister's identities as preacher, historian, citizen, and father become one: "*And to think,* Hickman thought, stirring suddenly in his chair. *We had hoped to raise ourselves that kind of man . . .*" Hickman's remembrance is his enactment of lines from T. S. Eliot that Ellison chose as epigraph:

> *This is the use of memory:*
> *For liberation—not less of love but expanding*
> *Of love beyond desire, and so liberation*
> *From the future as well as the past. . . .*

On many levels *Juneteenth* is a narrative of liberation, literally a celebration of June 19, 1865, the day two and a half years after the Emancipation Proclamation was decreed when Union troops landed in Galveston, Texas, and their commanding officer told the weeping, cheering slaves that they were free. The delay, of course, is symbolic acknowledgment that liberation is the never-ending task of self, group, and nation and that, to endure, liberation must be self-achieved and self-achieving. In his narrative Ellison, who took part in more than one "Juneteenth ramble" as a boy in Oklahoma, speaks of false as well as true liberation and of the courage required to tell the difference. Even in the face of deepest betrayal, Hickman keeps his word to stand by Bliss, although the little boy is now contained within the frame of a man whose public words and deeds repudiate Hickman's acts of kinship and fatherhood. Yet in the end perhaps Hickman's democratic faith is vindicated by the Senator's belated, never-to-be-consummated deathbed strivings toward the "way home"—the name Ellison gave in "Brave Words for a Startling Occasion" to "that condition of man's being at home in the world which is called love and which we term democracy." Dismissive at first of Juneteenth as "*the celebration of a gaudy illusion,*" the Senator realizes too late that his liberation is bound up with the Negro American communion expressed by and on Juneteenth Day. But, Ellison hints in his epigraph, it is not too late for those surviving "[t]o become renewed, transfigured, in another pattern," the pattern of art. Always in progress, Ellison's work may now find pause, not cessation but pause, in the gift of *Juneteenth* to his readers.

John F. Callahan
February 1999

POSTSCRIPT TO THE
INTRODUCTION (2021)

Brooding over what to say about this new edition, I remembered Albert Murray telling me something Ralph Ellison said one afternoon back in 1945, when the two men ran into each other in Harlem "on Seventh Avenue near 135th Street." Ellison reminded Murray "stories endure not only from generation to generation but also from age to age because literary truth amounts to prophecy." In the same conversation he was emphatic that "telling is not only a matter of retelling but also of foretelling." At the least foretelling is a riddle at the heart of *Juneteenth*'s provisional nature.

Certainly in *Invisible Man* telling, retelling, and foretelling play off one another. Invisible Man tells his story of invisibility through the prism of Jim Crow America; he retells time past from the 1920s to the early '50s, ending not long before the Supreme Court unanimously ruled segregation unconstitutional in *Brown v. Board of Education*, which was handed down in May 1954. In the epilogue of *Invisible Man*, Ellison retells the nation's founding, in particular the Declaration of Independence's embrace of "the principle" of equality alongside contradictory laws upholding the institution of slavery. That same epilogue foreshadows and foretells *Brown v. Board of Education*, as well as the civil rights movement, which advanced integration as the *actual* law of the land through nonviolent action.

Fifty years later, in *Juneteenth*, retelling leads to an astonishing act of foretelling in the last episode; in this case, the future arrives as an ominous, quasi-violent, guerilla action hallucinated in the delirious mind of the dying Senator Sunraider. Up to that point, call-and-response sequences between the two principal characters retell the past and drive the story forward in the present. Their exchanges reveal religious and paternal kinship in times past between the jazzman-turned-preacher Alonzo Hickman and Senator Adam Sunraider, the baby of "indeterminate race" whom Hickman midwives into the world and, after his white mother abandons him, names him Bliss and loves him like a son.

The catalyst for the novel's events occurs when a mysterious young man, Senator Sunraider's secret son Severen, white and "also somehow black," assassinates the Senator in a chaotic scene in the Senate ("circa 1955") before jumping to his death from the visitors' gallery. Immediately the grievously wounded Sunraider, against the wishes of his doctors, insists that Reverend Hickman be brought to his hospital room. Until the novel's last prophetic scene, the two men, Hickman and Bliss/Sunraider, take turns reimagining the events of the previous fifty years. Remote and urgent at the same time, their retelling becomes post-assassination communication and miscommunication tethered and untethered to reality.

Perhaps the best description of Ellison's complex telling and retelling is found in his note to "Night-Talk," an excerpt published in 1969 that comprises Chapter 13 of *Juneteenth*: the idea of the "sundered past." Ellison's "sundered past" phrase holds in relief the struggle by Reverend Hickman and Bliss/Sunraider to articulate the past they actually shared. The chaos of death and dying in the present vies complexly with the healing call-and-response through which Hickman and the man he trained as a boy preacher preach to the brothers and sisters of Hickman's beloved black congregation who raised Bliss as a person of faith and the *Word*.

Its telescoping of word and deed in African American history and culture makes Juneteenth the holiday the fulcrum of *Juneteenth* the novel. Ever since that day of celebration in Galveston, five months after the thirteenth amendment to the Constitution abolished slavery and two months after the unconditional surrender of the Confederate States of America at Appomattox, when former slaves in Galveston learned the news that they were free, the word *Juneteenth* has glowed with wonder.

With a contagious joy, from the crucible of slavery suffered and survived by individuals who had become (and who remain) a people, African Americans made up a vernacular word of elision. And Juneteenth quickly became an emblem of the past, present, and future destiny of that chosen people.

Fittingly, while Hickman and Bliss/Sunraider are alone in the hospital room, Juneteenth pivots them to the secrets and memories of their past. Hickman recalls preaching on Juneteenth night under a huge tent in Georgia a decade or two into the twentieth century. Wracked by pain and haunted by flickers of self-knowledge, Bliss, now the self-created, race-baiting Senator Sunraider, goes blank at Hickman's first mention of Juneteenth.

"I had forgotten the word," he replies. When memories do stir, he mocks Juneteenth as the "*celebration of a gaudy illusion*" and resists remembering: "No, the wounded man thought, Oh no! Get back to that; back to a bunch of old-fashioned Negroes celebrating an illusion of emancipation, and getting it mixed up with the Resurrection, minstrel shows and vaudeville routines." But soon, embraced by Hickman's consoling voice and presence, Sunraider falls under the old spell. He once more becomes Bliss, who was beloved. His heart sees and feels the prodigious, patriarchal life force of the man he loved as a boy. He remembers Hickman "carrying me on his shoulder so that I could touch the leaves of the trees as we passed. The true father, but black, black . . . Must I go back to the beginning when only he knows the start? . . ."

Despite longing to know "the beginning"—the circumstances of his birth, the actual identity of his parents, how and why he became beloved to Hickman—Bliss/Sunraider suppresses the quest. "*Not back to that me, not to that six–seven-year-old ventriloquist's dummy dressed in a white evening suit.*" Yet in his depths, Bliss/Sunraider enters Hickman's force field of magnetism. Before he knows it, he is helping the old preacher and father retell the Juneteenth sermon on the fatal night that would change both their lives for good.

Soon the Senator *is* Bliss responding fiercely to Reverend Hickman's call:

What was it like then, Rev. Bliss? You read the scriptures, so tell us. Give us a word.
WE WERE LIKE THE VALLEY OF DRY BONES!

Bliss's words echo the Book of Ezekiel's intimation of the Juneteenth themes of death and resurrection, slavery and liberation about to be preached by Hickman in necessary collaboration with his orphan son, Bliss/Sunraider.

Over and over he calls out—"Except what, Rev. Hickman?"—while Hickman tells him how the people are like the "dry bones" in Ezekiel's dream. At first they were dead. Dead!

The words rise and fall while Bliss and Hickman act out inter-changeably the call-and-response pattern of the black church.

> ". . . Except what, Rev. Hickman?"
>
> "Except for one nerve left from our ear . . ."
>
> "Listen to him!"
>
> "And one nerve in the souls of our feet . . ."
>
> ". . . Just watch me point it out, brothers and sisters . . ."
>
> "Amen, Bliss, you point it out . . . and one nerve left from the throat . . ."
>
> ". . . From our throat—right *here*!" . . .
>
> ". . . And another nerve left from our heart . . ."
>
> ". . . Yes, from our heart . . ."

Reverend Hickman approaches the culmination, crying out that "in the midst of all our death and buriedness, the voice of God spoke down the Word." From his hospital bed, as the boy had from his cof-fin, the man answers in the voice of God: ". . . Crying Do! I said, Do! Crying Doooo—these dry bones live?"

The people hang on every word, and as they do Hickman reveals that from slavery's suffering and injustice—and, yes, love—African Americans discovered "a secret" and "a new rhythm . . ." And Bliss affirms with his all-important call: "So tell us about this rhythm, Rev-erend Hickman."

"But we had the Word," Hickman replies, tying rhythm to "our kind of time." Unlike the enslavers' time, he explains, for the enslav-ers rode a "merry-go-round that they couldn't control" while slaves "learned to beat time from the seasons." The slave owners' sense of time is by rote, according to contraptions like the mechanical merry-go-round. For the slaves, temporality belongs to nature, to the rhythm and beat of the sun, the glow and dazzle of the moon, the fish-giving sea, and the rich black earth of seed and sustenance: belongs to the wondrous cycle of life and death and life again.

As he wraps up, Reverend Hickman spirals his story of time, rhythm, and the Word from the end of slavery through decades that celebrated the partial liberation captured in that single vernacular word created by the former slaves. From there he swings to the continuing present he shared with Bliss on the Juneteenth night retold from thirty-five or forty years ago. All this time the old preacher locates Juneteenth in the immediate present that whirls by while he speaks intimately to Senator Sunraider, who nears death beside him in the Washington hospital room.

In "our kind of time," he avows, each Juneteenth is alike and different in temporal distinctness. And Hickman's Word to Bliss, the grown man in that immediate moment "circa 1955," is that African American freedom remains part truth, part illusion. Hickman does not mince words or the Word: "There's been a heap of Juneteenths before this one and I tell you there'll be a heap more before we're truly free! Yes! But keep to the rhythm, just . . . keep to the way." He hopes his words will ease the orphan's loneliness and propel his heart toward personal liberation, while inspiring the Senator's public self to turn into "that kind of man" Hickman and his beloved congregation "had hoped to raise ourselves"—the old Abe Lincoln whom Hickman's "slavery-born granddaddy" told him about when he was a child.

Hickman's final words are his revelation. "I tell you," he prophesies, "time shall swing and spiral back around. . . ." He yearns to instill moral intent in the Senator's heart and actual transformation in individual lives and the life of the nation in the future. But tragically the Senator's response is one of swift, utter negation. He does not speak a word to Reverend Hickman. Instead he keeps a single silent thought trapped in the solitary confinement of his mind.

"*No*, the Senator thought, *no more of it! NO!*"

After deep silence, Hickman, with no idea of the sulfur burning through Sunraider's heart, eases into retelling how Juneteenth was "a great occasion" full of communion for those present, including Bliss. On display is a miniature of the "sundered past" Bliss/Sunraider chooses to keep veiled instead of seeking to overcome. Yes, there are moments of epiphany for Sunraider—such as his arresting memory of how long *after* seducing Lavatrice, the lovable and loving mixed-race American woman he meets while movie-making in Oklahoma, he remembers achingly that he loved her. And still has a melancholy memory of "how the likes of me could say, I love, I love . . . And having loved moved on." In a similar reverie about Hickman he wishes he could "have accepted you as the dark daddy of flesh and Word—Hickman? Hickman, you after all." But at the same time, as the Senator, Sunraider could fume about love's inadequacy: "HOW THE HELL DO YOU GET LOVE INTO POLITICS OR COMPASSION INTO HISTORY?"

Juneteenth has passage after passage of surpassing beauty and power, yet such moments of radiance and eloquence pass quickly. Time does not bring the reawakening Hickman prays will come to pass in Bliss/Sunraider's heart. When Senator Sunraider becomes conscious of what is happening, he is seized with the bitter gall of his orphan's loneliness and self-loathing. As *Juneteenth*'s last pages of the Senator's delirious, prophetic hallucinations reveal, in his dying moments his dream is a nightmare far from Reverend Hickman's dream that he develop into a man who is kin to the tragic Abraham Lincoln, who confronted and transcended his flaws, and in Hickman's view, "pointed the way for all of us who would be free—yes!"

A terrifying reversal is hidden in plain sight in these last pages of *Juneteenth*. Though farfetched, the hallucinatory details Senator Sunraider invents in a state of dying delirium belong to the extravagant junkyard of his mind. And their context foretells violent change in America—prophecy reversing Invisible Man's sense that gradual, peaceful change is coming. The indefinite "they" hiding in his mind are "moving out into the open and things are beginning to heave and the backwash is beginning." Their action fast-forwards to retell the past, tell the present, and foretell a future all the more real for being farfetched.

Sunraider riffs fabulously on American history: "Nine owls [the Supreme Court] have squawked out the rules [*Brown v. Board of Education* and other nation-changing decisions]." And Sunraider's own delirious fearful mind imagines (circa 1955) how things will play out in the American experience in the years to come when "the hawks will talk, so soon they'll come marching out of the woodpile and the woodwork—sorehead, sorefoot, right up close, one-butt-shuffling into history but demanding praise and kind treatment for deeds undone, for lessons unlearned. But studying war once more . . ." These words of protest, chaos, and perhaps even civil war prophesy a reversal of Invisible Man's forecast of nonviolent protest imbued with humane aspiration toward a beloved American community.

Invisible Man came to foretelling after being "hurt to the point of abysmal pain, hurt to the point of invisibility." By contrast, Bliss/ Sunraider has fueled his "orphan's loneliness" with a persistent "evasion of identity." That he runs away from Reverend Hickman and his beloved black community just before adolescence involves his obsession with finding a white mother in place of the actual woman, whose identity Hickman does not disclose to him. He is elected to the Senate because he uses the wit, wiles, and moves of a black preacher, Daddy Hickman, to master white power in the secular temple of Jim Crow America.

It is not surprising that in his post-assassination delirium he foretells vengeance on his person by three black militants. Their weapon is "no ordinary automobile," "no Cadillac" but "a mammy-made, junk-yard construction" that the three black men proudly and ironically call "DE JOE CAH." The car violates "mechanical tolerances" and defies "the laws of physics, property rights, patents—everything—they've forced part after part to mesh and made it run!" As he watches the car go forward, backward, sideways, and up in the air, Sunraider calls it "a rolling time bomb launched in the streets." What better poetic justice could there be than that this "bastard creation of black bastards" selects as its first victim this apparent white senator whose moniker for the Cadillac was the "Coon Car"?

On his vernacular "lower frequency," Ellison turns three black men each speaking a different African American idiom into descendants from the mythical boatman of the River Lethe about to ferry the Senator across his American river of forgetfulness (perhaps the Potomac). On still another frequency of time past and time future as well as time present, Ellison explores the implications of technology in the hands and minds of violent African Americans who, unlike Hickman and his "vanished tribe," regard violence and chaos as allies of their cause. These militant captains in the party of nemesis are determined to avenge all the violence, injustice, and invisibility visited upon them by the Sunraiders of America in the near future and beyond.

Yet, in a wonderful final touch, Hickman reappears in the mind of the same character who has just foretold the coming death and destruction to be inflicted by chaos. As the "dark hand" of one of the men reached down from the Joe Car, Sunraider "seemed to hear the sound of Hickman's consoling voice, calling from somewhere above" in the continuing struggle for his soul and the soul of America in this ever-provisional novel.

John F. Callahan
February 2021

Juneteenth

CHAPTER 1

Two days before the shooting a chartered planeload of Southern Negroes swooped down upon the District of Columbia and attempted to see the Senator. They were all quite elderly: old ladies dressed in little white caps and white uniforms made of surplus nylon parachute material, and men dressed in neat but old-fashioned black suits, wearing wide-brimmed, deep-crowned panama hats which, in the Senator's walnut-paneled reception room now, they held with a grave ceremonial air. Solemn, uncommunicative and quietly insistent, they were led by a huge, distinguished-looking old fellow who on the day of the chaotic event was to prove himself, his age notwithstanding, an extraordinarily powerful man. Tall and broad and of an easy dignity, this was the Reverend A. Z. Hickman—better known, as one of the old ladies proudly informed the Senator's secretary, as "God's Trombone."

This, however, was about all they were willing to explain. Forty-four in number, the women with their fans and satchels and picnic baskets, and the men carrying new blue airline take-on bags, they listened intently while Reverend Hickman did their talking.

"Ma'am," Hickman said, his voice deep and resonant as he nodded toward the door of the Senator's private office, "you just tell the Senator that Hickman has arrived. When he hears who's out here he'll know that it's important and want to see us."

"But I've told you that the Senator isn't available," the secretary said. "Just what is your business? Who are you, anyway? Are you his constituents?"

"Constituents?" Suddenly the old man smiled. "No, miss," he said, "the Senator doesn't even have anybody like us in *his* state. We're from down where we're among the counted but not among the heard."

"Then why are you coming here?" she said. "What is your business?"

"He'll tell you, ma'am," Hickman said. "He'll know who we are; all you have to do is tell him that we have arrived. . . ."

The secretary, a young Mississippian, sighed. Obviously these were Southern Negroes of a type she had known all her life—and old ones; yet instead of being already in herdlike movement toward the door they were calmly waiting, as though she hadn't said a word. And now she had a suspicion that, for all their staring eyes, she actually didn't exist for them. They just stood there, now looking oddly like a delegation of Asians who had lost their interpreter along the way, and were trying to tell her something which she had no interest in hearing, through this old man who himself did not know the language. Suddenly they no longer seemed familiar, and a feeling of dreamlike incongruity came over her. They were so many that she could no longer see the large abstract paintings hung along the paneled wall, nor the framed facsimiles of State Documents which hung above a bust of Vice-President Calhoun. Some of the old women were calmly plying their palm-leaf fans, as though in serene defiance of the droning air conditioner. Yet she could see no trace of impertinence in their eyes, nor any of the anger which the Senator usually aroused in members of their group. Instead, they seemed resigned, like people embarked upon a difficult journey who were already far beyond the point of no return. Her uneasiness grew; then she blotted out the others by focusing her eyes narrowly upon their leader. And when she spoke again her voice took on a nervous edge.

"I've told you that the Senator isn't here," she said, "and you must realize that he is a busy man who can only see people by appointment. . . ."

"We know, ma'am," Hickman said, "but . . ."

"You don't just walk in here and expect to see him on a minute's notice."

"We understand that, ma'am," Hickman said, looking mildly into her eyes, his close-cut white head tilted to one side, "but this is something that developed of a sudden. Couldn't you reach him by long distance? We'd pay the charges. And I don't even have to talk, miss; you can do the talking. All you have to say is that we have arrived."

"I'm afraid this is impossible," she said.

The very evenness of the old man's voice made her feel uncomfortably young, and now, deciding that she had exhausted all the tried-and-true techniques her region had worked out (short of violence) for getting quickly rid of Negroes, the secretary lost her patience and telephoned for a guard.

They left as quietly as they had appeared, the old minister waiting behind until the last had stepped into the hall, then he turned, and she saw his full height, framed by the doorway, as the others arranged themselves beyond him in the hall. "You're really making a mistake, miss," he said. "The Senator knows us and—"

"*Knows* you," she said indignantly. "I've heard Senator Sunraider state that the only colored he knows is the boy who shines shoes at his golf club."

"Oh?" Hickman shook his head as the others exchanged knowing glances. "Very well, ma'am. We're sorry to have caused you this trouble. It's just that it's very important that the Senator know we're on the scene. So I hope you won't forget to tell him that we have arrived, because soon it might be too late."

There was no threat in it; indeed, his voice echoed the odd sadness which she thought she detected in the faces of the others just before the door blotted them from view.

In the hall they exchanged no words, moving silently behind the guard who accompanied them down to the lobby. They were about to move into the street when the security-minded chief guard observed their number, stepped up, and ordered them searched.

They submitted patiently, amused that anyone should consider them capable of harm, and for the first time an emotion broke the immobility of their faces. They chuckled and winked and smiled, fully aware of the comic aspect of the situation. Here they were, quiet, old, and obviously religious black folk who, because they had attempted to see the man who was considered the most vehement enemy of their people in either house of Congress, were being energetically searched by uniformed security police, and they knew what the absurd outcome would be. They were found to be armed with nothing more dangerous than pieces of fried chicken and ham sandwiches, chocolate cake and sweet-potato fried pies. Some obeyed the guards' commands with exaggerated sprightliness, the old ladies giving their skirts a whirl as they turned in their flat-heeled shoes. When ordered to remove his wide-brimmed hat, one old man held it for the guard to look inside; then, flipping out the sweatband, he gave the crown a tap, causing something to fall to the floor, then waited with a callused palm extended as the guard bent to retrieve it. Straightening and unfolding the object, the guard saw a worn but neatly creased fifty-dollar bill, which he dropped upon the outstretched palm as though it were hot. They watched silently as he looked at the old man and gave a dry, harsh laugh; then as he continued laughing the humor slowly receded behind their eyes. Not until they were allowed to file into the street did they give further voice to their amusement.

"These here folks don't understand nothing," one of the old ladies said. "If we had been the kind to depend on the sword instead of on the Lord, we'd been in our graves long ago—ain't that right, Sis' Arter?"

"You said it," Sister Arter said. "In the grave and done long finished mold'ing!"

"Let them worry, our conscience is clear on that. . . ."

"Amen!"

On the sidewalk now, they stood around Reverend Hickman, holding a hushed conference; then in a few minutes they disappeared in a string of taxis and the incident was thought closed.

Shortly afterwards, however, they appeared mysteriously at a hotel where the Senator leased a private suite, and tried to see him. How they knew of this secret suite they would not explain.

Next they appeared at the editorial offices of the newspaper which was most critical of the Senator's methods, but here too they were turned away. They were taken for a protest group, just one more lot of disgruntled Negroes crying for justice as though theirs were the only grievances in the world. Indeed, they received less of a hearing here than elsewhere. They weren't even questioned as to why they wished to see the Senator—which was poor newspaper work, to say the least; a failure of technical alertness, and, as events were soon to prove, a gross violation of press responsibility.

So once more they moved away.

Although the Senator returned to Washington the following day, his secretary failed to report his strange visitors. There were important interviews scheduled and she had understandably classified the old people as just another annoyance. Once the reception room was cleared of their disquieting presence they seemed no more significant than the heavy mail received from white liberals and Negroes, liberal and reactionary alike, whenever the Senator made one of his taunting remarks. She forgot them. Then at about eleven A.M. Reverend Hickman reappeared without the others and started into the building. This time, however, he was not to reach the secretary. One of the guards, the same who had picked up the fifty-dollar bill, recognized him and pushed him bodily from the building.

Indeed, the old man was handled quite roughly, his sheer weight and bulk and the slow rhythm of his normal movements infuriating the guard to that quick, heated fury which springs up in one when dealing with the unexpected recalcitrance of some inanimate object—the huge stone that resists the bulldozer's power, or the chest of drawers that refuses to budge from its spot on the floor. Nor did the old man's composure help matters. Nor did his passive resistance hide his distaste at having strange hands placed upon his person. As he was being pushed about, old Hickman looked at the guard with a kind of tolerance, an understanding which seemed to remove his personal emotions to some far, cool place where the guard's strength could never reach them. He even managed to pick up his hat from the sidewalk where it had been thrown after him with no great show of breath or hurry, and arose to regard the guard with a serene dignity.

"Son," he said, flicking a spot of dirt from the soft old panama with a white handkerchief, "I'm sorry that this had to happen to you. Here you've worked up a sweat on this hot morning and not a thing has been changed—except that you've interfered with something that doesn't concern you. After all, you're only a guard, you're not a mind-reader. Because if you were, you'd be trying to get me *in* there as fast as you could instead of trying to keep me out. You're probably not even a good guard, and I wonder what on earth you'd do if I came here prepared to make some trouble."

Fortunately, there were too many spectators present for the guard to risk giving the old fellow a demonstration. He was compelled to stand silent, his thumbs hooked over his cartridge belt, while old Hickman strolled—or more accurately, *floated*—up the walk and disappeared around the corner.

Except for two attempts by telephone, once to the Senator's office and later to his home, the group made no further effort until that afternoon, when Hickman sent a telegram asking Senator Sunraider to phone him at a T Street hotel. A message which, thanks again to the secretary, the Senator did not see. Following this attempt there was silence.

During the late afternoon the group of closed-mouthed old folk were seen praying quietly within the Lincoln Memorial. An amateur photographer, a high-school boy from the Bronx, was there at the time and it was his chance photograph of the group, standing facing the great sculpture with bowed heads beneath old Hickman's outspread arms, that was flashed over the wires following the shooting. Asked why he had photographed that particular group, the boy replied that he had seen them as a "good composition. . . . I thought their faces would make a good scale of grays between the whiteness of the marble and the blackness of the shadows." And for the rest of the day the group appears to have faded into those same peaceful shadows, to remain there until the next morning—when they materialized shortly before chaos erupted.

CHAPTER 2

. . . Suddenly, through the sonorous lilt and tear of his projecting voice, the Senator was distracted. As he grasped the dimly lit lectern and concentrated on the faces of colleagues seated below him behind circular, history-stained desks, his eyes had been attracted by a turbulence centering around the rich emblazonry of the Great Seal. High across the chamber and affixed midpoint in the curving sweep of the distant visitors' gallery, the national coat-of-arms had ripped from its moorings and was hurtling down toward him with the transparent insubstantiality of a cinematic image that had somehow gone out of control.

Increasing alarmingly in size while maintaining the martial posture of tradition, the heraldic eagle with which the Great Seal was charged seemed to fly free of its base. Zooming forward, it flared luminously as it halted, oscillating a few arms' lengths before the Senator's confounded head. There, pulsating with hallucinatory vividness, the rampant eagle aroused swift olfactory memories of dried blood and dusty feathers, and stirred within him fragmentary images of warfare tinged with heroism and betrayal. . . .

Stepping instinctively backwards and fighting down an impulse to duck, the Senator managed by benefit of long practice to continue the smoothly resonant flow of his address, but before what appeared to be an insidious practical joke contrived to test his equanimity, he felt a cascading weakening of muscular control. For now, armed of beak and claw, the barred inescutcheon shielding its breast and the golden ribbon bearing the mystic motto of national purpose violently aflutter, the emblematic bird quivered above him on widely erected wings—while the symbolic constellation of thirteen cloud-encircled stars whirled furiously against a spot of intense blue which flashed like cold lightning above its snow-white head.

Shutting his eyes in a desperate effort to exorcise the vision, the Senator projected his voice with increased vigor and was aware of distorting the shape of what he had conceived as a perfect rhetorical period. But when he looked again the eagle was not only still there, but become more alarming. For at first, clutching in its talons the ambiguous arms of olive branch and sheaf of arrows, the eagle's exposed eye had looked in profile toward the traditional right, but now it shuddered with mysterious purpose, turning its head with sinister smoothness leftward—until with a barely perceptible flick of feathers two sphinxlike eyes bore in upon the Senator with piercing frontal gaze. For a breathless interval they held him savagely in mute interrogation, causing him to squint and toss his head; then with the stroke of a scimitar the curved beak carved the air. And with its wingspread thrusting upward, the feathers of its white-tipped tail flexed fanlike between feathery, wide-spread thighs, the eagle was no longer scrutinizing his face, but staring blandly in the direction indicated by its taloned clutch of sharp-pointed arrows.

Alarmed by the image's stubborn persistence, the Senator felt imprisoned in an airless space from which he viewed the placid scene of the chamber as through the semitransparent scrim of a theatrical stage. A scrim against which the heraldic symbols in whose name he served flashed and flickered in wild enigmatic disarray. And even as he forced himself to continue his address, he was aware that his voice was no longer reaching him through the venerable chamber's acoustics but now, sounding muted, metallic and stridently strange, through the taut vibrations of his laboring throat. Leaning forward and controlling himself by grasping the lectern, he recalled the famous cartoon which presented a man struggling desperately to prevent a huge octopus from dragging him into a manhole while a crowd thronged past unnoticing. For despite the disorder within his vision, the chamber appeared quite normal. Listening attentively, his audience was apparently unaware of his distress.

In whose name and under what stress do they think I'm speaking? the Senator thought. *For whose hidden interests and by what manipulation of experience and principle would they hang the bird on me?* But now, upon a flash of movement from above, the eagle appeared to leap aloft, reducing the rich emblazonment of the Seal to an exploding chaos of red, white, blue and gold through which the Senator's attention flashed to the distant gallery where with the amplified roar of his echoing voice he became aware of a collectivity of obscure faces, staring down. . . .

Anonymous, orderly and grave, they loomed high across the chamber, receding upward and away in serried tiers, their heads protruding slightly forward in the tense attitude of viewers bemused by some puzzling action unfolding on a distant screen which they were observing from the tortured angle provided by a segregated theater's peanut gallery. And as the Senator's words sped out across the chamber's solemn air the faces appeared to shimmer in rapt and disembodied suspension, as though in expectation of some crucial and long-awaited revelation which would make them whole. A revelation apparently even now unfolding through the accelerating rhythms, the bounce and boom of images sent flighting across the domed and lucid space from the flex and play of his own tongue, throat and diaphragm . . .

The effect upon the Senator was electric. Reassured and pleasurably challenged by their anonymous engrossment, he experienced a surge of that gaiety, anguished yet wildly free, which frequently seized him during an oration, and now, with a smooth shifting of emotional gears, he felt himself carried swiftly beyond either a concern with the meaning of the mysterious vision or the rhetorical fitness of his words onto that plane of verbal exhilaration for which he was notorious. And thereupon, in the gay and reckless capriciousness of his virtuosity, he found himself attempting to match that feat, long glorified in senatorial legend, whereby through a single flourish of his projected voice the orator raises his audience to fever pitch and shatters the chamber's windowpanes.

Do that, the Senator thought, *and without a single dissenting Hehell-naw! the gentleman from Little Rock will call for changing the outlandish name—of Arkansaw!*

Stifling an upsurge of laughter the Senator plunged ahead, tensing his diaphragm to release the full resonance of his voice. But as he did so it was as though his hearing had been thrown out of phase. Resounding through the acoustics of the chamber, his voice seemed controlled by the stop-and-go fluctuations of a hypersensitive timedelay switch, forcing him to monitor his words seconds after they were uttered and feeding them back to him with a hollow, decaying echo. More puzzling, between the physical sensation of statement and the delayed return his voice was giving expression to ideas the likes of which he had never articulated, not even in the most ambiguous of rhetorical situations. Words, ideas, phrases were jetting from some chaotic region deep within him and as he strove to regain control it was as though he had been taken over by some mocking ventriloquistic orator of opposing views, a trickster of corny philosophical ambition.

"But . . . but . . . but . . . now . . . now . . . now . . ." he heard, "let let us consider consider consider, the broader broader implication . . . cations of of our our current state. In this land it is our fate to be interrogated not by our allies or enemies but by our conduct and by our lives. Our . . . ours . . . ours is the arduous burden burden . . . den privilege of *self*-regulation and *self*-limitation. We are of a nation born in blood, fire and sacrifice. Thus we are judged, questioned, weighed—by the revolutionary ideals and events which marked the founding of our great country. It is these transcendent ideals which interrogate us, judging us, pursuing us, in terms of that which we do or do *not* do. They accuse us ceaselessly and their interrogation is ruthless, scathing, seldom charitable. For the demands they make of us are limitless. Under the relentless pressure of their accusation we seek to escape the intricate game-work of our enterprises. We make for the territory. We plunge into the edenic landscape of our natural resources. We seek out the warm seacoasts of leisure, the quiet cool caverns of forgetfulness—all made possible by the very success of our mind-jolting revolution and the undeniable accomplishments of our labor and dedication. In our beginning our forefathers summoned up the will to break with the past. They questioned the past and condemned it and severed themselves from its entangling tentacles. They plunged into the future accepting its dangers and its glories. Thus with us it is instinctive to evaluate ourselves against the examples of those, humble and illustrious alike, who preceded us upon this glorious stage and passed on. We are a people of joy and anguish. Our joy made poignant by our anguish. Of us is demanded great daring, great courage, great insight, prudence and even greater self-discipline.

"For we are like those great birds which, moved by an inborn need to test themselves against the mystery and promise of the universe, take off on powerful wings to be carried by fierce winds and gentle currents to great heights and far places. Like them we are given to maneuvering miraculously through treacherous passages and above marvelous plateaus and fertile valleys. It is our nature to soar and by following the courses mapped through the adventurous efforts of our fathers we affirm and revitalize their awesome vision. We are reapers and sowers, destroyers and creators, wheelers and dealers, finders and keepers—and why not? Since we are also generous sharers of that which we discover through our dedication and daring.

"Time flows past beneath us as we soar. History erupts and boils with its age-old contentions. But ours is the freedom and decision of the New, the Uncluttered, and we embrace the anguish of our predicament, we accept the penalties of our hopefulness. So on we soar, following our dream. Sometimes our clouds are fleecy and translucent, veiling thinly the sun; sometimes dark and stormy, lashing us with the wickedness of winter. We toss and swirl, pivot and swoop. We scrape the peaks or go kiting strutless toward the void. Ofttimes, as appears to be true of us today, we plunge down and down, we go round and round faltering and accusing ourselves remorselessly until, reminded of who we are and what we are about and the cost, we pull ourselves together. We lift up our eyes to the hills and we arise.

"God enclosed our land between two mighty oceans and, setting us down on the edge of this mighty continent, he threw us on our own. Our forefathers then set our course ever westward, not, I think, by way of turning us against the past and its lessons, although they accused it vehemently—for we are a product of those lessons—but that we should approach our human lot from a fresher direction, from uncluttered perspectives. Therefore it is not our way, as some would have it, to reject the past; rather it is to overcome its blighting effects upon our will to organize and conduct a more human future. We are called a consumer society and much is made of what is termed the 'built-in obsolescence' of our products. But those who do so miss the point: Yes, we are a consumer society, but the main substance of our consumption consists of *ideals*. Our way is to render ideals obsolescent by transforming them into their opposites through achieving and rejecting their promises. Thus do our ideals die and give way to the new. Thus are they redeemed, made manifest. Our sense of reality is too keen to be violated by moribund ideals, too forward-looking to be too long satisfied with the comforting arrangements of the present, and thus we move ever from the known into the unknown, for there lies the more human future, for there lies the idealistic core.

"My friends, and fellow citizens, I would remind you that in this our noble land, memory is all: touchstone, threat and guiding star. Where we shall go is where we have been; where we have been is where we shall go—but with a difference. For as we proceed toward our destination, it is ever changed by the transformations wrought by our democratic procedures and by the life-affirming effects of our spirit. Here we move ever toward past-future, by moonlight and by starlight, soaring by dead reckoning along courses mapped by our visionary fathers!

"Where we have been is where we shall go. We move from the realm of dreams through the valley of the practical and back to the realm of rectified dreams. Yes, but how we arrive there is *our* decision, *our* challenge and *our* anguish. And in the going and in the arriving our task is to tirelessly transform the past and create and re-create the future. In this grand enterprise we dance to our inner music, we negotiate the unknown and untamed terrain by the soundings of our own inner ear. By the capacity of our inner eye for detecting subtleties of contour, landmark and underground treasure, we shape the land. Indeed, we *shall* reshape the universe—to the forms of our own inner vision. Let no scoffers demand of us, 'How high the moon?' for not only can we supply the answer, in time we shall indeed fly them there! We shall demonstrate once again that in this great, inventive land man's idlest dreams are but the blueprints and mockups of emerging realities, technologies and poems. Here in the fashion of our pioneer forefathers, who confronted the mysteries of wilderness, mountain and prairie with crude tools and a self-generating imagination, we are committed to facing with courage the enormous task of imposing an ever more humane order upon this bewilderingly diversified and constantly changing society. Committed we are to maintaining its creative momentum.

"Committed we are to maintaining its involved and complex equilibrium.

"Committed to keeping it soaring ever forward in the materialization of our sublime and cornucopian dream. We rush ever onward, and often violently, yes, but on the adventurous journey toward the fulfillment of that dream, no one . . . no . . . one . . . not one, I say, shall . . . shall . . . be . . . bee . . . bee . . . denied . . . denied. . . ."

Thinking, *Am I drunk, going insane?*, the Senator paused, sweeping the curve of anonymous faces above him with his eyes.

"No," he continued, "no one shall be denied. An enormous task, some might say, a rash dream. Yet ours is no facile vision. Each day we suffer its anguish and its cost. It requires effort of an order to which only a great and unified nation, a nation conditioned to riding out the chaos of history as the eagle rides out the whirlwind, can arise. Therefore it is our duty to confront it with subtle understanding. Confront it with democratic passion. Confront it with tragic insight, with love and with endless good humor. We must confront it with faith and in the awareness of that age-old knowl-

edge which holds that it is in the nature of the human enterprise
that great nations shall not, *must* not, *dare* not evade their own mysteries but must grapple with them and live them out. They must
solve their innermost dilemmas through the expenditure of great
physical and spiritual effort. Yes, for great nations evolve and grow
ever young in the conscious acceptance and penetration of their
own most intimate secrets.

"Thus it is that we must will to remember our defeats and divi-
sions as we remember our triumphs and unities so that we may
transcend and forget them. Thus we must forget the past. Indeed,
our history records an undying, unyielding quest for youthful sages,
for a newfound wisdom fired by a vibrant physicality. Thus again we
must forget the past by way of freeing ourselves so that we can re-
assemble its untidy remnants in the interest of a more human order.

"Oh, yes; I understand: To some this goal appears too difficult. To
others, too optimistic, too unworldly—even though they would
agree that we are indeed a futuristic people. Ah, but in the face of
this bright and inescapable intuition, dark doubts afflict them. Dark
realities inhibit their powers of decision. They succumb to the shallow, somber materiality of our bountiful power and pursue it
blindly, selfishly for itself. They yearn for a debilitating and self-
defeating tranquillity. They falter before the harsher necessities of
action, whether that action calls for the exercise of force or charity,
charity or force. And before those ever-present dilemmas requiring
the exercise of charity supported by force they oscillate pathetically
between olive branch and arrows. They lose their way and in their
stumbling indecision they reward aggression and justify indolence.
In their hands charity becomes a force of cancerous malignancy, and
power a self-destructive agency that destroys themselves, their children and their neighbors.

"Nevertheless, we must accept forthrightly that arduous wisdom which holds that those who reject the lessons of history, or who allow themselves to be intimidated by its rigors, are doomed to repeat its disasters. Therefore I call upon them to remember that societies are artifacts of *human* design and that they are *man*-determined. Human societies float like great spaceships between earth and sky, dependent upon both but enjoying the anguish of human will and initiative. Man is born to act, to make mistakes, and to die. This all men know. But in the graceful acceptance of his fate, and in his protracted and creative dying, man builds his monument, he structures and makes manifest his accusation of the universe. He secures his earthly gains, sets the course of the ever-receding future and makes art of his yearning.

"So again, my friends, we become victims of history only if we fail to evolve ways of life that are more free, more youthful, more human. We are defeated only if we fail in the task of creating a total way of life which will allow each and every one of us to rise high above the site of his origins, and to soar released and ever reinvigorated in human space!"

The Senator smiled.

"I need not remind you that I am neither seer nor prophet," he went on, "but history has put to us three fatal questions, has written them across our sky in accents of accusation. They are, How can the many be as one? How can the future deny the Past? And How can the light deny the dark? The answer to the first is: Through a balanced consciousness of unity in diversity and diversity in unity, through a willed and *conscious* balance—that is the key phrase, so easy to say yet so difficult to maintain.

"For the second, the answer lies in remembering that, given the nature of our vision, of our covenant, to remember is to forget and to forget is to remember selectively, creatively! Yes, and let us remember that in this land to create is to destroy, and to destroy—if

we will it so and *make* it so, if we pay our proper respect to remembered but rejected things—is to make manifest our lovely dream of
progressive idealism.

"And how can the light deny the dark? Why, by seeking ever the
darkness in lightness and the lightness in darkness. As we incorpo-
rate and humanize nature we filter and blend the spectrum, we
exalt and we anguish, we order the world.

The land was ours before we were the land's.

So saith the poet. And so it is as it was in Eden. In darkness and in
lightness it is ours to name and ours to shape and ours to love and
die for. So let us not falter before our complexity. Nor become confused by the mighty, reciprocal, enginelike stroking of our national
ambiguities. We are by no means a perfect people—nor do we desire to be so. For great nations reach perfection, that final static
state, only when they pass their peak-promise and exhaust their
grandest potentialities. We seek not perfection, but coordination.
Not sterile stability but creative momentum. Ours is a youthful nation; the perfection we seek is futuristic and to be made manifest in
creative action. A marvel of purposeful political action, it was designed to solve those vast problems before which all other nations
have been proved wanting. Born in diversity and fired by determination, our society was endowed with a flexibility designed to contain the most fractious contentions of an ambitious, individualistic
and adventurous breed. Therefore, as we go about confronting our
national ambiguities, let us remember the purposes of our built-in
checks and balances, those constitutional provisions which serve
like subtle hormones to regulate the ingenious metabolism of our
body politic. Yes, and as we check our checks and balance our balances, let us in all good humor balance our checks and check our

balances, keeping each in proper order, issuing credit to the cred-
itable, minus to plus, and plus to minus.

"E pluribus unum!" the Senator shouted, pointing toward the
Great Seal attached to the wall of the gallery. "Observe there the
message borne in the beak of the noble bird under whose aegis our
nation thrives! Note the olive branch and arrows! Contemplate its
prayer and promise—E PLURIBUS UNUM. Regard the barred
shield that protects us, the stars of state leaping high in the sunburst
of national promise. Mark the olive branch extending peace and
prosperity to all. Consider the historically established fact that its
ready arrows are no mere boast of martial preparedness. They are
symbolic of our aggressive determination to fulfill our obligations
to humankind in whatever form they take or wherever they might
arise. So let us take wing with our emblem. Let us flesh out its
ideals. Let us unite like the flexing feathers that lift it aloft. Let us
forge ahead in faith and in confidence—E PLURIBUS UNUM!"

In the hushed silence the Senator stared out across the chamber
as though taken with a sudden insight. Then, leaning forward with a
look of amazement, he stroked his chin and waved his hands in a
gesture of impatience.

"Recently," he continued in a quietly confidential tone, "our national self-confidence has come under attack from within. It is said
that too many of our national projects have gone astray; that problems of long existence are proving to be unresolvable; that our
processes of governance have broken down; and that we are become
a distraught and weary people. And I would agree that something of
a darkness, an overcast has come upon us. There are seasons in the
affairs of nations, and this is to be expected. But I disagree that the
momentary disruptions which rack our society are anything new or
sufficient reason for despair.

"My friends, in such a nation as ours, in a nation blessed with so much good fortune, with so much brightness, it is sometimes instructive when we are so compelled, to look on the *dark* side. It is a corrective to the bedazzlement fostered by the brightness of our ideals and our history. The gentlemen from Pennsylvania will recall that the dark and viscous substance which once fouled the water of their fair state gave way under scientific scrutiny and soon gave radiance to their gloom. It made bright their homes and cities, became a new source of wealth. The gentlemen from Alabama and Georgia will recall the life-giving resuscitation of the old legend of sailing ship days, in which sailors dying of thirst took what appeared to be black-humored advice from a passing ship's captain and, plunging their buckets into what appeared to be pure brine, drew sweet spring water from the depths of the sea. They'll recall too that during a dark time in a dark section of the South a miracle was discovered beneath the hull of the humble peanut which proved similar to that of the loaves and the fishes. Yes, and this to the well-being of their state and nation.

"So in dark days look steadily on the darker side, for there is where brightness sometimes hides itself.

"Therefore let us have faith, hope and daring. And who can doubt our future when even the wildest black man behind the wheel of a Cadillac knows— Please, please!" the Senator pleaded, his face a mask before the rising ripple of laughter, the clatter of applause, "Hear me out: I say that even the wildest black man rampaging the streets of our cities in a Fleetwood knows that it is not our fate to be mere victims of history but to be courageous and insightful before its assaults and riddles."

And then, with a face most serious in its composure, he went on: "We have reached a sad state of affairs, gentlemen, wherein this fine product of American skill and initiative has become so common in Harlem that much of its initial value has been sorely compromised.

Indeed, I am led to suggest, and quite seriously, that legislation be drawn up to rename it the 'Coon Cage Eight.' And not at all because of its eight superefficient cylinders, nor because of the lean, springing strength and beauty of its general outlines. Not at all, but because it has now become such a common sight to see eight or more of our darker brethren crowded together enjoying its power, its beauty, its neo-pagan comfort, while weaving recklessly through the streets of our great cities and along our superhighways. In fact, gentlemen, I was run off the road, forced into a ditch by such a power-drunk group just the other day.

"Let us keep an eye on the outrages committed by the citizens whom I've just described, for perhaps therein lies a secret brightness, a clue. Perhaps the essence of their untamed and assertive willfulness, their crass and jazzy defiance of good taste and the harsh, immutable laws of economics, lies in their faith in the flexible soundness of the nation.

"Yes"—the Senator smiled, nodding his head with mock Elizabethan swagger—"methinks there is much mystery here. But one mystery at a time, I say. In the meantime, let us seek brightness in darkness and hope in despair. Let us remind ourselves that we were not designated the supine role of passive slave to the past. Ours is the freedom and obligation to be ever the fearless creators of ourselves, the reconstructors of the world. We were created to be Adamic definers, namers and shapers of yet undiscovered secrets of the universe!

"Therefore let the doubters doubt, let the faint of heart turn pale. We move toward the fulfillment of our nation's demand for citizen-individualists possessing the courage to forge a multiplicity of creative selves and styles. We shall supply its need for individuals, men and women, who possess the highest quality of stamina, daring, and grace—

> *Ho, Build thee more stately mansions,*
> *Oh, my soul—Yes!*

"For we"—the Senator paused, his arms reaching out with palms turned upward in all-embracing gesture—"by the grace of Almighty God, are A-MERI-CANS!"

And it was now, listening to his voice becoming lost in an explosion of applause, accented here and there by enthusiastic rebel yells, that the Senator became aware of the rising man.

Up in the front row center of the Visitors' Gallery the man was pointing out across the guardrail as though about to hurl down a vehement denunciation. *For Christ sake,* the Senator thought, *why don't you sit down or simply leave? Only spare us futile theatrical gestures. I always lose a few—the old; the short-of-attention-spanned; the mama's boys answering Mother Nature's call—but use your ears. Most I'm holding hard, so what can you hope to do?* But just as he lowered his eyes to the faces of his colleagues applauding on the floor below, the Senator became aware of the abrupt rise and fall of the man's still-pointing arm. Then a sound of ringing that was erupting above seemed to trigger a prismatic turbulence of the light through which, now, fragments of crystal, fine and fleeting as the first cool-touching flakes of a fall of snow, had begun to shower down upon him, striking sleet-sharp upon the still-upturned palms of his gesturing hands.

My God, the Senator thought, *it's the chandelier! Could it be I've shattered the chandelier?* Whereupon something smashed into the lectern, driving it against him; and now, hearing a dry popping sound above, he felt a vicious stinging in his right shoulder, and as he stared through the chaotic refraction of the light toward the gallery he could see the sharp kick of the man's gesturing arm and felt a second flare of pain, in his left thigh this time, and was thrown into a state of dreamlike lucidity.

Realizing quite clearly that the man was firing toward the podium, he tried desperately to move out of range, asking himself as he attempted to keep the lectern before him, *Is it me? Am I his target?* Then something struck his hip with the force of a well-aimed club and he felt the lectern toppling forward and he was spun forcefully around to face the gallery. Coughing and staggering backwards now, he felt himself striking against a chair and lurching forward as he marked the sinister *pzap! pzap! pzap!* of the weapon.

I'm going . . . I'm going . . . he told himself, knowing lucidly that it was most important to fall backwards if possible, out of the line of fire; but as he struggled to go down it was as though he were being held erect by an invisible cable attached somehow to the gallery, from where the man, raising and lowering his arm in measured calm, continued to fire.

The effort to fall brought a burst of moisture streaming from his pores but even now his legs refused to obey, would not collapse. And yet, through the muffled sound of the weapon and the strange ringing of bells, his eyes were recording details of the wildly tossing scene with the impassive and precise inclusiveness of a motion-picture camera that was toppling slowly from its tripod and falling through an unfolding action with the lazy motion of a feather loosed from a bird in soaring flight; panning from the image of the remote gunman in the gallery down to those moving dreamlike on the floor before him, then back to those shooting up behind the man above; all caught in attitudes of surprise, disbelief, horror; some turning slowly with puppet gestures, some still seated, some rising, some looking wildly at their neighbors, some losing control of their flailing arms, their erupting faces, some falling floorward— And up in the balcony now, an erupting of women's frantic forms.

Things had accelerated but, oddly, even now, no one was moving toward the gunman—who seemed as detached from the swiftly accelerating action as a marksman popping clay birds on a remote shooting range.

Then it was as though someone had dragged a poker at white heat straight down the center of his scalp and followed it with a hammering blow; and at last he felt himself going over backwards, crashing against a chair now and hearing it skitter away, as, thinking mechanically, *Down, down* . . . he felt the jolt of his head and elbows striking the floor. Something seared through the sole of his right foot then, and sharply aware of losing control he struggled to contain himself even as his throat gave cry to words which he knew, whatever the cost of containment, should not be uttered in this place.

"Lord, LAWD," he heard, "WHY HAST THOU . . ." smelling the hot presence of blood as the question took off with the hysterical timbre of a Negro preacher who in his disciplined fervor sounded somehow like an accomplished actor shouting his lines. *"Forsaken . . . forsaken . . . forsaken . . ."* The words went forth, becoming lost in the shattering of glass, the ringing of bells.

Writhing on the floor as he struggled to move out of range, the Senator was taken by a profound sense of self-betrayal, as though he had stripped himself naked in the Senate. And now with the full piercing force of a suddenly activated sprinkler, streams of moisture seemed to burst from his face *and somehow he was no longer in that place, but kneeling on the earth by a familiar clearing within a grove of pines, trying desperately to enfold a huge white circus tent into a packet. Here the light was wan and eerie, and as he struggled, trying to force the cloth beneath chest and knee, a damp wind blew down from the tops of the trees, causing the canvas to toss and billow like a live thing beneath him. The wind blew strong and damp through the clearing, causing the tent to flap and billow, and now he felt himself being dragged on his belly steadily toward the edge of the clearing where the light filtered with an unnatural*

*brilliance through the high-flung branches of the pines. And as he struggled
to break the forward motion of the tent a cloud of birds took flight, spinning
on the wind and into the trees, revealing the low shapes of a group of weed-
grown burial mounds arranged beneath the pines. Clusters of tinted bottles
had been hung from wooden stakes to mark the row of crude country graves,
and as the tent dragged him steadily closer he could see the glint and
sparkle of the glass as the bottles, tossing in the wind, began to ring like a
series of crystal bells. He did not like this place and he knew, struggling to
brake the tent's forward motion by digging his toes into the earth, that
somewhere beyond the graves and the wall of trees his voice was struggling
to return to him.*

*But now through the amber and deep-blue ringing of the glass, it was an-
other voice he feared, a voice which threatened to speak from beneath the tent
and which it was most important to enfold, to muffle beneath the billowing
canvas. . . .*

Then he was back on the Senate floor again and the forbidden
words, now hoarsely transformed, were floating calmly down to
him from gallery and dome, then coming on with a rush.

"For Thou hast forsaken . . . me," they came. But they were no
longer his own words nor was it his own echoing voice. And now,
hearing what sounded like a man's voice hoarsely singing, he struggled to bring himself erect, thinking, *No! No! Hickman? But how here?
Not here! No time, no place for HICKMAN!*

Then the very idea that Hickman was there somewhere above
him raised him up, and he was clutching onto a chair, pulling himself into a sitting position, trying to get his head up so as to see
clearly above as now there came a final shot which he heard but did
not feel . . .

He lay on his back, looking up through the turbulent space to where
the bullet-smashed chandelier, swinging gently under the impact of

its shattering, created a watery distortion of crystal light, a light which seemed to descend and settle him within a ring of liquid fire. Then beyond the pulsing blaze where a roiling darkness grew he was once more aware of a burst of action.

Now he could hear someone shouting far off. Then a voice was shouting quite close to his ear, but he was unable to bring his mind to it. There were many faces and he was trying to ask them *Why the hell'd he do it and who else was it?*

I can't understand, can't understand. My rule was graciousness, was politeness in all private contacts, but hell, anything goes in public. What? What?

Harry said if it gets too hot hop out of the pot. I say, If the tit's tough no one asks for milk when the steaks are high.

Lord, Lord, but it's hot. HOT! It hurts here and here and there and there, a hell of a clipping. How many rounds?

Lawd . . . Say Lord! Why? Ha! No time to go West but no time to stay East either, so blow the wind westerly, there's grease for the East.

I said, Donelson, crank it, man! Who broke the rhythm of the crowd? Old fat, nasty Poujaque! Don't accuse me; if I could pay them I could teach them! If they could catch me I could raise them up. That's their God-given, historical, woodpile role! Where was Moses, I mean to say? . . . No, let the deal go down. And if the cock crows three, I'm me, ME!—in the dark.

Roll the mammy-scratching camera, Karp! On with the lights! Hump it now! Get them over to the right side. It hurts, it was worth something in the right body for the right hand. . . .

Then I said, Politics is an art of maneuvering, and to move them you must change home base. Now you tell 'em because Ah stutter, Donelson said. But minds like that will never learn. . . . Hell, I've out-galloped Gallup—New Mexico, wasn't it? What happened to Body? Well, so long, old buddy, I missed touch, lost right hand but didn't forget. How the hell explain stony-going over stony ground?

Karp, you high-minded S.O.B., will you please *get some light over here? And keep the action going! . . .*

Yes, yes, yes! I'm all cud, bud; all chewed up like a dog! Like a dog. It was like shooting fish in a barbell. Fall! Fall! Take a dive! Green persimmons . . .

She said "Mother" and screamed and I said "Mother" and it shot out of my throat and something ran like hell up the tent and I doubled back and when I lifted the flap—dark again!

Roll the cameras!

What? What?

Perhaps you're right, but who would have thought what I knew on the back of my neck and ignored was ripening? A bird balled! That was the way it was. Oh, I rose up and she said "Mother," and I doubled back and he looked down upon the babe and said, "Look, boy, you're a son of God! Isn't that enough for you?"

But still I said "Mother" and something ran up the tent like a flash and then they came on, grim-faced and glassy-eyed, like the wrath of God in the shape of a leaping, many-headed cat . . . a stewardess's cap . . . What dreams . . . what dread . . .

Don't ask me, please. Please don't ask me. I simply can't do it. There are lines and shadows we can't stand to cross or recross. Like walking through the sharp edge of a mirror. All will be well, Daddy. Tell them what I said.

ROLL THE CAMERA!

What? What?

Who was? Who did that against me? Who untuned Daddy's fork when he could have preached his bone in all positions and places? I might have been left out of all that— Ask Tricky Sam Nanton, there's a preacher hidden in all the old troms— Bam! Same tune in juke or church, only Daddy's had a different brand of anguish.

Lawd, Lawd, why?

What terrible luck! What a sad kind of duck! Daddy strutted with some barbecue and the hot sauce on the bread was red and good—good—good. Yes, but in Austin they chilled the beans.

"*Mother,*" *she said.*

"*But weren't the greens nice in Birmingham?*" *Sister Lacey said.*

And she said "Mother" and I came up out of the box and he said "Let there be light"—but she didn't really mean it. And she said "cud" and that should have been worth the revival. But he wouldn't tell.

Oh, Maggie, Jiggs, and Aunt Jemima! Jadda-dadda-jing-jing! I miss those times sometimes. . . .

This game of politics is fraught with fraud, Ferd said—and a kiyi yippi and a happy nappy! So praise the Lord now, Pappy, and pass the biscuits! Oh, yes, the A.G. said, give ole Razorback Bill a guitar and the room to holler "nigger" and he'll forget about trying to pass for an intellectual. . . . A slow train through East Razorback on Captain Billy's Whizbang more pious than the Pharisees. . . . Hell, it was easy, easy. I was working as the old gentleman's chauffeur and he caught me in bed with his madam. He was amazed but calm. Who the hell are you, anyway? he said. And I thought fast and said, I'm a nigger; so you can forget it, it don't count. I'm outside the game. What? he said. Yes, I said, I am—or at least I was raised for one. So what are you going to do about it? And he said, Do? Hell, first I'm going to think about it. And then I'll decide. Was she satisfied? I don't know, I said, but I've had no complaints. Well, he said, taking that into consideration you might as well continue until she does. I'm a busy man and no old fool. Meanwhile I'll think about making you a politician. That should teach you to obey the Commandment. . . . So because she was years younger than the old gentleman I made a classical entry into the house. Bull-rushed the bully-raggers. . . . Yes, but you just wait, he said. The Spades'll learn to play the game and use their power and the old war will be ended. . . .

Oh, no! We'll legislate the hell against them. Sure, they must learn to play the game but power is as power does. Let's not forget what the hell this is all about. They'll have to come in as I did—through the living gate and sometimes it's bloody. But they ought to know from back in Seventy-four.

Mister Movie-Man . . . she said.

God is love, I said, but art's the possibility of forms, and shadows are the source of identity. And Donelson said, You tell 'em, buddy, while I go take a physic. . . .

Hold the scene, don't fade, don't fade . . . Seven's the number, Senator, I said. Fiscal problems come up seven, remember? Even for Joseph. . . . So she said, Mother, and I said me and she said cud was worth all that pain. But he still wouldn't tell.

Back away from me! Cat . . . cat . . . What's the rest?

I simply refused, that was all. Chicken in a casket was a no good-a union like-a da cloak. Too dark in there. Chick in this town, chick in that town and in the country. Always having to break out of that pink-lined shell.

No, not afraid after a while, but still against it. I was pretty little—little though not pretty, understand. Saw first snow in Kansas. The wind blows cold, but I can't tuck it.

Look, I have to climb out of here immediately, or the wires will flash Cudworth moos for Ma—a hell of a note from now on. And on the other side there's the dark. Daddy Hic, hic, what day?

To hell with it, I've stood up too long to lie down.

Lawd, Lawd, why?

Inevitable? Well, I suppose so. So focus in the scene. There, there. The Right Honorable Daddy— Where?

Karp! Karp, pan with the action— See! See! He's riding right out from under his old Cordoba. But watch him, Stack wore a magic hat— Listen for a bulldog!

Beliss?

No! What do you know about that? I can't hear him bark. . . .

Bliss be-eeee thee ti-ee that binds. . . .

CHAPTER 3

Forty-four in all, they were sitting in the Senate's Visitors' Gallery when Senator Sunraider arose to address the body. They sat in compact rows, their faces marked by that impassive expression which American Negroes often share with Orientals, watching the Senator with a remote concentration of their eyes. They barely moved while the Senator developed his argument, sitting like a row of dark statuary—until, during an aside, the Senator gave way to his obsession and made a quite gratuitous and mocking reference to their people.

It was then that a tall, elderly woman wearing steel-rimmed glasses arose from her chair and stood shaking with emotion, her eyes flashing. Twice she opened her mouth as though to hurl down some retort upon the head of the man holding forth below; but now the old preacher glimpsed her out of the corner of his eye, and, without turning from the scene below, gravely shook his head. For a second she ignored him, then feeling her still standing, he turned, giving her the full force of his gaze, and she reluctantly took her seat, the muscles ridged out about her dark prognathous jaws as she bent forward, resting her elbows upon her knees, her hands tightly clasped, listening. But although a few whites departed, some angrily shaking their heads over the Senator's remarks, others extending them embarrassed smiles, the rest made no sign. They seemed bound by some secret discipline, their faces remaining composed, their eyes remote as though through some mistake they were listening to a funeral oration for a stranger.

Nevertheless, Reverend Hickman was following the speech with close attention, his gaze playing over the orderly scene below as he tried to identify the men with their importance to the government. So this is where he came to rest, he thought. After all his rambling, this was the goal. Who would have imagined? At first, although he was familiar with his features from the newspapers, he had not recognized the Senator. The remarks, however, were unmistakable. These days, much to the embarrassment of his party and the citizens of his New England state, only Senator Sunraider (certain Southern senators were taken for granted) made such remarks, and Hickman watched him with deep fascination. He's driven to it, Hickman thought, it's so much with him that he probably couldn't stop if he wanted to. He rejected his dedication and his set-asideness, but it's still on him, it's with him night and day.

"Reveren' . . ." Sister Neal had touched his arm and he leaned toward her, still watching the scene.

"Reveren'," she said, "is that him?"

"Yes, that's him all right," he said.

"Well, he sho don't look much like his pictures."

"It's the distance. Up close, though, you'd recognize him."

"I guess you right," she said. "All those white folks down there don't make him any more familiar either. It's been so long I don't recognize nothing about him now."

"You will," Hickman whispered. "You just watch—see there . . ."

"What?"

"The way he's using his right hand. See how he gets his wrist into it?"

"Yeah, yeah!" she said. "And he would have his little white Bible in his other hand. Sure, I remember."

"That's right. See, I told you. Now watch this. . . ."

"Watch what?"

"There, there it goes. I could just see it coming—see the way he's got his head back and tilted to the side?"

"Yeah—why, Reveren', that's *you!* He's still doing you! Oh, my Lord," he heard her moan, "still doing you after all these years and yet he can say all those mean things he says. . . ."

Hearing a catch in her voice, Hickman turned; she was softly crying.

"Don't, Sister Neal," he said. "This is just life; it's not to be cried over, just understood. . . ."

"Yes, I know. But *seeing* him, Reveren'. I forgave him many times for everything, but seeing him *doing you* in front of all these people and humiliating us at the same time—I don't know, it's just too much."

"He probably doesn't know he's doing it," Hickman said. "Anyway, it's just a gesture, something he picked up almost without knowing it. Like the way you can see somebody wearing his hat in a certain way and start to wearing yours the same way."

"Well, he sure knows when he says something about us," she said.

"Yes, I guess he does. But he's not happy in it, he's driven."

"I'd like to drive him the other way a bit," she said. "I could teach him a few things."

Hickman became silent, listening to the Senator develop his argument, thinking, She's partly right, they take what they need and then git. Then they start doing all right for themselves and pride tells them to deny that they ever knew us. That's the way it's been for a long time. Sure, but not Bliss. There's something else, I don't know what it was but it was something different. . . .

"Reveren'!" It was Sister Neal again. "What's he talking about? I mean what's back of it all?"

"This is how the laws are made, Sister."

I guess that's the way it is, he thought. Power is as power does—for power. If I knew anything for sure, would I be sitting here?

Silently he listened to the flight of the Senator's voice and searched for echoes of the past. He had never seen the Senate in session before and was mildly surprised that he could follow most of the course of the debate. It's mainly knowing how to manipulate and use words, he thought. And reading the papers. Yes, and knowing the basic issues, because they seldom change. He sure knows how to use the words; he never forgot that. Imagine, going up there to New England and using all that kind of old Southern stuff, our own stuff, which we never get a chance to use on a broad platform—and making it pay off. It's probably the only thing he took with him that he's still proud of, or simply couldn't do without. Sister Neal's right, some of that he's doing is me all right. I could see it and hear it the moment she spotted it. So I guess I have helped to spread some corruption I didn't know about. Just listen to him down there; he's making somebody mighty uncomfortable because he's got them caught between what they profess to believe and what they feel they can't do without. Yes, and he's having himself a fine time doing it. He's almost laughing a devilish laugh in every word. Master, is that from me too? Did he ever hear me doing that?

He leaned toward Sister Neal again.

"Sister, do you follow what's happening?"

"Some, but not quite," she said. "He's got no principles but he's as smart as ever, ain't he?"

Hickman nodded, thinking, Yes, he's smart all right. Born with mother wit. He climbed up that high from nowhere, and now look, he's one of the most powerful men on the floor. Lord, what a country this is. Even his name's not his own name. Made himself from the ground up, you might say. But why this mixed-up way and all this sneering at us who never did more than wish him well? Why this craziness which makes it look sometimes like he does everything else, good and bad, clean-cut and crooked, just so he can have more opportunity to scandalize our name? Ah, but the glory of that baby boy. I could never forget it and that's why we had to hurry here. He has to be seen, and I'm the one to see him. I don't know how we're going to do it, but soon's this is over we have to find a way to get to him. I hope Janey was wrong, but any time she goes to the trouble of writing a letter herself, she just about knows what she's talking about. So far though we're ahead, but Lord only knows for how long. If only that young woman had told him we were trying to reach him . . .

He leaned forward, one elbow resting upon a knee, watching the Senator who was now in the full-throated roar of his rhetoric, head thrown back, his arms outspread—when someone crossed his path of vision.

Two rows below, a neatly dressed young man had stood up to leave, and, moving slowly toward the aisle as though still engrossed in the speech, had stopped directly in front of him, apparently to remove a handkerchief from his inside jacket pocket. Why doesn't he move on out of the way, Hickman thought, he can blow his nose when he gets outside—when, leaning around so as to see the Senator, he saw that it was not a handkerchief in the young man's hand, but a pistol. His body seemed to melt. Lord, can this be it? Can this

be the one? he thought, even as he saw the young man coolly bracing himself, his body slightly bent, and heard the dry, muffled popping begin. Unable to move he sat, still bent forward and to one
side, seeing glass like stars from a Fourth of July rocket bursting
from a huge chandelier which hung directly in the trajectory of the
bullets. Lord, no, he thought, no Master, not this, staring at the
dreamlike world of rushing confusion below him. Men were throwing themselves to the floor, hiding behind their high-backed chairs,
dashing wildly for the exits; while he could see Bliss still standing as
when the shooting began, his arms lower now, but still outspread,
with a stain blooming on the front of his jacket. Then, as the full
meaning of the scene came home to him, he heard Bliss give surprising voice to the old idiomatic cry,

Lord, LAWD, WHY HAST THOU . . . ?

and staggering backwards and going down, and now he was on his
own feet, moving toward the young man.

For all his size Hickman seemed suddenly everywhere at once.
First stepping over the back of a bench, his great bulk rising above
the paralyzed visitors like a missile, yelling, "No. NO!" to the young
man, then lumbering down and reaching for the gun—only to miss
it as the young man swerved aside. Then catching sight of the guards
rushing, pistols in hand, through the now standing crowd, he
whirled, pushing the leader off balance, back into his companion,
shouting, "No, don't kill him! Don't kill that Boy! Bliss won't want
him killed!" as now some of his old people began to stir. But already
the young man was moving toward the rail, waving a spectator away
with his pistol, looking coolly about him as he continued forward;
while Hickman, grasping his intention from where he struggled
with one of the guards, now trying in beet-faced fury to club him

with his pistol, began yelling, "Wait, wait! Oh, my God, son—WAIT!" holding the guard, for all his years, like a grandfather quieting a boy throwing a tantrum. "WAIT!" Then calling the strange name, "Severen, wait," and saw the young man throwing him a puzzled, questioning look, then climb over the rail to plunge deliberately headfirst to the floor below. Pushing the guard from him now, Hickman called a last despairing "Wait!" as he stumbled to the rail to stand there crying down as the group of old people quickly surrounded him, the old women pushing and striking at the angry guards with their handbags as they sought to protect him.

For a moment he continued to cry, grasping the rail with his hands and staring down to where the Senator lay twisting upon the dais beside an upturned chair. Then suddenly, in the midst of all the screaming, the shrilling of whistles, and the dry ineffectual banging of the chairman's gavel, he began to sing.

Even his followers were startled. The voice was big and resonant with a grief so striking that the crowd was halted in mid-panic, turning their wide-eyed faces up to where it soared forth to fill the great room with the sound of his astounding anguish. There he stood in the gallery above them, past the swinging chandelier, his white head towering over his clustered flock, tears gleaming bright against the darkness of his face, creating with his voice an atmosphere of bafflement and mystery no less outrageous than the shooting which had released it.

"Oh, Lord," he sang, "why hast thou taken our Bliss, Lord? Why now our awful secret son, Lord? . . . Snatched down our poor bewildered foundling, Lord? LORD, LORD, why hast thou . . . ?"

Whereupon, seeing the Senator trying to lift himself up and falling heavily back, he called out: "Bliss! You were our last hope, Bliss; now Lord have mercy on this dying land!"

As the great voice died away it was as though all had been stunned by a hammer and there was only the creaking sound made by the serenely swinging chandelier. Then the guards moved, and as the old ladies turned to confront them, Hickman called: "No, it's all right. We'll go. Why would we want to stay here? We'll go wherever they say."

They were rushed to the Department of Justice for questioning, but before this could begin, the Senator, who was found to be still alive upon his arrival at the hospital, began calling for Hickman in his delirium. He was calling for him when he entered the operating room and was still calling for him the moment he emerged from the anesthetic, insisting, for all his weakness, that the old man be brought to his room. Against the will of the doctors this was done, the old man arriving mute and with the eyes of one in a trance. Following the Senator's insistence that he be allowed to stay with him through the crisis, he was given a chair beside the bed and sank his great bulk into it without a word, staring listlessly at the Senator, who lay on the bed in one of his frequent spells of unconsciousness. Once he asked a young nurse for a glass of water, but beyond thanking her politely, he made no further comment, offered no explanation for his odd presence in the hospital room.

CHAPTER 4

When the Senator awoke he did not know if it was the shape of a man which he saw beyond him, or simply a shadow. Nor did he know if he was awake or dreaming. He seemed to move in a region of grays which revolved slowly before his eyes, ceaselessly transforming shadow and substance, dream and reality. And yet there was still the constant, unyielding darkness which seemed to speak to him silently words which he dreaded to hear. Yet he wished to touch it, but even the idea of movement brought pain and set his mind to wandering. It hurts here, he thought, and here; the light comes and goes behind my eyes. It hurts here and here and there and there. If only the throbbing would cease. Who . . . why . . . what . . . *LORD, LORD, LORD WHY HAST THOU* . . . Then someone seemed to call to him from a long way off, *Senator, do you hear me?* Did the Senator hear? Who? Was the Senator here? And yes, he did, very clearly, yes. And he was. Yes, he was. Then another voice seemed to call, *Bliss?* And he thought,

Is Bliss here? Perhaps. But when he tried to answer he seemed to dream, to remember, to recall to himself an uneasy dream.

It was a bright day and Daddy Hickman said, Come on out here, Bliss; I got something to show you. And I went with him through the garden past the apple trees on under the grape arbor to the barn. And there it was, sitting up on two short sawhorses.

Look at that, he said.

It was some kind of long, narrow box. I didn't like it.

I said, What is it?

It's for the service. For the revivals. Remember me and Deacon Wilhite talking about it?

No, sir.

Sho, you remember. It's for you to come up out of. You're going to be resurrected so the sinners can find life everlasting. Bliss, a preacher is a man who carries God's load. And that's the whole earth, Bliss boy. The whole earth and all the people. And he smiled.

Oh! I said. I remembered. But before it hadn't meant too much. Since then, Juney had gone away and I had seen one. Juney's was pine painted black, without curves. This was fancy, all carved and covered with white cloth. It seemed to roll and grow beneath my eyes, while he held his belly in his hands, thumbs in trousers top, his great shoes creaking as he walked around it, proudly.

How you like it?

He was examining the lid, swinging it smoothly up and down with his hand. I couldn't see how it was put together. It seemed to be all white cloth bleeding into pink and pink into white again, over the scrolls. Then he let the lid down again and I could see two angels carved in its center. They were blowing long-belled valveless trumpets as they went flying. Behind them, in the egg-shaped space in which they trumpeted and flew, were carved clouds. Their eyes looked down. I said,

Is it for me?

Sho, didn't I tell you? We get it all worked out the way we want it and then, sinners, watch out!

Suddenly I could feel my fingers turn cold at the tips.

But why is it so big, I said. I'm not that tall. In fact, I'm pretty little for my age.

Yeah, but this one has got to last, Bliss. Can't be always buying you one of these like I do when you scuff out your shoes or bust out the seat of your britches.

But my feet won't even touch the end, I said. I hadn't looked inside.

Yeah, but in a few years they will. By the time your voice starts to change your feet will be pushing out one end and your head out the other. I don't want even to have to think about another one before then.

But couldn't you get a littler one?

You mean "smaller"—but that's *just* what we don't want, Bliss. If it's too small, they won't notice it or think of it as applying to them. If it's too big, they'll laugh when you come rising up. No, Bliss, it's got to be this size. They have to see it and feel it for what it is, not take it for a toy like one of those little tin wagons or autos. Down there in Mexico one time I saw them selling sugar candy made in this shape, but ain't no use in trying to sugar-coat it. No, sir, Bliss. They have got to see it and know what they're seeing is where they've all got to end up. Bliss, that there sitting right there on those sawhorses is everybody's last clean shirt, as the old saying goes. And they've got to realize that when that sickle starts to cut its swath, it don't play no favorites. *Everybody* goes when that wagon comes, Bliss; babies and grandmaws too, 'cause there simply ain't no exceptions made. Death is like Justice is *supposed* to be. So you see, Bliss, it's got to be of a certain size. Hop in there and let's see how it fits. . . .

No, please. Please, Daddy Hickman. PLEASE!

It's just for a little while, Bliss. You won't be in the dark long, and you'll be wearing your white dress suit with the satin lapels and the long pants with the satin stripes. You'll like that, won't you, Bliss? Sure you will. In that pretty suit? Course! And you breathe through this here tube we fixed here in the lid. See? It comes through right here—you hear what I'm saying, Bliss? All right then, pay attention. Look here at this tube. All you have to do is lay there and breathe through it. Just breathe in and out like you always do; *only through the tube.* And when you hear me say, Suffer the little children . . . you push it up inside the lid, so's they can't see it when Deacon Wilhite goes to open up the lid. . . .

But then I won't have any air. . . .

Now don't worry about that, there'll be air enough inside the box. Besides, Deacon Wilhite will open it right away. . . .

But suppose something happens and . . .

Nothing's *going* to happen, Bliss.

Yes, but suppose he forgets?

He won't forget. How's he going to forget when you're the center of the services?

But I'm scaird. In all that darkness and with that silk cloth around my mouth and eyes.

Silk, he said. He looked down at me steadily. What else you want it lined with, Bliss? Cotton? Would you feel any better about it if it was lined with something most folks have to work all their lives and wear every day—weekdays and Sunday? Something that most of our folks never get away from? You don't want that, do you?

He touched my shoulder with his finger. I said, Do you?

I shook my head, shamed.

He watched me, his head to one side. I'd do it myself, Bliss, but it wouldn't mean as much for the people. It wouldn't touch them in the same way. Besides, I'm so big most towns wouldn't have men strong enough to carry me. We don't want to have to break anybody's back just to save their souls, do you, Bliss?

I don't guess so, but . . .

Of course not, he said quickly. And it won't be but a few minutes, Bliss. You can even take Teddy with you—no, I guess you better take your Easter bunny. With your Easter bunny you won't be afraid, will you? Course not. And like I tell you, it will last no longer than it takes for the boys to march you down the aisle. I'll have you some good, strong, big fellows, so you don't have to worry about them dropping you. Now, Bliss: You'll hear the music and they'll set it down in front of the pulpit. Then more music and preaching. Then Deacon Wilhite will open the lid. Then I'll say, Suffer the little children, and you sit up, see? I say, Do you see, Bliss?

Yessuh.

Say *Sir!*

Sir.

Good. Don't talk like I talk; talk like I *say* talk. Words are your business, boy. Not just *the* Word. Words are everything. The key to the Rock, the answer to the Question.

Yes, sir.

Now, when you rise up, you come up slow—don't go bolting up like no jack-in-the-box, understand? You don't want to scair the living daylights out of anybody. You want to come up slow and easy. And be sure you don't mess up your hair. I want the part to be still in it, neat. So don't forget when we close you in—and don't be chewing on no gum or sucking on no sourballs, you hear? Hear me now. . . .

Yes, sir, I said. I couldn't turn away my eyes. His voice rolled on as I wondered which of the two with the trumpets was Gabriel. . . .

. . . It depends on the size of the church, Bliss. You listening to me?

Yes, sir.

Well, now when you hear me say, *Suffer the little children,* you sit up slow and, like I tell you, things are going to get quiet as the grave. That's the way it'll be.

He stood silently for a moment, one hand on his chin, the other against his hip, one great leg pushed forward, bending at the knee. He wore striped pants.

Bliss, I almost forgot something important: I better have the ladies get us some flowers. Roses would be good. Red ones. Ain't nobody in this town got any lilies—least not anybody we know. I'm glad I thought of it in time.

Now, Bliss. We'll have it sitting near the pulpit so when you rise up you'll be facing to the side and every living soul will see you. But I don't want you to open your eyes right off. Yes, and you better have your Bible in your hands—and leave that rabbit down in there. You won't forget that, will you?

No, sir.

Good. And what are you suppose to say when you rise up?

I ask the Lord how come he has forsaken me.

That's right. That's correct, Bliss. But say it with the true feeling, hear? And in good English. That's right, Bliss; in Good Book English. I guess it's 'bout time I started reading you some Shakespeare and Emerson. Yes, it's about time. Who's Emerson? He was a preacher too, Bliss. Just like you. He wrote a heap of stuff and he was what is called a *philosopher*. Main thing though is that he knew that every tub has to sit on its own bottom. Have you remembered the rest of the sermon I taught you?

Yes, sir; but in the dark I . . .

Never mind the dark—when you come to *Why hast Thou forsaken me,* on the *me,* I want you to open your eyes and let your head go back. And you want to spread out your arms wide—like this, see? Lemme see you try it.

Like this?

That's right. That's pretty good. Only you better look sad, too. You got to look like you feel it, Bliss. You want to feel like everybody has put you down. Then you start with, *I am the resurrection and the life*—say it after me:

I am the resurrection . . .

I am the resurrection . . .

. . . and the life . . .

. . . and the life . . .

That's good, but not too fast now. I am the lily of the valley. . . .

I'm the lily of the valley. . . .

Uh-huh, that's pretty good—I am the bright and morning star. . . .

. . . the bright and morning star.

Thy rod . . .

Thy rod and thy staff.

Good, Bliss. I couldn't trap you. That's enough. You must remember that all of those *I*'s have got to be in it. Don't leave out any of those *I*'s, Bliss; because it takes a heap of *I*'s before they can see the true vision or even hear the true word.

They pain here and here and there and there. How far the sight? The Scene? . . . In Tulsa, after the tent meeting, they gave me a Black Cow, sweet teat of root beer and cool glob of ice cream. . . . He taught me to ha and ah deep in my throat like a blues singer. Horehound honey and lemon drops.

Cool against the heat of all that fire . . . It hurts here and here and there and there. Long nails.

"Senator, can you see me?"

Ha! The merry-go-round broke down!

Up there on Brickyard Hill the octagonal tents shimmered white in the sunlight. Below, my God, sweet Jesus, lay the devastation of the green wood! Ha! And in the blackened streets the entrails of men, women and baby grand pianos, their songs sunk to an empty twang struck by the aimless whirling of violent winds. Behold! Behold the charred foundations of the House of God! Oh, but then, in those sad days came Bliss, the preacher . . . Came Bliss, the preacher . . . No more came Bliss.

Daddy Hickman, I said, can I take Teddy too?

Teddy? Just why you got to have that confounded bear with you all the time, Bliss? Ain't the Easter bunny enough? And your little white leather Bible, your kid-bound Word of God? Ain't that enough for you, Bliss?

But it's dark in there and I feel braver with Teddy. Because you see, Teddy's a bear and bears ain't afraid of the dark.

Never mind all that, Bliss. And don't you start preaching me no sermon; 'specially none of those you make up yourself. You preach what I been teaching you and there'll be folks enough out there tonight who'll be willing to listen to you. I tell you, Bliss, you're going to make a fine preacher and you're starting at just the right age. You're just a little over six and Jesus Christ himself didn't start until he was twelve. *But you have to go leave that bear alone.* The other day I even heard you preaching to that bear. Bliss, bears don't give a continental about the Word. Did you ever hear tell of a bear of God? Of course not. There's the Lamb of God, and the Holy Dove, and one of the saints, Jerome, had him a lion. And another had him a bull of some kind—probably an old-fashioned airplane, since he had wings—he said under his breath, and Peter had the keys to the Rock. But no bear, Bliss. So you think about that, you hear?

He looked at me with that gentle, joking look, smiling in his eyes, and I felt better.

You think you could eat some ice cream?

Oh, yes, sir.

You do? Well, here; take this four bits and go get us each a pint. You look today like you could eat just about a pint. What I mean is, you look kind of hot.

He leaned back and squinted down.

I can even see the steam rising out of your collar, Bliss. In fact, I suspect you're on fire, so you better hurry. Make mine strawberry. Without a doubt, ice cream is good for a man's belly, and when he has to sing and preach a lot like I do, it's good for his throat too. Wait a second—where'd I put that money? Here it is. I thought I'd lost it. Ice cream is good if you don't overdo it—but I don't guess I have to recommend it to you though, do I, Bliss? 'Cause you're already sunk chin deep in the ice cream habit. Fact, Bliss, if eating ice cream was a sin you'd sail to hell in a freezer. Ha, ha! I'm sorry, now don't look at me like that. I was only kidding, little boy. Here, take this dime and bring us some of those chocolate marshmallow cookies you love so well. Hurry on now, and watch out for those wagons and autos. . . .

Yes, the Senator thought, *that was how it began, and that was Hickman. When he laughed his belly shook like a Santa Claus. A great kettledrum of deep laughter. Huge, tall, slow-moving. Like a carriage of state in ceremonial parade until on the platform, then a man of words evoking action. Black Garrick, Alonzo Zuber, Daddy Hickman.*

God's Golden-voiced Hickman
Better known as
GOD'S TROMBONE,

they billed him. Brother A.Z. to Deacon Wilhite, when they were alone.
They drank elderberry wine beneath the trees together, discussing the Word;
me with a mug of milk and a buttered slice of homemade bread.

It was Waycross.

I came down the plank walk past the Bull Durham sign where a white, black-spotted dog raised his leg against the weeds and saw them. They were squatting in the dust along the curb, pushing trucks made of wood blocks with snuffbox tops for wheels. Garrets and Tube Rose but all the same size. Then I was there and one turned, fingering for a bugger in his nose, saying:

Look here, y'all, here's Bliss. Says he's a preacher.

They stood, looking with disbelieving eyes, dust on their knees, making me like Jesus among the Philistines.

Who, him? One of them pointed. A *preacher?*

Yeah, man.

Hi, I, Bliss said.

He looked at me, one eyebrow raised, his lips protruding. A dark, half-moon-shaped scar showed beneath his left cheekbone. The others were ganging up on me, their faces closing in.

What he doing all dressed up like Sunday for? he said.

Who?

Him.

'Cause he's a preacher, fool.

Heck, he don't look like no preacher to me. Just looks like another li'l ole hi-yaller. What you say's his name?

Bliss. They swear he's a preacher.

Sho do, the bow-legged one said. My mama heard him preach.

Grown folks talking 'bout him all over town. He real notoriety, man.

Shucks! Y'all know grown folks is crazy. What can this here li'l ole jaybird preach? A.B.C.? Hell, I can preach that just like ole Revum McDuffie does and he's the best.

I watched his hands go behind his back, his chin drawing down and his eyes looking up, as though peering over the rims of spectacles as he frowned.

Brothers and sisters, ladies and what comes with you, my text this mawning is A.B.C. Y'all don't like to think about such stuff as that but you better lissen to me. I said A—whew, Lord! I says A! Just lissen, just think about it. A! A! *Aaaay!* In the beginnin' there was A. B. and C. The Father, the son, and the son-of-a-gun! I want you to think about it. Git in it and git out of it. I said A.B.C., Lawd. . . .

He shook his head grimly, his mouth turning down at the corners, his tone becoming soft then rising as he hammered his palm with his fist. A.B.C.—double-down D! Think about the righteous Word. Where would we be without A? Nowhere 'cause it's the start. Turn b around and what you got? I'll tell you what you got, you got a doggone *d!* Y'all better mind! I say you sinners better mind y'all's Abc's and zees!

He grinned. If I had me a Bible and a pulpit I could really lay that stuff, he said. Is that the kind of preachin' he does?

And one in a blue suit and tettered head defended me on heard words.

You crazy, man. 'Cause he *really* preaches. . . . Any of us can do what you doing.

That's what *you* say. So what do he preach?

Salvation. What all the grown preachers preach.

Sali*vation?* Hey, that's when your mouth gits sore and your teeth fall out, ain't it? Don't he want folks to have no teeth?

I said sal-*va*tion. You heard me.

Oh! Well tell a poor fool!

Don't you min' him, Bliss. He's just acting a clown.

He grinned and picked up a pebble with his toes.

No I ain't neither, I just ain't never seen no half-pint preacher before. Hey, Bliss, say "when."

"When" what?

Just "*when*."

Why?

Just 'cause. Go head on, do like I tole you; say "when."

So maybe I wouldn't have to fight him—And blessed are the peacemakers—"When," I said.

Aw come on; if you a preacher say it strong.

WHEN!

WHEN THE HEN BREAKS WIND—See, I got you!

They laughed. I tried to grin. My lip wouldn't hold.

I sho got you that time, Bliss. Hell, you can't be no preacher, 'cause a preacher'd know better than to git caught that easy. You all right though. You want to shoot some marbles? Man, dressed up the way you is, you ought to be a *real* gambler.

Not now, I have to go to the store. Maybe I can tomorrow.

Say, Rev, if you so smart, what's the name of that dog who licked those sores poor Lazarus had?

He didn't have a name, I said.

Yes he did too. He name Mo' Rover! Dam', Rev, we got you agin!

I said, you mean *more*-over.

He said, Shucks, how can you have *Mo'* Rover when he ain't got *no* Rover?

They laughed.

He a nasty dog, licking blood, someone said.

Sho, there's a heap of nasty things in the Bible, man.

Hey y'all, he said, even for a yella he's a good fella. Let's teach him a church song before he goes. They crowded around.

Sing this with me, Rev, he said, beginning like Daddy Hickman lining out a hymn:

> Well, ah-mazing grace
> How sweet
> The sound . . .
> A bullfrog slapped
> His grand-mammy
> Down. . . .

He watched me, grinning like an egg-sucking dog. I looked back, feeling my temper rise.

Hey, whatsamatter, Rev, he said. Don't you like my song?

Man, Bowlegs said, you know don't no preacher go for none of that mess. Bliss here is a real preacher and that stuff you singing is sinful.

Oh, it is, he said. Then how come nobody never tole me? I guess I better hurry up and sing him a *real* church song so he'll forgive me. What's more, come Sunday I'm going to his church and do my righteous duty. Here's a real righteous one, Rev!

> Well, I'm going to the church house
> And gon' climb up to the steeple
> Said I'm going to Rev's little ole church house
> Gon' climb up on the steeple
> Gon' take down my britches, baby,
> And doo-doo——whew, Lawd!——
> Straight down on the people!

I looked at him and gritted my teeth. My face felt swollen. No bigger'n me and trying to be a great big sinner. I thought: Saint

Peter bit off an ear but still got the keys. Amen! I looked on the ground, searching for a rock.

Boy, I said, before you were just pranking with me; now you're messing with the Lord. And just for that He's going to turn you into a crow.

Shoots, he said. *Who?* You can't scair me. Less see you.

I said *He* will do it, not me. You just wait and see.

Hell, I can't wait that long. Goin' on a cotton-pick next month. Goin' hear all those big guys tell all those good ole lies. See, he said bending over and patting his bottom. I ain't no crow. Can't see no feathers shooting outta my behind. . . .

They laughed, watching me. I reproached him with all the four horses galloping in my eyes.

Suddenly Bowlegs stepped close and looked him up and down, frowning.

Yeah, man, you might be right about your behind, he said. But while I don't see no feathers, your *mouth* is getting awful long and sharp. And while you always been black now I be dam' if you ain't begun to turn *blue* black!

Man, he said, taking a swing at Bowlegs, you better watch that stuff 'cause I don't play with no chillun.

Hey, Rev, he said, here's a church song my big brother taught me. He up in Chicago and this one's *really* religious:

> *Well, the tomcat jumped the she-cat*
> *By the bank of a stream*
> *Started howling and begging for that*
> *Natural cream.*
> *Soon the she-cat was spitting and*
> *A-scratching and a-kicking up sand*
> *Then the he-cat up and farted*
> *Like a natural man.*

> *The she-cat she jumped salty, looked around*
> *And screamed,*
> *Said, Hold it right there, daddy,*
> *Until your mama's been redeemed.*

As they laughed he joined in with his juicy mouth, rearing back with his thumbs thrust in his suspenders.

Hell, he said, I'm a poet and didn't know it.

He did a rooster strut, flapping his arms and scuffing up the dust.

Hey, y'all, he said, listen to this:

> *Bliss, Bliss*
> *Cat piss miss!*

He flicked his fingers at me like a magician, taking my name in vain.

Man, you sho got a fine kinda name to put down a conjure with. If a man was to say your name at two dogs gitting they ashes hauled the he-dog'll git a dog-knot in his peter as big as a baseball! They be hung up for ninety-nine days. That's right y'all. You say ole Rev's name to a guy throwing rocks at you and he couldn't hit the side of a barn with a whiffletree! Heck, Bliss, you say your name and hook fingers with another guy when a dog's taking him a hockey and you lock up his bowels like a smokehouse! Yeah, man, the First National Bank! Constipate that fool for life!

They laughed at me. I saw a good egg rock now and looked at him, mad. I was going to sin. Saint Peter, he got the keys.

Since you think you're so smart now here's one for you, I said. *Meat whistle*. That's for you.

What?

He puzzled up his face.

You heard me, I said. *Meat whistle*.

He bucked his eyes like I had hit him. It was quiet. I bent and picked up the rock. Someone snickered.

What you mean, he said, I never heard of no *meat* whistle. . . .

They looked at us, changing sides now. Ha, he got you! one of them said. Ain't but one kind of meat whistle and us all got one, ain't we, y'all?

Yeah, yeah, that's right, they said.

The whites of his eyes were turning red. I backed away.

What kinda dam' whistle is that, he said. It bet' not be what I think it is.

He doubled up his fists.

I watched his eyes.

It blows some real bad-smelling tunes, don't it, Bliss? one of the others said.

I watched his eyes, red. You ain't the only one who knows stuff like that, I said. Just because I'm a preacher, don't think you can run over me.

They were laughing at him now.

Tell him 'bout it, Rev!

Ole Bliss is awright!

Watch out now, ole Rev's colored blood is rising. . . .

Indian, man! Look at him!

Ole Bliss is awright! Look at him, y'all. He probably got him some mean cracker blood too, man!

He looked angry, his lips pouting. Maybe you know this one, I said.

Clank, clank, clank, I said and waited, watching his eyes.

What you mean, "clank, clank, clank," little ole yella som'bitch?

Clank, clank, clank, I said, that's your mama walking in her cast-iron drawers.

Seeing his face looming close I moved.

He came on at me but too late, I wasn't there. Always switch the rhythm—

Watch out, Bliss! they called, but I missed him not. I struck hard seeing his surprise as the blood burst from his forehead like juice from a crushed blackberry. His face went gray as his hand flew to his forehead. I looked, then I ran backwards with sin running with me in my eyes. I held the rock cupped in my hand like an egg, feeling his blood on my fingers. On this rock I will build my . . . Kept it with Teddy, my leather-bound Bible.

You shoulda used some cat piss, man, their short cries sounded behind me. 'Cause he ain't missed *nothing.* Look at ole Rev run! Zoooom! Barney-O-Bliss, man! Barney-O-Blissomobile.

Put some salt on his tail. You aim to catch him you got to turn on the gas, man.

Man, he may be a reverend but he runs like hell!

Taking it on the lamb chop, man.

Aches, breaks. Crackers and wine, you're out, Bliss. Out!

No, I'll be there when he arrives. We agreed . . . I'll . . .

They relaxed in their chairs, the whiskey between them. Only the air-conditioning unit hummed below their voices. O'Brien was intense.

Listen, he said. Dam' it, Senator, we're losing your state and my state and even New York seems doubtful. You'll have to lay off the nigger issue because the niggers and the New York Jews are out to get us this year. They don't have to take it and they won't. Here, try one of these. No, smoke it. There's plenty where that comes from. But you restrain yourself, you hear? We want you to curb that mouth of yours or else. . . . Make me whole, patch my sole. . . . It hurts here and here and there and there.

We made every church in the circuit. Lights! Camera!

Suffer the little children to come suffer the little children to come suffer-thelittlechildrentocome Sufferthelittlechildrentohospodepomeli—

Why don't they hurry and open the light? Please. Please, Please Daddy!

I learned to rise up slow, the white Bible between my palms, my head thrusting sharp into the frenzied shouting and up, up, into the certainty of his mellow voice soaring isolated and calm like a note of spring water burbling in a glade haunted by the counterrhythms of tumbling, nectar-drunk bumblebees. . . .

Teddy, Teddy! Where's my bear? Daddy!

You bear as you've sown. A growl.

Then, he appeared out of the brilliant darkness, dark and handsome.

You must not be startled at this blessed boy-chile, sisters and brothers, he intoned. Not by this little jewel. For it has been said that a little child shall lead them. Oh, yes! Where he leads me, I shall *follow*. Amen! And our God said, "Go ye into the wilderness and preach the Word," and this child has answered the sacred call. And he obeys. Suffer the little children. Yes! And it is said that the child is father to the man. So why be surprised over the size, shape, color of the vessel? Why not listen to his small sweet voice and drink in the life-giving water of the Word . . . ?

Listen to the lamb, he said. But I heard the bear a-growling. Teddy! Teddy! Where? Gone on the lamb's chop.

I used to lie within, trembling. Breathing through the tube, the hot air and hearing the hypnotic music, the steady moaning beneath the rhythmic clapping of hands, trembling as the boys marched me down a thousand aisles on a thousand nights and days. In the dark, trembling in the dark. Lying in the dark while his words seemed to fall like drops of rain upon the resonant lid. Until each time just as the shapes seemed to close in upon me, Deacon Wilhite would raise the lid and I'd rise up slowly, as he taught me, with the white Bible between my palms, careful not to disturb my hair on the tufted pink lining. Trembling now, with the true hysteria in my cry:

LORD, LORD, WHY HAST THOU . . . ?

Mankind? What? Correct. Lights in. Camera!

Donelson, the makeup is too pasty. The dark skin shines through like green ghosts.

Yeah, but you tell me how to make up a flock of crows to look like swans.

Donelson, you can do anything that you really try. In the beginning is the image. Use your imagination, man. Imagine a nation. New. Look into the camera's omniscient eye, there's a magic in it. And the crows shall be . . .

Whiter than swans? Balls! Let's change the script and make them Chinamen or Indians. . . . What do you say, Karp?

And in the confusion birthed by women that world rolled on like rushes on a Moviola. There'd be shouting and singing and that big woman in Jacksonville came running down front, looking like a fullback in a nurse's helper's uniform, crying, He's the Lamb of God, he is! And trying to lift me out and Teddy coming up with my legs and my cap pistol catching in the lining and Daddy Hickman grabbing her just in time to prevent the congregation from seeing, saying sotto voce, Deacon Wilhite, *git* this confounded woman away from here even if you have to put a headlock on the fool! She's about to upset *everything!*

He took Teddy and refused to buy me a soda and the next night I refused to rise up. I refused the call, just lay there in the throbbing deathlike stillness with the top up and my eyes closed against the brilliant light and him looming with outstretched arms above me, until he got them singing strong and came down and promised me I could have Teddy back. . . . When? *Beary me not in lone Calv'ry.* . . . Then standing there above me the shadow leaving and the light bright to my opened eyes, saying, This boy-chile, brothers and sisters, lies here in a holy coma. No doubt he's seeing visions beyond this wicked world. Ah, but he shall rise up as all the saved shall rise up—on that morning. . . .

But I didn't budge, demanding an ice cream cone with silence. Vanilla I wanted.

Suffer the little children to come . . .

Flora was in the alley picking sunflowers. We were alone. I'll show you mine if you'll show me yours, I said.

What! Button up your britches, li'l ole boy, she said. You ain't even old enough to dogwater.

But I just want to *see.*

You goin' see stars, that's what you gonna see 'cause I'm goin' to tell my mama if you don't go 'way.

Nine stitches saved Choc Charlie, or so they say.

One morning as he was shining his shoes in Georgia, I heard Daddy Hickman singing:

> *I'm going to the Nation, baby,*
> *Going to the Territory.*
> *Says I'm going to the Nation. . . .*
> *Going to the Territory . . .*

like any lonesome sinner but making it sound like "Beulah Land," puzzling me.

It haunts here and there; in and out.

Why don't Revern Hickman open . . . They were all hicks; I told me then, that's why I renounced them beyond all recovery. What a hickery-docket was Hick hock—the camera, Donelson; we've got to keep moving west. Hail to the great hickocracy. It hurts there. The waters of life. Thirst. Texas hots. Ladies and gentlemen, I swear, it was a strange adventure.

> *I met Mr. Rabbit*
> *Down by the pea vine*
> *And I asked him where he's gwine*
> *Well, he said, just kiss my b'hin'*
> *And skipped on down the pea vine. . . .*

Mr. Speaker, Mr. Speaker! I should like to call to the attention of this great body the insidious activities of those alien-minded groups who refuse the sacred obligations of becoming true Americans. . . . *How here I reject them and out of my rejection rule them. They create their own darkness and in their embarrassment left all to chance my changed opportunity. It haunts hard in this moment.* . . . Oh, they sweep around us with their foreign ways. Yes, and in the second and third generations they reject even these foreign but respectable traditional modes of their parents and become barbarians, maimed men; moral terrorists, winos, full of self-pity. Men filled only with the defeatist spirit of rejection. They become whiners and complainers, demanding the deification of their sloth. The soft touch. Nothing here in our fine, hard-won American tradition is good enough for them. Always it is some other way of life which wins them. It is the false promises of our enemies for which they thirst and hunger. Yes, and sabotage! Mr. Speaker, in their arrogance they would destroy our tender vines. And in their fury they would weaken the firm foundation of our way of life. In their malicious frenzy to evade responsibility they would destroy that which has given them shelter and substance, and the right to create themselves. Oh yes! Yes! These rootless ones would uproot us all! Consider the time-scene: When they watch our glorious flag passing on parade they greet it with an inward sneer. When we honor our fallen dead, they secretly applaud the marksmanship of our enemies. When we set forth to preserve our honor and the sanctity of our homes and the health of our customs they would cast into the smooth machinery of our national life their intractable and treacherous wooden shoes. Abuse, abuse! In the name of lawful dissent they seek our destruction. They would poison the spring of our unity. They would destroy the horses of our power. They would reduce our sacred diversity and dominate us! They would send the sapper of their hate to mine the defenses of our belief. They would pull down the protective walls of our fortress. But leave us to the peaceful glories of this great land they will not!

Ah Bliss, Bliss, so you've come to this. And I believed . . .

Nay! Nay! They would sweep over us with their foreign ways. They would undermine us with their un-Christian doubt. They are a thorn in our flesh, a dagger in our back; a putrid offense in the nostrils of every true red-blooded American. And it is time that we defend ourselves. We have been asleep, Mr. Speaker, my fellow citizens; asleep in our dream of security! Asleep in our well-meaning, sportsmanlike way of wishing the other fellow well. Asleep in the false security of accepting all men of goodwill who would be free as men of honor. And, I'm sorry to say, we have not been vigilant enough in administering our heritage. Our stewardship has been indeed faulty, so the fault is our own. For while we've looked the other way these internal enemies have become, in the words of that great Irish poet, kinsman no doubt to many of our colleagues here—in the words of Yeats—these enemies have become all too full of passionate intensity! Though fluent and often multilingual, they have not learned to speak in the true spirit of our glorious tongue—and yet, they strive to destroy it! They have not earned the right to harbor such malice, for this country has been kind to them. It has demanded little of them, and yet, they declare us decadent, deceptive, immoral and arrogant. Nor has our social life given them justification for such cynical disillusionment, such loss of confidence. Indeed, the country has strengthened them. It has freed them of the past and its terror. Yes, we have given them the strength which they would use against us. They have not the right even when most sincere to criticize us in the name of other so-called democracies. For they believe in *no* democracy! For there are those among us who yearn for the tyrant's foot upon their necks! They long for authority, brutal and unyielding. It is their nature to lick the boots of the strong and to spit in the faces of those weaker than themselves. This is their conception of the good life. This is their idea of security! This is their way, the way they would substitute for our principle of individual freedom, the way in which man faces nature, society and the universe with confidence. Moving from triumph to triumph, ever increasing the well-being of all . . . Each and every true American is the captain of his fate, the master of his own conscience.

Ah, yes! But somewhere we failed. We let down the gates and failed to draw the line, forgetting in our democratic pride that there were men in this world who *fear* our freedom; who, as they walk along our streets, cry out for the straitjacket of tyranny. They do not wish to think for themselves and they hate those of us who do. They do not desire to make—they tremble with dread at the very idea of making—their own decisions; they feel comfortable only with the whip poised ever above their heads. They hunger to be hated, persecuted, spat upon and mocked so that they can justify their overwhelming and destructive pride and contempt for all who are different, for they are incapable of being American. They are false Americans, for to be an American is truly to accept the hero's task as a condition of our everyday living and to bring it off with conscious ease! It is to take the risk of loneliness with open eyes; to face the forest with empty hands but with stout heart. To face the universal chaos in the name of human freedom and to win! To win even though we die but win and win again each day! To win and take the suffering that goes with winning along with the joy. To look any man in the face, unhindered by Europe's deadweight of vicious traditions. It is to take a stand, a man alone . . . going West.

Ah, it holds hard. Camera! Lights! Lights! Never cut call—now action.

Bliss, he said, there's but one thing keeping you from being a great preacher—you just won't learn to sing! A preacher just has *got* to sing, Bliss. But I guess whoever it was give you that straight hair and white skin took away your singing voice. Of course you're still pretty young. I just don't know, Bliss. I guess I have to do a lot of praying over you, 'cause you're definitely a preacher. . . .

Preach, cried the King, and forty thousand strained out the words.

Mr. Speaker . . . How far the heights?

Yes, preach! But how could I sing the Lord's song, a stranger man?

Mr. Speaker, I will be recognized. . . .

I took her for a walk under the cottonwood trees. The sticky buds lay on the ground. Spring warned me but I was young and foolish and how could I not go on and then go on? How make progress with her along? I had nothing, I was a bird in flight. And it was as though I mounted her in midair, and we were like a falcon plummeting with its prey. Pray for me—now. No, I was gentle then. She melted me. She poised me in time tenderly. Pray, for it was so. A gentle bird, but I was high and flying faster, faster, faster. I traveled light, Donelson said, so I could roll up the moss. To make the most of circumstance, I flew. What was possible was possible in one way only, in a spiraling flight. Who could release more than vague hopes for heaven on a movie screen . . . Lights!

CHAPTER 5

Now the Senator could hear a voice quietly calling, *Bliss? You hear me, Bliss?* but was too weary to respond. His lips refused to answer, his throat throbbed with unstated things, the words starting up from deep within his mind and lodging there. He could not make them sound, and he thought, The circuit is out; I'm working with cables like those of Donelson's lights, scenes go dark and there's only a sputtering along the wire.

Yet his mind flowed dreamily and deep behind the purple shadows, welling from depths of time he had forgot, one short-lived self mysteriously surviving all the years and turns of face. Once I broke the string I whirled, I scudded the high places, bruised against tree-tops and building spires, snagged here and there for a time but always sailing. But once spring turned me turtle, I tried to sing—that's a part Daddy Hickman doesn't know. The old bliss still clung to me; childlike beneath my restlessness, stubborn. Liked the flight of birds then; cardinals streaking red across the fields, red wings on blackbirds and whistling quail at eveningtide. And metal-blue dragonflies and ladybirds in the dust, and catleaps in the sun. Black cat poised on hind feet like a boxer, waiting to receive a squirt of milk from a cow's teat, the milk white on the whiskers and the flash of small pink tongue.

Inwardly he smiled. Where—Kansas? Bonner Springs, Kansas City, buildings black from the riots. No one would believe it me, not even for that flash of time and pleasure which I have denied on platform and in the Senate a million times by word, gesture and legislation. Now it's like a remembered dream or screen sequence that—listen to the mockingbird up in his apple tree—that time-slain moment breathed in and cried out and felt ago. This Bliss that passeth understanding you never know, you Reverend H, but still a turn in the dance . . . Where am I?

Bliss? I say can you hear me, Bliss? You want the nurse? Just move your fingers if you do and I'll get the girl.

Girl? There was a girl in it, yes. What else? There and then. Out there where they thought the new state a second chance for Eden . . . Tell it to the Cherokees!

What are you trying to say, Bliss? Take it slow, boy. I'm still with you. I'll never leave now, so . . .

. . . We were under the trees, away from the town, away from Donelson, Karp and the camera. There, how glorious to have been there. Below the park-space showed; shade here, sun there, in a dreamy, dappled mid-afternoon haze. We were there. High up the trees flurried with birdsong, and one clear note sang above the rest, a lucid, soaring strand of sound; while in the grass cicadas dreamed. For a moment we stood there looking down the gentle rising-falling of the land, while far away a cowbell tinkled, small across some hidden field beyond the woods. Milkweed ran across the ground. Imagine to remember—was it ever? Still. Thistle purple-blue, flowers blue, wisteria loud against an old rock wall—was this the season or another time? Certainly there were the early violets among the fallen pine needles—ago too, but that was Alabama and lonesome. Here she was close beside me and as we moved down the grassy slope the touch of her cool sweat-dampened arm came soft against me and went and came coolly again and then again as we went down the hill into the sun. Oh keep coming coming— Then through the sun into the dappled shade. How long ago, this comes comesa fall? Aches here, aches in spring like a lost limb refusing to recognize its dismemberment, no need to deny. Then too, but sweet. Coming just above my shoulder her glossy head, her hair in two heavy braids, and I seeing the small gold ring sunk snug in the pink brown berry of her ear. A smile dreaming on her serenely profiled face. And I remembered the Bliss years. He, Bliss, returned. (Laly was like 'lasses candy, with charm of little red socks in little girl's black patent leather shoes on slim brown legs, her gingham panties playing peekaboo beneath a skirt flip as a bird's tail, and her hair done up in tight little braids. *Bliss loves Laly,* I wrote in the sand where the ladybirds lived but the me preacher wiped it out. Then I wrote, *Bliss loves you know who,* and the preacher me wiped that away. So only *Bliss* and *loves* remained in the sand.) But she coming now was no Laly and I no preacher for a long time now and Bliss no more, though blissful beside her moving there. Saying inside my head, Touch me, touch me, touch me, you . . . And remembered the one phrase, "teasing brown," and used it, feeling her cool bare flesh so thinly veiled with fragrant sweat against my short-sleeved arm and said aloud,

Are you one?

One what? she answered me, turning her face with her eyes dreaming a smile. What're you talking about, Mister Man?

You, I said. Are you a teasing brown?

She laughed and I could feel her coming to me in waves, heavy around me, soft like hands pressing gently along the small of my back, sounding the column of my spine. I breathed her in, all the ripeness, all the sweetness, all the musky mysterious charm and the green afternoon approving. She smiled, her eyes turned up to mine, her irises soft as scuppernongs in their gentle, blue-white orbs.

It must have been some ole blues singer you learned that from, she said.

Maybe so, you're probably right, but are you?

I'm brown, and that's a plain fact for anybody to see, she said. And the full black eyes were on me now, softly laughing. But I'm not teasing anybody. I'm the country one, Mister Big-City Man. Mister Moving-Picture Man. You teasing me. Don't you like brown-skinned folks?

Now just what do you think? I said.

I think a lot of things, she said, but—

She smiled again and the whole afternoon seemed to swing around her glossy head. I breathed deeply the blossoms and sunlight and there was a sigh in it. I thought, Here is the place to stay, grow up with the state, take root. . . . Yes, here. Come, come. She pointed:

You want to go down yonder under those trees? It looks to me like a fine place to lay the spread.

Yes, I said, swinging the basket in my hand. Yes, I want to go anywhere you say, Miss Teasing Brown, yes I do. He was trying to break out of my chest. Bliss, fighting me hard. But you're looking at *me,* she said. Look down yonder where I mean, she pointed. See, under that tree with the blossoms.

A fine peach-fuzz of hair showed on her leveled arm, almost golden in the sunlight.

It's fine, I said. Just the place for a time like this.

A bee danced by as on a thread. I felt a suspension of time. Standing still, my eyes in the tree of blossoms, I let it move through me. Eden, I thought, Eden is a lie that never was. And Adam? His name was "Snake." And Eve's? An aphrodisiac best served with raw fresh oysters on the half-shell with a good white wine. The spirit's there. . . . She arose she rose she rose up from the waves.

Mister Movie-Man, she said, you sure have a lot of sleep in your voice.

And her laughter was gay in the afternoon stillness, shaping and making the quiet alive. And suddenly I wanted to say, Hey, I'm Bliss! I'm Bliss again, but there's hell in me. There was no alienation ringing in that laugh, so I joined her, startling the quiet. We laughed and laughed. I picked up a smooth stone and sent it sailing, a blossom bursting as it was kissed by a bee. Dreamer, I said, I'm full of dream—

And we came through the parklike space, into shade and out again, her cool skin touching mine. Touching and leaving and coming again unself-consciously, skin-teasing skin in gentle friction. Damn Bliss! And she was a fragrance mixed with the spicy odors of the parklike space broken by light and shadow. My purpose too. And I thought, Turn back now. Now is the time, leave her and go West. You've lingered long enough, so leave before complications. So I thought. But Bliss said, Come. Come. And I turned turtle and tried to sing. Suddenly she said,

Look!

And there beneath a bush I saw a white rabbit, its pink nose testing the air before its alerted, pink-veined ears. It watched us moving by, frozen beneath a flowering shrub.

That's somebody's Easter bunny lost out here in the woods, she said. I hope nothing gets him 'cause he don't look like he knows how to take care of himself. There's foxes and hawks out here. Even evil ole wildcats. Poor little ole thing.

And I was disturbed with memory. Sister Wilhite had nicknamed Bliss "Bunting" a bird. But some of the kids had changed it to "Bunny" a rabbit and this had led to fights. I had been lost too, in Atlanta—but later. I thought, He'll be all right, innocence is its own protection—or would be in the snows. Hey, Rev Hickman, gospel truth or pious lie?

We went on, in the shade now, the light softly filtering the high-branched trees, her shoulder touching my arm and that wave of her enfolding me as cool mist clings to a hot hollow at twilight; my mind saying, No, this is enough; leave now. Leave the moment unbroken in its becoming. Fly before you fall, flee before you fail— And then I stumbled over the buried stone and heard her saying,

Watch out there, Mister Movie-Man.

And I felt her hand upon my arm and I could not breathe. Then we moved on and I fought Bliss for my arm to keep in its place against my side, denying that sweet fugitive fulfillment. And somehow there were three of us now, although only two were actually within the trees, Bliss inside me but still I felt the stranger following. Twice I turned but couldn't see him. I should have run.

Pink blossoms were thick in the tree, the petals scattered broadside upon the grass, and as I breathed them in the fragrance mixed wildly with her own and that cool touching and going of her peach-brown arm sang in me like passionate words whispered in a dark place. Who spread the petals along our path, my mind asked, who arched this afternoon above our heads? And looking down at her feet twinkling in and out below her long, ankle-length skirt, I said, How beautiful are your feet in shoes, Miss Teasing Brown.

She stopped and looked at me full face, a question in her dark eyes.

You're the tease, she said. I think you're laughing at me, Movie-Man. Though he *was* part Cherokee my papa wasn't no prince and you know it. You see, I know where those words come from.

I looked at her, suddenly cold, and from far back I could hear a voice saying, Reveren Bliss, do you preach Job? And I thought, *Give Job back his boils, he deserved them* as I saw the sparks in her eyes' black depths. I said,

No, no I'm not laughing at all. To me they are beautiful, princess or no princess. And it doesn't take a Solomon to say how beautiful are thy feet in sandals.

I don't know about you, she said, I swear I don't know about you, Mister Movie-Man.

There's nothing to know, I said. I come like water, and like wind I go—only faster. I laughed, remembering:

> Said a rabbit to a rabbit
> Love ain't nothing but a habit
> Hello there, Mister Rabbit.

You're fast, all right, she said, kneeling and looking up past my head to the sky.

There's not a cloud to be seen, she sighed.

That's how it was, no clouds, only tall trees filtering the sunlight back across the clear space and the blossoms above. Standing there I watched her remove the cloth from the basket and begin spreading it upon the grass.

Why don't you sit down and stay awhile, she said, patting a place for me.

I sat, watching with my chin resting upon my knees as her hands came and went, removing sandwiches wrapped in wax paper from the basket, placing them on the cloth.

These here are chicken, she said, and these ham, and *these* are Texas hots.

And there were boiled eggs wrapped in twists of paper like favors for a children's party; and tomatoes, and a chocolate cake and a thermos of iced tea with mint leaves and lemon slices floating in it. She served with a gentle feminine flair of which I would have denied she was capable. I was on dangerous ground.

Do you like a drumstick? she said. Men usually like a drumstick, though we also have the breast.

I prefer the drumstick, I said. Do you know many men?

More than we have drumsticks. More than we have breasts too. She broke off. —What you mean, do I know many men?

Thanks, I said. It was crisp and flaky, a nice weight in the fingers. I mean *beaux,* I said.

Boy *beaux* but no men *beaux.* They all been boy *beaux,* Mister Movie-Man, and they don't really count. Lord, I almost forgot the coleslaw. Here it is in this mayonnaise jar. Let me help your plate to some.

I watched her, thinking wildly, What would happen to this natural grace under coaching? With a formal veil placed between it and the sharp world and all the lessons learned and carried out with this native graciousness to warm the social skills? Not a light against a screen but for keeps, Newport in July, Antibes with the proper costumes. Saratoga. Could she fly right? With a sari, say, enfolding her girlish charm? What if I taught her to speak and not to speak, to parry in polished tone the innuendoes dropped over cocktail crystal? To master the smile in time that saves lines? With a diamond of a certain size on that slender hand. Or an emerald, its watery green in platinum against that peach-brown skin. Who blushed this peach? . . . Did the blight I brought begin in fantasy? There was a part in her black hair; her scalp showed clearly through.

I said, The chicken is wonderful. How'd you get it so flaky?

I cooked it till it was done, she said. She made a face at me. How'd you learn to make moving pictures?

Oh that's a secret, I said.

Frying chicken is a secret too, she said.

I laughed. You baked the bread too. Is that a secret?

Uh-huh, sure I did. Most folks do their own baking in this town—only that's not a secret.

It's almost as good as the chicken, I said.

Thank you, Mister Movie-Man. It's right nice for you to say so. But I won't believe you unless you eat a lot. There's plenty and I expect a man to eat like a man.

And suddenly I had dressed her in a pink sari, swathing her girlish form in Indian silk, a scarlet mark of caste on her forehead, and me in tails and turban of immaculate white observing her with pride as now her head goes back with gay burst of laughter, her throat clean and curved and alive and as alive as a robin's, following some polished shaft of wit. No, the turban a mistake for me but the sari for her, yes. Gold brings out the blue of blue eyes. A gold turban for me. Walking her along Fifth Avenue with all the eyes reacting and she no flapper but something more formed, more realized, more magically achieved, and the crowds' imagination whirling like these blossoms tossed in a whirlwind and blown in the million directions of their hopes, hates, fancies, dreams, and we, she and I, become all things to all minds, drawing out their very souls, their potentialities set athrob by the passage of our forms through their atmosphere, sending them ever seeking for some finer thing. Angels and swine and bearers of divers flags and banners becoming more and less than themselves in the vortex of our ambiguity. . . . Thoughts like these while before me she nibbled a chicken wing undreaming of my wildness. Ah, my fair warrior, my cooing dove, we'll create possibility out of rags and bones and hanks of hair; out of silks and satins and bits of fur, out of gestures and inflections of voice and scents orchestrated funky-sweet; with emphatic nods and elusive sympathies and affirmations and every move to all of them a danced proclamation of "I believe you can, I know you can; we can in faith achieve the purest dream of our most real realities—look upon us two and be your finest possibilities."

Why are you looking at me like that? she said.

And there she was again, before me with her warm, high-cheeked face tilted to one side in question, the fine throat rising out of the white blouse, brown, be-peached, as alive and expressive as any singing bird's. She wore a small gold watch pinned to her waist and her napkin was tucked there and I said, I was dreaming. Did you realize that you make men dream?

Her mouth became a firm straight line beneath her smiling eyes.

You sitting here eating my fried chicken and can tell me you're dreaming? And her head went back in girlish pout. You give me back my something-to-eat this very minute!

But it's all part of the dream, I said. You and the blossoms and the lunch and the weather. All we need is some cold watermelon or perhaps some peach ice cream.

She arched her eyebrows and shook her head. Now just listen to him. Sounds like he wants everything. I can't figure you out, Mister Movie-Man, she said.

What do you mean?

The way you talk sometimes. Once in a while you sound just like one of us and I can't tell whether you mean it or just do it to make fun of me.

But you know I wouldn't make fun of you. You know I wouldn't. . . .

I hope not, she said, but you do sound like us once in awhile, especially when you get that dreamy look on your face. . . .

I haven't noticed, I said. I just talk as I feel.

Well, I guess you feel like us—every once in a while, I mean. Can I ask you a question?

Anything at all, Miss Teasing Brown, I said.

She smiled and lowered her sandwich. Where'd you come from to here, Mister Movie-Man?

From different places back East, I said.

Oh, she said, I kinda thought so. . . . You not from Chicago?

Never been there, I said. And looking at her nibbling the sandwich, her soft eyes on my face, I thought of some of them. *We had had a rough time, coming through all of that cloudburst of rain, having to avoid the towns where I might have been recognized and the unfriendly towns where the oil rigs pounded night and day, making the trip longer and our money shorter and shorter. Getting stuck in the mud here and having engine trouble there, the tires going twice and the top being split by hailstones the size of baseballs and almost losing all of the equipment off a shaky ferry when we crossed a creek in Missouri. Still, there was some luck with us—my luck or maybe Karp's—I have always honored my luck—and we managed to keep the film and the equipment dry and the patches and the boots held on the tires until we reached her town. But on our way, moving through the Ozarks and the roads steep and rocky and having to push the car out of ruts and Karp complaining of ever having left the East and complaining, as we strained and sweated in the mud, against all the goy world and all our troubles were goy and our journey goy and goy our schemes; complaining all the way of what we did and now several times a millionaire with air immaculate and still complaining only now more pious. But then along the way Donelson goaded him on:* Why the hell, Sweet Jesus, did you ever leave Egypt and all those spades? Why didn't you stay and lay Pharaoh's second-best daughter and make another Moses? Put your back into it, Jew boy. Act like a white man for once.

And having to step between them . . . What would she have made of it, the glamour she longed for locked in such grubby circumstance? *Driving them as I was driven and some towns suspicious and others without the proper places to work and the people uninterested or the days without* sun and the long hot stretches of green green green with no thoughts beyond continuing and little shade—Amen! Then back there in the town where Hickman had taken me long ago, a stop on the endless circuit and Donelson trying to get permission from the warden to shoot scenes (We cain't use them we'll sell them to Griffith or Zucker, he said) but getting nowhere. We were lucky they didn't keep us there, what with that cross-eyed bass drummer recognizing Donelson and dropping his cymbal and yelling Hey Rube! from the bandstand and how were Lefty Louie and Nick-the-Greek? How do you know them? I said. Lester Donelson said, Places where I've been there's always a Lefty Louie and a Nick-the-Greek. And in the hotel the whores were all so ladylike, with high-style airs and comic bitchery and the bellhops black—except for the fat, bald-headed, full-lipped captain whose pale, milky skin was so dense with freckles that he looked like a white man who'd rusted in the rain three days after drowning. He had our number when we first walked in, though how much of it I couldn't tell, but when I looked at him the spots seemed to detach themselves before my eyes and move to a tango rhythm across his broad expanse of face—da de dum dum—and back again. His eyes casing me as though to say, I know and you know that I know, so what are you going to do about it? I slipped him a five we couldn't afford and I swear those spots returned each to its alloted place—muy pronto.

Thank you suh! he said. It's awfully white of you.

He knew all right, and he knew someone important too, selling white women and bootleg whiskey to the leading white citizens and the drummer trade and to a few not-so-leading black ones who slipped in unctuously wearing starched waiter's jackets with the buttons missing. Yes, suh! and donating good sums of money to the Afro-American Episcopal Missionary Society and to a finishing school for young black upper-class ladies in Baltimore. He had it made all right, with certain complications of adjustment it's true, but made. He could have taught us all. Should find the bastard, make him a career diplomat. Chief of Protocol. He trained them all to

*Southern manners. Smarter than most men in the House—any house. I kept away from him while we waited for sun and opportunity in that town in which he appeared to be the only one with a capacity for fantasy. Dominated by those high gray walls and the freedom of both those inside and out seemed to be measured in days marked off on the calendar. I'm number so-and-so and I know my time and knowing my time I know the who-what-why-wherefore of me. No dreams, please. Well, so much the worse for you. . . . We tried everyone from the Chamber of Commerce to the bootleggers and no one interested in backing us in bringing a little poetry to the town. We almost starved, broke and cooking beans in our room, patching and pressing with a secret iron borrowed from one of the girls until her pimp threatened Donelson and I was forced to do once more that which I said I'd never do again. But we were hungry and the memory of Eatmore came to the rescue. That was long ago. Grant and forgive us our agos. Amen. We left before dawn, half drunk and unwashed and our bills unpaid, slipping into the damp streets by the baggage entrance, past seven stacks of pulp magazines abandoned by the drummers—*Argosy, Blue Book, Ace *and* Golden Book *being saved by the baggage man for the kids in his neighborhood—agent of cultural baggage—doing what he could to keep them reading, stopping on the outskirts of the town as the light grew and buying cheese and crackers in a lamp-lit general store where the men on the road gang bought their lunch. That smell of hogshead cheese, that greasy counter, that glass case with trays of dull penny candy. John Deere plows set in neat bull-tongued rows on a side of the porch and the boxes for benches the barrels the drums the baby crib, well used from its yellow pad a string of pecans strung end to end for a teething toy was dangling; that great crock of lye hominy setting on the counter looking white and sinister and garnished by a single blue-tailed fly yet making me twinge for home—Hickman? There were shelves of prison-made shoes and peg after peg hung with prison-made harness—Donelson, I said, shoot those horse collars hung round the walls, they're frames for portraits of future Presidents. Yeah, he said, I know a few bastards who'd look pretty natural with their heads stuck through one of those; the mayor, the mine owners, the*

Chamber-Pots-of-Commerce gang. And near Holdenville getting those shots of the motorcycle circling the overflow embankment around the storage tank in the refinery yard, leaning toward the parallel and his eyes like set points of madness behind his goggles, bent low close over the handlebars, roaring as though intent upon circling there forever . . . MOVIE TYCOONS VISIT CITY was the headline and there we were looking out from page one, my arms across their shoulders and all three looking dashing and devil-may-care, each with goggles on forehead and each with an air of potency, mystery. The camera in the foreground. It made it easy and I kept things simple, a pageant dedicated to the founding of the town with all the old-timers parading past the camera on horseback, or in buckboards, then sitting before the courthouse in funeral parlor chairs and an Indian or two in the background. Shot everything from low angles to make them tall and imposing, and the fire engines I made a half-block long. Holdenville, yes, the weather was fine and Holdenville couldn't hold us. No, but what we made there was lost in Ponca City. Roustabouts, Indians, 1001 ranch hands, and Wild Bill Tillman in the flesh in a white suit and white Stetson and astride a white horse every hour of every day in the streets. Yes, but in the middle of a roaring circus who has time for silent scenes? Donelson went wild in the town, getting hot on the dice and winning a thousand then losing our stake before they cooled him off. Then when he asked to see the dice they threw him into the street. There was hardly enough money for gas then Karp to the rescue, found a cousin who helped us on our way. And what a cousin, walking around in a blanket, a bullet-smashed derby, and a necklace of rattlesnake buttons, selling snake oil and mustard plasters. Morris, the Osage Indian Jew, of whom Karp disapproved. Listen, Morris said, here there's no minyan in fifty miles so what if I temporarily joined another tribe? And let me tell you something, wise guy: I been scalped like the best of them!

I wanted him to join us but Karp was against it. But what a town, everything in our grasp: gunplay and Indians, dance-hall girls, cowboys and gamblers, gunmen, bandits, rustlers and law officers, the real frontier atmosphere and Wild Bill acting himself right off a circus poster. But it was all too real and when we set up the camera on the street they gathered around, looking from everywhere. Then, understanding, they knocked us down and fifteen .45s were looking us dead in the eye.

What's the big idea, I said.

What's your name, the one-eyed one said.

We told him and what we were about.

Pictures, *he said. We don't need any dam' pictures around here.*

Maybe you *don't but other folks do, Donelson said. We'll put this town on the map.*

Map? the one-eyed one said. We don't want it on any goddam map. You want to ruin everything?

We're trying to help, Karp said. We can help it grow.

We don't need any help. We don't want no growing. Get up on your knees. He pointed the pistol.

We looked into their miscellaneous faces and did what he said.

All right, One-eye said, from now on you three cockies are going to be known as the three monkeys . . .

Why you—— Donelson began, starting up.

One-eye moved without bending. There was a flashing arc of movement and at the smackcrunch of impact Donelson sprawled in the dirt, his cheek flaming with the red imprint of a .45's long barrel.

Now shut up, Rebel, One-eye said, and you'll keep healthy.

God damn you, Donelson said, scrambling to his knees. But this time I grabbed him, holding on.

Shut up, I said, we're outnumbered. Can't you see that?

Now you're talking, One-eye said, glaring down. And don't you forget it! Outnumbered, outgunned and outmanned!

He grinned, shaking the whiskey to an oily foam, his thumb over the bottle-mouth. And you, he said, dowsing whiskey on Donelson's head, I now baptize Mister Speak-No-Evil. So from now on keep your big cotton-pickin' mouth shut tight as your daddy's smokehouse!

Then, pouring whiskey on Karp's bowed head, he said, And your buddy here is named forthwith, like the lawyers say, Hear-No-Evil.

Out of the corner of his swelling mouth Donelson's voice came harsh and violent. All right, Israelite, he said, Where's your goddam cunning now? Why don't you blow your fucking horn!

Karp looked straight ahead, kneeling there in the dust, his face calm, his eyes tragic and resentful yet resigned. As though the world was affirmed in the pattern of his forefathers' prediction. So he was prepared to die a stranger in a strange land, resigned before even this random fulfillment of prophecy. The goyim were repeating once more their transgression against him. . . .

I shook my head feeling the hot splash of whiskey soaking my skull. My eyes stung as it coursed down my face and I suppressed a scream, holding my breath. And I seemed to be walking under water and I no longer saw them there above me. For I was in the kingdom of the dead, tight and enclosed. Back in the box . . .

Don't appear to like it much, someone said and laughed.

And you, One-eye said, I name See-No-Evil.

I could see him then, his collar band held with a brass button, his rotten teeth, his drooped lid, stepping back and the others no longer threatening but laughing. My knees were aching but I could see very sharply now. The hair that showed on his knuckles, sprouted from his ear, his flared nostrils.

All right, boys, One-eye said, let 'em up.

We got up and I picked up the camera and folded the tripod. A drop of whiskey had splashed the lens and I polished it away with the end of my tie. I looked—Donelson's face was bright red and twitching as he watched One-eye take a drink and pass the bottle around. One-eye stuck the pistol in his waistband and rocked back and forth on his heels, smiling now and his missing eye giving his face the look of a battle-scarred, shell-shocked tomcat. Then the bottle came to Donelson, paused before him, and before he could open his mouth I said,

Drink up. Go ahead. . . . Then Karp took it, even though he didn't drink.

Now you got the right idea, One-eye said. You're getting the hang of how to live in this town. This here's a good town, you monkeys; the best town in the West. All you have to know is how to live in it. So I says: Go drink yourself some whiskey. Go diddle yourself some broads—we got all kinds from all kinds of places. Fact we got Frenchies, we got Poles, we got Irishers, Limeys, Eskimos, Yids, and even a few coal-shuttle blondes. That's right, and the price of poontang ain't high. So go shack up with a few and change your luck. We know the kind old Rebel here cottons after, don't we, boys? Let him sleep with Charleston Mary and he'll start to winning with the dice. What I mean is, enjoy yourself. Why, there's money laying around on the streets in this town. You can do most anything here as long as you can outdraw and outshoot the ones who don't like it. So like I say, you can do anything only don't let us see you poking that goddam piece of machinery at us. You understand?

We get it, Donelson said. But tell me something. . . .

What's that?

What time would you say it was?

Time? One-eye said. How the hell would I know? In this town we make our own fucking time. . . .

Mister Movie-Man, she said, you dreaming again?

Not now, I said. *Time is a juxtaposing of pains and pain hurts even after the object is gone, faded.*

You better not be while you're eating. But you were gone somewhere, flew right away from me. Or maybe you were thinking about the picture?

No, I said. Only about you. You make a very nice picture.

She looked a question, her head to one side. I sure hope I can act like you want me to, she said. I really never thought of being in a picture before but now I sure want to be able to do it. Will there be any fighting in it?

Some, I said.

And horses?

I'm not sure about that, I said. But there'll be love scenes. . . .

You mean I'll have to kiss somebody?

Sure, that's part of the love scene.

But in front of all those folks . . . and with his girl looking? She's angry with me already—

There'll be many more folks to see the picture, I said.

But that's different, she said. I won't be there. . . .

Don't worry about it, I said. I'll teach you how it's done. Now was the time to begin and I put down my sandwich and moved. I saw her large eyes and suddenly I ceased to dream.

You just work in the contest and win, I said. I'll take care of the rest. I was disturbed.

Oh, I will, she said. I'll raise more money than all the other girls put together. You'll have to give me the best part. . . .

Yes, I said, the best is yet to be, but you girls will have to work hard. Stir up the interest of everyone. Karp insists that we have the full cooperation of the community. . . .

Which one is Mr. Karp, the one with the camera?

No, that's Donelson. Right now Donelson is doing the shooting. Later on I'll take over. Karp is the other one.

Well, he won't have to worry because everybody is interested already. Two clubs are planning dances and another one—well, they're going to give a barbecue. Is Mr. Karp the boss?

Boss? No, he's just a partner like the rest of us. We're the three partners. What other plans do you have?

We're still thinking up things to do. We plan to give a combination hayride and trip-around-the-world.

What's a trip-around-the-world?

That's when you ride to different parts of town and go to different houses and in each house they have the food of some country—like Mexico for instance, and it's all decorated like a Mexican house and the boys and girls who give that part of the party will be dressed in Mexican costumes. And when you get there you buy the food and they give you some drinks and you can dance and have a good time. Then after a while everybody piles into the hay and the wagon goes to another house and there they'll find another country and another party. It keeps going on just like that.

That's interesting, I said, but you want to work hard on the popularity contest.

I mean to, she said, I really have to have that part. I like plays and things, they kind of take you out of yourself.

They do, I thought, and you have no idea how far.

Some English people were here last year and they put on some wonderful shows. With nice scenery and music and everything. You couldn't always understand what they were saying but it sounded so fine. Like listening to folks sing some of that opera music in a different language.

Did many folks go to see them?

Quite a few, she said. I went every night. A lot of folks did.

That's very good, but where'd they give the plays?

They gave them in the school auditorium. There's a stage there and they brought their own scenery for one of the plays. But you know something, Mister Movie-Man?

No, what?

When you listened to them real close you could see scenery that wasn't on the stage. They *said* the scenery and you could see it just as clear. You really could.

That's right, I said. Sometimes you can. But that's with a certain kind of play, movies are different. Everything has to be seen or scene. You've got good ears though. I touched where the gold wire

entered the soft lobe of her ear. She watched silently. Watched my
hand.

Thank you, Mister Movie-Man, she said, and have another drumstick. . . .

I thought about the contest and all their plans. A thousand would
get us to the coast and help us get a start. . . . Going to what nation
in what territory? And this time I'd let Karp hold the cash, he was
practical and more dependable than Donelson. He was down in the
business district picking up a few dollars at his jeweler's trade. He
could make a watch from the start, give him the tools, the metal
and the lathe. . . .

What will the story be about? she said.

I haven't decided yet, I said, but I'm working on it.

Well, I'm sure glad to hear that.

Why?

Because I saw your friends taking pictures all over the place.
What were they doing that for?

Oh that, I said, they're just chasing shadows, shooting scenes for
background. Later on when we start working we'll use them, splice
them in. Pictures aren't made in a straight line. We take a little bit
of this and a little of that and then it's all looked at and selected and
made into a whole. . . .

You mean you piece it together?

That's the idea, I said.

Well tell me something! she said. Isn't that just marvelous? Just
like making a scrap quilt, I guess; one of those with all the colors of
the rainbow in it——only more complicated. Is that it?

Just about, I said. There has to be a pattern though and we only
have black and white.

Well, she said, there's Indians and some of the black is almost
white and brown like me.

I looked up the hill, hearing the distant cowbell. Far above us the black and white coats of the herd lay like nomadic blankets against the close green hill, and higher still on the edge of the shade, two young bulls let fly at one another, head-on into the sun. They must have jarred the hill like thunder.

Hosan Johnny! Hosan Johnny!

Where'd I hear?

He shake his tail, he jar the mountain
He shake his tail, he jar the river.

A long time ago. I could see them back off and paw the earth preparing to let fly again. What was I doing here when there was so much to be done? Movement was everything. I had to move on, westward. How would I plot the scenario with these people? What line would engage them, tie them up in an image that would fascinate them to the maximum? Put money in thy purse, the master said. I needed it.

What time is it? I said.

She looked into the trees. A pink petal clung to her hair. About two-thirty, she said.

Two-thirty, I said. How can you tell without looking at your watch?

By the way the shadows slant against the trees, Mister Movie-Man.

By the shadows? Why don't you use your watch? Doesn't it run?

Sure, it runs, listen. . . .

I lowered my head to her blouse, hearing it ticking away. It was a little past two-thirty but she was close enough. She wore some faint scent—a trace of powder. I looked at her. There was no denying the charm of her.

You're right, I said. I wish I could do that. . . .

You could if you would stay in one town long enough, she said. Don't you have a watch?

I had it stolen back East, I said. I had pawned it in Newark.

Look, Donelson said, What's the plot of this thing?

We won't plot it, I said, we'll make it up as we go along. It depends upon how much dough they can raise. I'll think of something. Just shoot anything interesting you see.

Play it by ear, you mean? Karp said. With this little film we have?

That's right. By ear and by nose, by cheek and by jowl, by the foresight and the hindsight, by the foreskin and the rearskin, by the hair of my chinny chin chin and my happy nappy!

We stood in the street beneath a huge cottonwood tree, the camera resting on a tripod near the curb. For once there was no crowd. Sunlight, clear and unhazed, flooded the asphalt, and the odor of apple blossoms drifted to us from a pair of trees in a yard across the street. I could hear the bounce-rattle-scrape as a pair of little girls tossed jacks on the porch of a small house that sat behind a shallow lawn in which a bed of red poppies made bright red blobs in the sun. Beside me Donelson was rolling a Bull Durham cigarette and I fought my irritation under control. He was arrogant and impatient and he had no discipline. If I didn't guide him every minute he'd waste the film and antagonize the people. I'd look at the day's shooting and there would be nothing more than a jumble of scenes, as though the rambling impressions of an idiot's day had been photographed. With Donelson it was gelly, gelly, gelatine all day long and all images ran to chaos, as though Sherman's army had traumatized his sense of order forever. Once there was a sequence of a man whitewashing the walls of the slaughterhouse which stood at the edge of the town near the river, and this followed by a flock of birds strung out skimming over a stretch of field; then came shots of the courthouse clock at those moments when the enormous hands leaped across the gaps of time to take new positions but ever the same on the bird-fouled face, then a reversed flight of birds, and this followed by the clock hands whirling in swift reversal. Donelson ached to reverse time, I yearned to master it, or so I told myself. I edited a series of shots, killing time. The darkness between the frames longer than what was projected. Once there was a series consisting of a man and a boy and a boar hog, a cat and a great hairy spider—all shot in flight as they sought to escape, to run away from some unseen pursuer. And as I sat in the darkened hotel room watching the rushes, the day's takes, on a portable screen, the man seemed to change into the boy and the boy, changing his form as he ran, becoming swiftly boar and cat and tarantula, moving ever desperately away, until at the end he seemed, this boar-boy-spider-cat, to change into an old man riding serenely on an old white mule as he puffed a corncob pipe. I watched it several times and each time I broke into a sweat, shaking as with a fever. Why these images and what was their power?

And Donelson had sung, "Oh, while I sit on my ass on the ass of my ass a curious paradox comes to my mind: While three-fourths of my ass is in front of my ass the whole of my ass is behind." Oh, Donelson, that impossible Donelson. That bad boy with his toy. Sometimes I wondered if any of it had meaning for him beyond the joy of denying the reality of all that which he turned his lenses upon. . . .

From the walk I was listening to the dry, rhythmical, bounce-scrape-scrape-bounce of the knucklebone jacks and ball of the two little girls continuing, when suddenly from behind us a dark old fellow wearing a black Cordoba hat, a blue denim jacket and a scarf of fuchsia silk wrapped around his throat moved stiffly past on a fine black seven-gaited mare. Small and dry, he sat her with the stylized and monumental dignity of an equestrian statue and in the sun-slant the street became quite dreamlike. His leathery hands held the gathered reins upon the polished horn of a gleaming cowboy saddle and his black, high-heeled boots, topped by the neat, deep cuff of short tan cowhide riding chaps, rested easy and spurless in the stirrups as he moved slowly past as in meditation, his narrowed eyes bright glints in the shadow of his hard-brimmed hat. Donelson started to speak but I silenced him as I watched with whirling mind, filled with the sight and listening now to the mare's hooves beating with measured gait through the bright suspense of the afternoon—when suddenly a little boy in blue overalls exploded from between two small houses across the street and ran after the horseman, propelled by an explosion of joy.

Hi, there, Mister Love, he yelled. Make her dance, Mister Love, I'll sing the music. Will you, Mister Love? Won't you please, Mister Love? Please, *please,* Mister Love? clapping his hands as he ran pleading beside the mare's flank.

Dance her, Mister Love, he called, and I'll call the others and we'll all sing for you, Mister Love. . . .

Well, I'll be goddam, Donelson said beside me. What does the little bastard mean, he'll sing the music?

He means what he says, I guess, I said.

And who the hell is that, the Pied Piper on a gaited mare?

The children were singing now, following alongside the arch-necked mare as she moved, the old fellow holding his seat as though he were off somewhere in an elder's chair on a church platform— or on the air itself—watching the kids impassively as he stroked the horse's mane in time to its circus-horse waltzing.

There, I said, now *there's* something we can use. We could use that man, I said.

Donelson looked at me. So write a part for the nag and the kids, he said. You decided all of a sudden to make it a horse opera? He laughed. Now, by God, I've seen everything, he said.

No, I said. I was looking at the children move; some were waltzing in a whirl along the sidewalk, their arms outstretched, shouting and singing. They went past the houses, whirling in circles as they followed the dancing mare. A dog barked along a fence and through it all I could hear the first little boy's pure treble sounding high above the rest.

Suddenly I looked at Donelson— Why the hell aren't you shooting? I said, and saw his mouth drop open in surprise.

No film in the camera, he said. You told me to shoot exteriors of that mansion up in the north section of town. I forgot to reload. Besides you know we're short of film.

And all this happening right before our eyes, I said.

Maybe we could get them to run it through some other time, Donelson said. With a few chocolate bars and cones of ice cream you could buy all the pickaninnies in town. Though God knows what the horse and rider would cost. That old bastard looks like weathered iron. D'ya ever see anyone like him?

No, I said, and it'll never happen like this again. How often do I have to tell you that you have to have film in the camera at all times? We don't have the dough to make up everything, we have to snatch whatever passes, and in places like this anything can happen and *does*.

I cursed our luck.

A woman came out to stand on the porch of one of the houses shaking her head and hugging her body as though she were cold.

That Love, that ole hoss and those chillen, she said. They ought to put them all out in the meadow somewhere.

What is his name? I called.

That's ole Love, she said. That's ole Love New.

Then another voice spoke up and I became aware of an old woman sitting in a rocking chair on a porch two houses away down the street.

That's him all right. He's just the devil hisself and he's going to take those chillen off to Torment one of these days. You just mark my words.

She spat into the yard. Calling hisself an Indian and hound-dogging around. The old black tomcat. She spat again and I saw the snuff flash brown through the sunlight then snake across the bare yard to roll into a ball, like quicksilver across the face of a mirror.

Find out where the old fellow lives, I told Donelson. I watched them dancing on past the big cottonwood tree, the glossy horse moving with ceremonial dignity, its neck beautifully arched, and heard the children's bright voices carrying the melody pure and sweet along the air. They were coming to the corner now and suddenly I saw the old man rear the horse, the black Cordoba hat suddenly rising in a brisk salute above his white old head, freezing there for a moment, the mare dancing a two-step on her well-shod hooves. Then, as he put her down, I could hear the hooves ringing out on the road as he took the corner at a gallop, the children stringing after, cheering.

Damn, Donelson said, where do you think he comes from? Is there a circus in town?

Only you, I said. Only us out here without film.

We found Karp with one of his faith who ran a grocery store. They were discussing politics. We drank a soda and went back to the hotel to discuss the film. So how do we start? Donelson said. With a covered wagon? There must be enough of them rotting away in barns around this town.

Or how about an Indian attack? Karp said. Enough of them look like Indians to make things go fairly well. . . .

I was watching the little boy in blue overalls who had been left by the others. He had suddenly become a centaur, his back arched as he waltzed horse-style to his own *Taaa ta ta ta taaa ta ta,* back between the houses. At that age I preached Job, boils and all, but I didn't dance, and all his losses my loss of mother . . .

What about doing the Boston Tea Party, Donelson said, with these coons acting both the British and the Beantowners. That would be a riot. Make some up as Indians, take the rest and Harvard-up their talk. Even the camera would laugh. Too bad we can't film sound. We could out-do the minstrels 'Lasses White and all. I understand enough of them around here are named Washington and Jefferson and Franklin—put them in powdered wigs, give them red coats, muskets, carpetbags . . .

Some are named Donelson too, I said, watching the smile die out on his face.

So why not, he said. I'd feel awful bad if my folks didn't get their share.

No, I said, it'll be a modern romance. They'll have dignity and they'll play simple Americans. Good, hardworking, kindly ambitious people with a little larceny here and there. . . . Let's not expect to take their money and make fools of them while doing it.

What! And how the hell are we going to make these tar babies look like God's fair chosen creatures?

That's your problem, Donelson, I said.

God's going to turn you into a crow for that. . . . Who? You, that's who.

You must think you're a magician, Donelson said. Sometimes I have the feeling that you think you can do anything with a camera. So what's the romance all about? What'll we call it?

The Taming of the West, I said, or *The Naming of the Baby,* or *Who's Who in Tamarac* . . .

That's enough, Donelson said, I'll get it bye and bye.

Donelson, I said, we can shoot the scene right here. See, the lights should shine from above there, at an angle, cutting the shadow. And the leading lady will move through just as the hero comes into the door. . . .

Okay, okay, but who's going to play the part?

Never mind, there's bound to be some good-looking young gal in this town who'll be anxious to play it. There's bound to be plenty of talent here. I have a hunch.

Donelson looked at his glass. Say, he said, what you say they call this drink?

Black Cow.

You sure it isn't white mule? From the way you're talking I'd think so.

You just wait, you'll see.

I'll have to wait but we'd better get something going quick, because the dough is going fast. Go West, young man, where the pickings are easy—that's still the best idea for us.

We'll go West but for the while we'll linger here.

So we'll stay, but what about a script?

She smiled, her head back, and I could see the sweet throbbing of her throat. Thinking, *Time—time is all I need to take the mountain.* But now her mind was on the sheerest shadow she hoped to be upon the wall. I looked into the trees, the shadows there. Blossoms . . . fall.

He had called me to him on a bright day. . . .

I would like to have seen you when you were a little boy, she said.

That was a long time ago, I said.

Did you have a happy childhood?

I looked into her serious eyes. She was smiling.

It was blissful, I said.

I'm happy. I'm very happy because now there's something sad about you, she said. Something lonesome-like.

Like what?

She turned to rest on her elbow, looking into my eyes.

I don't rightly know, she said. It's something moody, and in the way you look at me sometimes. Do you feel sad?

No, I said, I just have a lot on my mind these days.

Yes, I guess you do, she said. Must be a lot on your hands too, judging from the way it's wandering.

I removed my hand. I'm sorry.

And is your hand sorry?

Yes.

Then give it here.

I gave it and she looked at me softly, taking my hand and holding it against her breast.

I didn't mean to be mean, she said.

I came close now, breathing the fever, the allure playing about her lips, her quick breath.

Please, I said, *Please.* . . .

You'll be good to me? *Really* good? Her eyes were frightened, the whites pale blue.

Oh yes, I said. Oh yes!

Ho, all that the seed for all that became the seed of all this, the Senator thought—hearing, *Bliss? What are you trying to tell me, boy? Want me to get you the nurse?*

Tell? Ah yes, tell . . . How she looked when I took her there in the shade, beneath the flowering tree, that warm brown face look-

ing past my head to the sky, her long-lashed eyelids dreamily accepting me, the stranger, and lifelove the sky—What? Who? Fate?
All creation, the rejected terms I fled?

Mister Man, she said, you're making me a problem I never had
before.

What kind of a problem?

She teased me with an elfish smile, then for a while she seemed
to dream.

What is the problem?

Well, I'll tell you the truth, Mister Movie-Man—I'm so country
I don't know where the long nose you have is supposed to go. . . .

She laughed then, placing the tips of her fingers there, tweaking
my nose. Her own was barely flatter than mine and I was provoked,
sweetly. My face suspended in her breath, the moisture came and I
went through, upon the sweet soft lips I rested mine. . . .

Bliss?

. . . And I could tell you how I drew her close then and how her
surrender was no surrender but something more, a materialization
of the heart, the deeper heart that lives in dreams—or once it
did—that roams out in the hills among the trees, that sails calm seas
in the sunlight; that sings in the stillness of star-cast night . . . The
heart's own that rejoins its excited mate once in a lifetime—like
Adam's rib returned transformed and glorious. I can tell you of her
black hair waved out upon the grass with leaves in it; the demands
of her hand, soft and soothing, with the back of my neck in it; her
breath's sweet fever inflaming my face. Even after all these years I
can tell you of passion so fierce that it danced with gentleness, and
how the whole hill throbbed with silence, the day gathering down,
ordered and moving radiant beneath the firm pumping of our enraptured thighs, I can tell you, tell you how I became she and she me
with no questions asked and no battle fought. We grasped the secret

of that moment and it was and it was enough. I can tell you as though it were only an hour past, of her feel within my arms, a girl-woman soft and yielding. Innocent, unashamed, yet possessing the necessary knowledge. How I was at rest then, enclosed in peace, obsessionless and accepting a definition for once and for once happy. How I kissed her eyes, pushed back the hair from her smooth forehead, held that face between my palms as I tried to read the mystery of myself within her eyes. Spoke words into her ear of which only then I was capable—how the likes of me could say, I love, I love . . . And having loved moved on.

CHAPTER 6

Bliss, boy?

Leaning forward, mountainous in the dwarfed easy chair, the old man watched the Senator's face now, observing the expressions flickering swiftly over the restless features of the man tossing beneath the sheet. He called again, softly, *Bliss?* Then heaved with a great sigh. I guess he's gone again, he thought.

Hickman searched his lower vest pockets with a long finger, extracting a roll of Life Savers and placing one of the hard circles of minty whiteness upon his tongue as he rested back again. Before him the Senator breathed more quietly now, the face still fluid with potential expressions, like a rubber mask washed by swift water. He looks like he's trying to smile, Hickman thought. Every now and then he really looks as though he would, if he had a little help. Maybe that's the way. When he wakes up I'll see what I can do. Anyway, he looks a little better. If only I could do something besides talk. Those doctors are the best though; the Government and his

Party saw to that. He'll have the best of everything, so there's nothing to do but wait and hope. The fact that they let *me* in here when he asked them is proof of something—I hope that they mean to save him. . . . There's such a lot I have to ask him. Why didn't I hop a plane and go and find out just what Janey Mason was telling me in her letter? I *knew* she didn't know how to say very much in a letter. Why? And who was that young fellow who did the shooting? Was it really that boy who Janey mentioned? It'll all come out, they'll find it out even if they have to bring him back from the dead— Ha! Bliss lost all sense of reason; he should have known that he couldn't do what he did to us without making somebody else angry or afraid. This here is a crazy country in which politicians have been known to be shot; even presidents. Pride. Let it balloon up and some sharpshooter's going to try to bring you down. What did Janey mean? Who? I remember back about twenty-five years ago when Janey sent word that a preacher showed up out there. That may have been Bliss. That's when he started whatever she was trying to tell me. One thing is sure, I heard that young fellow speak to the guard, he wasn't from Oklahoma and he wasn't one of us. A Northern boy, sounded like to me . . .

Suddenly he was leaning forward, staring intently into the Senator's face. The eyes, blue beneath the purplish lids, were open, regarding him as from a deep cave.

"Are you still here?" the Senator whispered.

"Yes, Bliss, I'm still here. How do you feel?"

"Let's not waste the time. I can see it on your face, so go ahead and ask me. What is it?"

Hickman smiled, moving the Life Saver to the side of his mouth with his tongue. "You feel better?" he said.

"I still feel," the Senator said. "Why don't you leave? Go back where you came from, you don't owe me anything and there's nothing I can do to help your people. . . ."

"My people?" Hickman said. "That's interesting; so now it's *my* people— But don't you realize we came to help *you,* Bliss? Remember? You should've seen us when we first arrived; things might have been different. But never mind all that. Bliss, was it you who went out there to McAlester and fainted on the steps of Greater Calvary one Sunday morning? That would be about twenty-five years ago. Was that you, Bliss?"

"Calvary?" The Senator's weak voice was wary. "How can I remember? I was flying above all that by then. I was working my way to where I could work my way to . . ." He sank to a safer depth. It was hot there but he could still hear Daddy Hickman.

"Think about it now, Bliss. Didn't you light there for a while and didn't you land on the Bible? In fact, Bliss, haven't you landed on a church each and every time you had to come down?"

Twenty-five years? He thought, Maybe he's right. "Perhaps the necessities, as they say, of bread brought me to earth. But remember, they always found me and took me in. It was in their minds. They saw what they wanted to see. It was their own desire. . . . It takes two as with the con game and the tango—ha!"

"Maybe so, Bliss," Hickman said, "but you allowed them to find you. Nobody went to get you and put you up there in the pulpit. Look here, can you see me? This is Daddy Hickman, I raised you from a little fellow. Was it you? Don't play with me."

"So much has happened since then. I was at McAlester, yes; but they were white. Or were they? Was it Me? Are you still here?"

"You mean you preached in a white church? That early?"

I think it's all mixed up. He closed his eyes, his voice receding. Is it my voice?

"Yes, High Style," the Senator said. "Huge granite columns and red carpets. Great space. Everyone rich and looking hungry; full of self-denial for Sunday. Ladies in white with lacy folding fans. Full bosoms, sailor straws. White shoes and long drawers in July. Men in shiny black alpaca, white ties. Stern Puritan faces, dry concentrate of pious Calvinist dilution distilled and displayed for Sunday. Yes, I was there. Why not? They sang and I preached. The singing was all nasal, as though God was evoked only by and through the nose; as though He lived, was made manifest in that long pinched vessel narrowly. That was a long time ago. . . ."

"So what happened?"

"I've told you, I preached."

"So what did you preach them, Bliss? Can you remember?"

Where can I hide? Nowhere to run here. It's a joke.

Yes, but what kind of joke?

"I preached them one of the famous sermons of the Right Reverend John P. Eatmore. In my, *our,* condition, what else?"

"Ha, Bliss, so you remembered Eatmore, Old Poor John. Now that there was a great preacher. We did our circuit back there. Revivals and all. Don't laugh at fools. Some are His. Holy, Holy, Holy, Lord God Almighty. Which of Eatmore's did you preach 'em, Bliss? Which text?"

Dreamily the Senator smiled. "They needed special food for special spirits, I preached them one of the most subtle and spirit-filling—one in which the Right Reverend Poor John Eatmore was most full of his ministerial eloquence: *Give a Man Wood and He Will Learn to Make Fire* . . . Eatmore's most Promethean vision . . ." Hot here.

No, Reverend Hickman seemed to say, his eyes twinkling, that's one that I've forgotten. I reckon I'm getting old. But Eatmore was the kind of man who was *always* true to his name and reputation. He put himself into everything he did. Preach me a little of it, Bliss; I'll lean close so you won't have to use up your voice. Let's hear you, it'll probably do us both some good. Go on, son.

But how? the Senator thought. Where are the old ones to inspire me? Where are the amen corner and old exhorters, the enviable shouting sister with the nervous foot tapping out the agitation on which my voice could ride? . . .

I don't think I can, he said. But his throat was silent and yet Hickman seemed to get it, to understand.

I taught you how, Bliss. You start it, you draw your strength and inspiration out of the folks. If they're cold, you heat them up; when they get hot, you guide the flame. It's still the same. You did it in the Senate when you told them about those Nazi fellows and swung the vote. . . .

What? the Senator said. You knew even then?

Eatmore, Bliss. Never mind the rest; let's talk about you preaching Eatmore in a white church. Do I have to start you off like I used to do when you were a baby? Didn't Eatmore begin something like this: He'd be walking back and forth with his head looking up at the ceiling and his hands touching prayer-like together? Then stop suddenly and face them, still looking out over their heads, saying:

Brothers and sisters, I want to take you on a trip this morning. I want to take you back to the dawn of Time. I want to let you move at God's rate of speed. Yes, let's go way back to the time of that twilight that had settled down upon the earth after Eden. Ah, yes! I want you to see those times because Time is like a merry-go-round within a merry-go-round, it moves but it is somehow the same even if you're riding on an iron tiger. Eden's fruit had done gone bad with worms and flies. Yes! The flowers that had been the dazzling glory of Eden had run wild and lost their God-given bloom. Everything was in shambles. It was a mess. Things were hardly better than jimson and stinkweeds. The water was all muddy and full of sulfur. The air back there stunk *skunk*-sharp with evil. And the beasts, the beasts of the jungle had turned against Man who had named them, and they no longer recognized him as the head of the animal kingdom.

In fact, they considered him the lesser of the animals instead. Oh, Man had come down so low that he was eating snakes. Brothers and sisters, it was an unhappy time— Yes, but even then, even in his uncouth condition, Man somehow remembered that he was conceived in the image of Almighty God. He had forgotten how to take a bath and John the Baptist was yet unborn, but still he was conceived in the image of the Almighty and even though he had sinned and strayed, he still knew he was Man. He was like that old crazy king I once heard about, who had messed up his own life and that of everyone else because he demanded more of everybody than they were able to give him and was living off of roots and berries in the woods but who knew deep down in his crazy mind that he was still a king, and knew it even though the idea made him sick at the stomach. Kingship was so *hard* and manship was so disgusting! He wanted to have it both ways. He wanted folks to love him like he wasn't king when he was carrying around all that power. Yes, Man had sinned and he had strayed; he was just doing the best he could, and that wasn't much.

Now that's enough for me, Bliss; you take it from there. Let's hear the old Eatmore, boy.

It's been a long time.

Bliss, all time is the same. Preach. Time is just like Eatmore used to say, a merry-go-round within a merry-go-round; only people fall off or out of time. Men forget or go blind like I'm going. But time turns, Bliss, and remembering helps us to save ourselves. Somewhere through all the falseness and the forgetting there is something solid and good. So preach me some Eatmore. . . .

You won't like it, the Senator said, closing his eyes.

I'll be the judge, Hickman said.

Amen. Yes, Man had sinned, brothers and sisters, and he had strayed. But he was still the handiwork of a merciful God. He car-

ried within him two fatal weaknesses—he was of little faith and he
had been contaminated by the great gust of stardust that swept over
the earth when Proud Lucifer fell like a blazing comet from the
skies. For Man had breathed the dust of pride, and it wheezed in his
lungs like a hellish asthma. Thus even though he mingled with the
beasts of the forest and Eden had become a forgotten condition
rankling with weeds and tares, a lost continent, a time out of his
brutish mind, still he retained his pride and his knowledge that he
was conceived in the image of God. Two legs God gave him to walk
around, two hands to build up God's world, and his two eyes had
seen the glory of the Lord. His voice and tongue had praised the fir-
mament and named the things of the earth.

Thus it was, brothers and sisters, that remembering his past
grace Man called upon the Lord to give him fire. Fire now! Just
think about it. In *those* times—fire! Even God in his total omni-
science must have been surprised. Man crying for *fire* when he
couldn't even deal with water. Remember, Old Noah was *long* since
forgot. Man drank dregs standing unpurified in the muddy tracks of
the tigers and the rhinoceroses! Fire! Why my Lord, what did he
want with *fire?*

He ate raw roots and the raw, still-quick flesh of beasts.

He drank the living blood jetting from the severed jugular veins
of cattle—and yet he cried for fire. Ah yes, today, long past we now
know it! Give a man wood and he will *learn* to make fire. But back
there in those days Man knew *nothing* about wood. Oh yes, oh
sure—he slept in trees, he swung from vines. He dug in the earth
for tender roots—but wood? What in the world was wood? He used
clubs of hickory and oak and even ebony . . . but wood—what was
wood? Did old Nero know about steel? Man knew no more about
wood than a hill of butter beans!

Ha! Now that was a true Eatmore line, Bliss. Preach it.

Suddenly Hickman turned. The door had opened and he saw a severe-looking, well-scrubbed young nurse, her blond hair drawn back severely beneath her starched cap, looking in.

"Don't you think you should leave and get some rest?" she said.

The Senator opened his eyes. "Leave us, nurse. I'll ring when I want you."

She hesitated.

"It's all right, daughter," Hickman said. "You go on like he said."

She studied the two men silently, then reluctantly closed the door.

Don't lose it, Bliss, Hickman said. Where did Eatmore go from there?

. . . knew no more about wood than a hill of butter beans . . . And still, this ignorant beast, this dusty-butted clown, this cabbagehead without a kindergarten baby's knowledge of God's world—brothers and sisters, this lowest creature of creatures was asking God for fire! I imagine that the Holy Creator didn't know whether to roar with anger or blast Man from the face of the earth with holy laughter. Fire! Man cried, *Give me fire!* I tell you it was unbelievable. But then time and circumstance caught up with him. *Give me fire!* he cried. *Give me fire!* Man became so demanding that finally God did rage in righteous outrage at Man's mannish pride. Oh yes!

For Man was beseeching the Lord for warmth when it was the *Sun* itself he coveted. And God knew it. For he knoweth all things. Not fire, oh no, that wasn't what Man was yelling about, he wanted the Sun!

Oh, give a man *wood* and he will *learn*—to make fire!

Amen!

So God erupted Hell in answer to Man's cries of pride. For Man had told himself he no longer wished to wear the skins of beasts for warmth. He wanted to rise up on his two hind legs and *be* somebody. That's what he did! He had seen the sun and now coveted the warmth of the blue vault of heaven!

Ah Man, ah Man, thou art ever a child. One named Hadrian, a Roman heathen, he built him a tomb as big as a town. Well, brothers and sisters, it's a jailhouse now!

One named Morgan built the great *Titanic* and tried to out-fathom one of God's own icebergs. Even though they should have known God's icebergs were still God's and not to be played with. Where are they now, Lord?

Full fathom five thy father lies, that's where. Down in the deep six with eyes frozen till Judgment Day. There they lie, encased in ice beneath the seas like statues of stone awaiting the Day of Judgment to blast them free.

Ho, ho they forgot to sing as the poet was yet to sing:

> *Lo, Lord, Thou ridest!*
> *Lord, Lord, Thy swifting heart*
>
> *Nought stayeth, nought now bideth*
> *But's smithereened apart!*
>
> *Ay! Scripture flee'th stone!*
> *Milk-bright, Thy chisel wind*
>
> *Rescindeth flesh from bone*
> *To quivering whittlings thinned—*
>
> *Swept, whistling straw! Battered,*
> *Lord, e'en boulders now outleap*
>
> *Rock sockets, levin-lathered!*
> *No, Lord, may worm outdeep*
>
> *Thy drum's gambade, its plunge abscond!*
> *Lord God, while summits crashing*

Whip sea-kelp screaming on blond
Sky-seethe, dense heaven dashing—

Thou ridest to the door, Lord!
Thou bidest wall nor floor, Lord!

Bliss, that's not Eatmore but it's glorious.

No, it's Crane, but Eatmore would have liked it, he would have sung it, lined it out for the congregation and they would have all joined in.

Yes, he would. Go on, boy. . . .

Thus did God send the lava streaming and scorching, searing and destroying, floating warmth and goodness within the concentric circles of evil which Man had evoked through his thunderous fall, his embrace of pride, though he had his chance. And now was time for God to laugh, because you see, sisters and brothers, just as today Man was blind to the mysterious ways of God, and thus Man ran screaming among the mastodons and dinosaurs. Ran footraces with the flying dragons, the hairy birds and saber-toothed tigers—tigers, Ha! Imagine it, with tusks as sharp, as long, as cruel as the swords of the Saracens who did attempt by bloodshed and fire to keep the Lord's message from the Promised Land, the land of Bathsheba's bright morning, of Solomon's enraptured song . . .

Preach it, Bliss. Now you're preaching Genesis out of Eatmore. . . .

Yes, ran screaming among the hellish beasts and his beastly fellowmen, all wrapped in the furs of beasts, with his hair streaming and his voice screaming. Running empty-handed, his crude tools and weapons, his stone axes and bows and arrows and knives of bone abandoned in his beastly flight before the fire of God! Ho, he stampeded in a beastly panic. Ha! He scrambled in terror under his own locomotion—for Ezekiel was not yet and Man knew not the wheel. Ho yes!

                          Yes!
                          Yes!
                          Yes!
                               Do you love?
                                    Ah,
                                         Ah,
                                              Ah, do

you *love?*

Man ran crying, Fire! And running as fast as Man can away from the true gift of God, crying Fire! and flinging himself in wild-eyed and beastly terror away from the fire that was his salvation had he but the eyes of faith to see. Running! Leaping!—Slipping and sliding!—Leaving in his wake even those lesser gifts, those side products of God's Holy Mercy and His righteous chastisement of Man's misguided pride. Man missed, brothers and sisters, missed in this flight the lesser good things: the huge wild boars, those great, great, *great* granddaddies of our greatest pigs, that in the fury of the eruption were now succulent and toasted to a turn by the unleashed volcanic fire. Ran past these most recent wonders, yes; and past whole sizzling carcasses of roasted beeves, and great birds covered with hair instead of feathers, for in those days *nothing* could look like angels' wings. Yes, and moose that stood some forty hands high, with noble countenance, a true and nobly cooked creature of God. But on Man ran, past rare cooked bears; those truly rare bears that made their lesser descendants of the far north, the Grizzlies, the great Kodiaks, the great Brown bears—yes, and the white Polar bears, even the Cinnamon bears, made all them bears seem like the pygmies of darkest Africa . . . Ah yes! Yes, yes-es-yes! Do-you-love? Doyoulove!

(Preach, Bliss. That's the true Eatmore now. Go get it!)

I say that Man ran! Ran in his headlong plunge, in hectic heathen flight, stumbling over acres of roasted swans and barbecued turkeys and great geese—yes, Lawd!—Great geese that fed on wild butternuts and barley grain—imagine, ignored and lost for centuries now but then there they were, cooked in that uncurbed fire. Yes, and God laughing at the godly joke of prideful, ignorant, limited Man.

For, Dearly Beloved, Man in his ignorant pride had called for that for which in his God-like ambition he was unwilling to suffer. So, having asked and received that for which he asked, he fled with ears that heard not and eyes that saw not, ran screaming away from this second Eden of fire, headlong to the highest hill he fled. He leaped out of there like popcorn roasting on a red-hot stove and with his nose dead to all that scrumptious feast God had spread for his enjoyment.

Now what should he have done? What was Man's mistake?

HE *SHOULD* have asked for *WOOD!* That's what he should have asked! Because give a man wood, and he will *learn* to make his own fire! But, Man-like, he asked for a gift too hot to handle. Yes indeed! So he bolted. He ran. He fled headlong to the highest hill. Yelling, *Fire! Fire! Fire,* Lawd! Then gradually he realized what had happened and Man yelled Ho! This hot stuff that's nipping me on the heels, this is fire!

This wind that's scorched my shoulder is *fire!*

This heat that's singeing my head bald is *fire!*

Yes! He yelled it so strong that God remembered in his infinite and mysterious mercy that now was not His time to destroy the world by fire and sent down the water from the rocks.

Yes, brothers and sisters, He sent down the cooling water. He unleashed the soothing spring within the heart of stones that lay where the wild red roses grew. Up there, up *yonder,* where the bees labored to bright humming music as they stored their golden grub. And He, God the Father, did give Man another chance. Ah, yes.

For although in his pride, Man had sacrificed whole generations of forests and beasts and birds, and though in the terror of his pride he had raised himself up a few inches higher than the animals, he was moved, *despite* himself he was moved a bit closer, I say, to the image of what God intended him to be. Yes. And though no savior in heathen form had yet come to redeem him, God in His infinite mercy looked down upon His handiwork, looked down at the clouds of smoke, looked down upon the charred vegetation, looked down at the fire-shrunk seas with all that broiled fish, looked down at the bleached bones piled past where Man had fled, looked down upon all that sizzling meat and natural gravy, parched barley, boiled roasting-ears and mustard greens . . . Yes, He looked down and said, Even so, My work is good; Man knows now that he can't handle unleashed hell without suffering self-destruction! The time will come to pass when he shall forget it, but now I will give him a few billion years to grow, to shape his hand with toil and to discover a use of his marvelous thumb for other than pushing out the eyes of his fellow-man. After all, I put a heap of work into that thumb of Man. And he'll learn that his index and second fingers are meant for something other than playing the game of stink-finger and pulling his bow. I'll give him *time,* time to surrender the ways of the beasts to the beasts, time to raise himself upright and arch his back and swing his legs. I shall give him *time* to learn to look straight forward and unblinking out of his eyes and to study the movement of the constellations without disrespecting My essential mystery, My prerogatives, My decisions. Yes, it will take him a few billion years before he'll discover pork chops and perhaps two more for fried chicken. It will take him time and much effort to learn the taste of roast beef and baked yams and those apples he shall name Mack and Tosh.

Until then he will only know charred flesh and a little accidental beer. And if he ever learns to take the stings along with the sweets, I'll let him have some of that honey those bees he's busy slapping at down there are storing up right beside him. He'll come to love it even as much as the burly bears and long before he learns about bear steaks and kidneys, and he'll take it from the hollow trees and learn to take his stings and like it. Yes, and I'll give him a little maize and breadfruit and maybe a squash or two. And it won't be long before he'll live in caves and then he'll start to worshipping me in magic and conjuration and a lot of other ignorant foolishness and confusion. But in time Man will learn to eat like a man and he'll rule his herds and he'll move slowly toward the birth of Time.

Oh yes, but now Man is but a babe, hardly more than a cub like the children of the bear or the wolf. And like these he soils himself. It will take him a few million years of a few seconds of My time. I shall watch and suffer with him as he goes his arduous way, and meanwhile I shall give him wood and I shall send him down a ray of light, send him a bright prismatic refraction of a drop of crystal dew and then onto a piece of dry wood and Man will in time see the divine spark and have his fire.

Give a man wood, and he will learn—to make fire. Give him a new land and he will learn to live My way.

Yes, and it took all that time, brothers and sisters. Man went on starving amid plenty; thirsting in the midst of all that knowledge being spelled out for him by the birds, the beasts, the lilies of the field. But in time the smoke cleared away and it all came to pass. . . .

The Senator's voice was silent now, his eyes closed.

Hickman shook his head and smiled. Amen, Bliss. You haven't forgot your Eatmore and you haven't forgot the holy laughter. I like that about the gift of roast pork, though I think Eatmo' used to throw in some pigs' feet and lamb chops. Yes, and those luscious chitterlings. And when he did he could make them cry over the sad fact of Man's missing such good grub out of his proud ignorance. He was a joke to some but a smart wordman just the same. He knew the fundamental fact, that you must speak to the gut as well as to the heart and brain. Then they've *got* to hear you one way or the other. Eatmore did all that, sure, but it's been a long time and you smoothed up his style a bit. Ole Eatmore had mush in his mouth too, till he worked up to the hollering stage, then it didn't really matter what he said because by then he was shaking them like the Southern Pacific doing a highball. By the way, you were signifying about that new state, weren't you?

Yes, but they were so surprised by the sermon that they forgot they were in a new state.

Bliss, the old man laughed, that was a pretty mean thing you did, springing Eatmore on those folks. But the last part was true. Even here in this aggravating land God gave Man a new chance. In fact, He gave him forty-eight new chances. And He's even left enough land for a few more—though I think by now the Lord's disgusted. . . . Well, don't let me get started on that; but how about Greater Calvary, Bliss, was that you too?

Ay, it was I, the Senator said. Yes, I was doing what I had to do at that time in that place. I stood there grown tall, but they didn't recognize me. My elbows rested where my hand couldn't reach in the old days, and I looked above their heads and into their hopes. They'd managed a stained-glass window divided into four equal parts and the strawberry light caressed their heads. They'd sweated and saved themselves an organ too, and it rose with its pipes behind me. In the floor at my feet, showing between the circular cut in the red carpet, I could see the zinc edge of the baptismal pool. Looking out at them from behind my face I had the sensation of standing on a hangman's trap, with only the rope missing. And later, I thought of it as the head of a drum because it throbbed beneath me. I made them make it throb— So yes, it was me; do I have to go on?

I know what you mean by the throbbing, Reverend Hickman said, because I've been there myself. I've made that whole church throb. The Word is a powerful force. Go on, Bliss, tell me.

So I knelt down like I'd seen you do when you were about to take over another man's pulpit, and when he came close to touch me with his hands he was chewing cinnamon to cover the fragrance of his morning's glass of corn. . . .

Suddenly the Senator struggled upward, his eyes wild as Hickman rose quickly to restrain him. "Bliss, Bliss!"

"Corn! Corn whiskey and the collection and the pick of the women! And you wouldn't even allow me ice cream. . . . In all that darkness, undergoing those countless deaths and resurrections and not even ice cream at the end . . ."

Hickman restrained him gently, a look of compassionate surprise shaping his dark face as the Senator repeated as from the depths of a forgotten dream, "Not even ice cream," then settled back.

"Steady, Bliss, boy," Hickman said, studying the face before him. The little boy is still under there, he thought. He never ran way from *him*. "I guess that must have been my first mistake with you. It wasn't my teaching you the art of saving souls before you were able to see that it wasn't just a bag of tricks, or even failing to make you understand that I wasn't simply teaching you to be another trickster or jackleg conman. No, it was that I refused to let you have a *payment*. You wanted to be paid. That was probably the first mistake I made. You coulda saved more souls than Peter, but you got it in your mind that you had a right to be paid—which was exactly what you weren't supposed to have. Even if you were going down into the whale's belly like Jonah every night. It wasn't that I begrudged you the ice cream, Bliss. It was just that you wanted it as payment. But that was my first mistake and yours too. Now you take that preacher, he probably took that drink of corn to help him reach up to the glory of the Word, but he took it *before* he preached, Bliss. And that made it a tool, an aid. It was like the box, or my trombone. But you now, you wanted the ice cream *afterwards.* Everytime you preached you wanted some. If you said 'Amen,' you wanted a pint. Which meant that you were trying to go into business with the Lord . . .

"I should have explained it to you better, and I sure tried. But, Bliss, you were stubborn. Stubborn as a rusted iron tap, boy. Well, I'm a man and like a man I made my mistakes. I guess you looked at the collection plates and got confused. But, Bliss, that money wasn't ours. After all these years I'm a poor man. That money went to the church, for the widows and orphans. It went to help support a school down there in Georgia, and for other things. So you went off for ice cream? Is that it? Is that why you left us? Come on now, we might as well talk this out right here because it's important. Anything you hold in your heart after so long a time is important and this is not the time for shame."

The Senator was silent for a moment; then he sighed.

"Meaning grows with the mind, but the shape and form of the act remains. Yes, in those days it was the ice cream, but there was something else. . . ."

"It had to be, but what?"

"Maybe it was the weight of the darkness, the tomb in such close juxtaposition with the womb. I was so small that after preaching the sermons you taught me and feeling the yawning of that internal and mysterious power which I could release with my treble pantomime . . . Oh you were a wonder, if only in quantitative terms. All the thousands that you touched. Truly a wonder, yes. I guess it was just too much for me. I could set off all that wild exaltation, the rending of veils, the grown women thrown into trances; screaming, tearing their clothing. All that great inarticulate moaning and struggle against what they called the flesh as they walked the floor; up and down those aisles of straining bodies; flinging themselves upon the mourners' bench, or rolling on the floor calling to their God—didn't you realize that afterwards when they surrounded and lifted me up, the heat was still in them? That I could smell the sweat of male and female mystery?"

"But Bliss—all small children and animals do that. . . ."

"Yes, but I had *produced* it. At least, I *thought* I had. Didn't you think of what might be happening to me? I was bewitched and repelled by my own effects. I couldn't understand my creation. Didn't you realize that you'd trapped me in the dead-center between flesh and spirit, and that at my age they were both ridiculous . . . ?"

"You were born in that trap, Bliss, just like everyone was born in it. We all breathe the air at the level that we find it, Bliss."

"Yes, but I couldn't put the two things together. Not even when you explained about the Word. What could I do with such power? I could bring a big man to tears. I could topple him to his knees, make him shout, crack him up with the ease with which shrill whistles split icebergs. Then when they gathered shouting around me, filling the air with the odor of their passion and exertion, the other mystery began. . . ."

"What was it, Bliss? Was it that you wanted the spirit without the sweat of the flesh? The spirit *is* the flesh, Bliss, just as the flesh is the spirit under the right conditions. They are bound together. At least nobody has yet been able to get at one without the other. Eatmore was right. . . ."

"Yes, but back there between my sense of power and the puzzling of my nose there were all those unripe years. I was too young to contain it all."

"Not *your* power, Bliss; it was the Master's. All you had to do was live right and go along with your God-given gift. Besides, it was in the folks as well as in you."

"Well, I was in the middle and I was bringing forth results which I couldn't understand. And those women, their sweat . . ."

Hickman was silent, his gaze suddenly turned inward, musing.

"Bliss, come to think about it, it just dawned on me where you might be heading—didn't you misbehave once on the road some-where?"

Suddenly the Senator's expression was that of a small boy caught in some mischief.

"So you knew all along? Did she tell you?"

"She told me some, but now I'm asking you."

"So she did after all. How old was she, Daddy Hickman?"

"Well sir, Bliss, I thought you'd forgot you used to call me Daddy." Hickman's eyes were suddenly moist.

"Everyone did," the Senator said.

"Yes, but *you* gave me the pleasure, Bliss. You made me feel I wasn't a fraud. Let's see, she must've been thirty or so. But maybe only twenty. One thing is sure, she was a full-grown woman, Bliss. As grown as she'd ever get to be. She was ripe-young, as they used to say."

"So. I've always wondered. Or at least I did whenever I let myself remember. It was one of your swings around the circuit and she'd taken me to her house afterwards. A tent meeting on that old meet-ing ground in Alabama . . ."

"That's right."

". . . that they had been using since slavery days. Thinking about it now, I wonder why they hadn't taken it away from them and planted it in cotton. I remember it as rich black land."

"It wasn't taken because it was ours, Bliss. It used to be a swamp. The Choctaws had it before that but the swamp took it back. So then we filled it in and packed it down with our bare feet—at least our folks did—long before we had any shoes. Sure, back in slavery times we buried our dead out around there, and the white folks recognized it as a sacred place. Or maybe just an unpleasant place because of the black dead that was in it. You've been on the outside, Bliss, so you ought to know better'n me that they respect *some* things of ours. Or at least they leave them alone. Maybe not our women or our right to good food and education, but they respect our burying grounds."

"Maybe," the Senator said. "It's a game of power."

"Yes, and maybe they're scared of black ghosts. But you ought to know after all this time, Bliss, and I hope you'll tell me sometimes. . . . Anyway, boy, it was out there. You remember what it was, don't you?"

"The occasion? It was another revival, wasn't it?"

"Course, it was a revival, Bliss—but it was Juneteenth too. We were celebrating Emancipation and thanking God. Remember, it went on for seven days."

"*Juneteenth,*" the Senator said, "I had forgotten the word."

"You've forgotten lots of important things from those days, Bliss."

"I suppose so, but to learn some of the things I've learned I had to forget some others. Do you still call it 'Juneteenth,' Revern' Hickman? Is it still celebrated?"

Hickman looked at him with widened eyes, leaning forward as he grasped the arms of the chair.

"Do we still? Why, I should say we do. You don't think that because you left . . . Both, Bliss. Because we haven't forgot what it means. Even if sometimes folks try to make us believe it never happened or that it was a mistake that it ever did . . ."

"Juneteenth," the Senator said, closing his eyes, his bandaged head resting beneath his hands. Words of Emancipation didn't arrive until the middle of June so they called it Juneteenth. *So that was it, the night of Juneteenth celebration,* his mind went on. *The celebration of a gaudy illusion.*

CHAPTER 7

No, the wounded man thought, Oh no! Get back to that; back to a bunch of old-fashioned Negroes celebrating an illusion of emancipation, and getting it mixed up with the Resurrection, minstrel shows and vaudeville routines? Back to that tent in the clearing surrounded by trees, that bowl-shaped impression in the earth beneath the pines? . . . Lord, it hurts. Lordless and without loyalty, it hurts. Wordless, it hurts. Here and especially here. Still I see it after all the roving years and flickering scenes: Twin lecterns on opposite ends of the rostrum, behind one of which I stood on a wide box, leaning forward to grasp the lectern's edge. Back. Daddy Hickman at the other. Back to the first day of that week of celebration. Juneteenth. Hot, dusty. Hot with faces shining with sweat and the hair of the young dudes metallic with grease and straightening irons. Back to that? He was not so heavy then, but big with the quick energy of a fighting bull and still kept the battered silver trombone on top of the piano, where at the climax of a sermon he could reach for it and

stand blowing tones that sounded like his own voice amplified; per-
suading, denouncing, rejoicing—moving beyond words back to the
undifferentiated cry. In strange towns and cities the jazz musicians
were always around him. Jazz. What was jazz and what religion back
there? Ah yes, yes, I loved him. Everyone did, deep down. Like a
great, kindly daddy bear along the streets, my hand lost in his huge
paw. Carrying me on his shoulder so that I could touch the leaves of
the trees as we passsed. The true father, but black, black. Was he a
charlatan? Am I—or simply as resourceful in my fashion? Did he
know himself, or care? Back to the problem of all that. Must I go
back to the beginning when only he knows the start? . . .

Juneteenth and him leaning across the lectern, resting there,
looking into their faces with a great smile, and then looking over to
me to make sure that I had not forgotten my part, winking his big
red-rimmed eye at me. And the women looking back and forth
from him to me with that bright, birdlike adoration in their faces;
their heads cocked to one side. And him beginning:

On this God-given day, brothers and sisters, when we have come
together to praise God and celebrate our oneness, our slipping off
the chains, let's us begin this week of worship by taking a look at the
ledger. Let us, on this day of deliverance, take a look at the figures
writ on our bodies and on the living tablet of our heart. The Hebrew children have their Passover so that they can keep their history
alive in their memories—so let us take one more page from their
book and, on this great day of deliverance, on this day of emancipation, let's us tell ourselves our story. . . .

Pausing, grinning down . . . Nobody else is interested in it anyway, so let us enjoy it ourselves, yes, and learn from it.

And thank God for it. Now let's not be too solemn about it either, because this here's a happy occasion. Rev. Bliss over there is
going to take the part of the younger generation, and I'll try to tell

it as it's been told to me. Just look at him over there, he's ready and raring to go—because he knows that a true preacher is a kind of educator, and that we have got to know our story before we can truly understand God's blessings and how far we have still got to go. Now you've heard him, so you know that he can preach.

Amen! they all responded, and I looked preacher-faced into their shining eyes, preparing my piccolo voice to support his baritone sound.

Amen is right, he said. So here we are, five thousand strong, come together on this day of celebration. Why? We just didn't happen. We're here and that is an undeniable fact—but how come we're here? How and why here in these woods that used to be such a long way from town? What about it, Rev. Bliss, is that a suitable question on which to start?

God bless you, Rev. Hickman, I think that's just the place we have to start. We of the younger generation are still ignorant about these things. So please, sir, tell us just how we came to be here in our present condition and in this land. . . .

Not back to that me, not to that six–seven-year-old ventriloquist's dummy dressed in a white evening suit. Not to that charlatan born—must I have no charity for me? . . . Not to that puppet with a memory like a piece of flypaper. . . .

Was it an act of God, Rev. Hickman, or an act of man? . . .

We came, amen, Rev. Bliss, sisters and brothers, as an act of God, but through—I said through—an act of cruel, ungodly man.

An act of Almighty God, *my treble echo sounded,* but through the hands of cruel man.

Amen, Rev. Bliss, that's how it happened. It was, as I understand it, a cruel calamity laced up with a blessing—or maybe a blessing laced up with a calamity. . . .

Laced up with a blessing, Rev. Hickman? We understand you partially because you have taught us that God's sword is a two-edged sword. But would you please tell us of the younger generation just why it was a blessing?

It was a blessing, brothers and sisters, because out of all the pain and the suffering, out of the night of storm, we found the Word of God.

So here we found the Word. Amen, so now we are here. But where did we come from, Daddy Hickman?

We come here out of Africa, son; out of Africa.

Africa? Way over across the ocean? The black land? Where the elephants and monkeys and the lions and tigers are?

Yes, Rev. Bliss, the jungle land. Some of us have fair skins like you, but out of Africa too.

Out of Africa truly, sir?

Out of the ravaged mama of the black man, son.

Lord, thou hast taken us out of Africa . . .

Amen, out of our familiar darkness. Africa. They brought us here from all over Africa, Rev. Bliss. And some were the sons and daughters of heathen kings . . .

Some were kings, Daddy Hickman? Have we of the younger generation heard you correctly? Some were kin to kings? Real kings?

Amen! I'm told that some were the sons and the daughters of kings . . .

. . . Of kings! . . .

And some were the sons and daughters of warriors . . .

. . . Of warriors . . .

Of fierce warriors. And some were the sons and daughters of farmers . . .

Of African farmers . . .

. . . And some of musicians . . .

. . . Musicians . . .

And some were the sons and daughters of weapon makers and smelters of brass and iron . . .

But didn't they have judges, Rev. Hickman? And weren't there any preachers of the word of God?

Some were judges, but none were preachers of the word of God, Rev. Bliss. For we come out of heathen Africa . . .

Heathen Africa?

Out of heathen Africa. Let's tell this thing true; because the truth is the light.

And they brought us here in chains. . . .

In chains, son; in iron chains . . .

From half a world away, they brought us . . .

In chains and in boats that the history tells us weren't fit for pigs—because pigs cost too much money to be allowed to waste and die as we did. But they stole us and brought us in boats which I'm told could move like the swiftest birds of prey, and which filled the great trade winds with the stench of our dying and their crime. . . .

What a crime! Tell us why, Rev. Hickman. . . .

It was a crime, Rev. Bliss, brothers and sisters, like the fall of proud Lucifer from Paradise.

But why, Daddy Hickman? You have taught us of the progressive younger generation to ask why. So we want to know how come it was a crime?

Because, Rev. Bliss, this was a country dedicated to the principles of Almighty God. That *Mayflower* boat that you hear so much about Thanksgiving Day was a *Christian* ship—amen! Yes, and those many-named floating coffins we came here in were Christian too. They had turned traitor to the God who set them free from Europe's tyrant kings. Because, God have mercy on them, no sooner than they got free enough to breathe themselves, they set out to bow us down. . . .

They made our Lord shed tears!

Amen! Rev. Bliss, amen. God must have wept like Jesus. Poor Jonah went down into the belly of the whale, but compared to our journey his was like a trip to paradise on a silvery cloud.

Worse than old Jonah, Rev. Hickman?

Worse than Jonah slicked all over with whale puke and gasping on the shore. We went down into hell on those floating coffins and don't you youngsters forget it! Mothers and babies, men and women, the living and the dead and the dying—all chained together. And yet, praise God, most of us arrived here in this land. The strongest came through. Thank God, and we arrived and that's why we're here today. Does that answer the question, Rev. Bliss?

Amen, Daddy Hickman, amen. But now the younger generation would like to know what they did to us when they got us here. What happened then?

They brought us up onto this land in chains . . .

. . . In chains . . .

. . . And they marched us into the swamps . . .

. . . Into the fever swamps, they marched us . . .

And they set us to work draining the swampland and toiling in the sun . . .

. . . They set us to toiling . . .

They took the white fleece of the cotton and the sweetness of the sugarcane and made them bitter and bloody with our toil. . . . And they treated us like one great unhuman animal without any face . . .

Without a *face,* Rev. Hickman?

Without personality, without names, Rev. Bliss, we were made into nobody and not even *Mister* Nobody either, just nobody. They left us without names. Without choice. Without the right to do or not to do, to be or not to be . . .

You mean without faces and without eyes? We were eyeless like Samson in Gaza? Is that the way, Rev. Hickman?

Amen, Rev. Bliss, like baldheaded Samson before that nameless little lad like you came as the Good Book tells us and led him to the pillars whereupon the big house stood— Oh, you little black boys, and oh, you little brown girls, you're going to shake the building down! And then, oh, how you will build in the name of the Lord!

Yes, Reverend Bliss, we were eyeless like unhappy Samson among the Philistines—and worse . . .

And WORSE?

Worse, Rev. Bliss, because they chopped us up into little bitty pieces like a farmer when he cuts up a potato. And they scattered us around the land. All the way from Kentucky to Florida; from Louisiana to Texas; from Missouri all the way down the great Mississippi to the Gulf. They scattered us around this land.

How now, Daddy Hickman? You speak in parables which we of the younger generation don't clearly understand. How do you mean, they scattered us?

Like seed, Rev. Bliss; they scattered us just like a dope-fiend farmer planting a field with dragon teeth!

Tell us about it, Daddy Hickman.

They cut out our tongues . . .

. . . They left us speechless . . .

. . . They cut out our tongues . . .

. . . Lord, they left us without words . . .

. . . Amen! They scattered our tongues in this land like seed . . .

. . . And left us without language . . .

. . . They took away our talking drums . . .

. . . Drums that talked, Daddy Hickman? Tell us about those talking drums . . .

Drums that talked like a telegraph. Drums that could reach across the country like a church-bell sound. Drums that told the news almost before it happened! Drums that spoke with big voices like big men! Drums like a conscience and a deep heartbeat that knew right from wrong. Drums that told glad tidings! Drums that sent the news of trouble speeding home! Drums that told us *our* time and told us where we were . . .

Those were some drums, Rev. Hickman . . .

. . . Yes, and they took those drums away . . .

Away, amen! Away! And they took away our heathen dances . . .

. . . They left us drumless and they left us danceless . . .

Ah yes, they burnt up our talking drums and our dancing drums . . .

. . . Drums . . .

. . . And they scattered the ashes . . .

. . . Ah, aaaaaah! Eyeless, tongueless, drumless, danceless, ashes . . .

And a worse devastation was yet to come, Lord God!

Tell us, Revern Hickman. Blow on your righteous horn!

Ah, but Rev. Bliss, in those days we didn't have any horns . . .

No *horns?* Hear him!

And we had no songs . . .

. . . No songs . . .

. . . And we had no . . .

. . . Count it on your fingers, see what cruel man has done . . .

Amen, Rev. Bliss, lead them . . .

We were eyeless, tongueless, drumless, danceless, hornless, songless!

All true, Rev. Bliss. No eyes to see. No tongue to speak or taste. No drums to raise the spirits and wake up our memories. No dance to stir the rhythm that makes life move. No songs to give praise and prayers to God!

We were truly in the dark, my young brothers and sisters. Eyeless, earless, tongueless, drumless, danceless, songless, hornless, soundless . . .

And worse to come!

. . . And worse to come . . .

Tell us, Rev. Hickman. But not too fast so that we of the younger generation can gather up our strength to face it. So that we may listen and not become discouraged!

I said, Rev. Bliss, brothers and sisters, that they snatched us out of the loins of Africa. I said that they took us from our mammies and pappies and from our sisters and brothers. I said that they scattered us around this land . . .

. . . And we, let's count it again, brothers and sisters; let's add it up. Eyeless, tongueless, drumless, danceless, songless, hornless, soundless, sightless, dayless, nightless, wrongless, rightless, motherless, fatherless—scattered.

Yes, Rev. Bliss, they scattered us around like seed . . .

. . . Like seed . . .

. . . Like seed, that's been flung broadcast on unplowed ground . . .

Ho, chant it with me, my young brothers and sisters! Eyeless, tongueless, drumless, danceless, songless, hornless, soundless, sightless, wrongless, rightless, motherless, fatherless, brotherless, sisterless, powerless . . .

Amen! But though they took us like a great black giant that had been chopped up into little pieces and the pieces buried; though they deprived us of our heritage among strange scenes in strange weather; divided and divided and divided us again like a gambler shuffling and cutting a deck of cards; although we were ground down, smashed into little pieces, spat upon, stamped upon, cursed and buried, and our memory of Africa ground down into powder and blown on the winds of foggy forgetfulness . . .

. . . Amen, Daddy Hickman! Abused and without shoes, pounded down and ground like grains of sand on the shores of the sea . . .

. . . Amen! And God— Count it, Rev. Bliss . . .

. . . Left eyeless, earless, noseless, throatless, teethless, tongue-less, handless, feetless, armless, wrongless, rightless, harmless, drumless, danceless, songless, hornless, soundless, sightless, wrong-less, rightless, motherless, fatherless, sisterless, brotherless, plow-less, muleless, foodless, mindless—and Godless, Rev. Hickman, did you say Godless?

. . . At first, Rev. Bliss, he said, his trombone entering his voice, broad, somber and noble. At first. Ah, but though divided and scat-tered, ground down and battered into the earth like a spike being pounded by a ten-pound sledge, we were on the ground and in the earth and the earth was red and black like the earth of Africa. And as we moldered underground we were mixed with this land. We liked it. It fitted us fine. It was in us and we were in it. And then— praise God—deep in the ground, deep in the womb of this land, we began to stir!

Praise God!

At last, Lord, at last.

Amen!

Oh the truth, Lord, it tastes so sweet!

What was it like then, Rev. Bliss? You read the scriptures, so tell us. Give us a word.

WE WERE LIKE THE VALLEY OF DRY BONES!

Amen. Like the Valley of Dry Bones in Ezekiel's dream. Hoooh! We lay scattered in the ground for a long dry season. And the winds blew and the sun blazed down and the rains came and went and we were dead. Lord, we were dead! Except . . . Except . . .

. . . Except what, Rev. Hickman?

Except for one nerve left from our ear . . .

Listen to him!

And one nerve in the soles of our feet . . .

. . . Just watch me point it out, brothers and sisters . . .

Amen, Bliss, you point it out . . . and one nerve left from the throat . . .

. . . From our throat—right *here!*

. . . Teeth . . .

. . . From our teeth, one from all thirty-two of them . . .

. . . Tongue . . .

. . . Tongueless . . .

. . . And another nerve left from our heart . . .

. . . Yes, from our heart . . .

. . . And another left from our eyes and one from our hands and arms and legs and another from our stones . . .

Amen, hold it right there, Rev. Bliss . . .

. . . All stirring in the ground . . .

. . . Amen, stirring, and right there in the midst of all our death and buriedness, the voice of God spoke down the Word . . .

. . . Crying Do! I said, Do! Crying Doooo—

—these dry bones live?

He said: Son of Man . . . under the ground, ha! Heatless beneath the roots of plants and trees . . . Son of Man, do . . .

I said, Do . . .

. . . I said Do, Son of Man, Doooooo!—

—these dry bones live?

Amen! And we heard and rose up. Because in all their blasting they could not blast away one solitary vibration of God's true word. . . . We heard it down among the roots and among the rocks. We heard it in the sand and in the clay. We heard it in the falling rain and in the rising sun. On the high ground and in the gullies. We heard it lying moldering and corrupted in the earth. We heard it sounding like a bugle call to wake up the dead. Crying, Doooooo! Ay, do these dry bones live!

And did our dry bones live, Daddy Hickman?

Ah, we sprang together and walked around. All clacking together and clicking into place. All moving in time! Do! I said, Dooooo—these dry bones live!

And now strutting in my white tails, across the platform, filled with the power almost to dancing.

Shouting, Amen, Daddy Hickman, is this the way we walked?

Oh we walked through Jerusalem, just like John— That's it, Rev. Bliss, walk! Show them how we walked!

Was this the way?

That's the way. Now walk on back. Lift your knees! Swing your arms! Make your coattails fly! Walk! And him strutting me three times around the pulpit across the platform and back. Ah, yes! And then his voice deep and exultant: And if they ask you in the city why we praise the Lord with bass drums and brass trombones tell them we were rebirthed dancing, we were rebirthed crying affirmation of the Word, quickening our transcended flesh.

Amen!

Oh, Rev. Bliss, we stamped our feet at the trumpet's sound and we clapped our hands, ah, in joy! And we moved, yes, together in a dance, amen! Because we had received a new song in a new land and been resurrected by the Word and Will of God!

Amen! . . .

. . . We were rebirthed from the earth of this land and revivified by the Word. So now we had a new language and a brand-new song to put flesh on our bones . . .

New teeth, new tongue, new word, new song!

We had a new name and a new blood, and we had a new task . . .

Tell us about it, Reveren Hickman . . .

We had to take the Word for bread and meat. We had to take the Word for food and shelter. We had to use the Word as a rock to build up a whole new nation, 'cause to tell it true, we were born again in chains of steel. Yes, and chains of ignorance. And all we knew was the spirit of the Word. We had no schools. We owned no tools, no cabins, no churches, not even our own bodies.

We were chained, young brothers, in steel. We were chained, young sisters, in ignorance. We were schoolless, toolless, cabin-less—owned . . .

Amen, Reveren Bliss. We were owned and faced with the awe-inspiring labor of transforming God's Word into a lantern so that in the darkness we'd know where we were. Oh, God hasn't been easy with us because He always plans for the loooong haul. He's looking far ahead and this time He wants a well-tested people to work his will. He wants some sharp-eyed, quick-minded, generous-hearted people to give names to the things of this world and to its values. He's tired of untempered tools and half-blind masons! Therefore, He's going to keep on testing us against the rocks and in the fires. He's going to plunge us into the ice-cold water. And each time we come out we'll be blue and as tough as cold-blue steel! Ah yes! He means for us to be a new kind of human. Maybe we won't be that people but we'll be a part of that people, we'll be an element in them, amen! He wants us limber as willow switches and he wants us tough as whip leather, so that when we have to bend, we can bend and snap back into place. He's going to throw bolts of lightning to blast us so that we'll have good footwork and lightning-fast minds. He'll drive us hither and yon around this land and make us run the gauntlet of hard times and tribulations, misunderstanding and abuse. And some will pity you and some will despise you. And some will try to use you and change you. And some will deny you and try to deal you out of the game. And sometimes you'll feel so bad that you'll wish you could die. But it's all the pressure of God. He's giving you a will and He wants you to use it. He's giving you brains and he wants you to train them lean and hard so that you can overcome all the obstacles. Educate your minds! Make do with what you have so as to get what you need! Learn to look at what *you* see and not what somebody tells you is true. Pay lip service to Caesar if you have to, but put your trust in God. Because nobody has a patent on truth or a copyright on the best way to live and serve Almighty God. Learn from what we've lived. Remember that when the labor's back-breaking and the bossman's mean our singing can lift us up. That it can strengthen us and make his meanness but the flyspeck irritation of an empty man. Roll with the blow like ole Jack Johnson. Dance on out of his way like Williams and Walker. Keep to the rhythm and you'll keep to life. God's time is long; and all short-haul horses shall be like horses on a merry-go-round. Keep, keep, keep to the rhythm and you won't get weary. Keep to the rhythm and you won't get lost. We're handicapped, amen! Because the Lord wants us strong! We started out with nothing but the Word—just like the others, but they've forgot it. . . . We worked and stood up under hard times and tribulations. We learned patience and to understand Job. Of all the animals, man's the only one not born knowing almost everything he'll ever know. It takes him longer than an elephant to grow up because God didn't mean him to leap to any conclusions, for God Himself is in the very process of things. We learned that all blessings come mixed with sorrow and all hardships have a streak of laughter. Life is a streak-a-lean—a streak-a-fat. Ha, yes! We learned to bounce back and to disregard the prizes of fools. And we must keep on learning. Let them have their fun. Even let them eat hummingbirds' wings and tell you it's too good for you.—Grits and greens don't turn to ashes in anybody's mouth—how about it, Rev. Eatmore? Amen? Amen! Let everybody say amen. Grits and greens are humble but they make you strong and when the right folks get together to share them they can taste like ambrosia. So draw, so let us draw on our own wells of strength.

Ah yes, so we were reborn, Rev. Bliss. They still had us harnessed, we were still laboring in the fields, but we had a secret and we had a new rhythm . . .

So tell us about this rhythm, Reveren Hickman.

They had us bound but we had our kind of time, Rev. Bliss. They were on a merry-go-round that they couldn't control but we learned to beat time from the seasons. We learned to make this land and this light and darkness and this weather and their labor fit us like a suit of new underwear. With our new rhythm, amen, but we weren't free and they still kept dividing us. There's many a thousand gone down the river. Mamma sold from papa and chillun sold from both. Beaten and abused and without shoes. But we had the Word, now, Rev. Bliss, along with the rhythm. They couldn't divide us now. Because anywhere they dragged us we throbbed in time together. If we got a chance to sing, we sang the same song. If we got a chance to dance, we beat back hard times and tribulations with the clap of our hands and the beat of our feet, and it was the same dance. Oh, they come out here sometimes to laugh at our way of praising God. They can laugh but they can't deny us. They can curse and kill us but they can't destroy us all. This land is ours because we come out of it, we bled in it, our tears watered it, we fertilized it with our dead. So the more of us they destroy the more it becomes filled with the spirit of our redemption. They laugh but we know who we are and where we are, but they keep on coming in their millions and they don't know and can't get together.

But tell us, how do we know who we are, Daddy Hickman?

We know where we are by the way we walk. We know where we are by the way we talk. We know where we are by the way we sing. We know where we are by the way we dance. We know where we are by the way we praise the Lord on high. We know where we are because we hear a different tune in our minds and in our hearts. We know who we are because when we make the beat of our rhythm to shape our day the whole land says, Amen! It smiles, Rev. Bliss, and it moves to our time! Don't be ashamed, my brothers! Don't be cowed. Don't throw what you have away! Continue! Remember! Believe! Trust the inner beat that tells us who we are. Trust God and trust life and trust this land that is you! Never mind the laughers, the scoffers—they come around because they can't help themselves. They can deny you but not your sense of life. They hate you because whenever they look into a mirror they fill up with bitter gall. So forget them, and most of all don't deny yourselves. They're tied by the short hairs to a runaway merry-go-round. They make life a business of struggle and fret, fret and struggle. See who you can hate; see what you can get. But you just keep on inching along like an old inchworm. If you put one and one and one together soon they'll make a million too. There's been a heap of Juneteenths before this one and I tell you there'll be a heap more before we're truly free! Yes! But keep to the rhythm, just keep to the rhythm and keep to the way. Man's plans are but a joke to God. Let those who will despise you, but remember deep down inside yourself that the life we have to lead is but a preparation for other things, it's a discipline, Reveren Bliss, sisters and brothers; a discipline through which we may see that which the others are too self-blinded to see. Time will come round when we'll have to be their eyes; time will swing and turn back around. I tell you, time shall swing and spiral back around. . . .

No, the Senator thought, *no more of it! NO!*

"Yes, Bliss; Juneteenth," he could hear Hickman saying. "And it was a great occasion. There had been a good cotton crop and a little money was circulating among us. Folks from all over were in the mood for prayer and celebration. There must've been five thousand folks out there that week—not counting the real young chillun and the babies. Folks came all the way from Atlanta, Montgomery, Columbus, Charleston and Birmingham, just to be there and hear the Word. Horse teams and mule teams and spans of oxen were standing under the grove of trees around the clearing, and the wagon beds were loaded down with hay and feed for the animals and with quilts for the folks who had come in from the far sections, so they could sleep right there. All those wagons made it look as though everybody in the whole section was waiting for the Word to move on over across Jordan. Or maybe migrate West, as some later did. The feel of those days has gone out of the air now, Bliss. And the shape of our minds is different from then, because time has moved on. Then we were closer to the faceless days, but we had faith. Yes, and ignorant as we knew we were, we had more self-respect. We didn't have much but we squeezed life harder and there was a warm glow all around. No, and we hadn't started imitating white folks who in turn were imitating their distorted and low-rated ideas of us. I'm talking now about how it felt when we were together and looking up the mountain where we had to climb. . . .

"But you remember how it was, Bliss: In the daytime hot under the tent with the rows of benches and folding chairs; and the ladies in their summer dresses and their fans whipping up a breeze in time to the preaching and the singing. And the choirs and the old tried and tested workers in the vineyard dressed in their white uniforms. That's right. All the solid substance of *our* way of doing things, of *our* sense of life. Everything ordered and in its place and everything and everybody a part of the ceremony and the evocation. Barrels of ice water and cold lemonade with the cakes of ice in them sitting out under the cool of the trees, and all those yellow cases of soda pop stacked off to one side. Yeah, and at night those coal-oil flares and the lanterns lighting things up like one of those country fairs.

"And the feasting part, you must remember that, Bliss. There was all those ladies turning out fried fish and fried chicken and Mr. Double-Jointed Jackson, the barbecue king, who had come out from Atlanta and was sweating like a Georgia politician on election day—excuse me, Bliss—supervising sixteen cooks and presiding over the barbecue pits all by hisself. Think about it for a second, Bliss; it'll come back to you, because even if you look at it simply from the point of eating it was truly a great occasion."

Hickman laughed, shaking his white head; then pushing back in his chair he held up his great left hand, the fingers spread and bending supple as he counted with his right index finger.

"Lord, we et up fifteen hundred loaves of sandwich bread; five hundred pounds of catfish and snapper; fifteeen gallons of hot sauce, Mr. Double-Jointed Jackson's formula; nine hundred pounds of barbecue ribs; eighty-five hams, direct from Virginia; fifty pounds of potato salad and a whole big cabbage patch of coleslaw. Yes, and enough frying-size chicken to feed the multitude! And let's not mention the butter beans—naw! And don't talk about the fresh young roasting-ears and the watermelons. Neither the fried pies, chocolate cakes and homemade ice cream. Lord, but that was a great occasion. A *great* occasion. Bliss, how after knowing such times as those you could take off for where you went is too much for me to truly understand. At least not to go there and *stay*. And don't go taking me simple-minded either. I'm not just talking about the eating. I mean the *communion,* the coming together—of which the eating was only a part; an outward manifestation, a symbol, like the Blood is signified by the wine, and the Flesh by the bread . . . Ah yes, boy, we filled their bellies, but we were really there to fill their souls and give them reassurance—and we *filled* them.

"We *moved* 'em!

"We preached Jesus on the cross and in the ground. We preached Him in Jerusalem and walking around Atlanta, Georgia. We preached Him, Bliss, to open up heaven and raise up hell. We preached Him till the Word worked in the crowd like a flash of lightning and a dose of salts. Amen! Bliss, we preached and you were with us through it all. You were there, boy. You . . ."

The Senator lay listening, feeling the pain rise to him again as he tried to surrender himself to the mellow evocation of the voice become so resonant now with pleasure and affirmation. For the moment, his powers to resist were weak, as though the word *daddy* in his mouth had opened a fresh flood of memory. Perhaps if he entered into the spell he could escape, could scramble the images that now were rising in his mind, could melt them down. . . .

"Think back, Bliss," Hickman was saying. "Seven preachers in black broadcloth suits and Stacy Adams shoes working full-time to bring them the Word of God. Starting with sunrise services, all kneeling in the dark down on the black earth, bending there on our knees and praying the sun right up out of the ground and into the sky there in the green dawn. Then preaching the clock around; sunup and sundown—from kin to cant. What I mean is seven *powerful* men; men who had the true feeling and the power to drive it home. Men who had the know-how of the human heart!

"What? *Who?* Seven grade-A-number-one first-class preachers. *Big* men. Sitting up there on the platform, big-souled and big-voiced; all worked up by the occasion and inspiring one another as well as the congregation. Seven great preachers, not to mention Eatmore and you, Bliss.

"And lots of unbelievers were there too; there just to hear those big Negroes preach. Ha! Some of them thought they came out there to hear a preaching contest—which was all right because when the good ones at anything get together there is just naturally going to be a battle. Men who love the Word are concerned with the way they preach it, that's how the glory comes shining through. . . . Oh, but

we caught our share of those who thought we were nothing but en-
tertainers. Reveren Eubanks got aroused there one evening and
started to preaching up under some sinner women's clothes and
brought 'em in like fish in a net. One got so filled up with the spirit
she started testifying to some things so outrageous that I had to grab
my trombone and drown her out. HA! HA! HA! Why she'd have
taught them more sin in trying to be saved than they'd have blun-
dered into in a whole year of hot Novembers. Don't smile, Bliss; it's
not really funny and you have to save your strength. Sho, I myself
preached fifteen into the fold—big gold earrings, blood-red stockings, short skirts, patent-leather shoes and all. Preached them right
out of the back of the crowd and down front to the mourners'
bench. Fifteen Magdalenes, Bliss. 'Fancy who's in fancy clothes.'
Yes, indeed. Brought them down humbled with hanging heads and
streaming eyes and the paint on their faces running all red and pink
with tears . . .

"But what could they do, Bliss? We were playing for *keeps;* we had
seven of the most powerful preachers you could find *any*where; we
had the best individual singers in the nation; we had the best choirs
from all over the southeastern division— And look who else we
had: Singing Williams was there—remember him? and Laura Min-
nie Smith, who could battle Bessie note for note and tone for tone,
and on top of that was singing the Word of God. Fess Mackaway was
there playing the piano most of the time and conducting the assembled choirs like the master he was. Young Tom Dorsey had come
down all the way from Chicago to sit in—even then flirting around
with God. Whitby's Heavenly Harmonizers were there, singing the
Word in a way that made everything from animals to birds and the
flowers of the fields to L & N Railroad trains sing in the sound and
give thanks to God. There, Bliss, were four Negroes who could
make everything of this earth burst into song. They played on Jew's

harps, hair combs, zu-zus, washtubs—anything. They blowed
Joshua on sorghum jugs—and harmony? Shucks, it ain't never been
writ down!

"So what could the poor sinners do? In fact, what could anybody
do? Bliss, let me tell you: Ole Eatmore, God bless his memory, Ole
Rev Eatmore unlimbered some homiletic there one evening that
had the hair standing up on *my* head—and I was already a seasoned
preacher! Why, I sat there listening to that Negro making pictures
rise up out of the Word and he lifted me plumb up out of my chair!
Bliss, I've heard you cutting some fancy didoes on the radio, but
son, Eatmore was romping and rampaging and walking through
Jerusalem just like John! Oh, but wasn't he romping! Maybe you
were too young to get it all, but that night that mister was ten thousand misters and his voice was pure gold. And it wasn't exactly what
he was saying, but how he was saying. That Negro was always a master, but that evening he was an *inspired* master. Bliss, he was a super-
master!"

Hickman chuckled, studying the Senator's face; thinking, *This
won't hurt him, not this part and the smile in it might catch him and help
him.* . . .

"And did he set *me* a hard row to hoe, Bliss, when it came my turn
I was so moved I could hardly make words. He had us up so high,
Bliss, that it called for pure song. I just took off and led them in 'Let
Us Break Bread Together' till I could get myself under control and
relieve the strain a bit. I taught you that song, Bliss. It was the very
first. It's a song of fellowship, so simple and yet so deep and powerful because in it the lion and the lamb lie down together. Out there
in Oklahoma, where they sometimes had the nerve and weren't
ashamed to be helped, I brought many a poor white sinner to God
with that song. . . . Well, as I stood there singing I looked out there
into all those faces shining there in the dark and in the light, and I

asked the Lord, 'Master, what does it all mean beyond a glad noise for Juneteenth Day? What does freedom, what does emancipation mean?' And the Lord said to me through all that sound, 'Hickman, the Word has found its flesh and there's salvation in the Word.' 'But, Master,' I said, 'back there in the night there's those mean little towns, and on beyond the towns there's the city, with police power and big buildings and factories and the courts and the National Guard; and newspapers and telephones and telegraphs and all those folks who act like they've never heard of your Word. All that while we here are so small and weak . . .' And the Master said, 'Still here the Word has found flesh and the complex has been confounded by the simple, and here is the better part. Hickman,' He said, 'Rise up on the Word and ride. All time is mine.' Then He spoke to me low, in the idiom: He said, 'You just be ready when the deal goes down. And have your people ready. Just be prepared. Now get up there and ride!' And Bliss, I threw back my head and rode! It was like a riddle or a joke, but if so, it was the Lord's joke and I was playing it straight. And maybe that's what a preacher really is, he's the Lord's own straight man.

"Anyway, Bliss, that night, coming after Eatmore and Pompey and Revern' Brazelton—yes, and that little Negro Murray, who had been to a seminary up North and could preach the pure Greek and the original Hebrew and could still make all our uneducated folks swing along with him; who could make them understand and follow him—and not showing off, just needing all those languages to give him room to move around in. Besides, he knew that ofttimes the meaning of the Word is in the way you make it sound. No, now don't interrupt me, save yourself. I know that you know these secrets; you have hurt us enough with them. . . . But as I was saying, what's more important, Revern' Murray's education didn't get him separated from the folks. Yeah, and he used to sit there in his chair bent forward like a boxer waiting for the bell, with his fists doubled up and his arms on his knees. Then when it came his turn to preach, he'd shoot forward like he was going to leap right out there into the congregation and start giving the Devil some uppercuts. Lord, what a little rough mister! One night he grabbed a disbelieving bully who had come out to break up the meeting, and threw him bodily out into the dark; tossed him fifteen feet or more into the mule-pissed mud. Then he came on back to the pulpit and preached like Peter. . . ."

"Yes," the Senator said, "I remember him. And there was the tongue-tied one. . . ."

"Yes, yes, I'm not forgetting Reverend Eubanks. He's the one who folks couldn't understand any more than they could Demosthenes before he put those rocks in his jaws—but when he got into the pulpit and raised his hands to heaven—then whoooo, Lord! didn't the words come down like rain!

"Well, Bliss, coming after all them and having to start up there in the clouds where Eatmore left those five thousand or more folks a-straining, I found myself knowing that I had to preach them down into silence. I knew too that only a little child could really lead them, and I looked around at you and gave you the nod and I saw you get up wearing that little white dress suit—you were a fine-looking little chap, Bliss; a miniature man of God . . . And I saw you leave the platform to go get ready while I tried to make manifest the Word. . . ."

Suddenly the Senator twisted violently upon the bed.

"Words, words," he said wearily. "What you needed was a stage with a group of actors. You might have been a playwright."

"Rest back, Bliss," Hickman said. "I preached them down into silence that night. True, there was preacher pride in it, there always is. Because Eatmore had set such a pace that I had to accept his challenge, but there was more to it too. We had mourned and rejoiced and rejoiced and moaned and he had released the pure agony and raised it to the skies. So I had to give them transcendence. Wasn't anything left to do but shift to a higher gear. I had to go beyond the singing and the shouting and reach into the territory of the pure unblemished Word. I had to climb up there where fire is so hot it's ice, and ice so cold it burns like fire. Where the Word was so loud that it was silent, and so silent that it rang like a timeless gong. I had to reach the Word within the Word that was both song and scream and whisper. The Word that was beyond sense but leaping like a tree of flittering birds with its *own* dictionary of light and meaning.

"I don't really know how I got up there, Bliss, there's no elevator for such things. First it was Eatmore and then I was leading them in 'Let us break bread together on our knees'—and it happened. Instead of sliding off into silence I started preaching up off the top of that song and they were still singing under me, holding me up there as I started to climb. Bliss, I was *up* there, boy. I was talking like I always talk, in the same old down-home voice, that is, in the beloved idiom, but I was no loud horn that night, I was blowing low—and we didn't have microphones either, not in those days. But they heard me. I preached those five thousand folks into silence, five thousand *Negroes,* and you know that's the next thing to a miracle. But I did it. I did it and it was hot summertime, and the corn whiskey was flowing out back of the edge of the crowd. Sure, there was always whiskey—and fornicating too. Always. But inside there was the Word and the Communion in the Word, and just as Christ Jesus had to die between two criminals, just so did we have to put up with the whiskey and the fornication. Even the church has to have its outhouse, just as it has to have a back door as well as a front door, a basement as well as a steeple. Because man is always going to be man and there's no true road without sides to it, and gulleys too, no true cross without arms that point away in two directions from the true way. But that Juneteenth night they all came quiet. And, Bliss, when I faded out they were still quiet. That's when ole Fess took over and got them singing again and I came down out of it and gave the nod to the boys and they started marching you down the aisle. . . ."

CHAPTER 8

Wait, Wait! the Senator's mind cried beneath the melodic line of Hickman's reminiscing voice, feeling himself being dragged irresistibly along. Yes, Bliss is here, for I can see myself, Bliss, again, on the night that changed it all, dropping down from the back of the platform with the seven black-suited preachers in their high-backed chairs onto the soft earth covered with sawdust, hearing the surge of fevered song rising above me as Daddy Hickman's voice sustained a note without apparent need for breath, rising high above the tent as I moved carefully out into the dark to avoid the ropes and tent stakes, walking softly over the sawdust and heading then across the clearing for the trees where Deacon Wilhite and the big boys were waiting. I moved reluctantly as always, yet hurrying; thinking, He still hasn't breathed. He's still up there, hearing Daddy Hickman soaring above the rest like a great dark bird of light, a sweet yet anguished mellowing cry. Still hearing it hovering there as I began to run to where I can see the shadowy figures standing around where it lies white and threatening upon a table set beneath the pines. Leaning huge against a tree off to the side is the specially built theatrical trunk they carried it in. Then I am approaching the table with dragging feet, hearing one of the boys giggling and saying, What you saying there, Deadman? And I look at it with horror—pink, frog-mouthed, with opened lid. Then looking back without answering, I see with longing the bright warmth of the light beneath the tent and catch the surging movements of the worshippers as they rock in time to the song which now seems to rise up to the still, sustained line of Daddy Hickman's transcendent cry. Then Deacon Wilhite said, Come on little preacher, in you go! Lifting me, his hands firm around my ribs, then my feet beginning to kick as I hear the boys giggling, then going inside and the rest of me slipping past Teddy and Easter Bunny, prone now and taking my Bible in my hands and the shivery beginning as the tufted top brings the blackness down.

And not even ice cream, nothing to sustain me in my own terms. Nothing to make it seem worthwhile in Bliss's terms.

At Deacon Wilhite's signal they raise me and it is as though the earth has fallen away, leaving me suspended in air. I seem to float in the blackness, the jolting of their measured footsteps guided by Deacon Wilhite's precise instructions, across the contoured ground, all coming to me muted through the pink insulation of the padding which lined the bottom, top, and sides, reaching me at blunt points along my shoulders, buttocks, heels, thighs. A beast with twelve disjointed legs coursing along, and I its inner ear, its anxiety; its anxious heart; straining to hear if the voice that sustained its line and me still soared. Because I believed that if he breathed while I was trapped inside, I'd never emerge. And hearing the creaking of a handle near my ear, the thump of Cylee's knuckle against the side to let me know he was out there, squinch-eyed and probably giggling at my fear. Through the thick satin-choke of the lining the remote singing seeming miles away and the rhythmical clapping of hands coming to me like sharp, bright flashes of lightning, promising rain. Moving along on the tips of their measured strides like a boat in a slow current as I breathe through the tube in the lid of the hot ejaculatory air, hushed now by the entry and passage among them of that ritual coat of silk and satin, my stiff dark costume made necessary to their absurd and eternal play of death and resurrection . . . Back to that? No!

"Bliss, I watched them bringing you slowly down the aisle on those strong young shoulders and putting you there among the pots of flowers, the red and white roses and the bleeding hearts—and I stood above you on the platform and began describing the beginning and the end, the birth and the agony, and . . ."

Screaming, mute, the Senator thought, Not me but another. Bliss. Resting on his lids, black inside, yet he knew that it was pink, a soft, silky pink blackness around his face, covering even his nostrils. Always the blackness. Inside everything became blackness, even the white Bible and Teddy, even his white suit. Not me! It was black even around his ears, deadening the sound except for Reverend Hickman's soaring song; which now, noodling up there high above, had taken on the softness of the piece of black velvet cloth from which Grandma Wilhite had made a nice full-dress overcoat—only better, because it had a wide cape for a collar. *Ayee,* but blackness.

He listened intently, one hand gripping the white Bible, the other frozen to Teddy's paw. Teddy was down there where the top didn't open at all, unafraid, a bold bad bear. He listened to the voice sustaining itself of its lyrics, the words rising out of the Word like Ezekiel's wheels; without breath, straining desperately to keep its throbbing waves coming to him, thinking, If he stops to breathe I'll die. My breath will stop too. Just like Adam's clay if God had coughed or sneezed.

And yet he knew that he was breathing noisily through the tube set in the lid. Hurry, Daddy Hickman, he thought. Hurry and say the word. Please, let me rise up. Let me come up and out into the light and air. . . .

Bliss?

So they were walking me slowly over the smooth ground and I could feel the slight rocking movement as the box shifted on their shoulders. And I thought, That means we're out in the clearing. Trees back there, voices thataway, life and light up there. Hurry! They're moving slow, like an old boat drifting down the big river in the night and me inside looking up into the black sky, no moon nor stars and all the folks gone far beyond the levees. And I could feel the shivering creep up my legs now and squeezed Teddy's paw to force it down. Then the rising rhythm of the clapping hands was coming to me like storming waves heard from a distance; like waves that struck the boat and flew off into the black sky like silver sparks from the shaking of the shimmering tambourines, showering at the zenith like the tails of skyrockets. If I could only open my eyes. It hangs heavy-heavy over my lids. Please hurry! Restore my sight. The night is black and I am far . . . far . . . I thought of Easter Bunny, he came from the dark inside of a red-and-white striped egg. . . .

> They took my Lord away
> They took my Lord
> Away,
> Please, tell me where
> To find Him. . . .

And at last they were letting me down, down, down; and I could feel the jar as someone went too fast, as now a woman's shout came to me, seeming to strike the side near my right ear like a flash of lightning streaking jaggedly across a dark night sky.

Jeeeeeeeeeeeeeeeeeeeee-sus! Have mercy, Jeeeeeee-sus! and the cold quivering flashed up my legs.

Everybody's got to die, sisters and brothers, Daddy Hickman was saying, his voice remote through the dark. That is why each and every one must be redeemed. YOU HAVE GOT TO BE RE-DEEMED! Yes, even He who was the Son of God and the voice of God to man—even *He* had to die. And what I mean is die as a *man*. So what do you, the lowest of the low, what do you expect you're going to have to do? He had to die in all of man's loneliness and pain because that's the price He had to pay for coming down here and putting on the pitiful, unstable form of man. Have mercy! Even with his godly splendor which could transform the built-in wickedness of man's animal form into an organism that could stretch and strain toward sublime righteousness—amen! That could show man the highway to progress and toward a more noble way of living— even with all that, even He had to die! Listen to me tell it to you: Even *He* who said, Suffer the little ones to come unto *Me,* had to die as a man. And like a man crying from His cross in all of man's pitiful puzzlement at the will of Almighty God! . . .

It was not yet time. I could hear the waves of Daddy Hickman's voice rolling against the sides, then down and back, now to boom suddenly in my ears as I felt the weight of darkness leave my eyes, my face bursting with sweat as I felt the rush of bright air bringing the odor of flowers. I lay there, blinking up at the lights, the satin corrugations of the slanting lid, and the vague outlines of Deacon Wilhite, who now was moving aside, so that it seemed as though he had himself been the darkness. I lay there breathing through my nose, deeply inhaling the flowers as I released Teddy's paw and grasped my white Bible with both hands, feeling the chattering and the real terror beginning and an ache in my bladder. For always it was as though it waited for the moment when I was prepared to answer Daddy Hickman's signal to rise up that it seemed to slide like heavy mud from my face to my thighs and there to hold me like quicksand. Always at the sound of Daddy Hickman's voice I came floating up like a corpse shaken loose from the bed of a river and the terror rising with me.

We are the children of Him who said, "Suffer . . ." I heard, and in my mind I could see Deacon Wilhite, moving up to stand beside Daddy Hickman at one of the two lecterns, holding on to the big Bible and looking intently at the page as he repeated, Suffer . . .

And the two men standing side by side, the one large and dark, the other slim and light brown; the other reverends rowed behind them, their faces staring grim with engrossed attention to the reading of the Word, like judges in their carved, high-backed chairs. And the two voices beginning their call and countercall as Daddy Hickman began spelling out the text which Deacon Wilhite read, playing variations on the verses just as he did with his trombone when he really felt like signifying on a tune the choir was singing:

Suffer, meaning in this workaday instance to surrender, Daddy Hickman said.

Amen, Deacon Wilhite said, repeating Surrender.

Yes, meaning to surrender with tears and to feel the anguished sense of human loss. Ho, our hearts bowed down!

Suffer the little ones, Deacon Wilhite said.

The little ones—ah yes! Our little ones. He was talking to us too, Daddy Hickman said. Our little loved ones. Flesh of our flesh, soul of our soul. Our hope for heaven and our charges in this world. Yes! The little lambs. The promise of our fulfillment, the guarantee of our mortal continuance. The little was-to-bes—Ha!—amen! The little used-to-bes that we all were to our mammies and pappies, and with whom we are but one with God. . . .

Oh my Lord, just look how the bright word leaps! Daddy Hickman said. First the babe, then the preacher. The babe father to the man, the man father to us all. A kind father calling for the babes in the morning of their earthly day—yes. Then in the twinkling of an eye, Time slams down and He calls us to come on home!

He said to come, Brother Alonzo.

Ah yes, to come, meaning to *approach*. To come up and be counted; to go along with Him, Lord Jesus. To move through the narrow gate bristling with spears, up the hill of Calvary, to climb onto the unyielding cross on which even li'l babies are turned into men. Yes, to come upon the proving ground of the human condition. Vanity dropped like soiled underwear. Pride stripped off like a pair of duckings that've been working all week in the mud. Feet dragging with the gravity of the trial ahead. Legs limp as a pair of worn-out galluses. With eyes dim as a flickering lamp-wick! Read to me, Deacon; line me out some more!

He said volumes in just those words. Brother Alonzo, COME UNTO ME, Deacon Wilhite cried.

Yes! Meaning to take up His burden. At first the little baby-sized load that with the first steps we take weighs less than a butter ball; no more than the sugar tit made up for a year-and-a-half-old child. Then, Lord help us, it grows heavier with each step we take along life's way. Until in that moment it weighs upon us like the headstone of the world. Meaning to come bringing it! Come hauling it! Come dragging it! Come even if you have to crawl! Come limping, come lame; come crying in your Jesus' name—but *come!* Come with your abuses but come with no excuses. Amen! Let me have it again, Rev. Wilhite. . . .

Come unto me, the Master said.

Meaning to help the weak and the downhearted. To stand up to the oppressors. To suffer and hang from the cross for standing up for what you believe. Meaning to undergo His initiation into the life everlasting. Oh yes, and to cry, cry, cry . . . Eyeeeee.

I could hear the word rise and spread to become the great soaring trombone note of Daddy Hickman's singing voice now and it seemed somehow to arise there in the box with me, shaking me fiercely as it rose to float with throbbing pain up to him again, who now seemed to stand high above the tent. And trembling I tensed myself and rose slowly from the waist in the controlled manner Daddy Hickman had taught me, feeling the terror gripping my chest like quicksand, feeling the opening of my mouth and the spastic flexing of my diaphragm as the words rushed to my throat to join his resounding cry:

Lord . . . Lord . . .

. . . Why . . .

. . . Hast Thou . . .

Forsaken me? . . . I cried, but now Daddy Hickman was opening up and bearing down:

. . . More Man than men and yet in that world-destroying, world-creating moment just a little child calling to His Father. . . . HEAR THE LAMB A-CRYING ON THE TREE!

LORD, LORD, I cried, WHY HAST THOU FORSAKEN ME?

Amen, Daddy Hickman said, amen!

Then his voice came faster, explosive with gut-toned preacher authority:

The father of no man, who yet was Father to all men—the human-son side of God—Great God A-mighty! Calling out from the agony of the cross! Ho, open up your downcast eyes and see the beauty of the living Word. . . . All babe, and yet in the mysterious

moment, ALL MAN. Him who had taken up the burden of all the
little children crying, LORD . . .

Lord, I cried.

Crying plaintive as a baby sheep . . .

. . . Baaaaaaaaa! . . .

Yes, the little Lamb crying with the tongue of man . . .

. . . LORD . . .

. . . Crying to the Father . . .

. . . Lord, LORD . . .

. . . Calling to his pappy . . .

. . . Lord, Lord, why hast . . .

Amen! LORD, WHY . . .

. . . Hast Thou . . .

Forsaken . . . me . . .

Aaaaaaaaaaah!

WHY HAST THOU FORSAKEN ME, LORD?

I screamed the words in answer and now I wanted to cry, to be
finished, but the sound of Daddy Hickman's voice told me that this
was not the time, that the words were taking him where they
wanted him to go. I could hear him beginning to walk up and down
the platform behind me, pacing in his great black shoes, his voice
rising above his heavy tread, his great chest heaving.

Crying—amen! Crying, Lord, Lord—amen! On a cross on a
hill, His arms spread out like my mammy told me it was the custom
to stretch a runaway slave when they gave him the water cure.
When they forced water into his mouth until water filled up his
bowels and he lay swollen and drowning on the dry land. Drinking
water, breathing water, water overflowing his earthbound lungs like
a fish drowning of air on the parched dry land.

And nailed NAILED to the cross-arm like a coonskin fixed to the
side of a barn, yes, but with the live coon still inside the furry gar-

ment! Still in possession, with all nine points of the Roman law a fiery pain to consume the house. Yes, every point of law a spearhead of painful injustice. Ah, yes!

Look! His head is lolling! Green gall is drooling from His lips. Drooling as it had in those long sweet, baby days long gone. AH, BUT NO TIT SO TOUGH NOR PAP SO BITTER AS TOUCHED THE LIPS OF THE DYING LAMB!

There He is, hanging on; hanging on in spite of knowing the way it would have to be. Yes! Because the body of man does not wish to die! It matters not who's inside the ribs, the heart, the lungs. Because the body of man does not sanction death. That's why suicide is but sulking in the face of hope! Ah, man is *tough*. Man is human! Yes, and by definition man is proud. Even when heaven and hell come slamming together like a twelve-pound sledge on a piece of heavy-gauged railroad steel, man is tough and mannish, and *ish* means like . . .

So there He was, stretching from hell-pain to benediction; head in heaven and body in hell—tell me, who said He was weak? Who said He was frail? Because if He was, then we need a new word for *strength,* we need a new word for *courage.* We need a whole new dictionary to capture the truth of that moment.

Ah, but there He is, with the others laughing up at Him, their mouths busted open like melons with rotten seeds—laughing! You know how it was, you've been up there. You've heard that contemptuous sound: IF YOU BE THE KING OF THE JEWS AND THE SON OF GOD, JUMP DOWN! JUMP DOWN, BLACK BASTARD, DIRTY JEW, JUMP DOWN! Scorn burning the wind. Enough halitosis alone to burn up old Moloch and melt him down.

He's bleeding from his side. Hounds baying the weary stag. And yet . . . And yet, His the power and the glory locked in the weakness of His human manifestation, bound by His acceptance of His

human limitation, His sacrificial humanhood! Ah, yes, for He *willed*
to save man by dying as *man* dies, and He was a heap of man in that
moment, let me tell you. He was man raised to his most magnifi-
cent image, shining like a prism glass with all the shapes and colors
of man, and dazzling all who had the vision to see. Man moved beyond mere pain to godly joy. . . . There He is, with the spikes in His
tender flesh. Nailed to the cross. First with it lying flat on the
ground, and then being raised in a slow, flesh-rending, bone-
scraping arc, one hundred and eighty degrees—up, up, UP!
Aaaaaaaaaaaah! Until He's upright like the ridgepole of the House
of God. Lord, Lord, Why? See Him, watch Him! Feel Him! His eyes
rolling as white as our eyes, looking to His, our Father's, the ten-
dons of His neck roped out, straining like the steel cables of a heavenly curving bridge in a storm. His jaw muscles bursting out like
kernels of corn on a hot stove lid. Yea! His mouth trying to refuse
the miserable human questioning of His fated words . . .

Lord, Lord . . .

Oh, yes, Rev. Bliss. Crying above the laughing ones whom He left
His Father to come down here to save, crying—

Lord, Lord, Why . . . ?

Amen! Crying as no man since—thank you, Jesus—has ever had
to cry.

Ah, man, ah, human flesh! This side we all know well. On this
weaker, human side we were all up there on the cross, just swarming over Him like microbes. But look at Him with me now, look at
Him fresh, with the eyes of your most understanding human heart.
There He is, hanging on in man-flesh, His face twitching and changing like a field of grain struck by a high wind—hanging puzzled. Bemused and confused. Mystified and teary-eyed, racked by the
realization dawning in the gray matter of His cramped human brain;
knowing in the sinews, in the marrow of His human bone, in the liv-

ing tissue of His most human veins—realizing totally that *man was born to suffer and to die* for other men! There He is, look at Him. Suspended between heaven and hell, hanging on already nineteen centuries of time in one split second of his torment and realizing, I say, realizing in that second of His anguished cry that life in this world is but a zoom between the warm womb and the lonely tomb. Proving for all time, casting the pattern of history forth for all to see in the undeniable concreteness of blood, bone and human courage before that which has to be borne by every man. Proving, proving that in this lonely, lightning-bug flash of time we call our life on earth we all begin with a slap of a hand across our tender baby bottoms to start us crying the puzzled question with our first drawn breath:

Why was I born? . . . Aaaaaaaah!

And hardly before we can get it out of our mouths, hardly before we can exhale the first lungful of life's anguished air—even before we can think to ask, Lord, what's my true name? Who, Lord, am I?—here comes the bone-crunching slap of a cold iron spade across our cheeks and it's time to cry, WHY, LORD, WHY WAS I BORN TO DIE?

Yes, why? Revern' Hickman, tell us why.

Why, Rev. Bliss? Because we're men, that's why! The initiation into the lodge is hard! The dues are outrageous and what's more, nobody can refuse to join. Oh, we can wear the uniforms and the red-and-purple caps and capes a while, and we can enjoy the feasting and the marching and strutting and the laughing fellowship—then Dong, dong! and we're caught between two suspensions of our God-given breath. One to begin and the other to end it, a whoop of joy and a sigh of sadness, the pinch of pain and the tickle of gladness, learning charity if we're lucky, faith if we endure, and hope in sheer downright desperation!

That's why, Reveren' Bliss. But now, thank God, because He

passed his test like any mannish man—not like a God, but like any pale, frail, weak man who dared to be his father's son. . . . Amen! Oh, we must dare to be, brothers and sisters. . . . We must dare, my little children. . . . We must dare in our own troubled times to be our Father's own. Yes, and now we have the comfort and the example to help us through from darkness to lightness, a beacon along the way. Ah, but in that flash of light in which we flower and wither and die, we must find Him so that He can find *us,* ourselves. For it is only a quivering moment—then the complicated tongs of life's old good-bad come clamping down, grabbing us in our tender places, feeling like a bear's teeth beneath the shortest of our short hairs. Lord, He taught us how to live, yes! And in the sun-drowning awfulness of that moment, He taught us how to die. There He was on the cross, leading His sheep, showing us how to achieve the heritage of our godliness which He in that most pitiful human moment—with spikes in His hands and through His feet, with the thorny crown of scorn studding His tender brow, with the cruel points of Roman steel piercing His side . . . crying . . .

Lord . . .

. . . Lord . . .

LORD! Amen. Crying from the castrated Roman tree unto his father like an unjustly punished child. And yet, Rev. Bliss, glory to God. . . . And yet He was guaranteeing with the final expiration of His human breath our everlasting life. . . .

Bliss's throat ached with the building excitement of it all. He could feel the Word working in the crowd now, boiling in the heat of the Word and the weather. Women were shouting and leaping up suddenly to collapse back into their chairs, and far back in the dark he could see someone dressed in white leaping into the air with outflung arms, going up then down——over backwards and up and down again, in a swooning motion which made her seem to float in the air stirred by the agitated movement of women's palm-leaf fans. It was long past the time for him to preach Saint Mark, but each time he cried Lord, Lord, they shouted and screamed all the louder. Across the platform now he could see Deacon Wilhite lean against the lectern shaking his head, his lips pursed against his great emotion. While behind him, the great preachers in their high-backed chairs thundered out deep staccato amens, he tried to see to the back of the tent, back where the seams in the ribbed white cloth curved down and were tied in a roll; past where the congregation strained forward or sat rigid in holy transfixion, seeing here and there the hard, bright disks of eyeglasses glittering in the hot, yellow light of lanterns and flares. The faces were rapt and owllike, gleaming with heat and Daddy Hickman's hot interpretation of the Word. . . .

Then suddenly, right down there in front of the coffin he could see an old white-headed man beginning to leap in holy exaltation, bounding high into the air, and sailing down; then up again, higher than his own head, moving like a jumping jack, with bits of sawdust dropping from his white tennis shoes. A brown old man, whose face was a blank mask, set and mysterious like a picture framed on a wall, his lips tight, his eyes starry, like those of a blue-eyed china doll——soaring without effort through the hot shadows of the tent. Sailing as you sailed in dreams just before you fell out of bed. A holy jumper, Brother Pegue . . .

Bliss turned to look at Daddy Hickman, seeing the curved flash of his upper teeth and the swell of his great chest as with arms out-spread he began to sing . . . when suddenly from the left of the tent he heard a scream.

It was of a different timbre, and when he turned, he could see the swirling movement of a woman's form; strangely, no one was reaching out to keep her from hurting herself, from jumping out of her underclothes and showing her womanness as some of the ladies sometimes did. Then he could see her coming on, a tall redheaded woman in a purple-red dress; coming screaming through the soprano section of the big choir where the members, wearing their square, flat-topped caps, were standing and knocking over chairs to let her through as she dashed among them striking about with her arms.

She's a sinner coming to testify, he thought. . . . But white? Is she white? hearing the woman scream,

He's mine, MINE! That's Cudworth, my child. My baby. You gypsy niggers stole him, my baby. You robbed him of his birthright!

And he thought, Yes, she's white all right, seeing the wild eyes and the red hair, streaming like a field on fire, coming toward him now at a pace so swift it seemed suddenly dreamlike slow. What's she doing here with us, a white sinner? Moving toward him like the devil in a nightmare, as now a man's voice boomed from far away, Madam, LADY, PLEASE—this here's the House of God!

But even then not realizing that she was clawing and pushing her way toward him. Cudworth, he thought, who's Cudworth? Then suddenly there she was, her hot breath blasting his ear, her pale face shooting down toward him like an image leaping from a toppling mirror, her green eyes wide, her nostrils flaring. Then he felt the bite of her arms locking around him and his head was crushed against her breast, hard into the sharp, sweet woman-smell of her. Me. She means me, he thought, as something strange and painful stirred within him. Then he could no longer breathe. She was crushing his face closer to her, squeezing and shaking him as he felt his Bible slipping from his fingers and tried desperately to hold on. But she screamed again with a sudden movement, her voice bursting hot into the sudden hush. And now he felt his Bible fall irretrievably away in the well-like echo punctuated by the heaving rasp of her breathing as he realized that she was trying to tear him from the coffin.

I'm taking him home to his heritage, he heard. He's mine, you understand? I'm his mother!

It sounded strangely dreamy, like a scene you saw when the big boys told you to open your eyes under the water. Who is she, he thought, where's she taking me? She's strong, but my mother went away, Paradise up high. . . . Then he was looking around at the old familiar grown folks, seeing their bodies frozen in odd postures, like kids playing a game of statue. And he thought, They're scaird; she's scairing them all, as his head was snapped around to where he could see Daddy Hickman leaning over the platform just above, bracing his hands against his thighs, his arms rigid and a wild look of disbelief on his great laughing-happy face, as now he shook his head. Then she moved again and as his head came around the scene broke and splashed like quiet water stirred by a stick.

Now he could see the people standing and leaning forward to see, some standing in chairs holding on to the shoulders of those in front, their eyes and mouths opened wide. Then the scene suddenly crumpled like a funny paper in a fireplace. He saw their mouths uttering the same insistent burst of words so loud and strong that he heard only a blur of loud silence. Yet her breathing came hard and clear. His head came around to her now, and he could see a fringe of freckles shooting across the ridge of the straight thin nose like a covey of quail flushing across a field of snow, the wide-glowing green of her eyes. Stiff copper hair was bursting from the pale white temple, reminding him of the wire bristles of Daddy Hickman's "Electric Hairbrush." . . . Then the scene changed again with a serene new sound beginning:

JUST DIG MY GRAVE, he heard. JUST DIG MY GRAVE AND

READY MY SHROUD, 'CAUSE THIS HERE AIN'T HAPPEN-
ING! OH, NO, IT AIN'T GOING TO HAPPEN. SO JUST DIG-A
MY GRAVE!

It was a short, stooped black woman, hardly larger than a little
girl, whose shoulders slanted straight down from her neck inside
the white collar of her oversized black dress, and from which her
deep and vibrant alto voice seemed to issue as from a source other
than her mouth. He could see her coming through the crowd, shaking her head and pointing toward the earth, crying, I SAID DIG IT!
I SAID GO GET THE DIGGERS! the words so intense with negation that they sounded serene, the voice rolling with eerie confidence as now she seemed to float in among the white-uniformed
deaconesses who stood at the front to his right. And he could see
the women turning to stare questioningly at one another, then back
to the little woman, who moved between them, grimly shaking her
head. And now he could feel the arms tighten around his body, gripping him like a bear, and he was being lifted up, out of the coffin;
hearing her scream hotly past his ear, DON'T YOU BLUEGUMS
TOUCH ME! DON'T YOU DARE!

And again it was as though they had all receded beneath the water
to a dimly lit place where nothing would respond as it should. For
at the woman's scream he saw the little woman and the deaconesses
pause, just as they should have paused in the House of God as well
as in the world outside the House of God—then she was lifting him
higher and he felt his body come up until only one foot was still
caught on the pink lining, and as he looked down he saw the coffin
move. It was going over, slowly, like a turtle falling off a log; then it
seemed to rise up of its own will, lazily, as one of the sawhorses
tilted, causing it to explode. He felt that he was going to be sick in
the woman's arms, for glancing down, he could see the coffin still in
motion, seeming to rise up of its own will, lazily, indulgently, like

Daddy Hickman turning slowly in pleasant sleep—only it seemed
to laugh at him with its pink frog-mouth. Then as she moved him
again, one of the sawhorses shifted violently, and he could see the
coffin tilt at an angle and heave, vomiting Teddy and Easter Bunny
and his glass pistol with its colored-candy BB bullets, like prizes
from a paper horn of plenty. Even his white leather Bible was
spurted out, its pages fluttering open for everyone to see.

He thought, He'll be mad about my Bible and my bear, feeling a
scream start up from where the woman was squeezing his stomach,
as now she swung him swiftly around, causing the church tent, the
flares, and the people to spin before his eyes like a great tin humming top. Then he felt his head snap forward and back, rattling his
teeth—and in the sudden break of movement he saw the deaconesses springing forward even as the spilled images from the toppling coffin quivered vividly before his eyes then faded like a splash
of water in bright sunlight—just as a tall woman with short, gleaming hair and steel-rimmed glasses shot from among the deaconesses
and as her lenses glittered harshly he saw her mouth come open,
causing the other women to freeze and a great silence to explode
beneath the upward curve of his own shrill scream. Then he saw her
head go back with an angry toss and he felt the sound slap hard
against him.

What? Y'all mean to tell *me?* Here in the House a God? She's
coming in *here*—who? WHOOOO! JUST TELL ME WHO BORN
OF MAN'S HOT CONJUNCTION WITH A WOMAN'S SINFUL
BOWELS?

And like an eerie echo now, the larger voice of the smaller
woman floated up from the sawdust-covered earth, JUST DIG MY
GRAVE! I SAY JUST READY MY SHROUD! JUST . . . and the
voices booming and echoing beneath the tent like a duet of angry
ghosts. Then it was as though something heavy had plunged from a

great height into the water, throwing the images into furious motion, and he could see the frozen women leap forward.

They came like shadows flying before a torch tossed into the dark, their weight seeming to strike the white woman who held him out of one single, slow, long-floating, space-defying leap, sending her staggering backward and causing her arms to squash the air from his lungs—Aaaaaaaah! Their faces, wet with wrath, loomed before him, seeming to enter where his breath had been, their dark, widespread hands beginning to tear at his body like the claws of great cats with human heads; lifting him screaming clear of earth and coffin and suspending him there between the redheaded woman who now held his head and the others who had seized possession of his legs, arms, and body. And again he felt, but could not hear, his own throat's Aaaaaaaaaaaaayee!

The Senator was first aware of the voice; then the dry taste of fever filled his mouth and he had the odd sensation that he had been listening to a foreign language that he knew but had neglected, so that now it was necessary to concentrate upon each word in order to translate its meaning. The very effort seemed to reopen his wounds and now his fingers felt for the button to summon the nurse but the voice was still moving around him, mellow and evocative. He recognized it now, allowing the button to fall as he opened his eyes. Yes, it was Hickman's, still there. And now it was as though he had been listening all along, for Hickman did not pause, his voice flowed on with an urgency which compelled him to listen, to make the connections.

" 'Well, sir, Bliss," Hickman said, "here comes this white woman pushing over everybody and loping up to the box and it's like hell had erupted at a sideshow. She rushed up to the box and . . ."

"*Box?*" the Senator said. "You mean 'coffin,' don't you?"

He saw Hickman look up, frowning judiciously. "No, Bliss, I mean 'box'; it ain't actually a coffin till it holds a dead man. . . . So, as I was saying, she rushed up and grabs you in the box and the deaconesses leaped out of their chairs and folks started screaming, and I looked out there for some white folks to come and get her, but couldn't see a single one. So there I was. I could have cried like a baby, because I knew that one miserable woman could bring the whole state down on us. Still there she is, floating up out of nowhere like a puff of poison gas to land right smack in the middle of our meeting. Bliss, it was like God had started playing practical jokes.

"Next thing I know she's got you by the head and Sister Susie Trumball's got one leg and another sister's got the other, and others are snatching you by the arms—talking about King Solomon, he didn't have but *two* women to deal with, I had seven. And one convinced that she's a different breed of cat from the rest. Yes, and the others chock-full of disagreement and out to prove it. I tell you, Bliss, when it comes to chillun, women just ain't gentlemen, and the fight between her kind of woman and ours goes way back to the beginning. Back, I guess, to when women found that the only way they could turn over the responsibility of raising a child to another woman was to turn over some of the child's love and affection along with it. They been battling ever since. One trying to figure out how to get out of the work without dividing up the affection, and the other trying to hold on to all that weight of care and those cords of emotion and love for which they figure no wages can ever pay. Because while some women work and others don't, to a woman a baby is a baby. She ain't rational about it, way down deep she ain't. All it's got to be is little and warm and helpless and cute and she wants to take it over, just like a she-cat will raise a litter of rabbits, or a she-

bitch dog will mama a Maltese kitten. I guess most of those deaconesses had been nursing white folks' chillun from the time they
could first take a job and each and every one of them had helped
raise somebody's baby and loved it. Yes, and had fought battles with
the white women every step of the way. It's a wonder those babies
ever grow up to have good sense with all that vicious, mute-
unspoken female fighting going on over them from the day they was
passed from the midwife's or doctor's hands into his mother's arms
and then from the minute it needed its first change of swaddling
clothes, into some black woman's waiting hands. Talking about God
and the Devil fighting over a man's soul, that situation must make a
child's heart a battleground. 'Cause, Bliss, as you must know by
now, women don't recognize no rules except their own—men
make the public rules—and they knew all about this so-called psychological warfare long before men finally recognized it and named
it and took credit for inventing something new.

"So there this poor woman comes moving out of her territory
and bursting into theirs. Mad, Bliss, mad! That night all those years
of aggravation was multiplied against her seven times seven. Because down there her kind always wins the contest in the end—for
the child, I mean—with ours being doomed to lose from the beginning and knowing it. They have got to be weaned—our women,
I mean, the nursemaids. And yet, it just seems to make their love all
the deeper and the tenderer. They know that when the child hits his
teens they can't hold him or help him any longer, even if she gets to
be wise as Solomon. She can help with the first steps of babyhood
and teach it its first good manners and love it and all like that, but
she can't do nothing about helping it take the first steps into manhood and womanhood. Ha, no! Who ever heard of one of us knowing anything about dealing with life, or knowing a better way of
facing up to the harsh times along the road? So the whole system's

turned against her then from foundation to roof; the whole beehive of what their folks consider good—'quality,' we used to say—is moved out of her domain. They just don't recognize no continuance of anything after that: not love, not remembrance, not understanding, sacrifice, compassion—nothing. Come the teen time, what we used to call the 'smell-yourself' time, when the sweat gets musty and you start to throb, they cast out the past and start out new—baptized into Caesar's way, Bliss. Which is the price the grown ones exact for the privilege of their being called 'miss' and 'mister.' So self-castrated of their love they pass us by, boy, they pass us by. Then as far as we're concerned it's 'Put your heart on ice, put your conscience in pawn.' Even their beloved black tit becomes an empty bag to laugh at and they grow deaf to their mammy's lullabies. What's wrong with those folks, Bliss, is they can't stand continuity, not the true kind that binds man to man and to Jesus and to God. My great-great-granddaddy was probably a savage eating human flesh, and bastardy, denied joy and shame, and humanity had to be mixed with my name a thousand times in the turmoil of slavery, and out of all that I'm a preacher. It's a mystery but it's based on fact, it happened body to body, belly to belly over the long years. But then? They're all born yesterday at twelve years of age. They can't stand continuity because if they could everything would have to be changed; there'd be more love among us, boy. But the first step in their growing up is to learn how to *spurn* love. *They have to deny it by law,* boy. Then begins the season of hate AND SHAMEFACED-NESS. Confusion leaps like fire in the bowels and false faces bloom like jimsonweed. They put on a mask, boy, and life's turned plumb upside down.

" 'Cause what can be right if the first, the *baby love,* was wrong, Bliss? Tell me then where's the foundation of the world? The tie that binds? You tell me, if with a boy's first buzz and a gal's first flow 'warm' has to become 'cold' and 'tenderness' calls forth 'harshness' and 'forthrightness' calls forth 'deviousness,' and innocence standing on the shady side of the street is automatically to be judged guilt? Hasn't joy then got to become flawed, just another name for sadness, like a golden trumpet with a crack in the valves and then with a pushed-in bell? Yes, and gratitude and charity and patience, endurance and hope and all the virtues Christ died to teach us become nothing but a burden and a luxury for black, knotty-headed fools? Speak to me, Bliss. You took their way, so speak to me and let me see by the light of their truth. I have arrived in ignorance and questioning. I'm old; my white head's almost forgot its blacker times and my sight's so poor I can almost look God's blazing sun straight in the face without batting my fading eyes. And I'm a simple man and nothing can change that. But I'm talking about simple things. For me, Bliss, the frame of life is round, and looking through I see the spirit does not die and neither does love when she smells of she and he smells of he, and the skirts git short and the voice cracks and deepens to mannish tones. No, but the way they've worked it out, tears become specialized, boy; and Jesus looked at the lot of man and wept for everybody. But those people put a weatherman in control of the sky. They cut the ties between the child and the foundation of his love. Laughter cracks down like thunder when tears ought to fall. And would have too, the year before. But standing in the doorway of manhood and womanhood you have to question yourself how to feel in the simplest things. You fall out of rhythm with your earliest cries, your movements. Little signs have to be stuck up and consulted in the heart: How must I feel, Mister Weatherman? His face over there is dark; though I used to know it, can I say howdy? She stretches forth the same old hand for charity that used to cook the fudge and plait my braids, can I acknowledge it? She cries for understanding and a recognition of that old cut nerve that twitches in my heart—can I afford to hear the voice of this bowed-down heart? How much money will it cost me, Mister Weatherman? He wrestles over there in pain; ain't this the time to laugh, with misery monkeying up his wrinkled face? Or he speaks polite and steps aside, isn't this the way of fear and a sign that God has spat on him? Bow down, bow down! Step aside and out of my exalted human sight.

"Then a little later, Bliss, when he's found a mate, that old severed nerve throbs again. They're laughing like fools out in the quarters—is it to mock my dignity? Is it zippered up? Listen to them praying, is it for my abject destruction? I built my house on King Mountain stone, will it crumble before their envying eyes? In the dark in the alley, in the summer night some mister man is making a woman howl and spit like a rapturous cat—could that black tomcat have prowled in my bed? Could he? Could he? How now! He's a buck stallion full of stinking sweat, I'm an eagle, bright with the light of God's own smile. His woman's a bitch and mine a doe . . . Ah, but think about it with the blue serge hanging on the rack: Has a black stallion ever mounted a snow-white doe at her frisky invitation when the sun was down? What goes on in that darkness I create when I refuse to see? What links up with what? Who reaches out to whom within that gulley, under that lid of life denied? You want me to hush and go away, Bliss?

"Not now, it's been too long and some things just won't stand not being said. Oh, all I've been talking about is human, Bliss. All human weakness and human pride and will—didn't Peter deny Christ? But you had a choice, Bliss. You had a chance to join up to be a witness for either side and you let yourself be fouled up. You tried to go with those who raise the failure of love above their heads like a flag and say, 'See here, I am now a man.' You wanted to be with those who turn coward before their strongest human need and then say,

'Look here, I'm brave.' It makes me laugh, because few are brave enough to be for right and truth above all their other foolishness. There wasn't a single man in that jail that night they beat me who didn't know I was innocent and there wasn't a single person in that town who didn't know that woman was crazy, but not a single one was brave enough and free enough simply not to beat me. I don't mean defend me, I don't mean take up the cause of Justice, but just say to the others, 'Listen, this man is innocent. He was preaching before a tent full of people and so couldn't have touched that woman with a ten-foot pole.' No, Bliss, I didn't expect that because I knew the score. But even knowing it I found I still had something to learn. I had to lay there while they beat me and what I learned was that there wasn't a mother's son among them who, knowing my innocence, had the manhood and decency to refuse to whip my head. I guess if there'd been a preacher among them he'd've got in his licks with the rest. I lay there and laughed, Bliss. Sure, I laughed. I laughed because there is some knowledge that's just too hopeless for tears.

"That was a long time ago and a few years before you were to make your choice, Bliss, but the devilment I'm describing has been going on for years and it's a process for blinding and all the hell un-leashed in the church that night sprang from it. The eye that was trained by two women's love to love and respond to life now must be blind to the spirit that shines from all but a special few human eyes, and now you can't look beneath the surface of a windowpane and see fire and the mirrors are rigged so you can't see what you would deny in those whom you would deny. Oh, sure, Bliss; you can cut that cord and zoom off like a balloon and rise high——I mean that cord woven of love, of touching, ministering love, that's tied to a babe with its first swaddling clothes——but the cord don't shrivel and die like a navel cord beneath the first party dress or the first long suit of clothes. Oh no, it parts with a cry like a rabbit torn by a hawk in the winter snows and it numbs quick and glazes like the eyes of a sledge-hammered ox and the blood don't show, it's like a wound that's cauterized. It snaps with the heart's denial back into the skull like a worm chased by a razor-beaked bird, and once inside it snarls, Bliss; it snarls up the mind. It won't die and there's no sun inside to set so it can stop its snakish wiggling. It bores reckless excursions between the brain and the heart and kills and kills again unkillable continuity. Bliss, when Eve deviled and Adam spawned we were *all* in the dark, and that's a fact."

Suddenly the old man shook his head. "Oh, Bliss; *Bliss,* boy. I get carried away with words. Forgive me. Maybe a black man, even one as old as me, just can't understand the mystery of a white man's pain. But one thing I do know: God, Bliss boy, is Love."

The Senator looked up at the fading voice, gripped by the fear that with its cessation his own breath would go. But there was Hickman still beside him, looking down as with the wonder of his Word for God.

"Perhaps," the Senator said, "but it makes the laces too tight. Tell me what happened while there's still time."

"Lord, Bliss," Hickman said, "here I've gone off and left you suspended in those women's hands and you crying to beat the band. Well, for a minute there it looked like they were going to snatch you limb from limb and dart off in seven different directions. *And* the folks were getting outraged a mile a minute. Because although you might have forgot it, nothing makes our people madder and will bring them to make a killing-floor stand quicker than to have white folks come bringing their craziness into the church. We just can't stand to have our one place of peace broken up, and nothing'll upset us worse—*unless* it's messing with one of our babies. You could just see it coming on, Bliss. I turned and yelled at them to regard the House of God—when here comes another woman, one of the deaconesses, Sister Bearmasher. She's a six-foot city woman from Birmingham, wearing eyeglasses and who ordinarily was the kindest woman you'd want to see. Soft-spoken and easygoing the way some big women get to be because most of the attention goes to the little cute ones. Well, Bliss, she broke it up.

"I saw her coming down the aisle from the rear of the tent and reaching over the heads of the others, and before I could move she's in that woman's head of long red hair like a wildcat in a weaving mill. I couldn't figure what she was up to in all that pushing and tugging, but when they kind of rumbled around and squatted down low like they were trying to grab better holts I could see somebody's shoe and a big comb come sailing out; then they squatted again a couple of times, real fast, and when they come up, she's got all four feet or so of that woman's red hair wrapped around her arm like an ell of copper-colored cloth. And Bliss, she's talking calm and slapping the others away with her free hand like they were babies. Saying, 'Y'all just leave her to *me* now, sisters. Everything's going to be all right. She ain't no trouble, darlings; not now. Get on away now, Sis' Trumball. Let her go now. You got rheumatism in you shoulder anyway. Y'all let her loose, now. Coming here into the House of God talking about this is *her* child. Since when? I want to know, since *when?* HOLD STILL DARLING! she tells the white woman. 'NOBODY WANTS TO HURT YOU, BUT YOU MUST UNDERSTAND THAT YOU HAVE GONE TOO FAR!'

"And that white woman is holding on to you for dear life, Bliss; with her head snubbed back, way back, like a net full of red snappers and flounders being wound up on a ship's winch. And this big amazon of a woman, who could've easily set horses with a Missouri

mule, starts then to preaching her own sermon. Saying, 'If this
Revern-Bliss-the-Preacher is her child then all the yellow bastards
in the nation has got to be hers. So when, I say, so when's she going
to testify to all that? You sisters let her go now; just let me have her.
Y'all just take that child. Take that child, I say. I love that child 'cause
he's God's child and y'all love that child. So I say take that child out
of this foolish woman's sacrilegious hands. TAKE HIM, I SAY! And
if this be the time then this is the time. If it's the time to die, then
I'm dead. If it's the time to bleed, then I'm bleeding—but take that
child. 'Cause whatever time it is, this is one kind of foolishness
that's got to be stopped before it gets any further under way!'

"Well, sir, there you were, Bliss, with the white woman still got
holt of you but with her head snubbed back now and her head bucking like a frightened mare's, screaming, 'He's mine, he's mine.'
Claiming you, boy, claiming you right out of our hands. At least out
of those women's hands. Because us men were petrified, thrown
out of action by that white woman's nerve. And that big, strong
Bearmasher woman threatening to snatch her scalp clean from her
head.

"And all the time Sister Bearmasher is preaching her sermon.
Saying, 'If he was just learning his ABC's like the average child in-
stead of being a true, full-fledged preacher of the Gospel you
wouldn't want him and you'd yell down destruction on anybody
who even signified he was yours—WHERE'S HIS DADDY? YOU
AIN'T THE VIRGIN MARY, SO YOU SHO MUST'VE PICKED
OUT HIS DADDY. WHO'S THE BLACK MAN YOU PICKED TO
DIE?'

"And then, Bliss, women all over the place started to taking it up:
'YES! That's right, who's the man? Let us behold him! Amen! Just
tell us!' and all like that. . . . Bliss, I'm a man with great puzzlement about life and I enjoy the wonderment of how things can happen and how folks can act, so I guess I must have been just standing

there with my mouth open and taking it all in. But when those
women started to making a chorus and working themselves up to
do something drastic I broke loose. I reached down and grabbed my
old trombone and started to blow. But instead of playing something
calming, I was so excited that I broke into the 'St. Louis Blues,' like
we used to when I was a young hellion and a fight would break out
at a dance. Just automatically, you know; and I caught myself on
about the seventh note and smeared into 'Listen to the Lambs,' but
my lip was set wrong and there I was half laughing at how my sinful
days had tripped me up—so that it came out 'Let Us Break Bread
Together,' and by that time Deacon Wilhite had come to life and
started singing and some of the men joined in—in fact, it was a
men's chorus, because those women were still all up in arms. I blew
me a few bars then put down that horn and climbed down to the
floor to see if I could untangle that mess.

"I didn't want to touch that woman, so I yelled for somebody
who knew her to come forward and get her out of there. Because
even after I had calmed them a bit, she kept her death grip on you
and was screaming, and Sister Bearmasher still had all that red hair
wound round her arm and wouldn't let go. Finally a woman named
Lula Strothers came through and started to talk to her like you'd
talk to a baby and she gave you up. I'm expecting the police or some
of her folks by now, but luckily none of them had come out to laugh
at us that night. So Bliss, I got you into some of the women's hands
and me and Sister Bearmasher got into the woman's rubber-tired
buggy and rode off into town. She had two snow-white horses
hitched to it, and luckily I had handled horses as a boy, because they
were almost wild. And she was screaming and they reared and
pitched until I could switch them around; then they hit that midnight road for a fare-thee-well.

"The woman is yelling, trying to make them smash us up, and
cursing like a trooper and calling for you—though by the name of

Cudworth—while Sister Bearmasher is still got her bound up by the hair. It was dark of the moon, Bliss, and a country road, and we took every curve on two wheels. Yes, and when we crossed a little wooden bridge it sounded like a burst of rifle fire. It seemed like those horses were rushing me to trouble so fast that I'd already be there before I could think of what I was going to say. How on earth was I going to explain what had happened, with that woman there to tell the sheriff something different—with her just *being* with us more important than the truth? I thought about Sister Bearmasher's question about who the man was that had been picked to die, and I tell you, Bliss, I thought that man was me. There I was, hunched over and holding on to those reins for dear life, and those mad animals frothing and foaming in the dark so that the spray from their bits was about to give us a bath and just charging us into trouble. I could have taken a turn away from town, but that would've only made it worse, putting the whole church in danger. So I was bound to go ahead since I was the minister responsible for their bodies as well as their souls. Sister Bearmasher was the only calm one in that carriage. She's talking to that woman as polite as if she was waiting on table or massaging her feet or something. And all the time she's still wound up in the woman's hair.

"But the woman wouldn't stop screaming, Bliss; and she's cussing some of the worst oaths that ever fell from the lips of man. And at a time when we're flying through the dark and I can see the eyes of wild things shining out at us, at first up ahead, then disappearing. And the sound of the galloping those horses made! They were hitting a lick on that road like they were in a battle charge.

" 'Revern'?' Sister Bearmasher yelled over to me.

" 'Yes, Sister?' I called back over to her.

" 'I say, are you praying?'

" 'Praying,' I yelled. 'Sister, my whole body and soul is crying out

to God, but it's about as much as I can do to hold on to these devilish reins. You just keep that woman's hands from scratching at my
face.'

"Well, Bliss, about that time we hit a straightaway, rolling past
some fields, and way off to one side I looked and saw somebody's
barn on fire. It was like a dream, Bliss. There we was making better
time than the Hambletonian, with foam flying, the woman screeching, leather straining, hooves pounding and Sister Bearmasher no
longer talking to the woman but moaning a prayer like she's bending over a washtub somewhere on a peaceful sunny morning. And
managing to sound so through all that rushing air. And then, there it
was, way off yonder across the dark fields, that big barn filling the
night with silent flames. It was too far to see if anyone was there to
know about it, and it was too big for anybody except us not to see
it; and as we raced on there seemed no possible way to miss it burning across the night. We seemed to wheel around it, the earth was
so flat and the road so long and winding. Lonesome, Bliss; that sight
was lonesome. Way yonder, isolated and lighting up the sky like a
solitary torch. And then as we swung around a curve where the road
swept into a lane of trees, I looked through the flickering of the
trees and saw it give way and collapse. Then all at once the flames
sent a big cloud of sparks to sweep the sky. Poor man, I thought,
poor man, as that buggy hit a rough stretch of road. Then I was
praying. Boy, I was really praying. I said, 'Lord, bless these bits, these
bridles and these reins. Lord, please keep these thin wheels and
rubber tires hugging firm to your solid ground, and Lord, bless
these hames, these cruppers, and this carriage tongue. Bless the
breast-straps, Lord, and these straining leather belly-bands.' And
Bliss, I listened to those pounding hoofbeats and felt those horses
trying to snatch my arms clear out of their sockets and I said, 'Yea,
Lord, and bless this whiffletree.' Then I thought about that fire and

looked over at the white woman and finally I prayed, 'Lord, please bless this wild redheaded woman and that man back there with that burning barn. And Lord, since you know all about Sister Bearmasher and me, all we ask is that you please just keep us steady in your sight.'

"Those horses moved, Bliss. Zip, and we're through the land and passing through a damp place like a swamp, then up a hill through a burst of heat. And all the time, Bliss . . ."

The voice had ceased. Then the Senator heard, "Bliss, are you there, boy?"

"Still here," the Senator said from far away. "Don't stop. I hear."

Then through his blurring eyes he saw the dark shape come closer, and now the voice sounded small, as though Hickman stood on a hill somewhere inside his head.

"I say, Bliss, that all the time I should have been praying for you, back there all torn up inside by those women's hands. Because, after all, a lot of prayer and sweat and dedication had gone into that buggy along with the money-greed and show-off pride. Because it held together through all that rough ride even though its wheels were humming like guitar strings, and it took me and Sister Bearmasher to jail and a pretty hot time before they let us go. So there between a baby, a buggy, and a burning barn I prayed the wrong prayer. I left you out, Bliss, and I guess right then and there you started to wander. But you, I left you in some of the sisters' hands and you misbehaved. Bliss, you was the one who needed praying for and I neglected you. . . ."

Hickman leaned closer now, gazing into the quiet face.

The Senator slept.

CHAPTER 9

Aaaaaaaayeeeee . . . ! It ripped his ears in a rising curve, choked and bubbling like the shout of a convert who had started screaming while Daddy Hickman was still raising his head from beneath the baptismal waters. . . . *Aaaaaaaaayeeeeee!* and he could feel it coming in sharp, shrill bursts but the redheaded woman was holding him so fiercely that he could not tell if they came from her heaving body or his own. Arms and hands were flying and he was plunging toward the coffin, catching sight of Teddy sprawled in the sawdust—only to be snatched up again, feeling a pain burning its way straight up his back as she screamed *He's mine! He's*—her head snapping back and the scream becoming the sound of Daddy Hickman's trombone and he saw the white sleeve of a tall sister's arm flash red, hearing, "Y'all leave her to me now," and thinking *Blood* as they whirled him around and her arms tightening and thinking That's flying *bloody blare of horn she's bleeding*—feeling himself being ripped completely away from her now, the sisters with faces hard and masklike coming on and twisting him from her arms like a lamb bone popped out of its socket, holding him kicking high and passing him between them as he looked wildly for the flowing blood. . . .

Catch him! someone shouted, and he then felt himself hanging by his heels and they were grabbing and slapping him across his burning back, lifting, and his head came up into a confusion of voices, hearing, *Here, let me take him. Let's get the poor child out of here,* seeing Sister Wilhite and another sister was saying *Better give him to Sister Mary,* holding her broad hand against his stomach, *Sister Mary's home, she's got kids of her own,* and another voice saying, *No, she's too crowded and lives too close to here. . . .* and *Then who?* Sister Wilhite was saying and long smooth fingers were reaching for him saying, *Me, Sister Wilhite, let me have him* and Sister Wilhite looking intensely at the young woman, her eyes sparkling, *You?* and the smooth Elberta peach brown face with curly hair covering her ears saying, *Let me, Sister Wilhite, I live far and I got no husband and I know my way through these woods like a rabbit. . . .* And Sister Wilhite turning her head, saying, *What you all think?* and he tried to open his mouth but she shook him—*Hush, Revern' Bliss*—and someone said, *She's right. Give him to Sister Georgia, only get him out of here.* And he was leaning forward, hearing Sister Wilhite's *Here, sister, take him,* and he began again, *I want Daddy Hickman,* and Sister Wilhite saying, *And you hurry.* He was being handed over once more and he said, *I want Daddy Hickman,* hearing, *Hush Revern' Bliss, honey,* in the hot blast of Sister Georgia's breath against his cheek. *You're going with me 'cause this ain't no place for you to be—not right now it ain't.* Then she turned and he caught sight of Daddy Hickman climbing down from the platform. Then he recognized the little slant-shouldered sister's deep voice—*Will y'all sisters get out of the woman's way?* she said—and the others were pushing and shoving and Sister Georgia was pushing him against them and the little sister said with her head on Sister Georgia's shoulder

Go with the speed of angels, love. Madame Herod done come, Mister Herod be coming soon; the snake! So take that child and let 'em diga my grave. . . .

And already Sister Georgia was rushing him along with her quick, swinging-from-side-to-side walk, away from the screaming white woman and the angry deaconesses in their ruffled baby caps, going straight through the strangely silent members, stepping over fallen folding chairs, lunch baskets and scattered hymnbooks, past the slanting tent ropes and a smoking flare, into the open. Beginning to run now as though someone was chasing them, on out across the sawdust-covered earth of the clearing, through the big trees into the bushes in the dark. She was saying baby words to him as she ran and he twisted around to see behind them, hearing, *"Hold still now, honey,"* as he looked back to the moiling within the yellow light of the tent. The woman was screaming again and a team of mules was pitching in their harness rising up and breaking toward the light, then plunging off into the shadow. Then Deacon Wilhite's voice was leading some of the members to singing and the sound rose up strong, causing the woman's screams to sound like red sparks shooting through a cloud of thick black smoke. Sister Georgia stumbled sending them jolting forward and he could hear her grunt and her breath coming hard and fast as she balanced herself, causing him to sway back and forth in her arms and his back to burn like fire.

"It's all right now, Revern' Bliss," she said as he began to cry.

"I want Daddy Hickman," he cried. "I want to go back."

"Not now, Revern' Bliss, darling, Right now he's got his hands full with that awful woman."

"But I hurt," he cried. "I hurt bad."

"Hurt? What's hurting you, Revern' Bliss?"

"I hurt all over. They scratched me. Please take me back."

"But the meeting's all over for tonight," she said. "That woman broke it up. Lord help us, but she *really* wrecked it. I hope the Lord makes her suffer for it too. Doing such an awful thing, and we supposed to act Christian toward them. Knocking over your coffin and everything . . ."

He thought, *I want Teddy and my Bible.* Then, remembering the look on the woman's face when she picked him up, he was silent. It was like a dream. He had been in the coffin, ready to rise up, and all of a sudden there she was, screaming. Now it was like a picture he was looking at in a book or in a dream—even as he watched the tear-sparkling tent falling rapidly away. And in the up-and-down swaying of the sister's movement he could no longer tell one member from another; he couldn't even see Daddy Hickman. *She was really one of them* passed through his mind, then the road was dipping swiftly down a hill in the dark and he was being taken where he could no longer see the peak shape of the tent rising white above the yellow light. Only the sound of singing came to him now and fading.

They were moving through low-branched trees where he could smell the sticky little blossoms which the honeybees and flea-flies loved so well; then the branches grew higher up on the trunks of the trees and the trees were taller and they were dropping down a slope. "Hold tight, Revern' Bliss," she said. "We have to cross over somewhere along here."

"Over water?" he said.

"That's right."

"Deep water?"

"Not very. You don't have to be afraid. Hush now, we be there in a minute."

"I'm not afraid of any water," he said.

She was moving carefully and he looked down, hearing the quiet swirl of the stream somewhere ahead before he could see its smoothly glinting flow. And she said, "Hold tight, honey, hold real tight, we got to cross this log," and was balancing and carrying him rapidly along a narrow tree trunk that lay across the stream, then breathing hard up the steep slope of a hill into the bushes. He could hear twigs snapping and plucking at her dress and raised his arm to keep the limbs from his face as she climbed. She was breathing hard and he could feel her softness sweating through the cloth of his full dress jacket and the heat of her body rising to him. And he could hear himself thinking just as Body would have said, *She's starting to smell kinda funky,* and was ashamed. Body said that ladies could smell a *good* funky and a *bad* funky but men just smelled like funky bears. But this was a good smell although it wasn't supposed to be and the sister was good to be carrying him so gently and she was nice and soft. Her pace slowed again now and suddenly they were out of the dusty bushes and he sneezed. They were moving along a sandy road.

"Wheew!" she said. "That was *some* thicket, Revern' Bliss, and you went through it like a natural man. You all right now?"

"Yes, mam," he said. "But I want to go back to Daddy Hickman."

"Oh, he'll be coming to get you soon, Revern' Bliss. He knows where you'll be. You're not afraid of me are you?"

"No, mam, but I have to go back and help him."

"I guess we can rest now," she said, bending, and he felt the sand give beneath his feet. She was breathing hard. Her white dress made it easier to see in the dark, just as his white suit did. She was younger than Sister Wilhite and the others. And he thought, *We are like ghosts on this road.*

"Of course you want to help, Revern'," she said, "and as much as I'd like to have a little boy as smart as you, I know you're a minister and not meant to be mine or anybody else's. So don't worry, Revern' Bliss, because as soon as Revern' gets through he'll be coming after you. That woman needs a good beating for doing this to you. . . ."

She was breathing easier now and looking up and down the dark road.

"She called me a funny name," he said.

"I could hear her yelling something when she broke in. What'd she call you?"

"Cudworth . . ."

"*Cudworth*—Revern' Bliss, are you sure?"

"I think so," he said.

"Well, I wouldn't be surprised. Doing what she done it's a wonder she didn't call you Lazarus . . . or Peter Wheatstraw . . . even Shorty George," and she laughed. "The old heifer. They always slapping us with some name that don't have nothing to do with us. The freckle-faced cow! You think you can walk now, Revern' Bliss? My house is just up the road behind those trees up yonder. See, up there."

"Yes, mam, I can walk," he said. But he couldn't see her house, only a dark line of bushes and trees. *This is a deep black night,* he thought. *She's got eyes like a cat.*

"Walk over here on the side," she said. "It's firmer."

"She made the members afraid," he heard himself saying.

"Afraid? Now where'd you get that idea, Revern' Bliss? As outraged as those sisters was and you talking about them being *afraid?* Were *you* afraid?"

"Yes, mam," he said, "but the sisters were hurting me. They were afraid too. I could smell them. . . ."

"*Smell* them? Well did I ever!" She stopped, her hands on her hips, looking down into his face. "Revern' Bliss, what are you talking about? You must be tired and near-half asleep, talking about *smelling* folks. Give me your hand so I can get you to bed."

She was annoyed now and he could feel the tug on his shoulder as she pulled him rapidly along. *She doesn't want me to know it,* he thought, *but they were afraid.*

"Revern' Bliss, you are *something,*" she said.

They went along a path through the trees; then they were climbing, and suddenly there was the house on a hill in the dark. He could smell orange blossoms as she led him up to it; then they were going across the porch up to a doorway.

"Stand right here a minute while I light the lamp," she said. Then the room was lighted and she said, "Welcome to my house, Revern' Bliss," and he went in. She was fanning herself with a handkerchief and sighing. "Lord, what a hot evening, and it had been going so good too—Revern' Bliss, would you like a piece of cold watermelon before you go to bed?"

"Yes, mam, thank you, mam," he said. And he was glad that she wasn't angry anymore.

"You don't think it'll make you have to get up in the night, do you?"

"Oh no, mam. Daddy Hickman lets me have watermelon at night all the time."

"Are you sure?"

"Yes, mam. He gives me melon and ice cream too. You wouldn't have any ice cream, would you, mam?"

"No I don't, Revern' Bliss, bless your heart. But if you come back on Sunday I'll make you a whole freezer full and bake you a cake, all for yourself. Would you like that, Revern' Bliss?"

"Yes, mam, I sure would," he said. And she bent down and hugged him then and the woman smell came to him sharp and intriguing. Then her face left and she was smiling in the lamplight and beyond her head two tinted pictures of old folks frozen in attitudes of dreamy and remote dignity looked down from where they hung high on the wall in oval frames, seeming to float behind curved glass. They had the feel of the statues of the saints he'd seen in that white church in New Orleans. It was strange. And he could see the reflection of his shadowed face showing above her bending shoulders and against the side of her darkened head. He felt her about to lift him then and suddenly he hugged her. And in the warm surge that flowed over him, he kissed her cheek, then pulled quickly away.

"Why, Revern' Bliss, that was right sweet of you. I don't remember ever being kissed by a minister before." She smiled down at him. "Let's us go get that melon," she said.

He felt the warmth of her hand as she led him out through a dark kitchen that sprang into shadow-shrouded light before them, placing the lamp on the blue oilcloth that covered the table, saying, "Come on, Revern' Bliss." And they went out into the dark, into the warm blast of the orange-blossom night and across the porch into the dark of the moon. Fireflies flickered before them as they moved across the yard.

"It's down in the well, Revern' Bliss; it's been down there cooling since yesterday."

She went up and leaned against the post that held the crosspiece, looking down into the wide dark mouth of the well, and he followed to stand beside her, looking at the rope curving up through the big iron pulley that hung above. And she said, "Look down there, Revern' Bliss; look down at the water before I touch the rope and disturb it. You see those stars down there? You see them floating down there in the water?"

And he boosted himself up the side, balancing on his elbows, as he looked down into the cool darkness. It was a wide well and there were the high stars, mirrored below in the watery sky, and he felt himself carried down and yet up. He seemed to fall down into the sky and to hang there, as though his darkened image floated among the stars. It was frightening and yet peaceful, and close beside him he could hear her breathing.

Then suddenly he heard himself saying, "I am the bright and morning star," and peered below, hearing her give a low laugh and her voice above him saying serenely, "You are too, at that," and she was touching his head.

Then her hand left and she touched the rope and he could see the sky toss below, shuddering and breaking and splashing liquidly with a dark silver tossing. And he wanted to please her.

"Look at them now," he said. "See there, the morning stars are singing together."

And she said, "Why, I know where that's from, it's from the book of Job, my daddy's favorite book of the Bible. Do you preach Job too, Revern' Bliss?"

"Yes, mam. I preaches Job *and* Jeremiah too. Just listen to this: *The word of the Lord came unto me, saying, Before I formed thee in the belly I knew thee; and before thou camest forth out of the womb I sanctified thee, and I ordained thee a prophet unto the nations. . . ."*

"Amen, Revern' Bliss . . ." she said.

". . . Ah, Lord, God!" he said, making his voice strong and full, *"Behold, I cannot speak: for I am a child,"* and it seemed to echo in the well, surprising him.

"Now ain't that wonderful?" she said. "Revern' Bliss, do you understand all of that you just said?"

"Not *all* of it, mam. Even grown preachers don't understand all of it, and Daddy Hickman says we can only see as through a glass darkly."

"Ah yes," she sighed. "There's a heap of mystery about us people."

She was pulling the rope now and he could hear the low song of the pulley and the water dripping a little uneven musical scale—a *ping pong pitty-pat ping ping pong-pat* back into the well, and he said,

"Sure, I preaches Job," and started to quote more of the scripture but he couldn't remember how it started. *It's the thirty-eighth chapter, seventh verse,* he thought, *that's where it tells about the stars singing together. . . .*

"Revern' Bliss, this melon's heavy," she said. "Help me draw it up."

"Yes, mam," he said, taking hold of the rope. And as he helped her he remembered some of it and said, "*Gird up now thy loins like a man; for I will demand of thee, and answer thou me. . . .*" He heard the pulley singing a different tune now and as the melon came up the water from the rope was running cool over his hands and his throat remembered some more of the lines and they came out hand over fist as the melon came up from the well:

> "*Where wast thou when I laid the foundations of the*
> *earth? declare, if thou hast understanding.*
> *Who hath laid the measures thereof, if thou knowest?*
> *or who hath stretched the line upon it?*
> *Whereupon are the foundations thereof fastened?*
> *or who laid the corner stone thereof?*
> *When the morning stars sang together, and all the*
> *sons of God shouted for joy?*
> *Or who shut up the sea with doors, when it brake forth,*
> *as if it had issued out of the womb? . . .*"

Then she said, "There!" and he saw the melon come gleaming from the well and she reached out and pulled it over to the side, setting the bucket on the rim. He could hear it dripping a quiet wet little tune far below as she removed it from the bucket.

"It's a mystery to me how you manage to remember so much, Revern' Bliss—Lord, but this sure is a heavy one we got us tonight! Come on over here where we can sit down."

So he followed her over the bare ground and sat on the floor of the porch beside the wet, cold melon, his feet dangling while she went into the kitchen. Behind him he could hear the opening of a drawer and the rattling of knives and forks; then she was back holding a butcher knife, the screen slamming sharply behind her.

She said, "Would you like to cut the melon, Revern' Bliss?"

"Yes, mam, thank you, mam."

"I thought you would," she said. "The men always want to do the cutting. So here it is, let's see how you do it."

"Shall I plug it, mam?" he said, taking the knife.

"*Plug* it? Plug this melon that I *know* is ripe? Listen to that," she said, thumping it with her fingers.

"Daddy Hickman always plugs *his* melons," he said.

"All right, Revern' Bliss, if that's the way it has to be, go ahead. I guess Revern' has plugged him quite a few."

And he took the knife and felt the point go in hard and deep to the width of the blade; then again, and again, and again, making a square in the rind. He felt the blade go deep and deep and then deep and deep again. Then he removed the blade, just like Daddy Hickman did and stuck the point in the middle of the square and lifted out the wedge-shaped plug, offering it to her.

"Thank you, Revern' Bliss," she said with a smile in her voice, and he could hear the sound of the juice as she tasted it.

"See there, I knew it was ripe," she said. "You try it."

It was cold and very sweet and the taste of it made him hurry. He cut two lengthwise pieces then, saying, "There you are, mam," and watched her lift them out, giving him one and taking the other.

And they sat there in the dark with the orange blossoms heavy around them, eating the cold melon. He tried spitting the seeds at the fireflies, hearing them striking the hard earth around the porch and the fireflies still blinking. Then Sister Georgia stopped eating.

"Revern' Bliss," she said, "I don't think we want to raise us any crop of melons this close to the porch, do you? 'Cause after all, they'd just be under our feet and getting squashed all the time and everything."

"No'm, I don't guess we do and I'm sorry, mam."

"Oh, that's all right, Revern Bliss. You care for some salt?"

"No'm, I like it just like it is."

"You really like it?"

"Oh yes, mam! It's 'bout the sweetest, juiciest melon I ever et."

"Thank you, Revern' Bliss. I told you it was a ripe one and I'm glad you like it."

"You sure told the truth, mam."

So they sat eating the melon and he watched the fireflies but held the slippery seeds in his fist. Then suddenly from far away he could hear boys' voices floating to them. "Abernathy!" they called. "Hey, you, Abernathy!" and waited. There was no answer. Then it came again. "Where you at, ole big-headed, box-ankled Abernathy!" And she laughed, saying "That Abernathy'll be looking to fight them tomorrow, 'cause he's got a real big head and don't like to be teased about it."

"Who's Abernathy?" he said.

"Oh, he's a little ole mannish boy that lives down the road over yonder. You'll see him tomorrow," she said. "You'll hear him too, 'cause his head is big and he's got a big deep voice just like a grown man."

He could hear the boys still calling as she talked on—until a grown woman's voice came clear as a note through a horn, "Abernathy's in bed, just where y'all ought to be. So clear on 'way from here."

"And who is you?" a voice then called.

"Who you think *you* is?" the woman's voice said.

"Don't know and don't care!"

"Well, I'm his mother, and you heard what I just said."

"Well 'scuse us, I thought you was his cousin," the voice yelled mocking her, and he could hear some of them laughing and running off into the night, calling "Hey, Abernathy—how's your ma, Abernathy? Hey you, Abernathy's ma, how's ole big-headed Abernathy?"

"That part about being in bed goes for you too, Revern' Bliss," she said, "considering all you been through with that terrible woman and all. You sleepy?"

"Yes, mam," he said. He'd had enough of the melon and his stomach was tight. "Where must I put this melon rind, mam?" he said.

"I'll take care of it," she said. "Don't you think you better pee-pee before you go to bed? The privy's right out there at the back of the lot."

"But I don't have to now," he said, thinking, *She must think I'm a baby. . . . Body says the first thing a man has to learn is to hold his water.*

"Well, you will by the time you get your clothes off, so you go on and do it now."

"No," he said, "because I don't have it."

"Then you do it for me, Revern' Bliss," she said. "Because while you might know all about the Bible, *I* know all about little boys from having to take care of a couple on my job—and even they ain't the first. So now don't be ashame and go make pee-pee. After all, I only have but one sofa and us don't want to ruin it, do us now?"

"No'm," he said.

So he walked back through the dark and came to grass and growing things and stopped, looking around. But then she called through the dark,

"You can do it right there if you scaird to go clear to the back, Revern' Bliss; just don't do it on my lettus."

He didn't answer, hearing her low laughter as he walked back until he could smell the hot dryness of lime and sun-shrunken wood.

He paused before it but didn't go in, standing looking down the hill where he could see a streetlight glowing near a house with a picket fence and a flowering tree. The blossoms were white and thick and motionless in the breathless dark and he stood looking at it and making a dull thudding upon the hard earth, his mind aware of the hush around him. Then he looked back toward the house and there was Sister Georgia, a black shadow in the door with the light behind her.

"I told you so," she said, her voice low but carrying to him sharp and clear. "I can hear you way up here. Sounded like a full-grown man."

And he could hear her laughing mysteriously, like the big girls when they teased him. He didn't answer, there were no words to say when a lady teased you like that. He could feel the pulsing of his blood between his fingers and the orange blossoms came to him mixed with the sharp smell of the lime. He turned and looked past the yard with the fence and the tree, to a row of houses where a single light showed. Then the confusion in the tent seemed to break through the surface of his mind, bringing a surge of fear and loneliness. . . .

"Come on in, Revern' Bliss," she called. "You can sleep on the sofa without my having to worry now. We'll leave the door open so the breeze can cool you."

So he went back across the yard into the house and sat up on the sofa, looking around the room as she stood near the doorway, smiling. There was an old upright piano across the room and he went to it and struck a yellowed key, hearing the dull shimmer of its tone echoing sadly out of tune.

"Don't tell me you play on the piano too, Revern' Bliss," she said.

"No, mam, but Daddy Hickman does."

"Oh him," she said, "Revern' can do just about anything, and I suspect he has too."

"He sure can do a heap of things," he said, yawning.

"Oh, oh! Somebody's sleepy; I better make down the bed."

He watched her go into a dark room and light a lamp; then he took off his shoes and socks, then his soiled white dress trousers. Then she came back with a sheet and pillow in her arms and he stood up, watching her spread the sofa and fluffing up the pillow and putting it in place. She left then and he could hear her humming softly and the sound of a bedcover being shaken as he removed his tie and shirt. In his undersuit now, he sat looking up at the people in the frames on the wall and at a paper fan with the picture of a colored angel pinned below them to the wallpaper. *Wonder are they her mother and father,* he thought. *Daddy Hickman has some little pictures of his mother and father in his trunk. . . . He had a brother too.*

She came through the door with a glass of milk in her hand and gave it to him.

"You tired, Revern' Bliss?" she said.

"Not very much, mam," he said.

"You lonesome?"

"No mam."

She shook her head. "Well, you sure ought to be tired. After all that preaching you did this week. And all those women pulling on you. Anyway, I bet you're sleepy, so I'm going to say nighty-night now. That is, unless you want me to hear you say your prayers. . . ."

"No thank you, mam," he said, taking a sip of the milk. "A preacher like me has to pray to the Lord strictly by hisself."

He could see the question in her eyes as she looked down into his face. "I guess you right, Revern' Bliss," she said, "but I still just can't get it out of my head that you needs your mama. . . ."

"I don't have a mama," he said firmly. "I just have Daddy Hickman and my Jesus." He sat the milk on the table and pushed it away.

"Yes, I know," she said. "And no papa either, have you?"

"No mam. But Daddy Hickman teaches us that the Father of all the orphans is God."

"Poor li'l lamb," she said. And he could see her moving toward him with tears welling in her eyes and stuck out his hand to halt it there. She hesitated, staring down at his extended hand in puzzlement with that sudden suspension of movement just as the deaconesses had done when the woman had taken hold of him. For a long moment her eyes swam with tears; then she moved past and turned back the sheet, and waited silently for him to lie down. He could see the hurt still there in her eyes but was afraid to feel sorry. She smiled sadly as he moved past and got in and he lay looking straight up at the dim ceiling. She turned to the table and blew out the light. Now she moved to the doorway of her room, her face half in shadow.

"Nighty-night," she said. "Night-night, Revern' Bliss."

"Good night, mam," he said. He felt sad, lying down now and watching her standing there watching him. She seemed to be there a long time, and then suddenly someone was calling *Cudworth, Cudworth,* and he looked toward her and she was still standing there and he could hear someone shaking a tambourine and he began to preach and call for converts, looking lonely and yearning as the others responded to the Word, and still there watching as a woman wearing a black veil came down the aisle past the rows of members wearing a thick veil over her face, and he thought, *This is my mother.* Without surprise but a surge of peace, he took her hand with deep joy and pointed to the bench and watched her going over to take her place upon it. And he was filled with pride that with his voice he had brought her forward at last, had brought her forth from the darkness, and he turned now to exhort the others to witness the power and the glory and the living Word. . . . But when he looked again she had disappeared. The congregation was gone and a great body of water swirled up where it had been, shooting toward him to wash him from the pulpit. And he was screaming and trying to run, as now the waterspout became a spray of phosphorescent fish shooting at him, sweeping him off his feet now and pulling him across the floor with a loud thump. And now he could hear screaming. And through the dream into the dark he saw Sister Georgia still there bending over him, saying, "Lord, Revern' Bliss, I *thought* you was eating too much of that melon for so late at night. Hush now, you'll be all right. You really are having yourself a time. All scratched and bruised purple like a grape and now this here bad dream. And all you was trying to do was convert a few sinners. . . ."

"No! I wasn't dreaming," he said. "It wasn't a dream. I don't want it to be a dream. . . ."

"Wasn't a dream? Well, you might be a preacher but I know all about li'l-boy dreams and nightmares." She lit the lamp, looking down upon him with a puzzled frown.

"You was having a nightmare, all right, and judging from that slobber drying on your mouth you was sucking the old sow too. So don't try to tell me, Revern' Bliss, 'cause once in a while the li'l boys where I work have trouble just like you been having."

She came over and helped him back onto the sofa. "Let me see your back, Revern' Bliss," she said. "That's it, take off your undershirt. Now turn round here so's I can see."

He saw her bend and could feel the tips of her fingers on his skin. "Lord, look what she did to you! All those scratches. I better get the salve."

He saw her take the light into the kitchen; then she returned with a small jar in her hand.

"Will it burn?" he said.

"Burn? Not this salve, Revern' Bliss. It'll soothe and heal you, though. Hold still now."

"Yes, mam." He could feel the cool spreading over his back beneath the soft circular motion of her hand. Then she was doing the scratches on his arms and legs. His eyes were growing heavy again and she said, "There, that ought to do it. This is a wonderful salve, Revern' Bliss, and it don't burn or make grease spots either. You'll feel good by morning."

"Thank you, mam," he said.

"You welcome, Revern' Bliss; and I'll tell you what we'll do about that nightmare—you just come and get in bed with me awhile and it'll be sure not to come back."

She lifted him gently then and he could feel the heat of the lamp come close as she bent to blow out the flame; then they were moving carefully through the dark and he was being lowered to her bed.

"Go to sleep now," she said. "You'll be all right here."

He lay feeling the night and the strangeness of the room and the bed. He could not remember ever being in bed with a woman before and it seemed like another dream. And he thought, *So this is the way it is. This is what Body and the others have.* . . . Then far off in the dark a train whistle blew and he could feel a slight breeze sweeping gently across the bed, bringing the orange blossoms into the room to fade away in the heat as it died, and he could see the stars in the well again and there came again the rising feeling of falling wellward into the watery sky, falling freely, well and sky, uply downly skyly, starly brightly well-ly wishing her mother No finish go to sleep No this out there She welly she was she very nice to let me see them there she was very nice as sugar and spice nicely well-ly nice are made of are you a lady or a girl Sister Elberta—I sleep? Shake the tree run hide and seek No are you no are you not one like Georgia peaches no shake not the tree was very nice Will there be any seeds in the well? Asleep? Awake. No stars in my crown. And now he moved close I curl beside, she sighing sleeping soft. Not she close Awake how here? It's her—

"Thank you for being so nice to me, Sister Georgia," he said very quietly, and waited. But she didn't stir. Zoom! Slide down the hill. *She a-snoring? She sleep pretending?* I rise up, her face flowed my eyes rock heavy my head wandering in here out there stars *She there she gone she dreaming? She see she sigh she saw the morning stars she singing she well she ward her father who our awake* . . . There she is. I see like watching real quiet while a mouse came out of its hole and ran around the floor. A feeling of tingling delight came over him. He stared hard, trying to see her clearly in the dark, nodding, thinking *She there* Then before he was aware he had thrust himself forward and was kissing her softly on the cheek. Mother, he said, Mother . . . you are my mother. And something unfolded within him and he kissed her again. She was what he'd never allowed himself to yearn for. She was what Body's mother meant to him when he hurt himself or felt so sad. She's what she said I need. *Mother,* he thought, *Mother,* and suddenly he could feel his eyelids stinging and tried to hold it back, but it came on anyway. He stuffed the corner of the sheet into his mouth, rolling to the edge of the bed, crying silently.

Before him the window opened onto the porch and he lay looking through his tears into the shimmering night now lighted with a lately risen moon. Brightness lay beyond the shadows and on the tops of trees and the tears were coming now, steadily, as though they flowed straight from the moon. *Mother, mother* . . . He could feel the bed giving as she stirred in sleep and held his breath, thinking *Mother, I wish—Mother* until it was as though he had yearned to the end of the world, to the point where the night became day and the day night and on until he seemed to float . . . Then he was back in the hands of the angry woman, seeing the members freezing and the redheaded woman taking hold of him and her hands white against his own and his own white, not yellow as Body said and he thought *We are the same—Cudworth am I* she called and the others were afraid beneath Daddy Hickman's sliding horn *Cudworth* she called me out of darkness for a mother, not you not you not you just one of the sisters . . . Then Body was there and they were walking through the thick weeds beside a road and Looka yonder, man, Body said, pointing to something half-concealed in the dirt, saying *Peeeeew!* And he could see Body hold his nose and spit. Ain't on my mama's table, Body said. And he looked again wondering what it was and saying Mine neither. You better spit then, Body said. But when he tried his mouth was too dry to spit and he looked around and the women had him again and his hands had turned white as the belly of a summer flounder. . . .

Suddenly the sound of fighting cats streaked across the night with a swirl of flashing claws and he was sitting up in the bed, looking wildly around him. She was still there, sleeping quietly. The room was breathless and her odor, warm and secret, came to him, and just then she turned to rest on her back, her breathing becoming a quiet, catchy snore. Somehow all had changed. He shook his head, "No, I can't sleep with you," he said to her sleeping face. "I don't want you for my mother. I'm going back to the sofa."

Then it was as though a hand had reached down and held him, forcing him to look at her once more, and before he realized it he was looking at the hem of her gown resting high across her round, wide-spread thighs. *I've got to get out of here,* he thought. *I got to move.* But suddenly he was caught between the movement of his body and the new idea welling swiftly in his mind, feeling his foot dangling over the side of the bed while in the dreamlike, underwater dimness of the light, he seemed to be looking across a narrow passage into a strange room where another, bolder Bliss was about to perform some frightful deed. *No,* he thought, *no no!* seeing his own hand reaching out like a small white paw to where the hem of her nightgown lay rumpled upon the sheet, and lifting it slowly back, stealthily, cunningly, as though he had done so many times before, lifting it up and back. He watched from far back in a corner of his mind, disbelieving even as he saw the gauzelike cloth lifted like a mosquito net above a baby's crib—then he had crossed the passage and was there with the other Bliss, peering down at what he had uncovered, peering into the shadow of the mystery. Peering past the small white paw to where the smooth flesh curved in the dim light, into the thing itself, the dark impression in the dark. *But what,* he almost said. . . . He saw yet he didn't see what he saw. There was nothing at all, a little hill where Body'd said he'd find a lake, a bushy slope where he thought he'd find a cave. . . . It was as though he had opened a box and found another box inside in which he was sure he'd find another and in that, still another—and by then she'd wake up. Yet he couldn't leave. Fragments of stories about digging for buried treasure whirled through his mind and suddenly he was standing in a great hole reaching for an iron-bound chest which he had uncovered, but just as he took hold of it a flock of white geese thundered up and around him, becoming as he watched with arms upraised a troop of moldy Confederate cavalry galloping off into the sky with silent rebel yells bursting from their distorted faces. He wanted desperately to move away but the cloth seemed to hold him, and now she gave a slight movement and his eyes were drawn to her face, seeing faint lights where before there had been dark shadows. . . . He jumped, hearing himself say "Oh!" and feeling the film of cloth rolling like a grain of sand between his fingers.

"Revern' Bliss, is that you?" she said from far away.

"I didn't mean to do it, mam. . . ."

She sighed sleepily. "Do? What'd you do, honey?"

He held his breath, hearing *dodododododododododododo!*

And again, "Revern' Bliss?" . . . *dododo* . . .

She stirred and he saw her arm go over as she started to turn only to halt with a deep intake of breath which suddenly stopped and he realized that he had trapped himself. *It's happening and it will be like Daddy Hickman says Torment is, forever and forever and ever. . . .* Then, as though the other Bliss had spoken in an undertone, he thought, *You're It this time for sure but you must never be caught again. Not like this again—move. When they come toward you, move. Be somewhere else, move. Move!*

But he couldn't move. He was watching her hand reaching out searchingly, patting the spot where he had lain. And he thought, *She thinks I wet the bed and I didn't and now her fingers are telling her that it's dry and if I only had, like the Jaybirds spying on you and telling the ants and telling the Devil, and she's raising up and her eyes growing wide and I shall be punished for what I can't even see. Please Lady God Sister Mother.*

"Oh!" Sister Georgia said, sitting up with a creaking of the bedsprings, and he felt the sheet swing across his leg and up around her body so swiftly that it was as though she or I'd never been exposed. He could see his upraised thumb and finger making an "O" of the darkness and she was saying, "Oh, oh, oh," very fast and the night seemed to rush backwards like a worm sliding back into its hole. And he told himself, *It was only a dream I am in the other room lying on the sofa where I went to bed and that woman with the veil is coming toward me and I know who she is and I'm overjoyed to see her save her and now dodging waterspout of fish and falling and screaming and now this one will come in a second and lift me from the floor, save me from——*

"No!" she said. "OH NO! Revern' Bliss, Revern' Bliss! YOU WERE LOOKING AT MY NAKEDNESS! YOU WERE EXPOSING MY NAKEDNESS!"

He was mute, shrinking within himself, his head turning from side to side as he thought, *If I could fall off the bed it would go away. If I had wings I could——*

But her words were calling up dreadful shapes in his mind. A black horse with buzzards tearing at its dripping entrails went galloping across a burning field, making no sound. . . . A naked, roaring-drunk Noah stumbled up waving a jug of corn whiskey and cursing in vehement silence while two younger men fought with another trying to cover his head with a quilt of many-colored cloth and he could feel her words still sounding. All the darkness seemed to leave the room. Nearby the cats which had hurtled across the night like a swirling wheel of knives had cornered now, filling the air with an agony of howling.

"You were, weren't you, Revern' Bliss?" she said. "Tell me, what was you doing!" And the minor note of doubt in her voice warned him that there was still time to lie, to erase it all with words and he seemed to be running, trying to catch up but he wasn't fast enough and felt the chance slipping through his hand like a silver minnow. He seemed to hear his voice sounding unreal even before he spoke.

"I didn't mean to do it, mam, honestly, I didn't. . . ."

"But you *did!*" she said in a fierce whisper. "You ought to be ashamed of yourself, peeping at my nakedness and me asleep. Sneaking up on me like a thief in the night, trying to steal me in my sleep! You, who's *supposed* to be Revern' Bliss, the young preacher!"

"Please, mam, *please* mam. I really didn't mean to do it. Forgive me. Please, forgive me. . . ."

She shook her head sadly, sitting higher and clutching the sheet around her.

"Oh you really ought to be ashamed," she said. "That's the least you can do. Acting like that, like an old rounder or something that's had no training or anything. What I want to know is ain't there *any* of you men a God-fearing woman can trust! I thought you was a real genuine preacher of the gospel and I was proud to have you staying in my house. You never would've had to sleep in any hay around here. But now just look what you done. I guess I been offering my hospitality to an old jackleg. A midnight creeper. I guess you just another one of these old no-good jacklegs. You're not good and sanctified like Revern' Hickman at all and it'll probably break his heart to hear what you done."

He cried soundlessly now, wanting to go to her, his whole body, even his guilty fingers crying *Mother me, forgive me.* He felt cast into the blackest darkness, the world being transformed swiftly into iron.

"Please," he cried, touching her arm, but she pulled away, refusing to touch him as he reached out to her.

"No," she said, "oh no. You get out of my bed. Get on out!"

"Please, Sister Georgia."

"I said, get!"

"Yes, mam," he said. He dragged himself from the bed now and found his way back to the sofa and lay sobbing in the dark.

"Sister Georgia," he called to the other room. "Sister Georgia . . ."

"What is it, ole jackleg?"

"Sister Georgia, please don't call me that. Pleeease . . ."

"Then you oughtn't to act like one. What is it you want?"

"Sister Georgia," he said, "are you a lady or a girl?"

"Am I *what?*"

"Are you a lady or a girl?" he said.

She was silent; then: "After what you done you shouldn't have to ask."

"But I have to know," he said.

"I'm a woman," she said. "What difference does it make, ole jackleg preacher?"

"Because . . . maybe if you're a girl what I did isn't really so bad. . . ."

She was silent and he lay straining to hear. Finally, she said, "You go to sleep. It won't be long before day and I have to have my sleep."

She won't tell me, he thought, *she won't say.*

His tears were gone now and he lay face downward, thinking, *I don't care, the other one is the one for a mother. . . .*

CHAPTER 10

He, Bliss, sat at the kitchen table drinking the ice-cold lemonade and listening to the tinkle the chunk of ice made when he stirred it with his finger. The others were sitting quietly in the room with Daddy Hickman and he could see Sister Wilhite nodding in her chair over near the window. Sister Wilhite's tired, he thought. She's been up all night and Deacon has too. He looked at the cooking stove, dull black with shining nickel parts around the bottom made in the shape of scrolls. They're the same shape as the scrolls on the lid of my coffin, he thought. Why do they put scrolls on everything? Sister Wilhite's sewing machine has scrolls made into the iron part where her feet go to pedal and it has scrolls painted in gold in the long shining block that holds the shiny wheel and the needle. Scrolls on everything. People don't have scrolls though. But maybe you just can't see them. Sister Georgia. . . . Scroll, Scroll Jellyroll. . . . That's a good rhyme—but sinful. . . . Jellyroll.

The stovepipe rose straight up and then curved and went out

through a hole up near the ceiling. The wallpaper up there was black where the smoke had leaked through. The stove was cold. No fire was showing through the airholes in the door where the wood and coal went, and he thought, It's sleeping too. It's resting, taking a summer vacation. It works hard in the winter though, it goes all day long eating up wood and coal and making ashes. From early in the morning till late at night and sometimes they stoke it and it burns all night too. It's just coasting then though, but it's working. Summertime is easy except for Sunday when a lot of folks have to eat string beans, turnip greens, cabbage and salt pork, sweet potato pie, ham hocks and collards, egg-cornbread and dandelion greens is good for you. Make you big and strong. Summer is easy except for those good things so the stove can take a rest. It wakes up for oatmeal for breakfast and eggs and grits and coffee but then it goes out. Not a stick of wood in the corner or bucket of coal. No heat for lemonade but it's good. In the fall is the busy time. In the fall they'll be killing the hogs and taking the chitterlins and the members will be bringing a whole pig to Daddy Hickman all scalded and scrubbed clean, then he'll give it to Deacon Wilhite and Deacon'll give it to Sister Wilhite and that's when the stove will really have to work. The door where the fire goes'll be cherry red and the stovepipe too.

That big pot on the back there will be puffing like a steam engine. Meshach, Shadrach and Abednego and I like black-eyed peas and curly pigtails and collards, hogshead hopping John—Pa don't raise no cotton or corn and neither no potatoes, but Lord God, the tomatoes. I like candied yams, spare ribs and Sister Wilhite's apple brown Betty with that good hard sauce. Sister Lucy, Daddy Hickman said that time, don't let the you-know-who's learn how good you can cook, because they're liable to chain you to a kitchen stove for ninety-nine years and a day. Chained? she said. I already been chained for fifteen years. *I wouldn't want to be chained to any stove* but

Sister Lucy just laughed about it and looked at Deacon. He looked at Sister Wilhite sleeping in the chair. She's really getting it, that sleep, he thought. She's making up for lost time. . . .

Then he must have dreamed because Sister Georgia was there in the kitchen and she was leading him over to the red-hot stove and asking him about Meshach, Shadrach and old big-headed Abernathy and shaking him—

But it wasn't Sister Georgia, it was Sister Wilhite.

"Wake up, Revern' Bliss," she said, "Revern' is calling you," And he got up sleepily and yawned and she guided him into the bedroom. The others were still there, sitting around and talking quietly. Then he was at the bed looking once more at the bandaged face. Daddy Hickman's eye was closed, hidden beneath the bandages and he thought, *He's asleep* when Sister Wilhite spoke up.

"Here's Revern' Bliss, Brother A.Z." And there was Daddy Hickman's eye, looking into his own.

"Well, there you are, Bliss," Daddy Hickman said. "Did you have enough lemonade?"

"Yes, sir."

"That's fine. That's very good. So what have you been doing?"

"I had a nap and I've been wondering . . ."

"Wondering, Bliss? What about?"

He hesitated, looking at Deacon Wilhite who sat with his legs crossed smoking. He was sorry he had said it, but it had come out.

"About that lady," he said.

"No, Revern' Bliss," Sister Wilhite said from behind him. "Let's forget about that. Now let Revern' rest. . . ."

"It's all right," Daddy Hickman said. Then the eye bored into his face. "She frightened you, didn't she, boy?"

He bowed his head. "Yes, sir, she sure did."

Then he tried to stop the rest from coming out, but it was too late. "She said she was my mama. . . ."

Daddy Hickman lifted his hands quickly and lowered them back to the sheet. "Poor Bliss, poor baby boy," he said, "you really had yourself a time. . . ."

"Revern'," Sister Wilhite said, "don't you think you should rest?"

Daddy Hickman waved his hand toward Sister Wilhite.

"Is she, Daddy Hickman?" he said.

"Is she what, Bliss?"

"My mother?"

"That crazy woman? Oh no, Bliss," Daddy Hickman said. "You took her seriously, didn't you? Well, I guess I might as well tell you the story, Bliss. Sit here on the bed."

He sat, aware that the others were listening as he watched Daddy Hickman's eye. Daddy Hickman was making a cage of his big long fingers.

"No, Bliss," he said. "The first thing you have to understand is that this is a strange country. There's no logic to it or to its ways. In fact, it's been half-crazy from the beginning and it's got so many crazy crooks and turns and blind alleys in it, that half the time a man can't tell where he is or who he is. To tell the truth, Bliss, he can't tell reason from *un*reason and it's so mixed up and confused that if we tried to straighten it out right this minute, half the folks out there running around would have to be locked up. You following me, Bliss?"

"You mean everybody is *crazy?*"

"In a way of speaking, Bliss. Because the only logic and sanity is the logic and sanity of God, and down here it's been turned wrong-side out and upside down. You have to watch yourself, Bliss, in a situation like this. Otherwise you won't know what's sense and what's foolishness. Or what's to be laughed at and what's to be cried over. Or if you're yourself or what somebody else says you are. Now you take that woman, she yelled some wild words during our services and got everybody upset and now you don't know what to think about her and when you see me all wrapped up like the Mummy or

old King Tut or somebody like that, you think that what she said has
to have some truth in it. So that's where the confusion and the craziness comes in, Bliss. We have to feel pity for her, Bliss, that's what
we have to feel. No anger or fear—even though she upset the meeting and got a few lumps knocked on my head. And we can't afford
to believe in what she says, not that woman. Nor in what she does
either. She's a sad woman, Bliss, and she's dangerous too; but when
you step away and look at her calmly you have to admit that whatever she did or does or whoever she is, the poor woman's crazy as a
coot."

"She's crazy, all right," Sister Lucy said. "Now you said something
I can understand."

"Oh, you can understand, all right, Sister Lucy," Daddy Hickman
said, "but you don't want to let yourself understand. You want
something you can be angry about; something you can hold on to
with ease and no need to trouble yourself with the nature of the
true situation. You don't want to worry your humanity."

"Maybe so," Sister Lucy said. "But I see that frightened child and
I see you all wrapped in bandages and I can still see that woman
dressed in red interrupting in the House of God, claiming that
child— And I'm supposed to feel sorry for—"

"*Yes,*" Daddy Hickman said. "Yes, you are. Job's God didn't
promise him any easy time, remember."

"No, he didn't," Sister Lucy said. "But I never been rich or had all
the blessings Job had neither."

"We'll talk about that some other time," Daddy Hickman said.
"You have your own riches. You just have to recognize what they
are. So Bliss, not only is that woman sad, she's crazy as a coot. That
woman has wilder dreams than a hop fiend."

"What's 'hop,' Daddy Hickman?"

"It's dope, Bliss, drugs, and worse than gin and whiskey. . . ."

"Oh! Has she been taking some?"

"I don't know, Bliss; it's just a way of speaking. The point is that the woman has wild ideas and does wild things. But because she's from a rich family she can go around acting out any notion that comes into her mind."

"Now that's something I can understand," Sister Lucy said.

"They taught that they own the world," Sister Wilhite said.

"Just like they got it in a jug, Revern' Bliss," another sister said.

"Here," Sister Lucy said, and she held out a licorice cigar.

"Thank you, Sister Lucy."

"So listen," Daddy Hickman said. "Let me tell Revern' Bliss a bit about that woman. A few years back she was supposed to get married. She was going to have a big wedding and everything, but then the fellow who she was supposed to marry was killed when his buggy was struck by the Southern at the crossroads and the poor woman seemed to strip her gears. . . ."

"So *that's* what started it," Sister Wilhite said.

"That's the story anyway," Daddy Hickman said. "For a while the poor woman couldn't leave her room, just lay in the bed eating ambrosia and chocolate eclairs day and night."

A new tone had come into Daddy Hickman's voice now. He looked at the eye set in the cloth, searching for a joke. "Eating what?" he said, removing his cigar.

"That's right, Revern' Bliss. Ambrosia and chocolate eclairs."

"Day and night?"

"That's what they say."

"But didn't it make her sick?"

"Oh, she was already sick," Daddy Hickman said. "Anyway, when she finally could leave her room she came up with some strange notions. . . ."

"What kind of notions?"

"Well, she thought she was some kind of queen."

"Did she have a crown?"

"Come to think about it, she did, Revern' Bliss, and she had a great big Hamilton watch set right in the middle of it and she used to walk around the streets wearing a long white robe and stopping everybody and asking them if they knew what time it was. It wasn't a bad idea either, Bliss—except for the fact that her watch was always slow. Folks who didn't want to set their watches according to her time was in for some trouble. She'd start to screaming right there in the street and charging them with all sorts of crimes. You have no idea how relieved folks were when she misplaced that watch and crown and went off to Europe with her auntie on her father's side."

Daddy Hickman's voice stopped and Bliss could see the eye looking from deep within the cloth.

"Then what happened?" he said.

"Oh she stayed over there about a year, taking the baths and drinking that sulfur water and mineral water and consorting with the crowned heads of Europe. And I heard she was at a place called Wiesbaden where she enjoyed herself losing a lot of money. Then I went up north to Detroit and worked in the Ford plant for a while and I didn't hear any more about her. Then I came back and I heard she had come home again and how she had a new mind and a new notion. . . ."

"What kind of new mind and notion?"

"Well, now she not only insisted she was a queen but she had the notion that all the young children belonged to her. She had the notion she was the Mary Madonna. Bliss, pretty soon she was making off with other folks' children like a pack rat preparing for hard times. The story is that she grabbed a little *Chinee* baby and took him off to New Orleans and named him Uncle Yen Sen, or something like that. . . ."

"She really stole him?"

"Yes she did, Bliss. And she rented a room and opened up what *she* called a Chinese laundry in one of those old houses with the iron lace around the front. It was on a street where a bunch of first-class washerwomen lived too and she had that poor little baby lying up there on the counter in a big clothes basket wearing a diaper made out of the United States flag. . . ."

"Oh, oh!" someone behind him said.

"Now how patriotic can you get," Sister Wilhite said.

"Didn't anyone come looking for the baby, Daddy Hickman?"

"Oh sure they did, Bliss. But she had covered her tracks like an Indian. She was supposed to be up in Saratoga, that's in New York, you see, but instead she went up to Washington, D.C., with the baby dressed up in a Turkish turban and little gold shoes that turned up at the toe and they spent two days up there riding up and down the Washington Monument, and after that they doubled back. That's how that was. You see?"

"Yes, sir," he said. "They probably had them a good time."

"I don't know, Bliss. They just might have got awfully dizzy."

"So what happened then, Revern'?" one of the women said.

"Well, things went along for a while. She wasn't doing much business but things were quiet and nobody bothered them and they ate a lot of buttered carrots and shoofly pie, but mostly carrots . . . and—"

"Why they eat all those carrots?"

"Because she thought they would improve the baby's vision, Bliss."

"He means she was trying to straighten out his eyes, Revern' Bliss," Deacon Wilhite said and suppressed a laugh.

"I hear that carrots make you beautiful," Sister Lucy said.

"And did they ever find the baby?"

"That's right, after a while they did, Bliss. And it happened like this. They was down there waiting for the Mardi Gras to come. One day an old Yankee veteran from the Civil War walked in there to get some shirts washed and ironed and when he looked in that basket and saw Old Glory pinned around that Chinese baby he like to bust a gut. Excuse me, ladies. He saw that, Bliss, and wanted to start the war all over again. He called the police and the fire department and wired the President up in Washington and raised so much Cain that they ran him out of town for a carpetbagger—while she was treated like she'd done the most normal thing in the world. The poor Chinese lady had a world of trouble getting her little boy back again, because folks tend to take what rich women like that say as the truth—*and*, on top of that, the child had come to like her, didn't think he was a Chinese at all. . . ."

"What'd he think he was?"

"A Confederate named Wong E. Lee."

"So what happened to them then?"

"Well, Bliss, the news got around and her folks heard about it and came and took her home and they gave the Chinese lady some money for all her trouble and grief and they turned over the laundry to them and they stayed there and made a fortune and now the little boy is glad he's a Chinese."

"Wong E. Lee," Bliss said.

"They should've put that woman under lock and key right then and there," Sister Wilhite said. "If they had we would've been saved all this trouble."

"That's right, Bliss," Daddy Hickman said. "That's one of the points. Down here a woman like that can get away with anything because not only is her family rich, it's old and has standing position. They're quality—of some kind. But no sooner did she get out of that mess than she ups and grabs a little Mexican boy. This was down in Houston, wasn't it, Deacon?"

"Dallas," Deacon Wilhite said, his head back, his eyes gazing at the ceiling. "Dallas is where it happened."

"That's right, Bliss; Dallas, Texas. She kidnaps this little boy and names him Pancho Villa Van Buren Starr and rushes him up to the Kentucky Derby—which was being held at the time. That was Louisville. Sports and hustlers from all over were there making bets and drinking mint juleps, having a little sport—innocent and uninnocent. Well, up there after she had lost five thousand dollars, a piebald gelding and all the jewelry she had taken along, she tried to use the baby to place a bet with, like he was cash on the line."

"Now Revern'," Sister Lucy said, "she didn't do a thing like that!"

"Oh yes, she did. And it was logical from her point of view. To her way of thinking property like that is negotiable and she swore that little Mexican boy was a family heirloom that had been in the family for years. . . . So knowing who she was and how solid her background was and all they took Pancho for the bet and called the president of the Jockey Club about it but the horse she picked came in last."

"And did they get the baby?"

"They did, Bliss, but it was a long time afterwards. The boy took off and got lost. He had a hard time, Bliss, because she hadn't let him eat anything but chop suey and although he found a Chinese restaurant he couldn't eat because he only spoke Mexican and the restaurant folks couldn't understand him. So I guess you were lucky because she only *tried* to steal you. The sisters took care of that. So I want you to forget that woman, you hear?"

"Yes, sir."

"You forget all about her, Bliss; I'm talking to you seriously now. Forget her and the foolishness she was saying because she'd never seen you before and I hope she never sees you again. All right now, I better rest so I can help you preach next week. Meantime, I want you to do like I say and forget the woman and if you do I'll take you . . . Here, come close so I can whisper. . . ."

He bent close, smelling the medicine and then Daddy Hickman was whispering, "I'll take you to see one of those moving pictures you've been hearing about. Now that's a secret. You'll keep it, won't you?"

"Yes, sir. The secret."

He looked but suddenly the eye was gone—as though someone had turned down the wick on a lamp.

"Daddy Hickman—" he began, but now Sister Lucy had him by the arm.

"Shhh," she said, "he's sleeping now," and he was being led quietly away.

It's like trying to reconstruct your own birth as *cherchez la femme* and find the man. Sin, Hickman'd call it but all men are of larceny to the fourth power of the newborn heart then it's run not walk to avoid escape, ignore the recognition. Hairs bursting isolated and red out of the white temple and her strange voice screaming *Cudworth, Cudworth* and I followed I went I fled up and out of the darkness and she lived behind a wall so strong it had no need for altitude. No foot transgressed no alien bird's song aggrieved her privacy— Was this my home, my rightful place? Cudworth, she called—I heard dragonflies I saw the great house resting in the gentle shade of her cottonwood mimosa wisteria, the tulip trees. *No Mister Movie-Man,* she said, locking her legs before the rise of magnolias, smiling, no peach blossoms no not that. . . . She's my mother *she* said and I answered She is my mother she Get out the vote Senator, vote. Senator, promise them anything but wheel and deal. She said, Baby, baby, always insisting upon appellation the fruit

Eve conned Adam with I'll call you by your true name, Baby she
said—after the snake. Cudworth from the cow's belly a round ball
of hair regurgitated. Call me Hank, no Bone. Important not to get
lost—I followed Cudworth, Cudworth he's my— Yes sir by following the line of Body's mother and Mrs. Proctor discussing my
aborted emancipation from the dark down labyrinthine ways of
gossip being hung on lines in the sun, the hot air. Body's mother
was there before me, broad-backed and turning great curved hips
with intent face and mouth spiked with wooden clothespins we
used for soldiers in our games, her hair hidden beneath a purple
cloth. I yearned for her love of Body as my own. Mrs. Proctor, short
and fat rocking from side to side, gently as she slow-dragged from
left to right, her man's shoes shuffling over the earth leaving ridges
in the soil—her hips tossing languidly, a gentle, mysterious tide of
gingham beneath the line hanging the underskirts, slips, bloomers
as they talked up under her wet clothes. Red-white-blue democracy for you bleached and clean making transparent shadows upon
the red clay ground, the sun filtering pastel through the cloth and
the air clean to the smell with me crouching underneath, the first
well-hung line, my finger tracing upon the hard earth, wondering
how did I get out and get lost, did I come down from under these
thin petticoats out of these in order to ascend—clank-clank-clank
your mother.

  She's got to be a fool, from Body's mother. Coming into our
meeting like that. Either that or she was drunk or something, her
voice rising in invitation to a re-creation of my soul's agony. And
Mrs. Proctor accepting,

  Ain't it the truth? And there we was just wanting to be left alone
in peace to serve God for a few days and to praise Him—but can we
do it? Oh no. She so high and mighty she gon' take that chile without the hardship and pain, without even gitting struck good and

hard on the maidenhead—And not only take from us but from the Lord as well. . . . Looking around

Then, seeing me, Sssssh . . .

What is it, girl— Oh, Revern' Bliss, Body's mother said. She looked down at me, her hands on ample hips.

Mam? I, Bliss, said, my face feeling tight, wan.

Honey, will you go send Body to me, please?

I looked for judgment in her broad face. She held the clothespins fanned out between her fingers like a marksman holding shotgun shells during a trap shoot.

Yes, mam.

Thank you, Revern' Bliss.

And I arose and moved down the line of clothes and then under a line of stockings and pink and blue underthings and back three lines till I was behind drying sheets, hearing her softly saying. These children, I swear they all alike, even Revern' Bliss. They never stop trying to listen to grown folks talking, and they always rambling in trunks and drawers. Lord knows what they 'spect to find. Him and Revern' Bliss was playing with some toy autos one day and I looked out and Body has done found one of my old breast pumps somewhere and is making out it's a auto horn!

I went past bloomers billowing gently in the breeze *Clank-clank-clank, that's your ma's with a fleet of them big Mack trucks and nineteen elephants. A whole team of mules could walk through there.* I went toward the back door where the washtubs glinted dully on the low bench, trailing my finger and thumb as I went past and around to the front of the house, calling, Body! Hey Body! Your mother wants you, Body. Knowing all the while that he had gone to dig crawdads. He was my right hand but I had been told not to go there. Calling: Body? Hey! Body! Lying in word and deed while my mind hung back upon their voices like a feather upon a gentle breeze. Behind me, over the top of the house I could hear their voices rising clear with soft hoarseness, like alto horns in mellow duet across the morning air. I looked down the street. Except for a cat rubbing itself against a hedge down near the corner nothing was moving. I was alone and lonely, the porch was high and I crawled beneath and lay still in the cool shadows thinking about the crawdad hole over where the cotton press had burned down across from the railroad tracks, the tall weeds and muddy water. Body could swim, I wasn't allowed. Along the slippery bank the crawdads raised up their pale brown castles of mudballs. We fried their tails in cornmeal and bacon grease, ate them with half-fried Irish potatoes. In the gloom I lay, beside the discarded wheel of a baby buggy. Body's mother saved his baby shoes. They hung by a blue ribbon from the mirror of the washstand. Where were mine? Near my arm a line of frantic ants crawled down the piling, carrying specks of white sugar or crumbs. Piss ants, sugar ants, all in a row, coming and a-going like my breath, their feelers touch and go. Patty-cake. Then I could hear their sighful voices approaching full of heat and sounds of rest, and through the cracks between the steps I could see their broad bottoms coming down upon the giving boards and saw their washday dresses collapsing then stretching taut between their knees as they rested back, their elbows upon the floor of the porch as slowly they fanned themselves with blue bandannas.

So she keeps on asking me what I do to get her washing so white, Mrs. Proctor said, and I keep telling her I didn't do nothing but soak 'em and boil 'em and rub 'em and blue 'em and rinse 'em and starch 'em and iron 'em, but she never believed me. Said, Julia, *Nobody* does clothes like you do. The others don't get them so white and clean so you have got to have some secret. Oh, yes, Julia, you have a trick, I just know you have. So finally, girl, I gets tired and the next time she asked me I said, Well, Miz Simmons, you keep on asking me so I guess I have to tell you, but first you haveta promise me that you won't tell nobody. And she said, Oh I promise, you just tell me what you do. Ho ho! So I said, well, Miz Simmons, it's like this, after I done washed the clothes and everything I adds a few drops of coal oil in the last rinse water.

Girl, she slapped her hands and almost turned a flip. Talking about, I knew it! And she said, Is that all? And I said, Yessum, that's it and please don't forget that you promised you wouldn't tell any- body. Oh no, I won't tell, she said. But I just *knew* that you had a se- cret, because no one could do the clothes the way you do with just plain soap and water. So girl, I thought maybe now she'd let me alone and be satisfied, because you see, I knew that if I didn't tell her *something* pretty soon she was going to fire me.

So how'd it work out, Body's mother said.

Wait, Mrs. Proctor said. The next week I picked up her laundry and she was still talking about it. Said: Julia, you sure are a sly one. But you didn't fool me, because I knew you had some special secret for getting my clothes so clean. And I said, Yessum, I don't do it for everybody but I know how particular you all are and all like that. And she said, Yes that's right and it just proves that if you insist on getting the best you'll get it. And I said, Yessum, that sure is the truth.

Body's mother laughed. Girl, you oughtn't to told that woman that stuff.

Don't I know it? Mrs. Proctor said. It was wrong. Because as I was luggin' those clothes of her'n home something way back in the rear of my mind hunched me. It said: Girl, maybe you wasn't so smart in telling that woman that lie 'cause you know she's a fool— but I forgot about it. Well suh, I did her laundry just like I always done it and when I went to deliver it there she was, waiting for me—and I could tell from the way her face was all screwed up like she was taking a dose of Black Draught that I was in trouble. Said, Julia, I want you to be a little more careful when you do the wash this time. And I said, What's wrong, Miz Simmons, wasn't the clothes clean? She said, Oh yes, they was clean all right. But you didn't rinse them enough and you put in a bit too much of that coal oil. Last night when he got home, Mr. Simmons complained that he could smell it in his shirts.

Oh, oh, Body's mother said.

Mrs. Proctor said: Well, girl, I liked to bust. I said, I knew it, I knew it! You been snooping around for something to criticize about my work. Well now you have gone and done it and I'm here to tell you that you just been telling a big ole coal oil lie because I never put a thing in those clothes but plenty of soap and water and elbow grease. Just like that.

And what'd she say then?

Say? What could she say? She stomped out of there and slammed the door. Stayed a while and then, girl, she come back with her eyes all red and *fired* me! The ole sour fool!

Their voices ripped out and rose high above me as they laughed and I closed my eyes seeing the purple shadows dancing behind my lids as I held my mouth to keep my laughter in. I could hear it wheezing and burbling in my stomach. It was hard to hold and then when it stopped, their voices were low and confidential. . . .

. . . You'd think that with all her money and everything a woman like that wouldn't even know we was in the world, wouldn't you girl? Body's mother said.

Sho would, Mrs. Proctor said, but that ain't the way it seems to work. Seems like they can't be happy unless they know we're having a hard time. Some folks just wants it all, the prizes of this world and God's own anointed. It's outrageous when you think about it. Imagine, coming into the meeting and trying to snatch Revern'

Bliss out of the Lord's own design. She's going to interrupt the *Resurrection of the spirit from the flesh!* Next thing you know she be out there in her petticoat telling the Mississippi River to stand still. I tell you that woman is what they call *arragant,* girl. She so proud she's like a person who done drunk so much he's got the blind staggers. . . .

You telling me! But she's always cutting up in some fashion so I guess that sooner or later she had to get around to us. But to interfere with the Lord's . . .

Girl, Mrs. Proctor said, I saw her one morning just last week. She was riding one of those fine horses they have out there and she's acting like she was a Kentucky woman, or maybe a Virginian. One of those F.F.V.'s as they call them. Up on that hoss's back wearing black clothes with a long skirt and one of those fancy sidesaddles but riding a-straddle that hoss like a man in full, and with a derby hat with a white feather in it on her head. Early in the morning too, Lord. I was on my way to deliver some clothes and here she come galloping past me so fast I swear it liked to sucked all the air from round me. Had me suspended there like a yolk in the middle of an egg. It went SWOSH! just like a freight train passing a tramp and that hoss was steaming and lathering like he been racing five miles at top speed. And in this weather too. You shoulda seen it, girl. I whirled around to look and there she went with that red hair streaming back from under that derby. Done almost knocked me down now but when she went past with that wild look on her face it's like she ain't seen me.

It's a sin and a shame, Body's mother said. You'd think that she'd at least respect how much labor and pain goes into keeping her garments clean. Washerwomen have rheumatism like a horse has galls.

Yes, and this is one who knows it, Mrs. Proctor said. But girl, that woman's a fool, that's the most Christian thing you can say about her. It ain't as if she was the mean kind who'd run a person down just for fun or to see you jump and get scaird, *she just naturally don't see nobody.*

That might be true, Body's mother said, but she saw Revern' Bliss, all right. Now just why would she decide to come out there and break up our meeting?

Crazy, girl! That's all there is to it, the woman's crazy and while we sitting here talking between ourselfs we might as well go ahead and admit it. You and me don't have to deny the truth when we talking between ourselfs. Rich and white though she be, the po' thing's nuts.

No, no, no, she's my mother, my mind said and I lay rigid, listening.

I don't know, Body's mother said, Maybe she is and maybe she ain't. Maybe she just knew she could get away with it and went on and did it.

You mean she started to do it but she didn't count on us women. . . . Neither on the outrage of the Lord.

That's right, she didn't take the child but she busted up the meeting. She still got no regard for other folks but this time *she went too far.* She's strong-willed even for a high-tone white woman, girl. Let me tell you something! One day I was out there to see Irene and just as I got around in the back I heard all this shooting and yelling and what do I see? Over there down where the grass runs down to the lake she's got a half-dozen or so little black boys and has them pitching up those round things rich white folks shoot at all the time when they ain't shooting partridges or doves, and girl, I tell you, it was something to *see.* Girl, she's got them standing in a big half-circle and she's yelling at first one and then the other to sail those things up in the air and *bang!* she's shooting them down just—

WHO? NOT THOSE CHILDREN?

No, *noo,* girl, those clay birds.

Thank goodness, that's what I thought, but with her you can't be too sure.

I know, Body's mother said. But girl, you never saw such a sight. She's yelling and those little boys are raring back and flinging those round black things into the air with all their might, and her dancing from side to side with that shotgun and busting them to dust. And as fast as she empties one gun here comes another little boy running up with a fresh one all loaded, and *bang! bang! bang!* she's busting 'em again. I stood there with my mouth open trying to take it all in and looking to see if Body was amongst those boys—thank God he wasn't, because the way she looked, with her red hair all wild and wearing pants and some kind of coat with leather patches on the shoulder she's liable to—

Girl, Mrs. Proctor said, that was a shooting jacket.

A *shooting* jacket?

Mrs. Proctor laughed a high falsetto ripple. Why sho, girl. You know these rich folks have a different set of clothes for everything they do. They have tea gowns for drinking tea, cocktail dresses for drinking their gin and whiskey, *ball* gowns for doing what they call dancing. Yes! And riding habits, then they got their riding habits on—that's what she was wearing when she almost run me down. Then they even have dressing gowns for wearing when they're putting on their other clothes.

Oh yes? Body's mother said. Well, I guess they have to have *something* to do to take up all the time they have on their hands. But tell me something—

What's that?

What was the red thing she was wearing when she tried to take our little preacher?

Well, Mrs. Proctor said, without making a joke about something religious I'd say maybe it was a maternity dress. . . .

If it was, Body's mother said, she was dressed for the wrong occasion. She surely was. Anyway, girl, she was really shooting that day. Jesse James couldn't have done no better. She ain't hardly missed a one. And if one of those children didn't pitch in time to suit her she'd cuss him for a little gingersnap bastard and the rest of them would just laugh. Oh, but it made me mad, hearing her abuse those children like that. Not that it seemed to bother those little boys though. In fact, when she cussed one of 'em he just laughed and sassed her right back. Said, Miss Lor, don't come blaming me 'cause you cain't shoot a shotgun. You missed that bird a country mile. . . .

And what happened then? Mrs. Proctor said.

Something crazy just like always with her. She started to laughing like a panther and gave out one of those rebel yells. Said, Enloe, you *are* a sassy little blue-gummed bastard, but if I miss the next twenty birds I'll have Alberta freeze you a gallon of ice cream!

Now you see what I mean: That woman is dangerous! You take that boy Enloe, she oughtn't to treat him that way, because he's liable to pull that with some *other* white woman and git hisself kilt.

You're right, and somebody had better speak to his mama about him. And that's the truth. Only when children reach the size of those boys they usually know when they dealing with a fool. But it's her I'm worried about. Anybody who plays around with the Lord's work that way is heading for trouble. In fact, that po' woman is *already* in trouble and I been thinking a heap about what she did. But did it occur to you that she might really *be* Revern' Bliss's mother?

Who, a child like that, girl? No!

She *said* he was hers, didn't she?

She surely did, wasn't I listening like everybody else? But how is a woman like that going to be *his* mamma? It would've made more sense if she'd a claimed Jack Johnson and all those white wives of his and his uncles and cousins too. How she going to be that child's mamma even in a dream *I* simply can't see.

How! Are you asking me? Man is born of woman, and skinny as she is she still appears to have all the equipment. Besides, does anybody know who his mamma is?

No, they don't; less'n it's Revern' and he ain't said. But remember now, Revern' *brought* that child here with him so he can't be from around here anywhere. . . .

And how do you know that? Half the devilment in this country caint be located on account of it's somewhere in between black and white and covered up with bedclothes in the dark.

That's the truth—but, girl, Revern' ain't no fool! He wouldn't bring that baby back here if that was the case. Not even if he'd found him in a grocery basket with a note saying the child was a present from Pharaoh's favorite daughter. Besides, that woman would have to either be drunk or out of her mind to claim him anyway. And you know that while a white man might recognize his black bastards once in a while, if they turn out *white* enough, and if he's stuck tight enough to the mother, he might even send them up north to go to school—but who in this lowdown South ever heard of a white *woman* claiming anything a black man had something to do with?

Yes, that's true, Mrs. Proctor said, 'cept he don't show no sign in his skin or hair or features, only in his talking. But this here ain't no ordinary chile and everything has its first time to happen. Besides, there's quite a few of them who have turned their heads and made their sweet-talking motions as if to say, "Come on, mister nigger, here's my peaches—you can shake my tree if you man enough or crazy enough to take the consequences." And as you well know, some of ours is both man enough and crazy enough and prideless enough to take hold to the branch and swing the dickens out of it— even knowing that if they git caught she gon' scream and swear he stole her.

Yes, I know all that. And as Mamma told me long ago, all those who cries denied in darkness ain't black, and a woman's lot is a woman's lot from the commencing of her flow on. It sure does make you wonder. Still, a woman like that is apt to do what she did just for the notoriety and the scandal for the rest of her own folks. But what can you expect from somebody who got started out wrong like she done?

What you mean? Mrs. Proctor said. Who?

Their voices fell and I strained to hear, finally rolling over softly and over again, until I was directly beneath them, hearing:

. . . And Irene told me her ownself that whenever Miss Lorelli comes around, which ain't too regular, she screams like a cat in heat. Says she has such pain they almost have to tie her to the bed-posts and keep the ice packs on her belly all the time. Irene said it's worse than somebody birthing triplets.

Talking about the curse, she's got a real curse, Mrs. Proctor said. That woman is damned!

Ain't it the truth; Irene said it's really something to witness. Said that the first time it come down on her the poor child was tomboy-ing around up on top of the grape arbor. . . .

Well, I hope she was prepared, Mrs. Proctor said.

Prepared my foot! Is a sow prepared? Is a blue-tick bitch? Irene said that it was at a time when her mamma was entertaining some ladies on the lawn too, but instead of being there learning how to entertain like any other young girl would've been, this Miss Lorelli is so uncontrollable she's up there on that grape arbor climbing around! Well suh, Irene said it was like a dam bursting or some-thing. The po' thing come tumbling out of that tree like a scalded cat and come running across the lawn, straight to where Irene was serving those ladies. She almost knocked over the teacart and with it all over her hands and all. Irene said when she realized what was happening she got so mad at the child's mamma that she dropped a whole tray of fine china. Said she'd wanted to prepare the chile for what all the signs—her birthday, the calendar, and the sign of the moon—all of them. Said she was fixing to happen soon, but no, the mamma was so jealous and so vain about her age that she wouldn't let Irene tell the child a thing. She was going to do it herself when *she* got ready.

As though nature was going to wait on *her,* Mrs. Proctor said.

Well, girl, it didn't. Irene said it come right on schedule, right up on that grape arbor.

Girl, that's enough to make anybody act peculiar.

Are you telling me? So there it was, Irene has to stop serving and teach the child right then and there and she said she didn't bite her tongue in telling her either. Told her in plain language right there in front of all those fine ladies.

Oh no, girl! You must be yeasting this mess!

She sho did, told her all about her womanhood and about boys while she snatched off her apron and wrapped it around the child and carried her upstairs and went to work on her. Poor thing, she thought she was bleeding to death and giving birth, all at the same time. She had it all mixed up, poor thing. Irene said she asked her where her baby was and everything and Irene had some time calming her. Can you imagine that, having to fall out of a tree in order to pick up your woman's burden?

That woman shoulda been whupped for doing that to that child, Mrs. Proctor said. One woman acts a fool out of her vanity and pride and ignorance. So now everybody has to suffer for it. That woman was just plain ignorant! Yes, that's what it is. Whenever I think about it I remember what the monkey said when the man cut off his tail with the lawn mower. Poor monkey just looked at his tail laying there in the grass, and tears came to his eyes, and he shook his head and said: My people, my people! . . .

CHAPTER 11

Bliss, Daddy Hickman said, you keep asking me to take you even though I keep telling you that folks don't like to see preachers hanging around a place they think of as one of the Devil's hangouts. All right, so now I'm going to take you so you can see for yourself, and you'll see that it's just like the world—full of sinners and with a few believers, a few good folks and a heap of mixed-up and bad ones. Yes, and beyond the fun of sitting there looking at the marvelous happenings in the dark, there's all the same old snares and delusions we have to sidestep every day right out here in the bright sunlight. Because you see, Bliss, it's not so much a matter of where you *are* as what you *see*. . . .

Yes, sir, I said.

No, don't agree too quick, Bliss; wait until you understand. But like old Luke says, "The light of the body is the eye," so you want to be careful that the light that your eye lets into you isn't the light of darkness. I mean you always have to be sure that you *see* what you're looking at.

I nodded my head, watching his eyes. I could see him studying the Word as he talked.

That's right, he said, many times you will have to preach goodness out of badness, little boy. Yes, and hope out of hopelessness. God made the world and gave it a chance, and when it's bad we have to remember that it's still his plan for it to be redeemed through the striving of a few good women and men. So come on, we're going to walk down there and take us a good look. We're going to do it in style too, with some popcorn and peanuts and some Cracker Jacks and candy bars. You might as well get some idea of what you will have to fight against, because I don't believe you can really lead folks if you never have to face up to any of the temptations they face. Christ had to put on the flesh, Bliss; you understand? And I was a sinner man too.

Yes, sir.

But wait here a second, Bliss—

He looked deep into me and I felt a tremor. Sir? I said.

His eyes became sad as he hesitated, then:

Now don't think this is going to become a habit, Bliss. I know you're going to like being in there looking in the dark, even though you have to climb up those filthy pissy stairs to get there. Oh yes, you're going to enjoy looking at the pictures just about like I used to enjoy being up there on the bandstand playing music for folks to enjoy themselves to back there in my olden days. Yes, you're going to like looking at the pictures, most likely you're going to be bug-eyed with the excitement; but I'm telling you right now that it's one of those pleasures we preachers have to leave to other folks. And I'll tell you why, little preacher: Too much looking at those pictures is going to have a lot of folks raising a crop of confusion. The show hasn't been here but a short while but I can see it coming already. Because folks are getting themselves mixed up with those shadows spread out against the wall, with people that are no more than some smoke drifting up from hell or pouring out of a bottle. So they lose touch with who they're supposed to be, Bliss. They forget to be what the Book tells them they were meant to be—and that's in God's *own* image. The preacher's job, his main job, Bliss, is to help folks find themselves and to keep reminding them to remember who they are. So you see, those pictures can go against our purpose. If they look at those shows too often they'll get all mixed up with so many of those shadows that they'll lose their way. They won't know who they *are* is what I mean. So you see, if we start going to the picture-show all the time, folks will think we're going to the devil and backsliding from what we preach. We have to set them an example, Bliss; so we're going in there for the first and last time—

Now don't look at me like that; I know it seems like every time a preacher turns around he has to give up something else. But, Bliss, there's a benefit in it too; because pretty soon he develops control over himself. *Self-control*'s the word. That's right, you develop discipline, and you live so you can feel the grain of things and you learn to taste the sweet that's in the bitter and you live more deeply and earnestly. A man doesn't live just one life, Bliss, he lives more lives than a cat—only he doesn't like to face it because the bitter is there nine times nine, right along with the sweet he wants all the time. So he forgets.

You too, Daddy Hickman? I said. Do you have more than one life?

He smiled down at me.

Me too, Bliss, he said. Me too.

But how? How can they have nine lives and not know it?

They forget and wander on, Bliss. But let's us leave this now and go face up to those shadows. Maybe the Master meant for them to show us some of the many sides of the old good-bad. I know, Bliss, you don't understand that, but you will, boy, you will. . . .

Ah, but by then Body had brought the news:

We were sitting on the porch-edge eating peanuts—goober peas, as Deacon Wilhite called them. Discarded hulls littered the ground below the contented dangling of our feet. We were barefoot, I was allowed to be that day, and in overalls. A flock of sparrows rested on the strands of electric wire across the unpaved road, darting down from time to time and sending up little clouds of dust. Body was humming as he chewed. Except in church we were always together, he was my right hand. Body said,

Bliss, you see that thing they all talking about?

Who? I said.

All the kids. You see it yet?

Seen what, Body. Why do you always start preaching before you state your text?

You the preacher, ain't you? Look like to me a preacher'd *know* what a man is talking about.

I looked at him hard and he grinned, trying to keep his face straight.

You ought to know where all the words come from, even before anybody starts to talk. Preachers is suppose to see visions and things, ain't they?

Now don't start playing around with God's work, I warned him. Like Daddy Hickman says, Everybody has to die and pay their bills— Have I seen what?

That thing Sammy Leaderman's got to play with. It makes pictures.

No, I haven't. You mean a Kodak? I've seen one of those. Daddy Hickman has him a big one. Made like a box with little pearly glass windows in it and one round one, like an eye.

He shook his head. I put down the peanuts and fitted my fingers together. I said,

> Here's the roof,
> Here's the steeple,
> Open it up and see
> the people.

Body sneered. That steeple's got dirt under the fingernails. Why don't you wash your hands? You think I'm a baby? Lots of folks have those Kodaks, this here is something different.

Well, what is it then?

I don't rightly know, he said. I just heard some guys talking about it down at the liberty stable. But they was white and I didn't want to ask them any questions. I rather be ignorant than ask them anything.

So why didn't you ask Sammy, he ain't white.

Naw, he a Jew; but he looks white, and sometimes he acts white too. 'Specially when he's with some of those white guys.

He always talks to me, I said, calls me *rabbi*.

The doubt came into Body's eyes like a thin cloud. He frowned. He was my right hand and I could feel his doubt.

You look white too, Rev. Why you let him call you "rabbit"?

I looked away, toward the dusting birds.

Body, can't you hear? I said he calls me *rabbi*.

Oh, it sounds like my little brother trying to spell rabbit. Re-abbi-tee, *rabbit,* he say. He a fool, man.

He sure is, he's your brother, ain't he?

Don't start that now, you a preacher, remember? How come you let Sammy play the dozens with you, you want to be white?

No! And Sammy ain't white and that's not playing the dozens, it means preacher in Jewish talk. Quit acting a fool. What kind of toy is this you heard them talking about?

His lids came down low and his eyes hid when I tried to look for the truth in them.

All I know is that it makes pictures, Body said.

It makes pictures and not a Kodak?

That's right, Rev.

I chewed a while and thought of all I had heard about but hadn't seen: airplanes and angels and Stutz Bearcats and Stanley Steamers. Then I thought I had it:

It makes pictures but not a Kodak? So maybe he's got hold to one of those big ones like they use to take your picture at the circus. You know, the kind they take you out of wet and you have to wait around until you dry.

Body shook his head, No, Rev, this here is something different. This is something they say you have to be in the dark to see. These folks come out already dry.

You mean a nickelodeon? I heard them talking about one of those when we were out there preaching in Denver.

I don't think so, Rev, but maybe that's what they meant. But, man, how's Sammy going to get something like that just to play with. A thing like that must cost about a zillion dollars.

I don't know, I said. But remember, his papa has that grocery store. Besides, Sammy's so smart he might've made him one, man.

That's right, he a Jew, ain't he? He talk much of that Jew talk to you, Bliss?

No, how could he when I can't talk back? I wish I could, though, 'cause they're real nice to you, man.

How you know if you cain't talk it?

Because once when Daddy Hickman took me with him to preach out there in Tulsa and we got broke he ran into one of his Pullman porter friends from Kansas City and told him about it, and this porter took us to one of those big stores run by some Jews—a real fancy one, man—and the minute we stepped through the door those Jews left everything and came gathering round Daddy Hickman's friend to hear him talk some Jewish. . . .

He was colored and could talk their talk?

That's right, man. . . .

Body doubted me. How'd he learn to do that, he go to Jew school?

He was raised with them, Daddy Hickman said. And he used to work for some up there in Kansas City. Daddy Hickman said they used to let him run the store on Saturday. He was the boss then, man; with all the other folks working under him. Imagine that, Body, being the *boss.*

Yeah, but what happened on Monday?

He went back to being just the porter.

So why'd he do it? That don't make much sense.

I know but Daddy Hickman said he went to running on the road because he couldn't stand pushing that broom on Monday after handling all that cash on Saturday.

I don't blame him, 'cause that musta been like a man being made monitor of the class in the morning, he can bet a fat man against a biscuit that one of those big guys will knock a hicky on his head after school is out— So what happened?

Well, Daddy Hickman's friend laughed and talked with those Jews and they liked him so well that when he told him that we needed some money to get back home with, they took up a collection for us. We walked out of there with fifty dollars, man. And they even gave me a couple of new bow ties to preach in.

Honest, Bliss?

Honest, man. Those Jews was crazy about that porter. You'd

have thought he was the Prodigal Son. Here, eat some of these goobers.

Wonder what he said to talk them out of all that money, Body said. He know something bad on them?

There you go thinking evil, I said. They were happy to be talking with somebody different, I guess.

Body shook his head. That porter sure was smart, talking those Jews out of that money. I like to learn how to do that, I *never* be out of candy change.

Those Jews were helping out with the Lord's work, fool. I wish you would remember some more about that box. It's probably just a magic lantern—except in those the pictures don't move.

I hulled seven peanuts and chewed them, trying to imagine what Body had heard while his voice flowed on about the Jews. Somehow I seemed to remember Daddy Hickman describing something similar but it kept sliding away from me, like when you bob for apples floating in a tub.

Say, Rev, Body said, can't you hear? I said do you remember in the Bible where it tells about Samson and it says he had him a boy to lead him up to the wall so he could shake the building down?

That's right, I said.

Well answer me this, you think that little boy got killed?

Killed, I said; who killed him?

What I mean is, do you think old Samson forgot to tell that boy what he was fixing to do?

I cut my eyes over at Body. I didn't like the idea. Once Daddy Hickman had said: *Bliss, you must be a hero just like that little lad who led blind Samson to the wall, because a great many grown folks are blind and have to be led toward the light. . . .* The question worried me and I pushed it away.

Look, Body, I said, I truly don't feel like working today. Because, you see, while you're out playing cowboy and acting the fool and going on cotton picks and chunking rocks at the other guys and things like that, *I* have to always be preaching and praying and studying my Bible. . . .

What's all that got to do with what I asked you? You want somebody to cry for you?

No, but right now it looks to you like we just eating these here good goobers and talking together and watching those sparrows out there beating up dust in the road—*I'm* really resting from my pastoral duties, understand? So now I just want to think some more about this box that Sammy Leaderman's supposed to have. How did those white guys say it looked?

Man, Body said, you just like a bulldog with a bone when you start in to thinking about something. I done told you, they say Sammy got him a machine that has people in it. . . .

People in it? Watch out there, Body. . . .

Sho, Rev—folks. They say he points it at the wall and stands back in the dark cranking on a handle and they come out and move around. Just like a gang of ghosts, man.

Seeing me shake my head, his face lit up, his eyes shining.

Body, you expect me to believe that?

Now listen here, Bliss; I had done left that box because I wanted to talk about Samson and you didn't want to. So don't come trying to call me no lie. . . .

Forget about Samson, man. Where does he have this thing?

In his daddy's basement under the grocery store. You got a nickel?

I looked far down the street, past the chinaberry trees. Some little kids were pushing a big one on a racer made out of a board and some baby buggy wheels. He was guiding it with a rope like a team of horses, with them drawn all up in a knot, pushing him. I said:

Man, we ought to go somewhere and roast these goober peas. That would make them even better. Maybe Sister Judson would do it for us. She makes some fine fried pies too, and she just might be baking today. I have to remember to pray for her tonight, she's a nice lady. What's a nickel got to do with it?

'Cause Sammy charges you two cents to see them come out and move.

I looked at him. Body had a round face with laughing eyes and was smooth black, a head taller than me and very strong. He saw me doubting and grinned.

They *move,* man. I swear on my grandmother that they move. And that ain't all: they walk and talk—only you can't hear what they say—and they dance and fist-fight and shoot and stab one another; and sometimes they even kiss, but not too much. And they drink liquor, man, and go staggering all around.

They sound like folks, all right, I said.

Sho, and they ride hosses and fight some Indians and all stuff like that. It's real nice, Bliss. They say it's really keen.

I willed to believe him. I said: And they all come out of this box? That's right, Rev.

How big are the people he has in there, they midgets?

Well, it's a box about this size. . . .

Now I *know* you're lying. . . . I said, Body?

What?

You know lying is a sin, don't you? You surely ought to by now, because I've told you often enough.

He looked at me then cut his eyes away, scowling. Listen, Bliss, a little while ago you wouldn't tell me whether that boy who led Samson got killed or not, so now don't come preaching me no sermon. 'Cause you know I can kick your butt. I don't have to take no stuff off you. This here ain't no Sunday, no how. Can't nobody make me go to church on no Friday, 'cause on a Friday I'm liable to boot a preacher's behind until his nose bleeds.

I rebuked him with my face but now he was out to tease me.

That's the truth, Rev, and you know the truth is what the Lord loves. I'll give a doggone preacher *hell* on a Friday. Let him catch me on Sunday if he wants to, that's all right providing he ain't too long-winded. And even on Wednesday ain't so bad, but please, *please,* don't let him fool with me on no Friday.

I flipped a goober at his boasting head. He didn't dodge and tried to stare me down. Then we dueled with our faces, our eyes, but I won when his lips quivered and he laughed.

Rev, he said, shaking his head, I swear you're my ace buddy, preacher or no—but why do preachers always have to be so serious? Look at that face! Let's see how you look when you see one of those outrageous sinners. One of those midnight-rambling, whiskey-drinking gamblers . . .

I rebuked him with my eyes, but he kept on laughing. Come on, Rev, let's see you. . . .

I've told you now, Body. . . .

Man, you too serious. But I'm not lying about that box though, honest. It's suppose to be about this size, but when they come out on the wall they git as big as grown folks—hecks, *bigger.* It's magic, man.

It must be, I said. What kind of folks has he got in that box? You might as well tell a really big lie.

White folks, man. What you think— Well, he *has* got a few Indians in there. That is if any of them are left after they're supposed to have been killed.

No colored?

Naw, just white. You know they gon' keep all the new things for theyselves. They put us in there about the time it's fixing to wear out.

We giggled, holding one hand across our mouths and slapping our thighs with the other as grown men did when a joke was outrageously simpleminded and yet somehow true.

Then that's got to be magic, I said. Because that's the only way they can get rid of the colored. But really, Body, don't you ever tell the truth?

Sure I do, all the time. I know you think I'm lying, Rev, but I'm telling you the Lord's truth. Sammy got them folks in that machine like lightning bugs in a jug.

And about how many you think he's got in there?

He held his head to one side and squinted.

About two hundred, man; maybe more.

And you think I'm going to believe that too?

It's true, man. He got them jugged in there and for four cents me and you can go see him let 'em come out and move. You can see for yourself. You got four cents?

Sure, but I'm saving 'em. You have to tell a better lie than that to get my money; a preacher's money comes hard.

Shucks, that's what you say. All y'all do is hoop and holler a while, then you pass the plate. But that's all right, you can keep your old money if you want to be so stingy, because I seen it a coupla times already.

You saw it? So why're you just now telling me?

I felt betrayed; Body was of my right hand. I saw him skeet through the liar's gap in his front teeth and roll his eyes.

Shoots, you don't believe nothing I say nohow. I get tired of you 'sputing my word. But just the same I'm telling the truth; they come out and move and they move fast. Not like ordinary folks. And last time I was down there Sammy made them folks come out big, man. They was twice as big as grown folks, and they had a whole train with them. . . .

A whole train?

Sho, a real train running over a trestle just like the Southern does. And some cowboys was chasing it on they hosses.

Body, I'm going to pray for you, hear? Fact is, I'm going to have Daddy Hickman have the whole church pray for you.

Don't you think you're so good, Bliss. You better ask him to pray for yourself while you doing it, 'cause you believe nothing anybody says. Shucks, I'm going home.

Now don't get mad—hey, wait a minute, Body. Come back here, where you going? Come on back. *Please,* Body. Cain't you hear me say "please"? But now the dust was spurting behind his running feet. I was sad, he was of my right hand.

So now I wanted to say, No, Daddy Hickman; if that's the way it has to be, let's not go. Because it was one more thing I'd have to deny myself because of being a preacher, and I didn't want the added yearning. Better to listen to the others telling the stories, as I had for some time now, since Body had brought the news and the movies had come to town. Better to listen while sitting on the curbstones in the evening, or watching them acting out the parts during recess and lunchtime on the school grounds. Any noontime I could watch them reliving the stories and the magic gestures and see the flickery scenes unreeling inside my eye just as Daddy Hickman could make people relive the action of the Word. And seeing them, I could feel myself drawn into the world they shared so intensely that I felt that I had actually taken part not only in the seeing, but in the very actions unfolding in the depths of the wall I'd never seen, in a darkness I'd never known; experiencing with the excruciating intensity a camel would feel if drawn through the eye of a needle a whole world uncoiling through an eye of glass.

So Daddy Hickman was too late, already the landscape of my mind had been trampled by the great droves of galloping horses and charging redskins and the yelling charges of cowboys and cavalry-men, and I had reeled before exploding faces that imprinted themselves upon one's eyeball with the impact of a watersoaked snowball bursting against the tender membrane to leave a felt-image of blue-white pain throbbing with every pulse of blood propelled toward vision. And I had sat dizzy with the vastness of the action and the scale of the characters and the dimensions of the emotions and responses; had seen laughs so large and villainous with such rotting, tombstone teeth in mouths so broad and cavernous that they seemed to yawn wellhole-wide and threaten to gulp the whole audience into their traps of hilarious maliciousness. And meanness transcendent, yawning in one overwhelming face; and heroic goodness expressed in actions as cleanly violent as a cyclone seen from a distance, rising ever above the devilish tricks of the badguys, and the women's eyes looking ever wider with horror or welling ever limpid with love, shocked with surprise over some bashful movement of the hero's lips, his ocean waves of hair, his heaving chest and anguished eyes. Or determined with womanly virtue to escape the badguy and escaping in the panting end with the goodguy's shy help; escaping even the Indian chief's dark clutches even as I cowered in my seat beneath his pony's flying hooves, surviving to see her looking with wall-wide head and yard-wide smiling mouth melting with the hero's to fade into the darkness sibilant with young girls' and women's sighs.

Or the trains running wild and threatening to jump the track and crash into the white sections below, with smoke and steam threatening to scald the air and bring hellfire to those trapped there in their favored seats—screaming as fireman and engineer battled to the death with the Devil now become a Dalton boy or a James or a

Younger, whose horses of devil flesh outran again and again the iron horses of the trains, upgrade and down, with their bullets flying to burst ever against the sacred sanctuary of Uncle Sam's mail cars, where the gold was stored and the hero waited; killing multitudes of clerks and passengers, armed and unarmed alike, in joy and in anger, in fear and in fun. And bushwhacking the Sheriff and his deputies again and again, dropping them over cliffs and into cascading waterfalls, until like the sun the Hero loomed and doomed the arch-villain to join his victims, tossed too from a cliff, shot in the belly with the blood flowing dark; or hung blackhooded with his men, three in a row, to drop from a common scaffold to swing like sawdust-filled dolls in lonely winds.

All whirled through my mind as filtered through Body's and the others' eyes and made concrete in their shouting pantomime of conflict, their accurately aimed pistol and rifle blasts, their dying falls with faces fixed in death's most dramatic agony as their imaginary six-shooters blazed one last poetic bullet of banging justice to bring their murderers down down down to hell, now heaving heaven high in wonder beneath our feet . . .

So I wanted to leave the place unentered, even if it had a steeple higher than any church in the world, leave it, pass it ever by, rather than see it once, then never to enter it again—with all the countless unseen episodes to remain a mystery and like my mother flown forever.

But I could not say it, nor could I refuse; for no language existed between child and man. So I, Bliss the preacher, ascended, climbed, holding reluctantly Daddy Hickman's huge hand, climbed up the steep, narrow stairs crackling with peanut hulls and discarded candy wrappers through the stench of urine—up into the hot, breathing darkness, up, until the roof seemed to rest upon the crowns of our heads. . . . And as we come into the pink-tinted light with its tiered, inverted hierarchical order of seats, white at bottom, black at top, I pull back upon his hand, frightened by what I do not know. And he says, Come along, Bliss boy—deep and comforting in the dark. It's all right, he says, I'm going with you. You just hold my hand.

And I ascended, holding on. . . .

Mr. Movie-Man, she said . . . and I touched her dark hair, smiling, dreaming. Yes, I said . . . still remembering . . .

The pink light faded as we moved like blind men. All was darkness now and vague shapes, the crackling of bags and candy wrappers, the dry popping of peanut hulls being opened and dropped to the floor. Back and forth behind us voices sounded in the mellow idiom as we found seats and waited for the magic to begin. Daddy Hickman sighed, resting back, overflowing his seat so that I could feel his side pressing against me beneath the iron armrest. I settled back.

Why don't they hurry and get this shoot-'em-up started, someone behind us said. It was a sinner.

Git *started?* a deep voice said. Fool, don't you know that it was already started before we even sat down. Have you done gone stone blind?

It was another sinner. I could tell by the don't-give-a-damn tease in his gravelly voice.

No, the first sinner said. I don't see nothing and you don't neither. Because when it comes to looking at shoot-'em-ups I'm the best that ever did it. What's more, I can see you, my man, and that ain't so easy to do in the dark.

Well, the deep voice said, it's starting and I'm already looking and you don't even know it. So maybe you see me but you sho in hell don't see what I see.

Yeah, I know, but that because you drunk or else you been smoking those Mexican cubebs agin.

Listening, I looked to see how Daddy Hickman was reacting. Silently eating popcorn, he seemed to ignore them, feeding the white kernels into his mouth from his great fist like a huge boy.

See there, the second sinner said, because you black you're trying to low-rate me. All right, call me drunk if you want to but any fool knows that a shoot-'em-up don't have no end or beginning but go on playing all the time. They keep on running even when the lights is on. Hell, it's just like the moon in the daytime, you don't see it but it's dam' sho up there.

Now I *know* you been drinking, the first sinner said. Man, you high.

No, but I been studying this mess. Now when the man turns off the lights and tells everybody to take off, you think these folks in the shoot-'em-ups go away.

You dam' right . . .

Yeah, and you think they just wait around somewhere until the nighttime comes and then they come out again.

That's right.

I know, but that's because you're a fool. You ignorant. But in fact, it's just like the moon, and folks who got sense know that the moon is hanging up there all day long. . . .

Oh come on, man. Everybody knows about the moon.

Yeah, but you don't understand that the same thing happens with these shoot-'em-up guys. All those guys, even the houses and things, they don't go nowhere when the lights come on. Hell naw! They just stay right here, with shooting and fighting and hoss riding and eating and drinking and jiving them gals and having a ball after the man puts us out and locks the door downstairs and goes on home to inspect his jellyroll. That's how it really is.

Bull, the first sinner said. Bull!

No bull, man nothing! Folks like us get tired and have to get some sleep and maybe eat some grits and greens, but hell, those people in the shoot-'em-ups they lay right there in the bend. They don't need no rest. . . .

Dam' if you don't make it sound like they in slavery, cousin, another sinner said.

Now you got it, the deep-voiced one said. Ace, take it from me, they in slavery. And man, just like the old folks say, slavery is a war and war is hell!

They laughed.

I was disturbed. Could this be true? Could the people in the pictures always be there working even in the dark, even while they were crowded back into the machine? Forever and forever and forever?

I turned to look at the laughing men. They slouched in their seats, their heads back. One had a gold tooth that flashed in the dim light. Maybe they were just making up a lie for fun, like the boys did at school.

Bliss, Daddy Hickman said.

He touched my arm. Bliss, it's coming on, he said.

I tensed and it was as though he knew before it happened, as though it switched on at his word. For there came a spill of light from behind us, flooding past our heads and down to become a wide world of earth and sky in springtime. And there was a white house with a wide park of lawn with flowers and trees in mellow morning haze. . . . *Far shot to medium, to close: poiema, pathema, mathema—who'd ever dream I'd know? Me, hidden in their very eyes . . .* Then it happened, I went out of me, up and around like a butterfly in a curve of flight and there was moss in the trees and a single bird flipped its tail and flew up and away, and I was drawn through the wall and into the action. Over there, graceful trees along a cobblestone drive now occupied by a carriage with a smooth black coachman in livery sitting high and hinkty proud holding the reins above the gleaming backs and arched necks and shining harness of the horses, sitting like a king, wearing a shiny flat-topped hat with a little brush in its band. I am above them as it moves to stop before the big house and a man opens the coach door and descends, hurrying along the walk to the porch, and I descend and go along behind him. He wears a uniform with saber and sash, boots to his knees. *Ep-aul-ets* (that's the way to say it) show as his cape swings aside and hangs behind him like a trail as he takes long strides, handsome and tall. A black man in a black suit with white ruffles at the neck meets him at the columns of the porch and in answer to a question points to a great doorway, then moves ahead to open the door and then steps aside with a little bow, like Body's when he has to recite a verse on an Easter program at church. *Jesus wept, Body says and bows, looking warily at his mother across the pews. She had taught him a longer verse but either he's forgot it, or refuses to recite it on a bet. It's the shortest verse in the Bible and the other boys snicker. He'd gotten away with it again. . . . Body bowed and hurried back to his seat. . . .* The servant's bow is lower and he holds it until the man sweeps past and I go in behind the man and now I can see past him, over his shoulder, into a large room bright with sunlight and vases of flowers. Near a big window a pretty lady with hair parted in the middle and drawn down to her ears in little curls sits at a piano and as she looks up surprised and then with pleasure I think suddenly, *What is the color of her hair?* And I wish to get past the man to see if she has freckles on her nose, but he keeps coming towards me and I strain to get behind him. I press on as in a dream. It's very hard to do but I made it—only she doesn't see me as she looks up at the man who is still ahead of me. And as I strain to draw closer something happens—and I feel myself falling out. . . .

Disturbed, I fly back to my seat, hearing in my mind Body saying *Man, them ghosts don't wear no shoes* as I sat back beside Daddy Hickman watching her loom shy and strange, smiling out into the dark not even seeing me in the cool sweet flooding of light. I feel high and lonely. My eyes tickled with tears, until she grew soft and hazy, still looking outward, dreamy-eyed into the darkness and then I knew.

Look, I said, Daddy Hickman, it's her. . . .

Unh-huh, he said. He shifted contentedly beside me. Unh-huh.

But he doesn't hear me, I thought, *because he's still in the room. He's still there back in the wall.* I couldn't see him there because he was also here, his body pressing forward in the seat. And as she moved toward the man in the elegant room, I searched his face for a sign of recognition. I touched his arm twice, then saw him looking down at me with a smile. Then his hand came up, holding the bag of popcorn towards me.

Excuse me, Bliss boy, he said. Take some.

No thank you, sir, I said. It's her, the same one. You see?

Huh?

It's *her,* I said.

He glanced at me and back again to the screen. Oh sure, he said. She's the lead, Bliss, the heroine. She'll be all through the picture. Because, you see, everything turns around her. Have some. He pushed the bag toward me and I took some, thinking, *He doesn't want to hear me. He doesn't want to tell me. . . .*

Looking back to the wall, I watched them talking earnestly in the room below, then suddenly Daddy Hickman turned listening to something behind us and I felt myself slip in again and then the man was outside the house and I was above it a ways, watching some men on horses come cantering along the curving drive, moving past the hedges and the tulip trees. They wore uniforms and flowing capes and were proud. And some had whiskers and wore swords. Then I went over their heads and was looking behind the house where some of our own people were watching them coming on. I could tell that they were excited but trying not to show it, leaning forward with hands on hips or holding the handles of their rakes and hoes, looking. Some of the women wore headcloths and had no shoes. I saw a big lazy dog come out of the hedge and bark at the horses. One of the horses, a white one, shied. Then I moved along behind the horses again. I couldn't smell, only see. Couldn't hear clearly either, but some. Where has she gone? I wondered.

Above the house now, I could see a road curving through rolling countryside and on it another body of horsemen, riding hard, in close formation, the dust rising from the horses' hooves. Their buckles and buttons sparkled along the lines. They were coming on. The banner streaming, riders slanting forward in the wind.

And now they were passing some croppers' cabins and some of our people wearing old clothes, head rags, bonnets and floppy straw hats came out and stood, and some others who were dragging cotton sacks raised up in the fields and looked at the men up high and all our people waved. . . . Then a sinner behind me said something and I fell out again, hard. I was mad.

Here they go again, y'all, the sinner said. Dad blame it! In a second them peckerwoods will be fighting over us again. I sho be glad when they git it over with and done.

Me too, the second sinner said. You'd think they'd git taird of the same thing over and over again.

They already taird, but they have to keep on fighting till they can tell it straight. Oh yeah, they taird all right.

Hell, Ace, they ain't never going to get it straight. That's why they keep on messing with it, so that they won't *have* to get it straight.

Listen, you granny dodgers, a voice behind them commanded, I want you to *hush up!*

Hey, granny dodger, who you calling a granny dodger?

You, granny dodger, so shut up before I kick yo' granny dodgin' butt!

They were quiet. I moved behind my eyes as when I tried to fall asleep, then I slipped in again, looking for her.

I was back in the big house now and she was coming out of the door and I thought, *It's her all right,* and I started in close to see her when her face swelled up—then something snapped and I fell out. My face felt slapped. High up behind me I could hear a flapping sound, very fast—like a window shade when the spring is too tight—then slowing down to a whirr.

From my seat now I could see only a series of black numbers flashing before me in a harsh white light that danced with specks and squiggles. I was breathing hard and my eyes tickled like tears. I was straining to keep it, thinking *Please don't say anything. Please don't say* . . . I closed my eyes tightly and throbbed my eardrums but I heard anyway.

That was the end of the reel, Bliss, Daddy Hickman said. Just sit tight a second and it'll take up where it left off. . . .

Yes, sir, I said. I wanted to ask him again but was afraid that now he'd understand and say no. . . .

I chewed some popcorn. My throat was dry, thick. The sinners were laughing behind us.

They call this doo-doo *history,* one of them said.

I closed my eyes. *Why doesn't Daddy Hickman shut them up?* I thought. Then the sound of flapping began again and for a second the light came back, again very bright, then faded to become soft and full of wiggles and there was Daddy Hickman's face smiling in the dim light.

You see, Bliss? he said.

Yes, sir. I was looking hard.

You like it, Bliss?

Oh, yes, sir.

Does it come up to what you expected?

It's better, I, Bliss, said; it's pretty keen.

Yes it is, Daddy Hickman said. It's marvelous and at the same time it's terrible, but that's the way the world is, Bliss. But *shhh* now, it's started again.

She was back, sitting down at a distance in the room looking at a book and I strained to be there and went in. She wore pointed white shoes, with buckles. I was glad. . . . But then the house . . . *The house was not there and that old fool high coffin and that strumpet doing splits without her drawers on the floor what the*— Then I was with a soldier galloping on a white horse through a tree-lined lane. Fast, this time, the trees tear at my face, his long cape streaming in the wind. Things tossed. The road ran wobbling up and down before us, the trees tearing at my face, as the hot horse went tearing along with a smell of oak and leather. Too fast now to see all but suddenly I could hear the leather and the brass creaking and straining and it was like sitting in the barber chair and hearing Mr. Ivey say, *Gentlemen, I swear, when that ole hoss went into that backstretch he was running so fas' you could hear him sucking air straight up through his ass!* I held on tight, ducking the branches. Then someone was rushing behind us but I couldn't see. We were stretched out now and suddenly we turn and fire a pistol and now I can see the man on the black horse coming on. Then we're through the trees and approaching a big house with cabins behind it. It's her house and we leap off while the horse is still in motion, tossing its head as we yank on the bit and throw the reins to a servant who looks like he knows us. But his face isn't happy. Then we're inside the house and coming into the room where she stands wearing a long white cape and as she comes forward and sees us, suddenly she stops short, then throws out her arms and runs forward and, her face painful with eyes closed, flies toward me, filling the room and I screamed. . . .

Daddy Hickman whirled in his chair. What's the matter, Bliss?

It's her, the lady . . . I was crying.

What lady, Bliss. Where? This is a moving picture we're watching. I pointed toward the light.

She's the one. She tried to take me out. The one who said she was my mother. . . . Goodehugh. . . .

He sighed. Oh no, Bliss, he said, and talk low. We can't be disturbing the other folks like this. . . . This is a *moving picture* we're watching, Bliss.

But it's her, I whispered.

No, Bliss. That's not that woman at all. She only looks a bit like her, but she's not the one. So now you sit back and enjoy yourself. And don't be afraid, she cain't hurt you, Bliss boy; she's only a shadow. . . .

No, I thought, *it's her. He doesn't want me to know, but just the same, it's her.* . . . And I tried to understand the play of light upon the dark whiteness, the rectangle of cloth that would round out the mystery of my mother's going and her coming.

They're only shadows, Bliss, Daddy Hickman whispered. They're fun if you keep that in mind. They're only dangerous if you try to believe in them the way you believe in the sunlight or the Word.

Yes, sir, I, Bliss, said.

But for me now the three had become hopelessly blended in mystery: my mother gone before memory began, then she who called me Goodehugh Cudworth, and now she I saw as once more I entered the shadows.

Say there, Mister Dreamer-Man, she beside me said.

Goodehugh-cudworth, she called me Goodehugh. If not my mother, who moves in the shadows? And again as I look through the beam of pulsing light into the close-up looming wide across the distant yet intimate screen, I'm enthralled and sweetly disintegrated like motes in sunlight and I listen, as when in the box, straining to hear some sound from her moving lips, holding my breath to catch some faint intonation of her voice above the printed word which Daddy Hickman reads softly to me, explaining the action. And I knew anguish. Yes. There was the wavery beam of light. There was the smokelike weaving of the light now more real than flesh or stone or pain pouring at a slant down to the living screen. And there behind me now I hear a whirring, a grinding, a hum, broken by the clicking of cogs and rapid wheels. But from her no sound . . .

CHAPTER 12

It was a bigger tent than ours. The seats went up and around the sides and we had to sit up high at the end over near where the animals were coming through. I was looking down at the pumping and swaying of their backs and at the tops of the heads of the men in red coats walking beside them as they came through. I said, "What kind of elephants are those?"

"Those are Africans, Bliss," Daddy Hickman said. "There's African elephants and Indian elephants."

"But how do you tell them apart?"

"By their ears, Bliss. The African ones have big ears," Daddy Hickman said.

"What about the noses?"

"You mean *trunks*. They're about the same."

They were strung out like fat boys moving around the ring holding trunk to tail.

"How about those lions?" I said. The man in the white and gold coat and the shiny boots was shooting a pistol in the air and waving an ice cream parlor chair at the lions.

"What do you mean, Bliss?"

"I mean, where do they come from?"

"They're from Africa too, little boy."

I looked at the lions, sitting up on some stools with their lips rolled back, snarling. One struck at the air with his paw, like Body trying to shadow-box. The man snapped the whip and he stopped. I said,

"Why don't they catch him?"

Daddy Hickman was bent forward, looking hard.

"Why don't they catch him?" I said.

"They're mastered, Bliss. He's scared them. They could destroy him like a cat with a mouse if they weren't scared. But that's the test of his act. He can outthink them from the start because he's a man, but in order to get in there with those animals and master them he has to master his nerves." He laughed. "Bliss, you can't tell it from up here, but he's probably popping his whip and shooting off that pistol at his own legs about as much as he's doing it at the lions. Because sometimes the trainer makes a mistake and that's it, the lions take over. But we don't want that to happen, do we? It's enough to know it's a possibility. Is that right, Bliss?"

"Yes, sir."

Now the man was popping the whip and making the lions gallop around in a circle, while he stood in the same spot, making them gallop around and around him. I said,

"Could you do that, Daddy Hickman?"

He laughed and looked down at me.

"What's that, Bliss?"

"I say could you make those lions do like he's doing?"

"No, Bliss, I'm only a man-tamer. Lions are not in my line." He laughed again.

"Daniel could," I, Bliss, said.

"Yes, but Daniel wasn't a lion-tamer either, Bliss. It was the Lord who controlled those lions. What Daniel had to do was to have faith."

"But don't you have faith?"

"Sure. But if the Lord ever wants to test me with a lion, He'll do it, Bliss. And He'll put the lion in my path. I won't have to go looking for him. I don't think he intends for me to go bothering with these lions. Would you want to get in there with them?"

"Unh-unh—no sir. I'm too little."

"What if you were big, Bliss?"

"Maybe. If I was as big as you I might."

"What if they were little lions?"

"That would be better. I'm not afraid of little ones. How long do you think it took that man to learn to scare them?"

"I don't know, Bliss. He probably started when he was your age. Maybe he started with dogs, little puppies or little kittens. . . . Look yonder, Bliss, here come the clowns. My, my! Now watch this, you'll like the clowns."

He was smiling.

They came through the tent flap in a burst beneath us, all dressed up in funny clothes. I could see down on top of their heads. Seven clowns, one of them short and black, another tall and skinny in underwear and a fat one wearing a barrel, running to the center of the tent and they were hitting one another over the head with clubs that exploded and sent flowers and bird cages shooting out of their hats and heads, while the black one runs in and out, holding on to his britches with one hand and hitting at them with the other like a girl, a washerwoman, in and out between their legs. Then the others were turning and hitting him on the head and each time they hit he dropped his britches, showing his short bowed legs and his flour sack drawers with printing on them and a big red star in the center and one of them hits him there with a big paddle and he sounds like a hoarse jackass, hoarse and disrespectful early in the morning, while he skips around trying to pull up his britches and falls and turns a flip and gets up and rolls and skips and runs real fast, still holding on. Then the one with the big red nose pulls out a big mallet and hits him on his head and he squashes down to his knees and a big red rooster flies out and runs squawking around in the ring with the others chasing him over the sawdust and he hits him again and again, real fast, and hams and sides of bacon and cabbage and spurts of flour and eggs start falling out of his clothes and he starts running out of his bloomers and a clown dog drops out and starts barking and chasing him along with the others and him skipping and running and turning double flips and more chickens squashing out and a little pink clown pig with a black ring around one eye and the whole tent is laughing while the big clowns are hitting one another with the eggs and hams and sides of bacon and it sounds like the Fourth of July. He was just my size.

"Why does he just run, Daddy Hickman?"

He was laughing. I pulled his sleeve.

"What's that, Bliss?" Tears were running down his cheeks from laughing.

"Why does he always run?"

"Because that's his part in the act, Bliss."

"But why can't he hit and see what he can knock out of them?"

"That would be good, too, Bliss. But he's acting his part. Don't you like him? Listen to how all the folks are laughing. These are real fine clowns, Bliss."

"I don't like him," I said.

"Why?"

"Because I don't like him to be hit all the time. It would be better if *he* hit *them*. They're hitting him because he's the littlest. Are they real people?"

"Of course, Bliss. What's wrong with you? I bring you to see the circus and to have a good time so you can see the clowns and you asking if they're people."

"What kind of people are they?"

"*People*. Humans."

"Like us?"

"Sure, Bliss. —Look at that little dog do his act."

He was walking on his front legs.

"Colored?" I said.

"Oh——" He gave me a quick look. "No, Bliss, they're white folks—at least as far as I know. Look at the little dog, Bliss." He was doing a backflip now.

"Back there some were Germans," he said. "Billy Kersans is colored but you haven't seen him. But they're supposed to be funny, Bliss. That's the point. This is all for fun. So when we laugh at them we can laugh at ourselves."

I looked at the little one. "Him too?" I said.

"Sure, he's just short, a dwarf."

"I mean is he white?"

"Sure, Bliss. Don't you feel good? You think you want to go to the toilet?"

"No, sir, not now. Is that little one really white?"

"Sure, Bliss. Of course that's not the point. He's a clown. He's there to make us laugh just like the rest. That's burnt cork he's wearing on his face. Underneath it he's white."

"Is he a grown man like the others?"

"Of course— Look a-there, he's turning flips. See, there he goes. Now there's what you wanted to see. He's hitting the great big fellow. See, Bliss, he's hitting him on his feet and the big one is hopping around—look, look, there's a stalk of corn growing out of the shoe where he hit him. Oh, oh, the others are chasing him again, look at him go! Right under that elephant!"

I watched. He, the little one, was running around the circle now, with the little clown pig under his arm, feeding it from a baby bottle.

The little pig was still after the bottle as they chased him out of the tent and everybody was laughing. Then the band started playing and two horses galloped in with women standing on their backs in very short flip-up skirts and shiny things in their hair, and down at the center of the tent the music was going and I could see the band-master swaying in time as he played a short little horn. They were pretty ladies on horseback and they bowed up and down and turned flips in the air and came down still on the backs of the cantering horses, all in time with the music and their little skirts flipped up and down like a bird's tail or a branch of peach blossoms swaying in the wind. I wanted some ice cream, and started to ask when a man in tights came running in and the music speeded up the horse to a gallop that was like a fast merry-go-round and the man was running beside him and jumping on top along with the lady and they were galloping galloping and then she was standing on top of his shoul-ders and the horse still galloping along.

"Daddy Hickman," I said, "I'm hungry."

"What do you want now, Bliss, some popcorn?"

"No, sir."

"What?"

"Some ice cream."

"Do you know how to go to get it and come back without getting lost?"

"Yes, sir. I can do it. I'm kinda hungry."

"Here," he said, "go get yourself a cone of cream. And hurry right back, you hear?"

I got a mix, vanilla and strawberry. I didn't like chocolate. Body did. *I'm dark brown, chocolate to the bone,* Body liked to brag about everything but I couldn't, not about that. As I started back, I licked the cone slow to make it last.

Some ladies were dancing on a platform in front of a tent. Behind them and up high was a picture of a gorilla taking a white lady into the jungle. He had big red eyes and sharp teeth and she was screaming and her clothes were torn and her bubbies were showing. I went on. The next tent had pink lemonade and watermelon on ice. I watched a man throwing baseballs at some wooden milk bottles. He knocked them over the second time and won a Dolly Dimples Kewpie doll. He had three already. Out in front of another tent a man was saying something real fast through a megaphone and pointing to a picture of a two-headed man, and a lot of folks were listening to him. One of the heads was laughing but the other head was crying. I watched the man awhile. He waved his arm in a circle in the air like he was doing magic and some of the people were going inside. Then two big white guys came up and pinched me and I said "Oh!" and they laughed and called me Rastus. They knew me. I didn't cry. I backed away and went behind the tent. It was quiet, the crowd was all out front. I saw the wagons and the ropes and cages for the animals. Some wet clothes were hanging on a line stretched between two of the wagons and I could hear the music coming up from the big tent and I could smell the hamburgers frying. My ice cream was running out so I ate it very slow, but it didn't last. It was all down in the little end and I bit it off and let the cream run down in my mouth. Then I thought of some fine little-end barbecue ribs and wanted some but nobody was selling any. Pig feet neither. I went on past the back of the tent where the fat lady lived. She looked like a Dolly Dimples too, and I went around and took a look at her. She was holding a handkerchief in her two fingers and her pinkie was crooked like Sister Wilhite's when she drinks her coffee and her hair was cut short in a bob with a pink ribbon around it. A man said, Hi there, to her and she said, Hello dear, and smiled and winked her eye. She looked just like a big fat Dolly Dimples doll and I wondered if she was made like Body said all the littler women were. She winked at me and smiled.

I went on. I was still hungry for ice cream but I saw those two big guys again and went behind the tent and over the staked ropes and sawdust. That's when I saw him. He was sitting on a little barrel looking down at a black and orange felt beanie with a little flower pot and a paper flower attached to the top and I didn't know what I was going to do but when I went up to him I could see that we were the same height, then he looked up and said, Hi, kid, and I hit him. I hit him real quick and it glanced off his cheek and I could see the blackness smear away and the white coming through and then I hit him again, hard and solid this time and he yelled, Git outta here, y'little bastard! What's the matter with you, kid? You nuts? trying to push me away and I hit and hit, trying to make all the blackness go away. He was surprised and his arms were too short to push me far and I was hitting fast with both fists, going as fast as I could go and he was cursing. Then something snatched me up into the air and I was trying to hit and kicking at him until Daddy Hickman shook me hard, saying, Boy, what's come over you? Don't you know that that's a grown man you're trying to fight? You trying to start a riot? And saying to the little clown, I'm sorry, I'm very sorry; I sent him to get an ice cream cone and here I find him trying to fight. Who are you? the little one said. You work for his folks? No, Daddy Hickman said, but I know him; he's with me. Then you better get him the hell out of here before I forget he's just a kid. In fact, I should get you instead. What the hell do you mean letting a wild kid like that run around loose? Don't worry, Daddy Hickman said, we're leaving and

I mean to take care of him. He won't do it again. . . . And then he was running with me under his arm, puffing around the tent and across the lot into an alley and someone behind us screaming, "Hey, Rube! Hey, Rube!" and the blackness was all over the back of my hands. . . .

CHAPTER 13

". . . Oh, yes," Hickman said, fanning the Senator's perspiring face, "you were giving us a natural fit! All of a sudden you were playing hooky from the services and hiding from everybody—including me. Why, one time you took off and we had about three hundred folks out looking for you. We searched the streets and the alleys and the playgrounds, the candy stores and the parks, and we questioned all the children in the neighborhood—but no Bliss. We even searched the steeple of the church where the revival was being held but that only upset the pigeons and caused even more confusion when somebody knocked against the bell and set it ringing as though there had been a fire or the river was flooding.

"So then we spread out and really started hunting. I had begun to think about going to the police—which we hated to do, considering that they'd probably have made things worse—because, you see, I thought that she—that is, I thought that you might have been kidnapped. In fact, we were already headed along a downtown street

when, lo and behold, we look up and see you coming out of a picture house where it was against the law for us to go! Yes, sir, there
you were, coming out of there with all those people, blinking your
eyes and with your face all screwed up with crying. But thank God
you were all right. I was so relieved that I couldn't say a word, and
while we stood at the curb watching to see what you would do,
Deacon Wilhite turned to me and said, 'Well, 'Lonzo—A.Z.—it
looks like Rev. Bliss has gone and made himself an outlaw, but at
least we can be thankful that he wasn't stolen into Egypt.' . . . And
that's when you looked up and saw us and tried to run again. I tell
you, Bliss, you were giving us quite a time. *Quite* a time . . ."

Suddenly Hickman's head fell forward, his voice breaking off;
and as he slumped in his chair the Senator stirred behind his eyelids,
saying, "What? What?" But except for the soft burr of Hickman's
breathing it was as though a line had gone dead in the course of an
important call.

"What? What?" the Senator said, his face straining toward the
huge, shadowy form in the bedside chair. Then came a sudden gasp
and Hickman's voice was back again, soft but moving as though
there had been no interruption.

"And so," Hickman was saying, "when you started asking me that,
I said, 'Bliss, thy likeness is in the likeness of God, the Father. Because, Reverend Bliss, God's likeness is that of *all* babes.' Now for
some folks this fact is like a dose of castor oil as bitter as the world,
but it's the truth. It's hard and bitter and a compound cathartic to
man's pride—which is as big and violent as the whole wide world.
Still it gives the faint of heart a pattern and a faith to grow by. . . .

"And when they ask me, 'Where shall man look for God, the
Father?' I say, let him who seeks look into his own *bed*. I say let him
look into his own *heart*. I say, let him search his own *loins*. And I say
that each man's bedmate is likely to be a Mary—no, don't ask me

that—is most likely a Mary even though she be a Magdalene. That's another form of the mystery, Bliss, and it challenges our ability to think. There's always the mystery of the one in the many and the many in one, the you in them and the them in you—ha! And it mocks your pride, mocks it to the billionth, trillionth power. Yes, Bliss, but it's always present and it's a rebuke to the universe of man's terrible pride and it's the shape and substance of all human truth. . . ."

. . . *Listen, listen! Go back,* the Senator tried desperately to say. *It was Atlanta! On the side of a passing streetcar, in which smiling, sharp-nosed women in summer dresses talked sedately behind the open grillwork and looked out on the passing scene, I saw her picture moving past, all serene and soulful in the sunlight, and I was swept along beside the moving car until she got away. Soon I was out of breath, but then I followed the gleaming rails, hurrying through crowded streets, past ice cream and melon vendors crying their wares above the backs of ambling horses and past kids on lawns selling lemonade two cents a glass from frosted pitchers, and on until the lawns and houses gave way to buildings in which fancy dicty dummies dressed in fine new clothes showed behind wide panes of shop-window glass. Then I was in a crowded Saturday-afternoon street sweet with the smell of freshly cooked candy and the odor of perfume drifting from the revolving doors of department stores and fruit stands with piles of yellow delicious apples, bananas, coconuts and sweet white seedless grapes—and there, in the middle of a block, I saw her once again. The place was all white and pink and gold, trimmed with rows of blinking lights red, white and blue in the shade; and colored photographs in great metal frames were arranged to either side of a ticket booth with thin square golden bars and all set beneath a canopy encrusted with other glowing lights. The fare was a quarter and I felt in my pocket for a dollar bill, moist to my touch as I pulled it out, but I was too afraid to try. Instead I simply looked on awhile as boys and girls arrived and reached up to buy their tickets then disappeared inside. I yearned to enter but was afraid. I wasn't ready. I hadn't the nerve. So I moved on past in the crowd. For a while I walked beside a strolling white couple pretending that I was their little boy and that they were taking me to have ice cream before they took me in to see the pictures. They sounded happy and I was enjoying their talk when they turned off and went into a restaurant. It was a large restaurant and through the glass I could see a jolly fat black man cutting slices from a juicy ham. He wore a white chef's cap and jacket with a cloth around his neck and when he saw me he winked as though he knew me and I turned and ran dodging through the sauntering crowd, then slowed to a walk, going back to where she smiled from her metal frame. This time I followed behind a big boy pushing a red-and-white-striped bicycle. A small Confederate flag fluttered from each end of the handlebars on which two rearview mirrors showed reflecting my face in the crowd, and two shining horns with red rubber bulbs and a row of red glass reflectors ridged along the curve of the rear fender, throwing a dazzled red diamond light, and the racing seat was hung with dangling coon tails. It was keen and I ran around in front and walked backwards a while, watching him roll it. He looked at me and I looked at him but mainly at his bike. A shiny bull with lowered horns gleamed from the end of the front fender, followed by a screaming eagle with outstretched wings and a toy policeman with big flat hands which turned and whirled its arms in the breeze as he guided it by holding one hand on the handlebar and the other on the seat. And on the fork which held the front wheel there was a siren which let out a low howl whenever he pulled the chain to warn the people he was coming. And as it moved the spokes sparkled bright and handsome in the sun. It was keen. I followed him back up the street until we reached the picture show where I stopped and watched him go on. Then I understood why he didn't ride: His rear tire had a flat in it. But I was still afraid so I walked up to the drugstore on the corner and listened a while to some Eskimo Pie men in white pants and shoes telling lies about us and the Yankees as they leaned on the handlebars of their carts, before going back to give it another try. This time I made myself go up to the*

booth and looked up through the golden bars where the blue eyes looked
mildly down at me from beneath white cotton candy bangs. I . . .

"Bliss?"

Was it Mary? No, here to forget is best. They criticize me, me a senator
now, especially Karp who's still out there beating hollow wood to hully
rhythms all smug and still making ranks of dead men flee the reality of the
shadow upon them, then Who? What cast it? stepping with the fetch to the
bank and Geneva with tithes for Israel while ole man Muggin has to keep
on bugging his eyes and rolling those bales so tired of living but they refuse
to let him die. Who's Karp kidding? Who's kidding Karp? making a for-
tune in bleaching cream, hair straightener and elevator shoes, buying fu-
tures in soy beans, corn and porkers and praising his God but still making
step fetch it for the glory of getting but keeping his hands clean, he says.
And how do they feel, still detroiting my mother who called me Goodrich
Hugh Cuddyear in the light of tent flares then running away and them
making black bucks into millejungs and fraud pieces in spectacularmythics
on assembly lines? Who'll speak the complicated truth? With them going
from pondering to pandering the nation's secret to pandering their pon-
dering? So cast the stone if you must and if you see a ghost rise up, make
him bleed. Hell, yes, primitives were right—mirrors do steal souls. So
Odysseus plunged that matchstick into Polyphemus' crystal! Here in this
country it's change the reel and change the man. Don't look! Don't listen!
Don't say and the living is easy! O.K., so they can go fighting the war but
soon the down will rise up and break the niggonography and those ghosts
who created themselves in the old image won't know why they are what
they are and then comes a screaming black babel and white connednation!
Who, who, who, boo, are we? Daddy, I say where in the dead place between
the shadow where does mothermatermammy—mover so moving on? Where
in all the world pile hides?

"Bliss?"

. . . but instead of chasing me away this kindly blue-eyed cotton-headed

Georgiagrinder smiled down and said, What is it, little boy? Would you like a ticket? We have some fine features today.

And trembling, I hid behind my face, hoping desperately that the epiderm would hide the corium and corium rind the natural man. Stood there wishing for a red neck and linty head, a certain expression of the eyes. Then she smiled, saying, *Why of course you do. And you're lucky today because it's only a quarter and some very very fine pictures and cartoons. . . .*

I watched her eyes, large and lucid behind the lenses, then tiptoed and reached, placing my dollar bill through the golden bars of the ticket booth.

My, my! but we're rich today. Aren't we now? she said.

No, mam, I said, *'cause it's only a dollar.*

And she said, *That's true and a dollar doesn't go very far these days. But I'm sure you'll get plenty more because you're learning about such things so early. So live while you may, I say, and let the rosebuds bloom tomorrow—— ha! ha!*

She pushed the pink ticket through the bars so I could reach it.

Now wait for your change, she said. *Two whole quarters, two dimes and a nickel——which still leaves you pretty rich for a man of your years, I'd say.*

Yes, mam. Thank you, mam, I said.

She shook her blond head and smiled. *We have some nice fresh buttered popcorn just inside,* she said, *you might want to try some. It's very good.*

Yes, mam, thank you mam, I said, knotting the change in the corner of my handkerchief and hurrying behind the red velvet barrier-rope. Then I was stepping over two blue naked men with widespread wings who were flying on the white-tiled lobby floor, only the smaller one was falling into the white tile water, and approached the tall man who took the tickets. He wore a jaunty, square-visored cap and a blue uniform with white spats and I saw him look down at me and look away disgusted, making me afraid. He stood stiff like a soldier and something was wrong with his eyes. I crossed my fingers. I didn't have a hat to spit in. Then suddenly he looked down again and smirked and though afraid I read him true. *You're not a man,* I thought, only a big boy. You're just a big old freckly face. . . .

> Peckerwood, peckerwood,
>> You can't see me!
> You're just a redhead gingerbread
>> Five-cents-a-cabbage head—

All right, kid, he said, where's your maw?

Sir?

You heard me, Ezra. I'm not supposed to let you little snots in here without your folks. So come on now, Clyde, where's ya maw?

Watching his face, I pointed into the dark, thinking I ain't your Clyde and I ain't your Ezra, I'm Bliss. . . . She's in there, I said. She's waiting for me.

She's in dere, he mimicked me, his eyes crossing upon my face and then quickly away. You wouldn't kid me would you, Ezra, he said.

Oh, no, sir, I said, she's really and truly in there like I said.

Then in the dark I could hear the soaring of horns and laughter.

Oh, yeah— he began and broke off, holding down his white-gloved hand for silence. Out on the walk some girls in white silk stockings and pastel dresses came to a giggling halt before the billboards, looking at the faces and going "Oooh! Aaah!"

Well did Ah evuh wet-dream of Jeannie and her cawn-sulk hair, he said, snapping his black bow tie hard against his stiff white collar. He stood back in his knees, like Deacon Wilhite, then drummed his fingers on the edge of the ticket hopper and grinned.

Inside the music surged and flared.

Hold it a minnit, Clyde, he said, Hold it! looking out at the giggling girls.

Sir? I said. Sir?

Hush, son, he said, and pray you'll understand it better bye 'n' bye. 'Cause right now I got me some other fish to fry. Y'all come on in, gals, he said in a low, signifying voice. Come on in, you sweet misstreaters, you fluffy teasers. I got me a special show for ever one of you lily-white dewy-delled mama's gals.

Yes, sir! You chickens come to Papa, 'cause I got the cawn right here on the evuh-lovin' cob!

Here mister, I said. . . .

He rubbed his white gloves together, watching the girls. What's that you say, kid?

I say my mamma's in there waiting for me, I said.

He waved his hand at me. Quiet, son, quiet! he said.

Then the girls moved again. Oh, hell, he said, watching them as they turned on their toes, their skirts swirling as they flounced away, laughing and tossing their hair.

Then he was looking down again.

Clyde, he said, what's your mamma's name?

Her name's "Mamma"—I mean Miz Pickford, I said

Suddenly his mouth came open and I could see the freckles bunch together across his nose.

Lissen, kid—you trying to kid me?

Oh, no sir, I said. That's the honest truth.

Well, I'll be dam'!

He shook his head.

Honest, mister. She's waiting in there just like I said. . . . I held out my ticket.

He pulled hard on the top of his glove, watching me.

Honest, I said.

Dammit, Clyde, he said, if that's the truth your daddy shore must have his hands full, considering all the folks who are just dying to help him out. I guess you better hurry on in there and hold on to her tight. Protect his interests, Ezra. Because with a name like that somebody big and black might get holt to her first.—Yas, suh! An' mah mammy call me Teebone!

Smirking, he took the ticket, tearing it in half and holding out the stub.

Here, Mister Bones, Mister Tambo, he said, take this and don't lose it. And you be quiet, you hear? I ain't here for long but don't let me come in there

*and find y'all down front making noise along with those other snotty-shitty
little bastards. You hear?*

Yes, sir, I said, starting away.

Hey, wait a minnit! Hold it right there, Clyde!

Sir?

Lissen here, you lying little peckerwood—why aren't you in school today?

I looked at him hard. Because it's Saturday, *mister, I said, and because my
mamma is in there* waiting *for me.*

*He grinned down at me. O.K., Ezra, he said, you can scoot—and watch
the hay. But mamma or no mamma, you be quiet, you hear? This is way down
south in de lan' uv cotton, as the nigger boys say, but y'all be quiet, y'all
heah-uh? An' Rastus, Ah mean it!*

I hesitated, watching him and wondering whether he had found me out.

Well, go on! he barked.

And I obeyed.

*Then I was moving through the sloping darkness and finding my way by
the dim lights which marked the narrow seat rows, going slowly until the
lights came up and then there were red velvet drapes emerging and eager
faces making a murmuring of voices, and golden cherubim, trumpets and
Irish harps flowing out in space above the high proscenium arch, while in the
hidden pit the organ played sweet, soothing airs. Then in the dimming of the
lights I found a seat and horses and wagons flowed into horses and wagons
and wagons surrounded by cowboys and Indians and Keystone Kops and
bathing beauties and flying pies and collapsing flivvers and running hoboes
and did ever so many see themselves comfortably, humorously in quite so few?
And ads on the backdrop asking "Will the Ladies Please Remove Their Masks
and Reveal Their True . . ." and everyone and everything moving too swiftly,
vertigoing past, so that I couldn't go in, couldn't enter even when they came
close and their faces were not her face. So in the dark I squirmed and waited
for her to come to me but there were only the others, big-eyed and pretty in
their headbands and bathing suits and beaded gowns but bland with soft-*

looking breasts like Sister Georgia's only unsanctified and with no red fire in green eyes. She called me Goodehugh Gudworthy and I couldn't go in to search and see. . . .

On the hill the cattle tinkled their bells and she said, Mister Movie-Man, I have to live here, you know. Will you be nice to me? and the blossoms were falling where the hill hung below the afternoon and we sprawled embraced and out of time that never entered into future time except as one nerve cell, tooth, hair and tongue and drop of heart's blood into the bucket. Oh, if only I could have controlled me my she I and the search and have accepted you as the dark daddy of flesh and Word— Hickman? Hickman, you after all. Later I thought many times that I should have faced them down—faced me down and said, Look, this is where I'll make my standing place and with her in all her grace and sweet wonder. But how make a rhyme of a mystery? If I had only known then what I came to know about the shape of honor and the smell of pride—I say, HOW THE HELL DO YOU GET LOVE INTO POLITICS OR COMPASSION INTO HISTORY? And if you can't get here from there, that too is truth. If he can't drag the hill on his shoulders must a man wither beneath the stone? Yes, the whole hill moved, the cattle lowed, birds sang and blossoms fell, fell gently but I was . . . I was going in but couldn't go in and then it ended and the lights came on. But still I waited, hoping she'd appear in the next run, so I sat low in my seat, hiding from the ticket man as they moved in and out around me. Then it was dark again and I knew I should leave but was afraid lest she appear larger than life and I would go in—why couldn't you, Daddy Hickman, say: Man is born of woman but then there's history and towns and states and between the passion and the act there are mysteries. Always. Appointive and elective mysteries. So I told myself: Man and woman are a baby's device for achieving governments— ergo ego and I'm a politician. Or again, shadows that move on screens and words that dance on pages are a stud's device for mounting the nightmare that gallops by day. And I told myself years ago, Let Hickman wear black, I, Bliss, will wear a suit of sable. Being born under a circus tent in the womb of wild women's arms I reject circumstance, live illusion. Then I told myself, speed up the process, make them dance. Extend their vision until they disgust themselves, until they gag. Stretch out their nerves, amplify their voices, extend their grasp until history is rolled into a pall. The past is in your skins, I cried, face fortune and be filled. No, there's never a gesture I've made since I've been here that hasn't tried to say, Look, this is me, me. *Can't you hear? Change the rules! Strike back hard in angry collaboration and you're free but I couldn't go in I have to live here, Mister Movie-Man, she said and I found a resistance of buttons and bows. Imagine, there and in those times, a flurry of fluffy things, an intricacy of Lord knows what garment styles, there beneath the hill. . . .*

"Bliss, are you there?"

So I waited, hoping I could get into it during the next show and she would be there and I waited yearning for one more sight word goodehugh even if seventy outraged deaconesses tore through the screen to tear down the house around us. But couldn't go in and sat wet and lonely and ashamed and wet down my leg and outside all that racing life swirling before me but once more the scenes came and tore past, sweeping me deeper into anguish yet when I came out of all that intensified time into the sun the world had grown larger for my having entered that forbidden place and yet smaller for now I knew that I could enter in if I entered there alone. . . . I ran—Bliss ran.

. . . Where are we? Open the damper, Daddy: It heats hard. So I told myself that I shall think sometime about time. It was all a matter of time; just a little time. I shall think too of the camera and the swath it cut through the country of my travels, and how after the agony I had merely stepped into a different dimension of time. Between the frames in blackness I left and in time discovered that it was no mere matter of place which made the difference but time. And not chronology either, only time. Because I was no older and although I discovered early that in different places I became a different me. What did it all mean? Was time only space? How did she who called Cud forth become shadow and then turn flesh? She broke the structure of ritual

*and the world erupted. A blast of time flooded in upon me, knocking me out
of the coffin into a different time.*

*. . . My grandpap said the colored don't need rights, Donelson said; they
only need rites. You get it? Just give niggers a baptism or a parade or a dance
and they're happy. And that, Karp said, is pappy-crap. . . . And I was
stunned.*

*So now when I changed places I changed me, and when I entered a place
that place changed imperceptibly. The mystery went with me, entered with
me, realigning time and place and personality. When I entered all was
changed, as by an odorless gas. So the mystery pursued me, shifting and
changing faces. Understand?*

*And later whenever instead of taking in a scene the camera seemed to
focus forth my own point of view I felt murderous, felt that justifiable murder was being committed and my images a blasting of the world. I felt sometimes that a duplicity was being commissioned, an ambuscado trained upon
those who thought they knew themselves and me. And yet I felt that I was
myself a dupe because there was always the question aroused by my ability to
see into events and the awareness of the joke implicit in my being me. Who?
So I said, What is the meaning of this arrangement of time place and circumstance that flames and dampens murder in my heart? And what is this
desire to identify with others, this need to extend myself and test my most farfetched possibilities with only the agency of shadows? Merely shadows. All
shadowy they promised me my mother and denied me solid life. Oh, yes, mirrors do steal souls. So indeed Narcissus was weird. . . .*

"Reverend Bliss," Hickman was saying, "in the dark of night, alone
in the desert of my own loneliness I have thought long upon this. I
have thought upon you and me and all the old scriptural stories of
Isaac and Joseph and upon our slave forefathers who killed their
babes rather than have them lost in bondage, and upon my life here

and the trials and tribulations and the jokes and laughter and all the endless turns-about that mark man's life in this world—and each time I return, each time my mind returns and makes its painful way back to the mystery of you and the mystery of birth and resurrection and hope which now seems endless in its complication. Yes, and I think upon the mystery of my involvement in it—me, a black preacher's willful son, a gambler-musician who rejoiced in the sounds of our little hidden triumph in this world of deceitful triumphs. Me, given you and your gifts, your possibilities in this whirlwind of circumstance. How and why did it happen? Why was I, the weakest of vessels, chosen to give so much and to have to try to understand so much which hardly seems understandable? Why did He give me this mysterious burden and then seem to mock me and challenge me and let men revile and despise me and wipe my heart upon the floor of this world after I had suffered and offered it up in sacrifice because in the coming together of hate and love and life and death that marked the beginning, I looked upon those I love and upon them who caused their death and was unable to accept it except as I'd already accepted the blues, the clap, the loss of love, the fate of man. . . . I bared my breast, I lowered my head into the ashes where they had burned my own, my loved ones, and accepted Thy will. Why didst Thou choose me, single me out for further humiliation who had been designated for humiliation by men unworthy, by men most unworthy, Lord? Why? Why me? Me who had accepted my blackness as my fate, in the dark and shadowy complication of Thy will? And yet, down there in the craziness of the Southland, in the madhouse of down home, the old motherland where I in all my ignorance and desperation was taught to deal with the complications of Thy plan, yes, and at a time when I was learning to live and to glean some sense of how Thy voice could sing through the blues and even speak through the dirty dozens if only the players were rich-spirited and resourceful enough, comical enough, vital enough and enough aware of the disciplines of life. In the zest and richness Thou were there, yes! But still, still, still, my question Lord! Though I say, quiet, quiet, my tongue. So teach me, Lord, to move on and yet be still; to question and not cry out, Lord, Lord, WHY? . . . Why?"

And Hickman slept.

CHAPTER 14

So now I suppose that the medicine is taking him over again, Hickman thought. *The needle has reached through his flesh into his mind. Those hypos into the vein then . . . The way he looks at me, still wanting to talk and his eyes dulling. But the hopeful thing is that he's fighting to live, to stay alive. Regardless of what it will all have to mean if he does, he still wants to live. So my task is simply to help him to keep on fighting, to keep on wanting to live. What else is there, other than what a minister always tries to do to help? Comfort and consolation—no, not just that, because there's still the mystery to be understood. Reverse the time. Lord, but I'm tired . . . cramped in muscle and confused in mind. . . . Maybe I ought to go out and stretch my legs, get a little fresh air in my lungs. No, you can't risk it because it would be just like him to come to while I'm out and if he did, what would be the next move? Forget it; you've waited all this long time so you can afford to sit still and wait awhile longer—tired or no tired. . . . Those hypos . . . He's sleeping hard, quiet in his body if not in his mind. Hypos. I sure hope so, because the time has come when everything has to be understood and I mean to be here to try. . . .*

Just look at him, Hickman, there he is: Bliss at last. Out of all the time and racked and tiered-up circumstance, out of all the pomp and power-seeking—there's ole Bliss. It makes you wonder all over again just what kind of being man really is; makes you puzzle over the difference between who he is and what he does. But how do you separate it? Body and soul are all mixed together and yet are something different just the same. One grows in the way it's destined to grow, flesh and bone, blood and nerves, skin and hair, from the beginning; while the other twists and turns and hides and seeks and makes up itself as it grows and moves along. So there he is and for whatever the world knows him to be, somehow he's still Bliss. . . . It's like hearing a fire-cracker go off at a parade and you look up and see the great and bejeweled king of the Mardi Gras, sitting high on his throne in all his shiny majesty, and he starts to shake and cough and there, before your eyes, a little ole boy looks out from behind his mask. Well, the child is father and somewhere back there in the past, back behind little Bliss's face, this twitching, wounded man was waiting. No point of dreaming about it either. I was in the picture and a lot of other folks too, and we made a plan, or at least we dreamed a dream and worked for it but the world was simply too big for us and the dream got out of hand. So we held on to what we saw, us old ones, and finally it brought us here.

But just look at him—who would have thought that it would come to this, that our little Bliss would come to this? But why, Master? Why did this have to be? Back there in our foolish way we took him as our young hope, as our living guarantee that in our dismal night You still spoke to us and stood behind Your promise, even when things were most hopeless. Now look at him, all ravaged by his denials, sapped by his running, drained and twitching like a coke-fiend from all the twistings and turnings that brought him here. All damaged in his substance by trying to make everything appear to be the truth and nothing really truthful, playing all the old lying, obscene games of denial and rejection of the poor and beaten down. And even at the very last moment, refusing to recognize us, refusing to even see us who could never forget the promise and who for years haven't asked anything except that he remember and honor the days of his youth—or at least his baby days. Honor, oh yes; honor. But not to us but honor unto Thy dying lamb. We asked nothing for ourselves, only that he remember those days and what he had been at that time. Remember the promising babe that he was and the hope we placed in him and his obligation to the babes who come after. Maybe that was our mistake, we just couldn't surrender everything, we just couldn't manage to burn out the memory and cauterize the wound and deny that it had ever happened . . . that he had ever existed. Couldn't treat all of that like a hobo walking along the tracks back of town who passes and looks up and sees your face and spits on the cinders and crunches on. Gone without a word . . . After having been born so close to the time of whips and cold iron shackles we could fly up here in an airplane—which is like the promise of a miracle fulfilled . . . which is no longer miraculous—but still there on the bed lies the old abiding mystery in its latest form and still mysterious. Why'm I here, Master? Why? And how is it that a man like him, who has learned so much and gone so far, never learned the simple fact that it takes two to make a bargain or to bury a hatchet, or even to forget words uttered in dedication and taken deep into the heart and made sanctified by suffering? Blood spilled in violence doesn't just dry and drift away in the wind, no! It cries out for restitution, redemption; and we (or at least I—because it was only me in the beginning), but we took the child and tried to seek the end of the old brutal dispensation in the hope that a little gifted child would speak for our condition from inside the only acceptable mask. That he would embody our spirit in the councils of our enemies—but, oh, what a foolish miscalculation! Way back there . . . I'm no wise man now, but then, Lord, how mixed-up and naive I was! There I was, riffing on Thy Word and not even sure whether I was conducting a con game or simply taking part and leading in a mysterious prayer— Forgive me my ignorance. . . . Yesterday after the shooting started. . . . Was it yesterday? It was, wasn't it, Hickman? How long? Have you been sitting here all that time? How many hours in this hos-

pital waiting and talking and talking and remembering and revealing and talking and not revealing? And all because I slipped up and was sitting there in that gallery looking on like a man watching a scene unfolding in a dream instead of acting on the facts already exploding in my face. I could have stepped in front of that boy—or at least have picked him out of the crowd and stopped and tried to talk some sense into his head. But my eyes, my old eyes failed me. So now this sitting and waiting. It was awful! Truly awful! But what's a man to do, Hickman? So you try, you do your best as you see your best. Yes, but you realize that there's no guarantee that it's going to work. The best intentions have cracks in them, man, and that'll never change. Not until somebody puts the Lord's sun into a bushel basket—ho now! So here we come all this way and after all these years and there was no stopping even a fraction of it. Talking about sending a boy to do a man's work, this coiled spring has been stretched out so far that when it started to snap back I'd almost reached my second childhood. Talking to myself and belching in crowds and in the deep of night dreaming kindly of my wicked days and all against my duties and my soul's need. Lucky my bladder's still what it was years ago and I still have good breath control because my strong old slave-borne body has held up pretty well as bodies go. . . . Still, you failed. You were in the right place but not enough in it. You saw what was coming because Janey had warned you. You knew something was going to happen but not its shape or its outrageous face. So I simply couldn't stop it. Sometimes everything mocks a man—even his own tongue, his eyes and hands. Then babes judge him and fools ignorant of his strengths leap on his weaknesses like a mosquito finding the one tender spot at the back of his knee where it knows it can draw his blood.

Like that reporter asking me how come I was crying over a man who hates my people so. First place, I didn't realize that I was crying. At a time like that was I supposed to be thinking of how I looked? Did those senators think about how they looked when they were breaking for those doors like a crowd of crapshooters when a raid is on? Sure, I must have looked pretty foolish cry-

ing in a place like that, but tell me, who can simply look at his own reflection at such a time? I guess that reporter, that McIntyre, was looking at himself looking at me while all I could see was a great part of my life blowing up to a snick-snick-snick of bullets. Was I supposed to observe some kind of etiquette that has nothing to do with how I feel about things? And surely he didn't understand my saying that I was crying because I didn't know what else to do——me, a man of prayer. But hadn't I been praying for Bliss all these long years? One thing is sure, I couldn't bat those bullets down in midair. Oh no, too much was riding with those bullets, and when I missed that boy I missed my chance to stop the outrage. Yes, and maybe we lost all those hard, hopeful years. . . . "Rejoice when your enemy is struck down, why aren't you rejoicing?" That's what that reporter was saying; but what if it's too mixed up for that? What if there's more than appears on the surface? You live inside it for years, moving with it and feeling it grow and change and getting more complicated and making you grow more confused and complicated——except that you keep the faith; while folks outside think it's simply just a matter of "a" or "b," or else they think that it disappeared and no longer matters; while all the time it has been growing and sending out its roots until it touches everything in sight and all the streets you walk and all the deep actions of a man's mind and heart——yes. So I was deep upset, that's all. I lost control. I admit it and no apologies. Because when something hits you where you live you have got to go. Dignity, I guess that's what that white boy was talking about. I suppose to his mind I should have been worrying about those senators who have never thought a single thing about my dignity except maybe as a joke. Dred Scott's cross is mine—— Anyway, I've known crowds that had sharper teeth and more searching and penetrating eyes just because they were my own and so knew something about what it really costs to keep your dignity under pressure. In the old days I kept playing even when the bullets got to flying. We all did. I shouldn't have paid that reporter any attention because when I reacted I almost let him provoke me into telling him something, which would have been a mistake arising out of pride. I almost let him know

*that there was a secret to be revealed. Asking me why I was crying—well, if
we can't cry for Bliss, then who? If we can't cry for the Nation, then who?
Because who else draws their grief and consternation from a longer knowledge or from a deeper and more desperate hope? And who've paid more in
trying to achieve their better promise?*

   But, Hickman, you almost gave the thing away!

   *Well, maybe so; but what if I had, nobody would believe it. And maybe
that's because everybody dreams in the night that in this land treachery is
the truth of life—so they can't stand to think about it in the light of day.
That reporter—McIntyre?—yes, waiting out there in the hall. He would've
just thought that I was crazy the same as he does anyway. He wouldn't know
how to add up the figures; couldn't get with the beat, even if I gave them to
him. It would be like him walking down into a deep valley in the dark and
looking up all at once to see two moons arising up over opposite hills at one
and the same time. Ha! He'd either go cross-eyed and fall on his face in trying to deal with the sight. Or maybe like the fellow in the depot who was too
tight to invest a nickel, he'd simply stand there twisting and turning and trying to make up his mind until he'd invented a new kind of dance and stank.
No, Hickman, not his kind; he'd simply shut one eye and swear that one of
those hills and one of those moons wasn't there—even if the one he was trying to ignore was coming streaking toward him like a white-hot cannonball. . . .*

   *Well, few men love the truth or even regard facts so dearly as to let either
one upset their picture of the world. Poor Galileo, poor John Jasper; they persecuted one and laughed at the other, but both were witnesses for the truth
they professed. Maybe it's just that some of us have had certain facts and
truths slapped up against our heads so hard and so often that we have to see
them and pay our respects to their reality. Maybe wise men are just those who
have had the power to stay awake and struggle. And who can blame those
who don't feel that they have to worry about the complicated truths we have
to struggle with? In this country men can be born and live well and die with-*

out ever having to feel much of what makes their ease possible, just because so much is buried under all of this black and white mess that in their ignorance some folks accept it as a natural condition. But then again, maybe they just feel that the whole earth would blow up if even a handful of folks got to digging into it. It would even seem a shame to expose it, to have it known that so much has been built on top of such a shaky foundation.

But look, Hickman—Alonzo . . . this is here and now and the stuff has begun to bubble. The man who fell and the man lying there on the bed is the child, Bliss. That's the mystery. How did he become the child of that babyhood . . . father to the man, as it goes? And how could he have been my child, nephew and grandchild and brother-in-Christ as he grew? The confounding mystery of it has to be struggled with and I wish it was all a lie and and we could go back home and forget it. Still there was Robert, my brotherson. He was the second, dropping out of all that confusion. Yes, and there were all those long years before I had learned not to puzzle out questions about the babe anymore and could come to accept the sheer quickening wonder of him growing up, a young life being lived without regard to the consequences of its being put there among us, and without regard to the violent circumstances of its bawling birth. There was blood on the land and blood on my hands. I made my peace with that beginning too long ago for vengeance and finally I found my way to my ministry. Yes, the Lord-and-Master calls a man in strange tongues and voices, yes, and among strange scenes in stranger weather. I was never one to argue Genesis, not even in my heathen days—a start is a start, and "is" is "is" not "was." Still, there had to be a beginning. Used to hear that crab lice came from a man and woman's unwashed secreting and that was ignorant superstition—even though there's no denying the biting and the scratching, or the fact that the big crabs made the little ones. . . . I'm so tired and sleepy that my mind's falling into the cracks and crevices. Wonder if that young nurse would bring me a cup of coffee? No, just hold on. Wait. You'll be asleep a long time and soon. Meanwhile stay awake and watch the story unfold. By right, he should be dead and cold, but he's *holding on so you couldn't let go even if you wanted to. Stay. Yea! I wait and hope for me, because ain't this the time for me as well as for him? Here in his condition, so late in the day, asking me to tell him and me holding back the little I do know to keep him holding on and still not knowing fully how I became the man I am but merely the start. It sure changed my life around. I was never the same afterwards and it left an ache and emptiness that I've had to live with ever since. Oh, yes, you tried to cover it over with rectitude, tried to move on up above it and grow on top of it and you didn't try to sermonize from it either. Not directly. You just allowed it to teach you to feel for others. . . . Hickman, you ache like he aches, and he aches, they ache, everybody aches and aches. Hickman, the guards outside the door think you want to get out, to leave. And that's the truth. . . . Most will to forget, they drink denial like they drink whiskey. Yes, but where's the true contrast coming from? Sugar without salt. Life without death, what kind of a world? What kind of reality? Yes, but I must live by what I've seen and remember. And I have seen my people face Death and even go a piece with him and then wrestle with him and get away, thank the Lord, and return. Yes, but how many have I seen pass on and die? How many, where there are no hospitals to take them in, passing on in little ole stuffy rooms lit by a dim flame guttering low in sooty chimneys? And me sitting in some rickety rocking chair on a bumpy boarded floor looking across the pain-racked face to ole Death crouching like a big bird on the head of the bed; just sitting and a-waiting like the great-granddaddy of all poker players. Just crouching there while I tried to give myself over to some poor soul's trial, trying to absorb his agony into my own inadequate flesh. Humming a little comfort from the scriptures, sometimes from one of his favorite hymns, and sometimes praying until I grew mute and numb with weariness, and then leaving it up to the Lord . . . Bliss, sometimes I've seen Death arise and leave like smoke from the chimney when dawn grayed the room. I've seen him wait with patience and then take off in silence, like a cat hunting in the grass that's waited until it sees the bird break his spell and fly away. And sometimes I've seen* him come down to claim the prostrate soul and heard the rattle in the dying throat as life left the body and the soul took flight. And sometimes in the quiet of the early morning, around the still point of three, the simmering time, when back there in the old days the dancers would have been bear-panting and rocking to the shouting of those horns, getting with it, while I played the blues. Then here comes the to-be-or-not-to-be time, the crisis time, and found me sitting and a-rocking along beside some sickbed with sleep weighing heavy on my lids and almost exhausted with the watching and the struggle and there heard some wife or mother give voice in the dark to woman's old cry of heart-loss. I have heard it rip and tear up suddenly out of sleep as though the whole night had drawn itself together and screamed, and me looking up then and amazed as always to see their nightgowned forms flashing past to get to the bed to confirm what their souls had already acknowledged and accepted across sleep and distance, known it the way a fisherman knows when his line goes slack in the water that the fish is gone. Then I've heard them screaming again with the full realization of eternity come down. That's something to remember and think about, here and now. Something to remember even beyond the question of being ready for the time when it comes. But who can stand to stare steady into Death's blank face and all-consuming eye all the time, every day—even as the tens of thousands fall around us? Better to lift up our eyes to the hills and prepare for what's on the other shore. A man has to live in order to have a reason for dying as well as for having a reason for being reborn—because if you don't, you're already dead anyway. Now hush, because you're simply thinking words, old saws. So hush . . . all is noise.

Yes, but what a time this has been. What an awful time this has turned out to be. And I thought we'd make it with something to spare. I still did, even after that young gal kept turning us away. I thought we'd contact him somewhere along the line and we'd talk awhile somewhere in private and tell him what we felt and hoped and prayed, both for him and for us and for the country, and then go on back home and wait. Just that. Just that; that was *all, even though there wasn't a thing to justify the feeling that it might come to pass except our old habit of hoping. Maybe it just sneaked up on me, stole me while we were out there where I took them so they could see it for the first time and probably for most of us the last, and that got my hopes up and made me reckless. Maybe I let them down right there. Maybe the place and the image and the associations got to me. But what a feeling can come over a man just from seeing the things he believes in and hopes for symbolized in the concrete form of a man. In something that gives a focus to all the other things he knows to be real. Something that makes unseen things manifest and allows him to come to his hopes and dreams through his outer eye and through the touch and feel of his natural hand. That's the dangerous shape, the graven image we were warned about, the one that makes it possible for him to hear his inner hopes sound and sing and see them soar up and take wing before his half-believing eyes. Faith in the Lord and Master is easy compared to having faith in the goodness of man. There are simply too many snares and delusions, too many masks, too many forked tongues. Too much grit in the spiritual greens. But then, there that something is. There sits his hopes made manifest and a man knows that it's not simply the mixed-up hopes and yearnings within his own mind and most secret heart that grab him and make him stand tiptoe inside his skin and reach up through the dark for something better and finer and more durable than he knows himself to be capable of, but something felt by a lot of other folks and even achieved and died for by a precious few. . . .*

So I walked them out there just so that we could ease off from the frustration and runaround that we were getting, and so that I could have time to figure out our next move. Then they—we—had arrived and there it was . . . there.

He slowly shook his head, staring across to the sleeping face and feeling it become almost anonymous beneath his inward-turning vision, the once-familiar cast of features fading like the light. He closed his eyes, his fingers clasped across his middle as the mood of the afternoon moment returned in all its awe and mystery, and he found himself once more approaching the serene, high-columned space. Once more they were starting up the broad steps and moving in a loose mass still caught up in the holiday mood evoked by seeing the sights and scenes which most had only read about or seen in photographs or in an occasional newsreel. Then he was mounting the steps and feeling a sudden release from the frame of time, feeling the old familiar restricting part of himself falling away as when, long ago, he'd found himself improvising upon some old traditional riffs of the blues, or when, as in more recent times, he'd felt the Sacred Word surging rapturously within him, taking possession of his voice and tongue.

And now his heartbeat pounded and his footsteps slowed and he was looking upward, hesitating with one foot fumbling for the step which would bring him flush into the full field of the emanating power, and he felt himself shaken by the sudden force of his emotion. Then once again he was moving, moving into the cool, shaded and sonorous calm of the edifice, moving slowly and dreamlike over the fluted shadows cast along the stony floor before him by the upward-reaching columns, and he advanced toward the great image slumped there above in the huge stone chair.

From far away he could hear some sister's softly tentative "Reveren'? Reveren'?" and now their voices fading in a hush of awed recognition; creating but for her echoing *Reveren'? Reveren'?* a stillness as resonant as the profoundest note of some great distant bell; still staring, still hearing the sister's soft voice, which sounded now through a deep and doom-toned silence, her *Reveren'? Reveren'?* reverberating through his mind with the slow, time-and-space-devouring motion of great wings silently flying. . . .

Then he, Hickman, was looking up through the calm and peaceful light toward the great brooding face; he, Hickman, standing motionless before the quiet, less-and-more-than-human eyes which seemed to gaze from beneath their shadowed lids as toward some vista of perpetual dawn which lay beyond infinity. And he thought, *Now I understand: That look, that's us! It's not in the features but in what that look, those eyes, have to say about what it means to be a man who tries to live and struggle against all the troubles of the world with but the naked heart and mind, and who finds them more necessary than all the power of wealth and great armies. Yes, that look and what put it there made him one of us. It wasn't in the dirty dozens about his family and his skin-tone that they tried to ease him into, but in that look in his eyes and in his struggle against the things which put it there and saddened his features. It's in that, in being the kind of man he made himself to be that he's one of us. Oh, he failed and he knew that he could only take one step along the road that would make us free, but in growing into that look he joined us in what we have been forced to learn about life and about being truly human in the face of life. Because one thing we have been forced to learn is that man at his best, when he's set in all the muck and confusion of life and continues to struggle for his ideals, is near sublime. So yes, he's one of us, not only because he freed us to the extent that he could, but because he freed himself of that awful inherited pride they deny to us, and in doing so he became a man and he pointed the way for all of us who would be free—yes!*

Staring upward into the great brooding eyes he felt a strong impulse to turn and seek to share their distant vision but was held, the eyes holding him quiet and still, and he stared upward, seeking their secret, their mysterious life, in the stone; aware of the stone and yet feeling their more-than-stoniness as he probed the secret of the emotion which held him with a gentle but all-compelling power. And the stone seemed to live and breathe then, its great chest appearing to heave as though, stirred by their approach, it had decided to sigh in silent recognition of who and what they were and had chosen to reveal its secret life for all who cared to see and share and remember its vision. And he was searching the stony visage, its brooding eyes, as though waiting to hear it resound with the old familiar eloquence which he knew only from the sound of the printed page—when a sister's voice came to him as from a distance, crying, "Oh, my Lord! Look, y'all, it's him! It's HIM!," her voice breaking in a quavering rush of tears.

And he was addressing himself now, crying in upon his own spellbound ears, as the sister's anguished "Ain't that him, Revern'? Ain't that Father Abraham?" came to him like the cry of an old slave holler called across a moonlit field.

And too full to speak, he smiled; and in silent confirmation he was nodding his head, thinking, *Yes, with all I know about him and his contradictions, yes. And with all I know about men and the world, yes. And with all I know about white men and politicians of all colors and guises and intentions, yes. And with all I know about the things you had to do to be you and stay yourself—yes! She's right, she's cut through the knot and said it plain; you are and you're one of the few who ever earned the right to be called "Father." George didn't do it, though he had the chance, but you did. So yes, it's all right with me; yes. Yes, and though I'm a man who despises all foolish pomp and circumstance and all the bending of the knee that some still try to force upon us before false values, yes, and yes again. And though I'm against all the unearned tribute which the weak and lowly are forced to pay to a power based on force and false differences and false values, yes, for you "Father" is all right with me. Yes . . .*

And he could feel the cloth of the sister's dress as he gently touched her arm and gazed into the great face; thinking, *There you sit after all this unhappy time, just looking down out of those sad old eyes, just looking way deep out of that beautiful old ugly wind-swept and storm-struck face. Yes, she's right, it's you all right; stretching out those long old weary legs like you've just been resting awhile before pulling yourself together again to go and try to bind up all these wounds that have festered and run and stunk in this land ever since they turned you back into stone. Yes, that's right, it's you just sitting and waiting and taking your well-earned ease, getting your second wind before getting up to do all over again what has been undone throughout all the betrayed years. Yes, it's you all right, just sitting and resting while you think out the mystery of how all this could be. Just puzzling out how all this could happen to a man after he had done all one man could possibly do and then take the consequences for having done his all. Yes, it's you— Sometimes, I guess . . . Sometimes . . .*

And then he was saying it aloud, his eyes held by the air of peace and perception born of suffering which emanated from the great face, replying to the sister now in a voice so low and husky that it sounded hardly like his own:

"Sometimes, yes . . . sometimes the good Lord . . . I say sometimes the good Lord accepts His own perfection and closes His eyes and goes ahead and takes His own good time and He makes Himself a *man*. Yes, and sometimes that man gets hold of the idea of what he's supposed to do in this world and he gets an idea of what it is possible for him to do, and that man lets that idea guide him as he grows and struggles and stumbles and sorrows until finally he comes into his own God-given shape and achieves his own individual and lonely place in this world. It don't happen often, oh no; but when it does, then even the stones will cry out in witness to his vision and the hills and towers shall echo his words and deeds and his example will live in the hearts of men forever—

"So there sits one right there. The Master doesn't make many like that because that kind of man is dangerous to the sloppy way the world moves. That kind of man loves the truth even more than he loves his life, or his wife, or his children, because he's been designated and set aside to do the hard tasks that have to be done. That kind of man will do what he sees as justice even if the earth yawns and swallows him down, and even then his deeds will survive and persist in the land forever. So you look at him awhile and be thankful that the Lord allowed such a man to touch our lives, even if it was only for a little while, then let us bow our heads and pray. Oh, no, not for him, because he did his part a long time ago. By word and by deed and by pen on paper he did the Lord's work and transformed the ground on which we stand. And in the words my slavery-born granddaddy taught me when I was a child:

> Ole Abe Lincoln digging in the sand,
> Swore he was nothing but a natural man.
> Ole Abe Lincoln chopping on a tree
> Swore a mighty oath he'd let the slaves go free.
> And he did!

So let us pray, not for him but for ourselves and for all those whose job it is to wear those great big shoes he left this nation to fill . . ."

And there in the sonorous shadows beneath his outspread arms they bowed their heads and prayed.

And to think, Hickman thought, stirring suddenly in his chair, *we had hoped to raise ourselves that kind of man . . .*

Opening his eyes in the semidarkness now, Hickman looked about him. While he had dozed, the nurse and security man had gone, leaving him alone with the man sleeping before him and now, still possessed by the experience at the Memorial, he looked upon the sleeping face before him and felt an anguished loss of empathy. He looked at the Senator's face half in shadow, half illuminated by a dim bed lamp as from a great distance, mist-hung and beclouded, thinking, *This is crazy; weird. All of it is. A crazy happening in a crazy place and I am the craziest of all. His being here is crazy, my being here is crazy, the reasons that brought us here are crazy as any coke-fiend's dream—and yet part of that craziness contains the hope that has sustained us for all these many years. . . . We just couldn't get around the hard fact that for a hope or an idea to become real it has to be embodied in a man, and men change and have wills and wear masks. So there he lies, wounded and brought low but still he's hiding from me, even in this condition he's still running, still hiding just as he did long ago— Only now I'll have to stay close and seek him out. For me it's Ho-ho, this a-way, woe-woe, that-a-way and the game is lost in the winning. Besides, they wouldn't let me leave here even if I told them that I only wanted to go back down home and forget all the things I've been forced by hope and faith to remember for all these years. What's worse, they won't want to hear the truth even if somebody could tell it. They're keeping me here for the wrong reasons and probably trying to keep him alive just because it seems the thing to do after they learned that someone faceless and out of nowhere could have the nerve and determination to do what that boy did in the place that he did it. So now they're shaking in their boots and looking for someone to give them the answer they want to hear. Not the truth, but some lie that will protect them from the truth. They really don't want to know the reason why or even the part of it I think I know because knowing will mean recognizing that they slipped up in places where they'd rather die than be caught slipping. A tint of skin—ha! They'd have to recognize that in this land there's a wild truth that they didn't blunt and couldn't bring to heel. . . . It's like a tamed river that rises suddenly in the night and washes away factories, houses, cities and all. Why can't they face the simple fact that you simply can't give one bunch of men the license to kill another bunch without punishment, without opening themselves up to being victims? The high as well as the low? Why can't they realize that when they dull their senses to the killing of one group of men they dull themselves to the preciousness of all human life? Yes, and why can't they realize that when they allow one group of men the freedom to kill us as evidence of their own superiority they're only setting the stage so that these killers will have to widen the game, since if anyone can kill niggers the only way left to prove themselves superior is by killing some white man high in the public eye? At-*

tack the head since the feet are too easy a target? We have suffered, trained ourselves against their provocations, have taken low and rejected their easy invitations to die, have kept to our own vision and for the most part put down the need for bloody retaliation as foolishness. But instead of being sat-isfied, they've sensed the life-preserving power of our humility and gone stark crazy to destroy even that! Hickman, how can you help despising these peo-ple? How can you resist praying for the day when they shall turn upon one another as they did once before and purge this land with blood? How can you resist praying for the day when the sacrificer will be sacrificed, when the many-headed beast will rend itself, tooth, nail and fiery tail, and die? . . .

How resist, Hickman? Why not pray for that?

Why not? Don't play me for a fool— Why not? Because this American cloth, the human cloth, is woven too fine for that, that's why. Because you are one of the few who knows where the cry of pain and anguish is still echoing and sounding over all that bloodletting and killing that set you free to set yourself free, that's why again. Because you know that we were born of sac-rifice, and that we have had to live by a different truth and that that truth is good and the vision of manhood it stands for is more human, more desir-able, more real. So you're in it, Hickman, and have been in it and there's no turning back. Besides, there's no single living man calling the tune to this crazy dance. Talking about playing it by ear, this is one time when everybody is playing it by ear because everybody in the band and out on the dance floor is as blind as a mole in a hole.

But why couldn't he have seen us, if only for a minute? Why? If he had, then all of this might not have happened. Oh, but it's the little things that find us out, the little things we refuse to do in order to avoid doing the big things that can save us. Well, there's nothing to do but wait and see. He's holding on even though Death is around somewhere close by—as he always is. I'll just have to try once more to outwait him, to outface him, even though I've seen enough even for an old preacher like me. . . .

CHAPTER 15

And I named him Bliss, Hickman thought, shaking his head. Resting back in his chair now, his hands shading his eyes from the light, he stared sadly at the man on the bed. Lord, he thought, here he is at last, stretched out on his bed of pain. Maybe his dying bed. After flying so far and climbing so high and now here. Just look at him, Lord. Why does this have to be? I know it's supposed to be this way because in spite of all our prayers it is; still, why does it have to be? I'm tired; for the first time I feel *old*-tired, and that's the truth. And this is what's become of our Bliss. He wasn't always ours and yet he first was mine. It wasn't easy either; far from easy. My hardest trial . . .

Hickman, maybe she was as Christian as she thought she was, maybe she was doing just what she had to do. . . . Then it seemed like Wickham said the Jews used to put it out there in K.C.: like killing your mother and father and then asking the court for mercy because you're an orphan. . . . Maybe she was driven, like those gamblers who couldn't stand to win. But just think about it—coming there wrapped in a black shawl through the rutted alley over all that broken glass shining in the starlight . . . past all those outhouses, yard-dogs, and chicken coops, long after dark had come down. Coming into *that* house at a time like that. Having the nerve, the ignorant, arrogant nerve to come in there after all that had happened. Hickman, do you know that that was *something?* Talking about Eliza crossing the ice!—Ha! But her—having the arrogance to come there after all that had happened.

Maybe she was innocent, Hickman.

Innocent?

I can't understand what people mean when they call somebody like her innocent. A man murders sixteen people on a city street at high noon he'd never seen before in his life, and they call him innocent? Maybe she had innocence *in* her but she was not *of* it. You couldn't believe it, could you?

The first, yes; all that about Mamma and Bob, I could. Because that terrible story has happened to so many that it's new only when it happens to you and to yours. You get to live with it like the springtime storms. So that it gets to be part of your sense of what life is. You learn to live with it like a man learns to live with only one arm and still get his work done—but not the Bliss part, *that* was the snapper, the stinger on the whip!

There you were, sitting again in the lamp-lit room feeling the weight of the rifle across your knees and a shotgun and two pistols on the table beside you; sitting dressed in your working tuxedo and your last white, iron-starched shirt, there staring into the blank wall at the end of time. Yes, and with death weighing down your mind. They'd already told you to get out of town, because you reminded them of what they'd done and you'd refused to go; yes, and maybe they recognized what it would cost some one or two of them at the least to force you, so after all those months you were still there. And instead of the end it was the beginning. Maybe it would help him to know. Yes, but in his condition it might *kill* him to know; the truth can humiliate those who refuse to meet it halfway. And I couldn't believe it myself when it was happening. You'd heard the expected knock on the door and said *Come in* with the rifle ready, taking a glance at the shotgun and the pistols on Mamma's table and at her Bible open to where you'd written the record, hers and Bob's; and with your own all written down to the month, feeling that this was to be the month, and just waiting for some unknown hand to write in the date. It's still waiting, after all these years, thank you, Master—my best-loved Bible to this day . . . I never thought of it before, but maybe it all began with my writing my death in the Book of Life, who knows? Yes, and with me sitting just like I'm sitting now . . . It's like I've never gotten up or recognized her presence in all these elapsed years. Ha! Sitting there in death's dry kingdom preparing myself for seven months to take a few of them along with me. Yes, ready to write your name in blood and to go to hell to pay for it. Hickman, you were too big and black for anybody to ever have called callow, but, man, you were *young!* Waiting for more liquored-up, ganged-up violence to come get you—and then seeing her standing there. There, Lord, after the double funeral and all, you thought you were seeing an evil vision, didn't you, Hickman? Yes, indeed, or at least that I had dozed. I shot bolt upright in the chair. Yes, you sure did. Standing there, looking at me out of those hollow eyes; not saying a word. I thought, *If I take a deep breath it'll go away,* then she stretched out her hand and kind of fluttered her fingers and tried to speak and I knew she was real. Shot up with a pistol in my hand, no longer surprised as Bob must have been, just dead sure her being there meant more deathblood to flow, and dead set to drown her in it along with me. A church organist, come to think of it. I never thought about that before, but, Hickman, look at the pattern it makes. . . . Tall and wrapped in a black shawl like those Mexican women in mourning, shaking her head at my pistol like I was some child she'd come upon in the woods about to go after a bear with an air rifle, saying,

No, no, it won't help us, Alonzo Hickman; you and I, we're beyond help; I had to come. Have you a woman here, a wife? You'd better call her because there isn't much time.

Just like that. And I felt the pistol throbbing beneath my hand like a hungry hound that's sighted game. So she wants me too, it's not simply the men who want me. She got Mamma and Robert and now she wants me. I'm supposed to be next. Less than seven months to pickle me in my pain and now she wants me. All right, if that's the deal, then all right. But she goes too. This time she'll lead the way.

There's not much time, she said.

All right.

Standing there, leaning—Lord, I can see her after all this time— leaning a little to one side with her fingers just touching the back of the chair as though she knew it was Mamma's, and so to her a rock- ing accusation, and me looking across the room at those black- smudged eyes in that chalk-white face, not even a tint of rouge to give it the color even a corpse would have nowadays . . . Me, look- ing at her and all dedicated to one last act and trying to hold on to my life and trying to live my life fully in those few seconds I felt I had left to live . . . Oh, Hickman, you'd been a rover and a rounder, but man, you were *young.* Young? Wasn't even born! No, and you couldn't see the side of a church house: There the lamp on the table was telling you to look at the facts of life staring you dead in the face and you seeing only the white paperish mask above that black lace shawl; standing there with that heavy Colt .45 so light in your hand that it seemed to be part of your own body; then her

coming toward me casting the shadow across the floor and the opposite wall and then across me, and that was the first time I noticed
that she was moving like a woman pushing a basket of clothes in a
wheelbarrow—that slow, heavy-laden walk, yet swift in the mind's
eye tightened with my feelings. Moving the omen or sign I couldn't
read. Yes, coming like a sick woman carrying a Christmas gift under
her coat to hide its shape from the children's eyes; seeing it floating
before her as I raised my hand towards her and still could not accept
what my eyes screamed to me was there and which my brain refused to deal with because it didn't want to give up its simple-
minded interpretation of the scene as through a glass darkly. Like
my eyes had jumped clean out of my head and flown up there beside
Papa's picture on the wall and were just sticking there watching and
recording and saving till later what I was trying to see through my
fingers or my skin. Yes, my brain refusing to accept the bold-faced
evidence because knowing that Bob hadn't been anywhere around
and wasn't the type. So it doubly wasn't him, and so making her big-
bellied ripeness a fact as meaningless to me as a mole on her shoulder blade beneath the shawl, or an offending tonsil that had been
removed and dropped in a jar of alcohol when she was twelve years
old.

And then we were joined together. Me without realizing it, sailing past the table with the lamp and the Bible and jamming the pistol barrel there where I knew the pain would wind slow and live
and give birth to death long after I was beyond the revenge of
screams . . . *Rest, Bliss— Wonder why they don't give him something to
really ease him?* . . .

Brother Bob, the only brother I had left; the good, true and duti-
ful son to Mamma while I the preacher's hellion son rambled and
gambled out there in the Territory, in Joplin, St. Joe, and K.C. You,
Hickman, that was you. Yes indeed. I had prayed for the end of her

and all like her, and for revenge, and here, I thought, was the answer. How many have shriveled with that pain? It was for me to
round out the order, to bring it to a halt, dead-end— But all the
time saying not a word to her, just thinking in snatches and hearing
breathing sounds, hers and mine. Standing there gripping her neck
in my hand like it was a bass fiddle's and with the sight of the barrel
pressing into the curving of her belly. Still refusing to recognize
what it all meant. Just trying to feel it all as I saw it, so that I could
say it all, so she could suffer it all and feel it keen in one red burst
like an abscessed tooth at midnight on a highballing train. No relief.
No red lights. No one to flag it down. So that she'd know what it
meant to let loose all that old viciousness out of the pit to strike
down some innocent man in his defenselessness; so that I could
throw her upon the same old disgusting sacrificial altar on all the ignored blood still screaming there for justice. Ay, so that in my anger
the high and mighty young priestess would for once sprawl where
her victim fell. . . . But those must have been the terms that came
afterwards, sitting in the chair; not then. Then was more blind feeling and thinking. I was swept backwards into deeper and older
depths of living, down where the life had gone out of the air and
only animals could breathe. Just why I didn't slap her backhanded
across the room and kick her into a corner like a bouncer or a
dance-hall floor-manager would have done any overbearing whore
who'd interrupted a dance just to win herself some cheap notoriety
at the expense of his good nature, I'll never know. Such I had
learned to watch without flinching back there in those places where
the music was more important than any violation of a woman's
womanliness by a man's male strength. I was sure a big heathen,
back there. *You sure were, although Lord knows you were taught better.*
Yes, but it's a fact that those women knew that the consequences of
fooling around like that was either a black eye, a lumped head or a

bruised behind. As Rush used to sing it, *Women all screaming murder. I never raised my hand. . . .* But that would have been too personal, I was beyond just that, I was as a thousand in my ache for vengeance. So I *must* have been changing. . . . Old clock used to work by weights passing one another, up and down. Maybe the shock of their death *had* to change me if I was to live even a second after I heard the news. Maybe the shock was so great that I knew even in my tongue-tied condition of wickedness that there was a moment when all heaven and hell had come together to purge men with the pill of eternal judgment, emptying us just like those old Greek folks were emptied after they committed some of their God-cursing crimes. And, in fact, the same kind of crime it was and just as holy-horrible even though we ignore it and let it happen year after year after year and no punishment or hope for justice. Thy must regulate thyself or take the pill. Ha, yes! But one day soon now it'll come back to us from strange places, seeking us out with sword and fire in a strange sunburned hand, saying, Here, you folks without recollection or feeling for the humiliation and the wasted blood, take some of old Dr. Time's Compound Cathartic. . . . *Thou shalt not bear false witness*— No, but that don't even begin to describe it, not what she did . . . they do. Maybe something like that went on under the old skin of my brain back there. Ah, Bliss, would knowing the story have helped you? . . . *With her breathing between my hands and me recognizing that here was more than we actually saw when we sat up there on the bandstand playing while they danced, or when we passed on the street and thought: That there now is a woman who flows with the moon and who squats in the morning like other women but who by law and custom can spread herself or smile only for those she knows as her own kind. She there is a woman who wills herself to believe that she's different from my women and better than my women simply by being born and not because of anything she can do that's more womanly or wifely or motherly, but who can prove she is*

what she's supposed to be when the chips are down only by letting hell yell
rape from the pit between her thighs and then pointing her lying finger at
me. Talking about having the power of life and death! Maybe the
shock of Bob's death—poor Mamma was old and sick and wore out
with trouble, so I had faced up to her leaving us before long, I had
only hoped to see her once more before— But Bob, Lord, their
doing that to him was such a shock that even in my lost condition I
understood that even if she, there in the palm of my hand and
curved hard against the pistol barrel, even if she were the finest of
the fine, a lady fair and gentle-wayed was now become a pus pot
slopping over with man's old calcified evil and corruption. What
kind of love and respect is that—raised up like a golden cow just to
plunge then in the raising lower than those poor whores perform-
ing daisy-chain circuses in dope-fiend cathouses and West Coast
opium dens. Lower! Those poor lost souls couldn't touch the
downright obscenity of one of these. Not even the ones who per-
verted themselves with dogs and goats before flyspecked spotlights
for money and then moved from table to table lifting their tips from
dirty, liquor-ringed tabletops with the shaved, raw, puffed, dry,
slack-mouthed lips of their corrupted and outraged businesses.
Those shameless whores with their guts fish-mouthing for filthy old
limp and wrinkled dollar bills that they had to straddle the corners
of the tables and grind down to in order to retrieve— No, Hickman, not even these— And back there you had seen life raw. You
had seen the bottom of the bucket and the hole in the bottom of the
bucket and the cruel jagged edges of the hole. Yes, and seen the bitter lees lying on the bottom, the very dregs and under the gritty
bottom level of the dregs those poor lost souls. But none so lost and
bound for perdition on Perdido Street could touch those who had
been armed with the power to kill with *that* lying cry. . . .

Lord, Hickman, I wonder what you'd done if she had been a man?

You know what you would've done; that's why women could do so much good if they would, they're meant to make us men put on brakes, meant to break our headlong pace. Ay! but anyone seeing us that night would have been justified in calling for the straitjackets! This here is insanity, I told myself. This here is the instant before you foam at the mouth and bite off your tongue; the split second when you see the man pull the trigger just five feet away and when you realize still without pain that you have been hit because you can't hear the gun go off and then he's turning cartwheels with the gun still pointing straight at you. . . . In Tulsa, that was, and lucky I threw my trombone and the bullet went through my shoulder. . . . Oh yes, indeed. That was me back there—wild and reckless. Who used to hit the poolroom's swinging doors yelling,

> *Fee fi fo fum*
> *Who wants to shoot the devil one?*
> *My name is Peter Wheatstraw,*
> *I'm the devil's son-in-law,*
> *Lord, God Stingerroy!*

Both of us must have risen up about three feet off the floor and been standing there in the air by now, because no floor in Alabama could support such goings-on. No, and no one could live through it without some modification of his deepest soul. So I was already changing, I suppose. Hearing her saying like someone in a trance:

If you've got to do it, go ahead; only hurry. But it won't help either of us, Alonzo Hickman, it wouldn't help a bit and I'm not worth what it'll cost you. . . .

And me repeating, *He didn't do it; Robert didn't do it and you know dam' well he didn't do it. . . .*

That's right, I lied. You don't have to say it again because I acknowledge it.

Just breathing, nervous between my hands like a scared convert standing chest-deep in the baptismal water. Then that word *lied* started banging around in my head. Like when you put a coin in one of those jukes, yes, and it takes a while before the machinery goes into action, then all of a sudden—wham! the red and blue lights go on and the sound comes blaring out:

Woman, is all you can say is that you lied? What's that word got to do with it? If you're going to use these last minutes to talk, then say something. Say you burned up all the cotton and polluted the waterworks. Say that you dried up all the cows; that you spread the hoof-and-mouth disease through-out the state and gave all the doctors the bleeding piles. Even that you brought everybody down with the galloping consumption and the sugar di-abetes— But don't come here telling me that you lied. Everybody, including the littlest children, know that you lied—what's all this death got to do with the truth?

What? What?

Tell me that you're responsible for the Johnstown flood.

What?

. . . That you can stir up cyclones just by waving your naked heels in the air. Tell me that you breathe fire and brimstone from your belly every time the moon comes full—but don't come talking about you lied! Don't you re-alize what you did?

Yes—shaking her head. Yes, can't you see that I'm here? I'm not a loose woman. . . . . I'm from a good family. . . . . I'm a Christian!

You're a *what?*

Yes, a *Christian.* I lied. Yes. I bore false witness and caused death. Yes, and I'm a murderess. Can't you see that I understand? How could I help but know? I'm here. Can't you see, I'm *here.* . . .

And Lord knows, she was. . . .

You couldn't deal with that about her being a Christian, could you A.Z. Ho, ho! No, she could just as well said she was the head

chief Rabbi of Warsaw, or the Queen of Sheba . . . or Madame Sis-
eretta Jones. So I ignored that one.

I said: Why Bob? You've been knowing me from when we were
children, but you didn't know him from Adam's off ox. . . .

But it wasn't him. I didn't wish to hurt him. Nor anyone. Can't
you understand that, Alonzo Hickman? You have to try. He just
didn't exist for me. He was just a name; just a name which by saying I could protect someone more precious to me than myself or
mother or father, or anything he and I might have together. But I
wanted only to protect my own. Not to destroy anybody. It was
fate. Please, is there a woman here? There's very little time. . . .

*A woman? Won't I be enough for you this time? Do you have to have an-
other woman as well as another man? Don't you know that what you did has
killed the only woman of this house, my mother?*

*Yes, I heard. You don't have to remind me. I'm here. I've put myself in
your hands but it's still beyond the two of us. Still I tell you, if you don't
hurry and shoot you'd better hurry and get a woman because you're going to
have too much on your hands for any man. . . .*

And even in the hard cold center of my anger I was confounded.
I simply couldn't link all that death back to life. No, I couldn't fit the
links into a chain. Said:

Another woman for what? To lay out our bodies? You want a
woman for that? Don't worry about it, because I'm putting a hot
bullet through that oil lamp sitting right there on the table; we
won't need her. Besides, we'll both be in hell watching the confusion long before she could even get here.

Oh, I was already feasting on revenge and sacrifice, telling myself: Those eyes for Bob's eyes; that skin for Bob's flayed skin; those
teeth for Bob's knocked-out teeth; those fingers for his dismem-
bered hands. And remembering what they had done with their
knives I asked myself, But what can I take that can replace his wasted

seed and all that's now a barbaric souvenir floating in a fruit jar of alcohol and being shown off in their barbershops and lodge halls and in the judge's chambers down at the courthouse? And then beginning to really see, my own eyes betraying my aim and my understanding growing and making me say,

Bob's; you know dam' well it can't be Bob's.

I tell you I didn't know him, she said. Can't you get a woman?

I said, Whose is it then?

All I can tell you is that it wasn't your brother. It's cost too much my trying not to tell to tell it now. But not his . . . He had nothing to do with it. . . .

Just like that. So Hickman, maybe *that's* when you started to change. It was like seeing all of a sudden the air falling apart so that you could recognize the separate gases and molecules that made up its substance and which you'd have to see gather quick and mix together again if you meant to continue breathing. She had been protecting her secret and her man. That's all it was for her. All of that destruction just to deny that little growing bit of truth. Gone and set fire to the whole house just to hide where she'd spilled a little grease on the rug. Talk about all those lives ground up to build the Pyramids, she'd have destroyed the nation just to protect her pride and reputation in that little old town. Slop the juice and cause a flood. Fire is more like it. So naturally she couldn't go to a doctor for help and in confidence. Not after screaming Robert's name, because then everybody would have yelled Bliss's question even before he could draw his first living breath. Just as surely as Mary had a baby, King Herod had him a daughter; thousands of 'em.

Where could she go? So not to her doctor, or to her pastor; both those ministering roles were scratched from the book and denied. Neither to her mother, nor to her father; nor to her sister or to any friends or kinfolks. Neither could she go to any maidservant, to no black cook or washerwoman, nor to any of our preachers, teachers, or doctors. The blind man could stand on the corner and cry, and folks would drop money in his cup so they could ignore his pain, but she bred and spread muteness and blindness and deafness. That poor girl had cut herself loose from both sides. She must have thought about each and every grown person in the whole town, like someone turning over each and every pebble on a mile-square stretch of seashore, hoping to find just one that would give her relief from that terrible loneliness. Misery doesn't just love company, it reaches out for its own through all the man-erected walls and then claims its own.

So *I* had to be the one. Me, the least likely, the anyone-else-but: She finally sifted the grains down to me. Oh, she could be willful and blot Bob out without ever bothering to think that there was a body attached to his name and life in that body, she could do it and be beyond the consequences—but now her own belly said, Let the disgusting, foul-aired truth come clean, and it turned her wrong-side out. Or maybe right-side, because she must have had to have more than simple arrogant nerve to come there that night.

But to who else could she go, Hickman? Who but to the one who had suffered deep down to the bottom of the hole, down where there's nothing to do but come floating up lifting you in his own arms into the air, or die? Oh, John the Baptist was a diver into those lonely depths, I do believe. I *do* believe. . . . In all that frenzied agitated searching she must have been like a man being chased West so hard and fast that he stumbles and falls into the ocean and has either got to swim or sink. Don't tell me a human don't live by instinct when he reaches bottom, because when he's just about to go to pieces his instinct tries to guide him to where he can save himself. That's when God shows you His face. That's when in a split second you're about to be nothing and you have a flash of a chance to be something. She must have been sore desperate, like backed into the corner of a red-hot oven. Hickman, that was when your heart stopped beating like a run-down clock. Oh, yes; and that's when you got your first peep through the crack in the wall of life and saw hell laughing like a gang of drunk farmers watching a dogfight on a country road. All at once you were standing there smelling her sour, feverish white woman's breath mixed up with that sweet soap they used to use and you were hearing the hellish yelling and tearing around and about of a million or so crazy folks. Ha, yes! That's when the alphabet in your poor brain was so shaken up that the letters started to fall out and spell "hope," "faith," and "charity"—it would take time for them to fall all the way into place, so you could recognize it, but it was beginning to happen. Yes, it was happening even while you were saying:

So now you come to me. Out of all the rest you come to me. I guess you think that old lady who died doesn't mean anything to me because she was only a black man's old worn-out mother who was soon to die anyway. I guess I'm supposed to forget about her. So now here you come to me after all that to demand that I get you aid to perpetuate all that you have done without even thinking. So I'm to stand here on the spot and switch over from the animal you consider me to be to the human you've decided I could never be, so that I can be understanding and forgiving— Woman, do you think I'm Jesus Christ? Do you think a man like me is even interested in the idea of trying to be Christ-like? Hell, my papa was a preacher while I'm a horn-blowing gambler. Do you think that after being the son of a black preacher in this swamp of a country I'd let you put me in the position of trying to act like Christ? Make it easy for you to destroy mine and me without even the need to remember, and humiliate mine and me, and, dam' you, expect me to understand and forgive you and then minister to your needs? Destroy me and mine so that you can cast me down into corruption and the grave and then dig me up next week so that I can serve you. Tell me, what kind of endless, bottomless, blind store of forgiveness and understanding am I supposed to have? Just tell me where I'm suppose to carry it. What kind of meat and bread am I suppose to eat in order to nourish it?

Hickman, you didn't know it at the time but when you started talking she had shifted out of your hands and put you into hers. She really had you then. You were talking so fast you were foaming at the mouth, but that instinct and life inside her had reached out and tagged you and you were It. A pair of purple smears sagging shuteyed in my hands and me standing there holding her and unable to let her fall. . . . If we ever learn to feel real revulsion of the flesh—any flesh—that's when hell will truly erupt down here and the whole unhappy history become an insane waste; if we ever learn to hate the mere rind in the same way we ignore the spirit and the heart and the hopeful possibility underneath. . . . And there I stood—me, cursing her for using a woman's weakness as a club to kill me there and to deny me anger and hate because I was my mother's boy child and my father's son whom they had brought up on the ideas and standards that made any human beings bearable one to the other. . . . That woman, coming there using my very black manhood to deny me grief and to deny me love and to deny me thirst and hunger and weakness and hope and joy—denying me even denial and rejection and contempt and vindictiveness against any claim her kind had upon mine . . . denying me even the need for anger or life. There she'd been feeding two for all those months and now sagging in my hands like the shadow of some little ole frightened bird about to take off and fly.

And then it really started, and me still cursing but helpless before the rhythm of those pains that started pulsing from him to her to me, as though some coked-up drummer was beating his snares inside her belly and I was being forced against my will to play or dance, and dance or play, even if I had nothing left but bleeding stumps for arms and legs. *Me,* a full-grown man crying, "Mamma, Mamma," with tears running down my face, while I was getting her to bed. Me, crying helpless at a time like that, as though my body had somehow to register a protest against what I was being forced to do, and getting her into Mamma's bed and starting to uncover all that that Bob had died for not even thinking about uncovering: white and blue-veined and bulging like that boa constrictor I saw back there during my days with the circus band after it had swallowed a lamb. Yes, and went about dressing her just the same in one of Mamma's gowns. Then going on to tear Mamma's sheets, and pouring the water I'd heated for my own last bath in case the men had come. . . . . Yes, almost convinced that I was in a dream. Too mad and outraged now to be afraid that she had been followed and still determined to make small-town history in blood. Determined, after letting out the life that bulged her belly, to let out the life that had drained me dry of love.

Oh, ashamed too; shamed and too outraged with myself to call a woman to come do the midwife's work. Asking myself, Man, where's your dignity, where's your pride? Where, at what point is my hate spilling out between my hands and my determination? What do you *call this* situation? Who's doing this to me? Who's got me hypnotized? And all the while doing the whole thing myself in spite of myself: Holding the damp cloth to her brow and placing the pillow beneath her quivering backside to ease and aid the flesh in its quaking and quickening, and holding firm to her weaving hands while she gave birth to that bawling, boiled-red and glistening baby flesh. Watching my own big black hands going in and out of those forbidden places, ha! into the rushing fluids, and despising it all. No mercy in my heart, Lord, no! Only the choking strangulation of some cord of kinship stronger and deeper than blood, hate or heart-break. And stopped from killing the two of us only by the third that was coming screaming in all his innocent-evil bewilderment into that death house. . . . Ho! if anyone passing in the night had heard him cry. . . . They had me battling against myself, but I went all the way, I suppose by then to prove to myself, even to the Lord, that I was mean enough to play the cards that life had dealt me and still stick to my will. They say a doctor is a butcher underneath, it's a wonder I didn't try to use those pistol barrels for forceps— No, but I took Papa's old straight-edged razor and boiled the blade to steril-ize it and divided the fruit from the tree. Yes, and tied up his navel cord with Mamma's embroidery thread, fixed his first belly band. Him, Bliss. Wiped his unseeing eyes and anointed his body with oil. You, Bliss. I wrapped you in the sheet around and placed you in the crook of her sleeping arm and saw her try after all of that to smile. Her face all beaded over with sweat and I wiped that too away; then sat way back in Mamma's rocking chair, just looking at them, dazed and defiant.

I was too tired to sleep or rest and my mind wouldn't stop. There she was, relieved of her burden and sleeping like a peaceful child, and him beside her with his little fists already balled up for the fight of life. I couldn't look at him too steady either. There was that one bright drop of blood on the white sheet and I watched it growing dark, thinking: Now there's two, one to accuse me and the other to hang me; one to point the finger and the other to rise up and shoot me down, or pull the rope to break my neck. Yes, and because of these there is no one of my own to come cut me down. There they are in Mamma's own bed, outraged and outrageous. I started think-ing about those old Hebrew soldiers who use to leave their prison-ers castrated on the battlefield—but for what Jehovah could I even

play Abraham to that little Isaac? Lord, my eyes must've been blood-
shot with my thoughts and frustrations. And there Bliss was, puckered up and so new he looked like if you were to drop him he would
bounce like a rubber ball. . . .

How long did I sit there? Nobody would come to mark the passage of time and I had long ago drawn the shades and let the clock
run down and she'd made me a pariah even to my own. Pariah and
midwife too, and raped me of my will and my manhood. Dehuman-
ized my human needs. Told myself, it won't stop here. When she
gets her strength she'll scream again. Yes, but now the life is out of
there and she'd beat me with a little child. . . . *Hickman, you were
crazy.* Yes, but I was sane too; because what I thought there was true,
though it took time to learn it in. She had torn me out of my heathen freedom so she could save herself, that was the truth. And all
with that baby. With just that little seven-pound rabbit. Not even a
few minutes of pleasure or relief either. Which was the last thing I
would have thought about. She wasn't even good-looking, with that
thin nose and high forehead; with just that ugly-sounding way of
talking through her lips and nostrils. I knew her before her skirts
went down, gangle-legging along the street like a newborn foal,
trying to walk with class. And him not even brown so that I could
have made some sensible meaning out of her coming here to me;
just nothing definite, just baby-mouse-red and wrinkled up like a
monkey with a strawberry rash. And me such a slave to what a
human is supposed to be that I couldn't refuse to help him into the
world. Helped him when I should, according to the way I felt then,
have left him stranded and choking with the cord wrapped around
his neck when her mammy-waters burst.

Now she's sleeping, I thought. Now she's in her woman's exhaus-
tion, resting out of time like a stranger to both good and evil—
while here I am, tired and feeling with no relief or rest inside me or

outside me. She, resting up so she can scream again and they'll hear it all the way to the State House. Yes, but now the life is out I'm going to put us all to sleep. I mean to clear the earth of just this one bit of corruption. Which is all one can do, just clean up his own mess or that which is dumped on top of him when he has the chance. . . . Just look at them sleeping there, fruit of all this old cancerous wrong. Why isn't he brown or black or kinky, so that I could see some logic in her coming here? At least allow me to see the logic of a mare neighing help from a groom who happened to be passing her stall during her foaling time. Oh no, but coming here to me . . . Easy, Hickman, don't fight old battles. Maybe it was the way the sacred decided to show Himself. Would you at this age still criticize God?

Lord, O Lord, you must have been preparing me all those twenty-six years for that ordeal; giving me this great tub of guts and muscle and deep, windy lungs and this big keg-sized head and all that animal strength I used to have and which I thought was simply meant for holding all the food and drink I loved so well and to contain all the wind necessary to blow my horn and to sing all night long, sure; and for the enjoyment of women and the pleasures of sin. . . . Ah, but right then and there I learned that you had really given me all that simply so I could contain and survive all I was to feel sitting there through those awful hours.

Just sitting there and hating. Just sitting there looking at the two generations of them in the ease of their sleeping, and thinking back three generations more of my people's tribulations and trying to solve the puzzle of that long-drawn-out continuation of abuse. That and why the three of us were thrown together in my house of shame and sorrow. It was a brain-breaker and a caustic in the naked eye all right, and the longer I sat there the stranger it seemed. I guess it couldn't have been stranger than if one of Job's boils had started addressing him, saying, "Look here now, Job; this here is your head-chief boil speaking to you. You just tell me my name and I'll jump off your neck and take all the rest of the boils along with me." Yes, and ole Job too used to trouble and straitjacketed in misery by then to even be surprised to learn that a boil could talk—even one of *his* boils—only wondering why his kin or hair or toenails or something didn't speak up and tell the boil to be silent in the presence of the Lord. Because, Master, you must have been there with me at the time, and probably with a sad smile on your face. Even after Mamma and Robert it was like waking up on mornings in some Territory town like Guthrie in the old days and discovering that my trombone mouthpiece had grown to my lips and my good right arm changed into a slide, but with no bell anywhere to let out the sound. . . . Hickman, you were in a fix. You and those two strangers in the most unlikely place in the world and you the strangest of all.

Yes, with the baby mewling and raising the dickens and me having to put him to that thin, white, blue-veined tit to suck. Yes, having to guide his red little gums to that blighted raspberry of a nipple so I wouldn't have to listen to him crying for a while. And my having to be gentle, not like a nursemaid who loves a child enough to give it a good hard pinch in the side when it vexes her too much, but just because of the murder in my heart having to be gentlest of the gentle. Just because he was a baby and me a man full of hate; and gentle with her because aside from everything else, she was a mother lying in the bed where my own mother had once lain. It was like the Lord had said, "Hickman, I'm starting you out right here— with the flesh and with Eden and Christmas squeezed together. Never mind the spirit and justice and right and wrong—or time— just now you're outside all that because this is a beginning. So, starting right here, what will you do about the *flesh?* That's what you have to wrestle with." He had called me and I had nothing in the hole and was in too far to pass and still couldn't take the trick by using the baby's life as my ace, no matter whether he were dealt in spades or in hearts.

So now I had to cook for her. Go out and get that little boy, Raymond, to go bring me milk and bread and meat from the store, pretending it was for his mamma, and me picking the vegetables that Robert had planted for Mamma's needs and then stand over the stove and prepare the meal and then feed it to her spoon by spoon. Yeah, and remembering . . . *A little bit of poison helped her along,* that old slave-time line, and coming as close to breaking out of my despair and grinning as I ever did for a long, long time. But still granting nothing to the facts. So all right, I told myself, you're just fattening her for the time she can understand what she did and pay for it. You just be patient, just count the rest until your solo comes up. This rhythm won't stop until you take your break; just keep counting the one-two-three-fours, the two-two-three-fours, the three-two-three-fours. . . .

So I didn't eat, only took water and a few sips of whiskey, never leaving the house, knocking on the windowpane in the afternoons to get little Raymond to go to the store, or to stand out on the back porch in the dark to get some fresh air. And with all that feeding and clumsy, grudging ministering to them I wouldn't let myself think a second about life and living, only about dying. About how to kill and the way our bodies would look when they found us. And the quickest way to get it over with, how the flames would announce the news in the night. Whether to just let them find us or to have little Raymond take a note to Mamma's pastor to tell the folks to keep off the streets . . .

Everything, but never whether I could save myself because that would have meant to run and I didn't believe I had anything left to run for.

Ah, but Hickman, you were caught deaf and blind. With eyes that saw not, and ears that heard nothing but the drums of revenge. And there was that baby growing more human every second nudging his way into your awareness and making his claim upon you, and her crying all the time—in fact more than the baby did. You had fallen into the great hole and they'd dropped the shuck in on you. There was simply too much building up inside of you for clear vision. I guess if I could have played I might have found some relief, but I couldn't play, even if I hadn't left my horn in Dallas when I got the word. And I couldn't sing and if I had after all she'd done to me I'd probably sung falsetto. Then came the day . . .

Poor Bliss, the terrible thing is that even if I told you all this, I still couldn't tell who your daddy was, or even if you have any of our blood in your veins. . . . Like when I was a boy and guessed the number of all those beans in that jar they had in that grocery window and they wouldn't give me the prize because one wasn't a bean, they said, but a rock! What a bunch of rascals. Ha! Ha! So outrageous that I just grinned and they had to laugh at their own bogusness. Gave me a candy bar . . . No, I'd still have to tell him as I told myself in the days that were to come: that who the man was was made beside the point by all that happened. Bliss started right there in that pain-filled room—or back when the fish grew lungs and left the sea. You don't reject Jesus because somebody calls Joseph a confidence man or Mary a whore; the spears and the cross and the crime were real and so was the pain. . . . So then came the day when I started in from the kitchen to find her sitting on the side of the bed, her bare bony feet on the bare boards of the floor as she sat there all heavy-breasted in Mamma's flannel nightgown; her hair swinging over her shoulder in one big braid and with eyes all pale in her sallow skin; and all weak-voiced, saying—

Listen, Alonzo Hickman, the time has come for me to leave.

Leave, I said, who told you you were ever going to leave here?

Yes, I know, but he's growing to me too fast. So if I'm ever to leave I must do it now. . . .

What makes you think . . .

No, let me tell you why I came here. . . .

Yes, I said. As though I don't know already; you tell me. Just why, other than the fact that you had no damn where else to turn?

Don't you be so sure, Alonzo Hickman. And don't quarrel with me after helping me. There's more to it than you think. . . .

So why? I'm listening.

I came to give you back your brother, do you understand?

You *what!*

Yes, it's true. I never knew your brother and I meant him no special harm. It was just that I am what I am and I was in trouble and so desperate that I couldn't feel beyond my heart. You must understand, because it's true and it's a truth that's cost us both all this. —No, let me finish. So now you must take the baby . . .

WHO?

. . . take him and keep him and bring him up as your own, looking at her feet, that braid swinging across her breast . . .

WHO? I said. WHO?

It's the only way, Alonzo Hickman. And don't just stand there in that doorway saying "Who" like that. Who else can save us both? I mean you. It's the only way. After what I've done you'll need to have him as much as I need to give him up. Take him, let him share your Negro life and whatever it is that allowed you to help us all these days. Let him learn to share the forgiveness your life has taught you to squeeze from it. No, listen: I've learned something; you won't believe me, but I have. You'll see. And you'll need him to help prevent you from destroying yourself with bitterness. With me he'll only be the cause of more trouble and shame and later it'll hurt him. . . .

And you expect me . . .

Yes, and you can. You have the strength and the breadth of spirit. I didn't know it when I came here, I was just desperate. But I've seen you hold him, I've caught the look in your eyes. Yes, you can do it. Few could but you can. So I want you to have him—and don't think I don't love him already at least as much as I love my own mother, or that I don't love his father. I do, only his father doesn't know about him; he's far away, and unless I do something to undo a little of what I've done there'll never be a chance for us. I could go to him— Oh, Alonzo Hickman, nothing ever stops; it divides and multiplies, and I guess sometimes it gets ground down to superfine, but it doesn't just blow away. Certainly none of the things between us shall. So you must take him. Later there'll be money and I'll get it to you. I'll help you bring him up and pay for his education. Somewhere in the North, maybe. He'll be intelligent like his father and he deserves a chance . . . and I'll see that you're taken care of. . . .

And I thought, So now I've got to be a pimp too. First animal, then nursemaid and now pimp, seeing her shake her head again:

No, please don't speak yet. I must do this for both of us. . . .

And you think that that child there can do all that?

No, but he's all I have—unless you still want my life. And if you take that, somebody will still have to take him. You don't just help a child to be born and then leave it alone. So very well, if you mean to kill me, all right, but could you destroy something as weak as that, as helpless as that?

I have killed snakes.

A snake? Can you even with death in your eyes call him a snake? Can you? Can you, Alonzo Hickman?

Ha! Hickman, and you couldn't. No, but if your heart had been weak I would have died right there of the sheer, downright nerve of

it. Here I had been pushed even in Alabama. Well, God never fixed
the dice against anybody, we have to believe that. His way may be
mysterious but he's got no grudge against the infants, not even the
misbegotten. It's a wonder I didn't split right down the middle and
step out of my old skin right then and there; because even after all
these years I don't see how I stood there in that doorway and took
it all without exploding. And yet, there we were, talking calm and
low like two folks who arrived late at the services and were waiting
in the vestibule of the church. She sitting on the edge of the bed,
kinda leaning forward, with arms spread out to the side and gripping the bedclothes to support herself. Still weak but with her crazy
woman's mind all set. And me telling myself that I was waiting to
learn just how far she intended to follow the trail of talk she'd
blazed before I would set the house afire; saying:

So supposing I say all right—what are you going to call him?

You mean what shall we name him?

Yes.

It's not for me to do, he's yours now. But why not Robert Hickman?

No!

Then just Robert, and you give him a last name. But I name him
Robert as he should be . . .

Just like that. She couldn't face life with him, wanted to give him
to me but wanted me to always remember all the circumstances
that brought him to me. So there it was. Like a payday, when all the
sweating and aching labor that went into a dirty job is reduced to
some pieces of dirty paper and silver and coppers, which the hate-
ful bossman handed to you in a little white envelope. As though that
was the end of it and Monday would never come to start you out all
over again. It was too much for me. I just listened to her and then
backed out of the doorway and went and lay down and tried to think

it clear. Ha! Hickman, you had wanted a life for a life and the relief of drowning your humiliation and grief in blood, and now this flawed-hearted woman was offering you two lives—your own, and his young life to train. Here was a chance to prove that there was something in this world stronger than all their ignorant superstition about blood and ghosts—as though half a town was a stud farm and the other half a jungle. Maybe the baby *could* redeem her and me my failure of revenge and my softness of heart, and help us all (was it here, Hickman, that you began to dream?). Either that or lead him along the trail where I had been and watch him grow into the wickedness his folks had mapped out for him. I thought, *I'll call him Bliss, because they say that's what ignorance is.* Yes, and little did I real-ize that it was the name of the old heathen life I had already lost.

So she got her way. She asked the impossible of a bitter man and it worked; I let her walk out of that house and disappear. Let her stay around and nurse the baby until dark, four or five hours more, and still let her leave. Let her come in crying and put him in my arms then walk out of the back door and gone. Oh, thank the Lord, I let her. Ah, but who but those who know life would believe that out of that came this? That out of that bed came this bed; that out of that sitting and a-rocking came this remembering, and this gold cross on my old watch chain?

That was the end of the old life for me, though I didn't know it at the time. But what does a man ever know about what's happening to him? She came in there heavy and when she went out I had his weight on *my* hands. What on earth was I going to do with a baby? I wasn't done with rambling, the boys were waiting for me out in Dallas. I hadn't ever met a woman I thought I'd want to marry, and later when I did she wouldn't have me because she insisted I had been laying around with a white gal because she thought I was trav-eling with a half-white baby. So not only had the woman placed a child on my hands, she made me a bachelor. And maybe after that night, after seeing what a woman could be, after that revelation of their boundless nerve and infinite will to turn a man's feelings into mush and rubber, I had lost the true will to join with one forever in matrimony. I was still young and full of strength but after that I could only come so close and no closer. I had been hit but I hadn't discovered how bad was the damage. Master, did you smile? Did you say, "Where's your pride now, young man? Did you say, "*How now, Hickman, can you hear my lambs a-crying? You've got to do something, son; you can't stand on the air much longer. How now, Hickman?*"

And didn't I try to get away! I must have sat there for hours, numbed. Then when the realization struck me I got up and put him in the bed with a bottle and went to Beulah's and ordered a pitcher of corn, broke in the door because she didn't want me in there and all the others leaving when they saw who I was. And I drank it and couldn't feel it so I left there. And walking down the railroad tracks, between the two shining rails not caring if a manifest struck me down or if I could get to Atlanta in one piece, stumbling between the gleaming rails like a man in a trance. Then finding myself at Jack's place and beginning to shoot craps with those farmhands and winning all the money and having to break that one-eyed boy's arm when he came at me with his blade after my winning with their own dice. Then stumbling out of there into another dive and then another, drinking and brawling, but always seeing that baby reaching out for me with his little hands that were growing stronger and stronger the farther I moved away from him. Till I could feel him snatching me back to the room as a dog leaping the length of his chain is snatched back to the stake driven in the ground.

That little ole baby, that li'l ole Bliss. So I had to go back and get him. Made up my mind. Slept all day and left the next night with him in a satchel. That was the beginning. Took him to Mobile where we stayed in a shack on the river. And him getting sick there, almost dying and getting him a doctor and pulling him through with the help of God; still mixed up over why I was trying to save him but needing to bad enough to learn to pray. The Master must have really smiled then, but I was still trying to leap my chain. Running out of money in Dallas because the boys were afraid to play with me because they had heard about Robert and Mamma and then I show up with the baby and they didn't know who would come looking for me and I wouldn't explain a thing. Pride, that's what it was, but I said that if they couldn't take me back for my way with a horn then they didn't need to know anything else about me. So I shined shoes and I swept the floors and cleaned the spittoons in that barbershop and paid for our room and his milk and my whiskey. Then Felix came and told me about Reverend McDuffie being in town and needing a musician for his tent meetings and I began playing my music for the Lord. That was Bliss then. He couldn't remember any of that even if he hadn't willed himself to forget us; now it was too far back. I lied that he was my dead sister's child and the ladies were kind and looked after him while I played and we were always traveling and that made it easier for me. Then a year old and never from my side, me still mixed up in my emotions about him but always having him with me. . . . Had to leave Memphis on a freight train once and just managed to grab a bottle of milk to feed him and them right behind me for kidnapping, running over those cinders with him under my arm like a bear cutting out with a squealing pig. Lord, but I could really pick 'em up and put 'em down in those days, kicking up dust for a fare-thee-well and making that last boxcar just in time. Poor little fellow, he didn't know what it was all about. Stripped the paper from the boxcar walls to make him a bed then setting there with the car bumping under me wondering why I hadn't let them have him and be free. . . . But what could I have told them, when any part of the truth meant trouble? Master, did you grin? So we went rolling through the land over the rhythm of those wheels clicking along the tracks and when he started to cry, me lullabying him "Make Me a Pallet on the Floor" till we were long gone to Waycross.

Then gradually beginning to find my way, finding the path in the fog, getting my feet on the earth and my head in the sky. Yes, my heathen freedom gone, I followed the only thing I really knew about, my music. Followed it, right into the pulpit at last. Had found a sanctuary where all babies could grow without too much questioning as to where they came from. After all, I testified to my sins before a crowd and sat down at the welcome table and learned to open up my heart—and I was heard.

They took us in and they loved him. That was Bliss then. All the love we gave him. Now no trust for me; none of us, even though we kept the faith through all those watchful and graveling years. We held steady, stood firm in face of everything; even after he ran away and we picked up his trail. I had been claimed by then and they loved him. Foolish to do but all those from the old evangelizing days felt the same need I felt to watch him travel and to hope for him and to learn. Yes, I guess we've been like a bunch of decrepit detectives trailing out of love. We didn't even have to think about it or talk it over, we all just missed him and keep talking about him and seeking for him here and there. Lord, but we missed little Bliss. We missed his promise, I guess, and we were full of sorrow over his leaving us that way, just up and gone without a word. So we kept looking for him and telling all those who had heard him when he was traveling with me throughout the country to keep a lookout. Some thought he had been kidnapped and some that he was dead, and others that his people had come and taken him away—though they didn't know who his people were and were too respectful to ask me about him.

So we started looking and asking questions, all the chauffeurs and Pullman porters and waiters, anybody who traveled in their work—till finally we picked up his trail again and I knew that it wouldn't do any good to go to him and say, Come home, we miss you, Bliss; and we need you. Oh no, he was on another track by then and it was up to him to miss us in his heart and need us. So we just watched and waited.

Someone was always near him to watch him; maids and butlers, dining-car waiters, cooks—anybody who traveled, anybody who could keep him in our sights. Even a few of the younger ones were recruited; a few every year or so given hints that he was one of us, telling them just enough so that they could feel the mystery and start to watching him and reporting back. And all of it building up our amazement. Even when what he did left our hopes pretty weak. I guess we hoped for the Prodigal's return. But in a country like this, where prodigal boys have so much that they can do and get that they can never waste it all which makes it easier for them to forget where home is and that made our hoping and waiting a true test of our faith or at least our love. There he lies, worth about three million dollars, I understand, and ran away with five saved dollars and a leatherbound Bible. Lord, I could laugh at the "laugh-cry" of it and I could cry sure enough right now. I was pretty bad when that child started shooting, pretty hysterical. But Lord forgive me for violating my manliness, because it was little Bliss I saw going down. Instead of this one lying here I saw a little boy with the white Bible as in a waking vision. I'm getting old, but how is a man who's had to do with children but only had one child suppose to act when he sees such as we were witness to? Yes, and who'll be a witness for my grief, my awful burden? Who, when nobody knows the full story? Still the old-timers were with me and they prayed that he'd find his way back home! Bliss. All the old ones and some of the young and some of the old ones committed so long ago, many forgot just why, but still. We came when we sensed the circle was closing in upon him. Poor Bliss, he had wrapped up his heart in steel, stainless steel, and I guess he'd put his memory down there in Fort Knox with all that gold. He wouldn't see us and he only had to remember us as we were and as he was to know that we didn't come here to rebuke him, his own heart would do enough of that, considering the line he's been taking against our people all these years. Still, that too is the way of man, so he couldn't trust even me, even though I told him way back when he seemed bent on leaving us that I would live a long time and that I would arrive in his presence when he was in sore need. And I tried. We arrived and he didn't trust me enough to see me. So why'd we come, why'd we hold on so hard to hope? What about this, Master? Is this one more test of faith put to us in our old days, or just our own foolishness, just some knotted strings of slavery-time weakness still clinging to us?

Well, that is what the baby boy became and there's no denying. Poor fellow, poor Bliss lost. He's lying there twitching and groaning and I can only talk and sit and wait. We're with you, Bliss. We arrived just as we said we would, way back there when you put us down. I don't know, Hickman, maybe the real one, the true Bliss got lost and this is somebody else. Because during all that time we could never ask if he really were the true son even though we knew in our hearts he ought to be. Maybe we've been following the wrong man all this time. Naw, Hickman, you're tired, this was Bliss. There's no doubt about that. It's him and there lies the nation on its groaning bed. Those Georgia politicians knew it twenty years or so ago, when they tried to make me admit our ties. Sure, and I lied and denied so he could climb higher into the hills of power hoping that he'd find security and in his security and power he'd find his memory and with memory use his power for the good of everyone. Oh yes, he's the one, Hickman, you won't get out of it that easy. You can't stop now by calling it all foolishness. Those politicians didn't threaten you for being foolish, they were playing for keeps. That's why they threatened to run you out of town. Well, I had been run out of better towns by then, sometimes with little Bliss with me, and always my sanctuary was the Word. Anyway there was nothing to lose as there's nothing to lose now and the sheer amazement of God's way is a wonder and well worth it. Let me laugh, I see the links in the chain. Bliss had to bribe and deny and deny and bribe somebody to get in the position he's in. They know it and I know it, only they don't know all I know. Just like I know that I had nothing to lose when they threatened me and that they probably made a deal back there, because Bliss did turn into this, there. Rest, boy. Lord, I wish I could reach him. That doctor ought to be coming in to look at him pretty soon. Janey. After all those long years, Janey writing me that something was brewing:

Dear Brother Alonzo, a young man I know about is come hereabouts from far away and after a long time. You will know who I mean. So I think you ought to know that he's stirring up old ashes and turning over old stones and he is taking down true names and asking questions. I know you will want to know about this because I am too old now to put him off for much longer. I mean he's pressing me too hard. I have dreaded it but it had to come. I always knowed it would. Brother Alonzo I'm not strong like I used to be and I have trouble keeping quiet. I betrayed him once a long time past and now I think my time is closing down. So I hope everything is all right with you and I know you will do what you can. May the good Lord be with you and all our old friends. May he rest you and keep you and them in faith. Tell them that I'm still praying on my bended knees. Tell them I'm remembering them all in my prayers. Your sister in Christ, Janey Mason . . .

I had to think about that one. I remember Janey from way back there in my heathen days, before Bliss came. Riding out of the bot-

toms during the springtime flood on a dripping horse with five little children rowed behind her and holding on to her nightgown and
to each other while she swam that horse out of the swift water and
her bare heels against his belly barrel till he came on up to higher
ground. Talking comfort to those children with weeds in her hair.
Saved all of 'em too. Walnut Grove. That was a woman. Oh yes. She
roused me then too, up there looking, standing on the bank of mud
and silt. Oh yes, in that wet nightgown she roused me. It wasn't
long before Bliss either, though I didn't know it. I was on the verge
of change—oh how odd of God to choose—yet playing Cotch and
Georgia-skin or Tonk every night I wasn't gigging or playing dances
in that hall overlooking the railroad tracks, blowing out my strength
and passion against those east- and west-bound trains.

No little Bliss then, but a lot of easy living in that frontier town.
This I could tell him, since he wandered there years later. A lot of
half-Indian Negroes, those "Natives," they called them, and a bunch
of hustlers and good-time gals. What times; what hard, young
wasteful living. Used to put a number-two washtub full of corn on
the table and drink your fill for a dime a dipperful. And there was
Ferguson's barbecued ribs with that good hot sauce, yes; and Pul-
hams. "Gimme a breast of Guinea hen," I'd say, "and make the hot
sauce sizzling." All that old foolishness. Ha! Me a strapping young
horn-blowing fool with an appetite like a bear and trying to blow
all life through the bell of a brass trombone. Belly-rubbing, dancing and a-stomping off the numbers and everybody trying to give
the music a drive like those express trains. Shaking the bandstand
with my big feet, and the boys romping by midnight and jelly-jelly-
jelly in the crowd until the whole house rocked. I should tell him
about those times; maybe it was the self-denial that turned him
away. Maybe he should have known all the wildness we had to
bring to heel. Surely the Lord makes an allowance for all that,

when you're in the heat of youth. He gave it to me, didn't He, and it was the new country which He gave us, the Indian Nation and the Territory then, and everything wide open and hopeful. You have to scream once maybe so you can know what it means to forbear screaming. That Chock beer, how I exulted in that; rich and fruity mellow. A communion there, back there in that life. Its own communion and fellowship. That Texas white boy who was always hanging around till he was like one of us, he knew it. *Tex, why you always out here hanging around with us all the time? You could be President, you know.*

Yeah, but what's the White House got that's better than what's right here?

Maybe Bliss could tell him. Old Tex. Heard he struck oil in his daddy's cotton patch but I hope he's still a witness for the good times we had. Forget the name of that State Negro with the Indian face . . . a schoolteacher, tall man, always smoking Granger Rough Cut in his pipe and talking politics and the Constitution? From Tennessee, walked all the way from Gallatin leading a whole party of relatives and friends and no preacher either. That scar on my skull to this day from going to the polls with ax handles and pistols, some whites and Indians with us, and battling for the right. Long back, now Oklahoma's just a song, but they don't sing about that. Naw, and why not, since that's what they want to forget. Run up a skyscraper and forget about the foundation, just hope there's oil waiting to get into the water pipes. Yeah, but we got it all in the music. They listen but hear not; they feel its call, but they act not. Drink of the Waters of Life, He said. And I drank until He sent the child and I realized that I had to change. Then I drank again of the true water. I had to change so the sound of life, the life I felt in me and in the others could become words and it's still too complicated for definition. But like the Lord Himself, I loved those sinners and I'll not deny even one. They had the juice of deep life in them, and I learned

to praise it to the transcending heat. Who knows? His ways are
strange ways, Hickman. Maybe it was all His plan, and you had to be
what you were then in order to lead His flock. It took all of that to
come to this and little Bliss was the father to the man and the man
was also me. . . .

CHAPTER 16

The air was stirring gently across his face now and the Senator could hear dimly the "Son, are you there?" of Hickman's voice softly murmuring—but when he tried to respond Bliss had moved on. . . .

. . . Stirring beneath the sterile grain of the sheet the Senator felt a binding pressure on heel and toe, and now alone in the hot world beyond the puckered seal of his lids he found himself wading through a sandy landscape bathed in an eerie twilight. In the low-hung sky before him, vaguely familiar images of threatening shapes appeared, flickering and fading as though to taunt him, and he found himself lunging desperately across the sandy terrain in a compulsive effort to grasp their meaning. But the closer he approached the more rapidly the images changed their shape, tearing apart in smokelike strands only to reappear in ever more ambiguous forms further, further ahead.

The Senator struggled on, his right foot flaming, and now as he paused for breath the sudden rhythmical gusting of a slight breeze irritated the feverish surface of his skin and he could hear Hickman's voice again, at first muted and low, then becoming a booming roar. Hickman was somewhere above him but suddenly as he strained toward the sound he was swept up and carried through the air with such force that his body slanted headfirst into the wind and he kept his balance only by rotating his arms in the manner of a skier soaring in exhilarating flight above the earth. Then came a burst of light followed by a shrilling of whistles and the clanging of bells and the Senator realized that he was standing atop a speeding freight train, his feet dancing unsteadily upon the narrow boards of a catwalk that ran the length of the car. It was a long freight, and far up the tracks he could see the engine, pouring a billowing plume of smoke against the sunny landscape as with a nervous, toylike shuttling of driving-rods it curved the rails to the west. . . .

Wondering at the sudden change of scene, the Senator fought desperately to keep his feet, holding on by flexing at ankle and knee in a bending, straightening, balancing, swaying, dancelike motion which moved his body with and against the erratic rhythms of the bounding car. In the blazing sun the train was hurtling downgrade now and the engineer seemed determined to send him flying into space, for he had the impression that every car in the train was being forced to knock the car just ahead into a capricious, offbeat, bucking increase of speed which nothing on top could withstand. For a while it caused him to bounce about like a manic tap dancer, rattling his teeth and fragmenting the landscape into a whirl of chattering images; then the grade was leveling off and with the going smoother the Senator looked about.

Beyond the rows of cross ties and gleaming rails to his left, wheat fields, turned tawny and dry by the sun, wheeled away at a slant accented by flashing telegraph poles: and below he could see his own thin shadow atop that of the car flickering swiftly along the grading. Flocks of blackbirds were whirling up from the strands of wire which fenced off the field and swinging in broad circles over the tilting land.

Sweeping ahead the train screamed shrilly as it gathered highball speed, its whistle sending snatches of vapor into the blaze of sun. Then to his right, past a sparse windbreak of trees, three dark dogs raced over a harvested field, the agitated music of their trailing cry reaching him faintly through the roar. The dogs ran with nose to earth and far beyond, where the land rolled down to a sparkling stream, he could see the white semaphore-flashing of a rabbit's tail as it coursed in curving flight away from the hounds.

Hurry, hurry, little friend, the Senator thought, hearing the engines whirling again, the sound distraught and lonely as he heard a woman's voice speaking to him in an intimate, teasing drawl, "So, honey, I tell you like the rabbit tole the rabbit, 'Darling, love ain't nothing but a habit—hello, there, Mister Babbitt Rabbit'— Now, now, honey, don't go getting mad on me. All I mean is that you can come see me again sometimes; 'cause short-winded and frantic as you is I still think you kinda cute. You kinda fly too, and I like that. So whenever you feel like coming down to earth, why, drop in on a poor soul and thank you kindly. . . ."

And in the cool shade of the back-alley porch he could see Choc Charlie pausing to drink from his frosty bottle of Chock beer then looking out bemusedly across the yard ablaze with a center bed of red canna flowers, shaking his head. Beyond the yard, the rutted roadbed of the alley was covered with broken glass of many colors and beyond its sparkling surface he could see a black cat yawning pinkly in the shade of the high, whitewashed fence which enclosed the yard beyond. Then Choc Charlie belched and turned, winking at Donelson, and he could see tiny wrinkles forming at the corners of Choc Charlie's eyes as his querulous voice resumed.

"So now," Choc Charlie said, "the dam' hound was so hot on Brer Rabbit's trail that he had to do something real quick because that hound was chasing him come hell for breakfast. So 'bout that time Brer Rabbit sees him a hole in some rocks—and, blip! he shoots into it like a streak of greased lightning—and too bad for him!"

"Looks like he made a mistake of judgment," Donelson said. "How come, how come?"

"How come? Man, do you know who was holed up in that hole?"

"Not yet," Donelson said. "You didn't say. . . ."

"Well, it was ole Brer Bear! That's how come. Man, Brer Rabbit liked to shit his britches then, because didn't nobody in his right mind mess with Brer Bear—and Brer Bear had done already looked up and seen him! . . ."

"Dramatic as hell, isn't it," Donelson said. "A turn in the plot; a 'reversal.' David and Goliath . . . Daniel in the goddamned lion's den! Ole J.C. couldn't do better."

"Drink some beer, man," Choc Charlie said. "I'm telling this lie and my initials ain't J.C., they're C.C. —You see, Brer Bear had been sleeping and when he sits up and rubs his eyes he's flabbergasted! He's hornswoggled! He's hyped! He's shucked! But he don't know who dropped it! He's looking right at him too but he can't believe his own God-given eyes! Here's Brer Rabbit in his very own bedroom! Somebody go get the chief of police, 'cause now Brer Bear is 'bout to move!"

"Ulysses alone in Polly-what's-his-name's cave," Donelson said. "And without companions . . ."

"Man, what are you talking about?" Choc Charlie said. "How the hell did she get in there?"

"She?" Donelson said, "I didn't say anything about 'she,' I said 'he'—but forget it. What happened then?"

"Man," Choc Charlie said, "you drinking too fast. —And sit back out of that sun— Anyway, don't nobody name of Polly mess with Brer Bear, male or female. Not when he's trying to get his rest . . ."

"That's his name," Donelson said, "Polly-fee-mess."

Choc Charlie took a drink and looked wearily at the Senator. "Make him quit messing with this lie, will you please? I appreciate your buying me this Chock and those ribs last night and all but it ain't really that good—know what I mean? Anyway, Brer Rabbit was there and he thought real hard and came up with what he hoped would be a solution. Because with Brer Bear in front of him and with that hound right on his heels Brer Rabbit had to come up with something quicker than the day before yestiddy . . . and that's no bull."

"We're with you, hanging on," Donelson said. "He's reached a moment of grave decision. . . ."

"Now you're talkin'," Choc Charlie said, "grave is right. He better do something quick or he's in his grave, and that's when Brer Rabbit made his move. Gentlemen," Choc Charlie said, "git this: He spins in front of Brer Bear like a wheel of fortune, he spits on the floor like a man among men, he spins back around and makes his white tail flash like the nickel-plated barrel of a .45 pistol, then he wheels around agin and jumps way back and slaps his hips like he's wearing two low-slung, tied-down holsters and a bushel of bullets, then he basses out at Brer Bear like he's all of a sudden ten feet tall and weighing a ton. Said, 'Let a motherfucker move and I'll mow him down!' "

Donelson let out a howl. "Oh no, man, I must protest! You can't do that, not add incest and insult to trickery. . . ."

"Man, hush," Choc Charlie said. "Now don't forget, while this was happening the hound is streaking in like a cannonball, but when he hears all that evil talk coming out of the hole that hound throws on the brakes and makes a turn so fast that not only is he running along the wall but his own tail is whipping his head like a blackjack in the expert hands of Rock Island Shorty, the railroad bull—and man, he highballs it the hell out of there yelling bloody murder.

"Gentlemen, by now Brer Bear is sitting there in a flim-flam fog and before he can git hisself together, Brer Rabbit reaches up and snatched off his cap in order to cut down on the wind resistance and bookety-bookety, bookety, he lit up out of there and is long gone!"

"Act five, scene one coming up," Donelson said. "What did they do then?"

"They? Hell, man, other than Brer Bear wasn't no one left in there—unless'n it was that Polly fellow you brought up, and if so I guess he musta been under the bed. But Brer Bear, poor fellow, he was in a hell of a fix. He's just sitting there rubbing his eyes, sweating gallons and shaking all over like he's got the palsy. Gentlemen, it was pathetic. . . ."

"Tragic," Donelson said.

"Whatever it was," Choc Charlie said, "it was a bitch and it gave Brer Bear the bad-man blues. Said, 'What on earth is this here country coming to, with these bad acting bub-bub-bub, bad-talking bad men breaking into folks' homes talking 'bout their mamas and threatening them with these outrageous, dum-dum-bullet-shooting pearl-handled .45's?' Poor Brer Bear thought Brer Rabbit's tail was a pearl-handled pistol grip and he felt so bad he started to cry like a baby. Said, 'What did I ever do to have a fellow like that come imposing on me? What this here dam' country needs is more law and order—and that's a fact! Where the hell did I put my Gatling gun . . . ?'

"But, gentlemen, Brer Bear was already too late, because by the time he located his shooting-iron Brer Rabbit was already going slam-bam-thank-you-mam through all those fine young lady rabbits back in the briar patch."

"And there," Donelson said, "you have a scenario with conflict of will, high skullduggery, gunplay, escape and rampant sex!"

Smiling into the sun, the Senator had begun to enjoy the familiar sensation of flying, the rush of wind against his face, but as he looked back along the tops of the swaying cars a cloud of black dust had begun to rise from where, several cars to the rear, three hulking figures were slipping and sliding through a gondola loaded with soft coal. The figures were shouting and gesturing in his direction and for a moment the Senator hesitated, but now, seeing a flash of metal burst from a gesturing hand he turned, and bending low, pushed hurriedly through the heavy pressure of the wind to the metal ladder attached to the forward end of the boxcar. Reaching it, he looked back and seeing the figures crawling in a line along the top of the boxcar he clambered down the ladder and held on. Looking along the top where the figures came slowly forward he looked quickly ahead, seeing a cindered path running beside the tracks and to the right of the path the roadbed was falling steeply down into a narrow field. Sunflowers grew tall in the field and at its edge a wall of closely planted trees arose. The trees were tall with sunlight filtering through the high-flung branches and flickering gloomily upon the

slender trunks and as the train swept him past, the Senator looked some
dozen cars ahead to where a sunny clearing was suddenly breaking and
growing wider and as now the car came abreast he braced himself and let go,
feeling his body flying away from the car and trying to run only to see the
cindered path slamming up to meet him as with a palm-searing, knee-
burning explosion of breath he landed hard upon the shuddering roadbed.

Fighting for breath against the heaving path, he lay as though paralyzed,
watching the wheels and undercarriages churning the light just beyond his
head. Dust and bits of trash were whirling furiously about and he could see
the rhythmical rise and fall of the sleepers as they took the pound and click
of wheel on rail. Then, his breath returning, he was sitting up and watching
the tail end of the train whipping swiftly up the track. The red lenses of
lanterns glinted like enormous jewels from either side of the caboose and a
flag was snapping briskly from the handrail as the three figures ran back
along its top, continuing doggedly to advance toward him even as the train
bore them smoothly away.

Sweeping on, with smoke and flame pouring from its stack, the engine
screamed again as it plunged toward a rise of rocky country that lay to the
west. And suddenly it was as though he were watching a scene from a silent
movie—with the train hurtling toward a point in the rocks where, as it approached, a spot grew like that which blossoms in a paper napkin at the
touch of a lighted cigarette. Widening mysteriously around its periphery, the
hole was turning rapidly inward upon itself and in a flash the three figures,
the train and sunlit surrounding scene had vanished, leaving behind only the
cindered grade, the cross ties and gleaming rails, now running in steely con-
vergence into the darkness of a void.

For a moment the Senator had the impression of gazing toward a huge
rumpled sheet which hung against the landscape with a mysterious hole
burned in its center, but still hearing the muffled, clicking sound of the receding train he got to his feet and plunged in jolting, stiff-legged bounds
down the grade and into the trees.

The Senator was moving through deep country now, the sound of the train a faint rumble in the distance. Here in the shade of the trees the air was clear and cool and he walked beneath stands of towering walnuts, oaks and cottonwoods that grew in clumps broken by parklike spaces of grass accented by bushes and trailing vines. His leg and palms smarted from his fall but now he moved ahead with a sense of relief, breathing the spicy air and trying to recall when he had passed through such woods before.

Off to his right an abandoned apple orchard stood with gnarled limbs in surreal disarray and farther beyond he could see a stand of elders displaying clusters of dark red berries in the sunlight. He was moving in silence, brushing embedded cinders from his palms and stepping carefully to protect his injured leg—when, suddenly, a covey of quail flushed at his feet, breaking the cathedral quiet with a roar that caused his heart to pound and his nerves to hum as he watched the rocketing birds reel off and sail with set wings into a nearby thicket. A dampness broke over his skin, chilling him as he watched where the birds had blended magically into the background, and for a moment he stood silent, searching in vain for the slightest telltale motion from the quail.

Now the afternoon was motionless, the brown and green foliage where the birds had gone inscrutable. But for the distant cry of a single bird the only sound was that of his own breathing and the Senator's mind stirred with excitement, thinking: Surprise, speed and camouflage are the faith, hope and charity of escape, and the essence of strategy. Yes, and scenes dictate masks and masks scenes. Therefore the destructive element offers its own protective sanctuary. Hunting codes are a concern of human hunters or otherwise. To imaginate is to integrate negatives and positives into a viable program supporting one's own sense of value. Flown before the unseeing hand the bird crouches safe in the bush. Therefore freedom is a willful blending of opposites, a conscious mixing of ungreen, unbrown things and thoughts into a brown-green shade. . . . Where's the light? What's the tune? What's the time?

For a moment he mused, his eyes playing along the quiet hedge. There was something missing from the formula but he would work it out later, for now he must move ahead.

But hardly had he approached a mossy clearing in the trees than the Senator froze again. Before him two foxes were moving past at a leisurely trot, their elegant brushes floating weightlessly upon the quiet air. One fox carried a limp rabbit retriever-wise in its jaws and he could see the lazy flopping of the rabbit's leaf-veined ears, observed its white powder puff of a tail. And now, reaching the center of the clearing the animals paused, delicately sniffing the air as they regarded him quietly out of the amber remoteness of vulpine eyes. One of the animals was gravid and the forgotten image of plump fox puppies playing upon the hard bare bone- and feather-strewn earth before a rocky burrow flashed through his mind and a fragment from the scriptures sang in his head:

> Oh, the foxes have holes in the ground
> But son of man . . . son of man . . .

And before the quiet confrontation of their eyes the Senator stood breathless, feeling a breeze passing over the dampness of his arms and watching a lazy rippling begin to play through the fur of the foxes. And he felt the hairs stirring lightly along his own forearms as the breeze blew slowly past pointed muzzles and alerted ears to part with a gentle, silklike ruffling the long fine fur of the high-held tails.

> Oh, the foxes have holes in the ground
> But son of man, son of man . . .

Then imperceptibly the foxes moved, becoming with no impression of speed twin streaks of red moving past the thicket of green, and he watched their brushes floating dreamlike into the undergrowth.

All this I've known, the Senator thought, but had forgotten. . . . Then in the sudden hush, accented by a pheasant's cry, he felt as though no trains nor towns nor sermons existed. He was at peace. Here was no need to escape nor search for Eden, nor need to solve his mystery. But again he moved, somehow compelled to go ahead. . . .

Soon the Senator was beyond the woods, his throat throbbing with nameless emotion stirred by the foxes, and he moved with inward-turning eyes—until, high above, where it flashed like a minnow in an inverted bowl of a clear blue lake, a small plane caught his eye and he moved beneath the boughs of a pine tree, watching the plane bank languidly into the sun to write in smoke across the sky:

Niggers
Stay
Away
From
The Polls

And watching the words expand and drift in ghostlike shapes he shook his fist at the sky and ran again, cursing the taut constriction of the sand.

Following the upward slant of the terrain the Senator found himself approaching a crowd gathered below the terrace of a clubhouse resting on the broad, level surface of a cliff which overlooked a winding river. Below the cliff and atop the river's farther bank, a flock of grazing sheep was strung out along a rolling meadow, making dark foreshortened shadows against the green; and far below, past the brown and gray outcroppings of the meadow's rocky edge, he could see the dark swirl and sparkle of the river as it flowed past a pile of boulders which protruded white and brilliant in the sun.

There was a feeling of holiday in the air now, and on the terrace he could see uniformed waiters serving pale yellow melon, frosted drinks and ices to smiling couples who lounged at tables set in the pastel shade of brightly colored parasols.

*Moving painfully through the fashionable crowd the Senator squeezed
past handsome women clad in sports clothing, and tweedy, heavily tanned
men sporting alpine hats decorated with the feathers of a game bird, silver-
mounted brushes of badger fur or tiny medals celebrating the hunt, and was
suddenly aware of the fresh scents the women wore, the fine, smooth texture
of their complexions. Then he had pressed to the front of the crowd and found
himself leaning against a low barrier that fenced off the broad semicircle of
a grassy shooting ring.*

*To his right, just inside the barrier a group of men with guns cradled in
the crooks of their arms were looking out to the center of the ring where three
workmen knelt in the grass working over a device attached to a length of rubber hosing. The hosing ran back to a truck parked at the rear where it was attached to the storage tank of a mobile air compressor. Other workmen,
wearing black berets and blue coveralls, were standing in groups of three at
four stations arranged at equal distances across the ring, all marked, like
that where the men were working, by stacks of bright yellow dovecotes. They
too were looking toward the kneeling, frantically busy men; and back near
the compressor truck the Senator could see dozens of dovecotes stacked high
on a wagon before which a small, bony horse with docked tail, wearing a
farmer's straw hat in which holes had been cut for its twitching ears, dozed
wearily between the shafts. Then, as though someone had pulled a switch, the
Senator was aware of the throbbing sound made by the cooing of many birds.
The dovecotes were crammed with pigeons and he could see the nervous motion of their beaked heads thrusting back and forth between the bars. The air
throbbed with the sound of their cooing reminding him of a crowd of summer passengers looking out of the grill of a trolley car as they commented on
something out in the passing scene.*

*And now as the annoyed voices of the spectators began drowning out the
noise of the birds, he saw the men drawing erect and heard one of them call
out to the men with guns:*

"O.K., gentlemen, it's now in working order."

"And it's damn well time," a spectator called; then a bell sounded and the

Senator could see a uniformed official wearing a green sun visor stepping across the springing turf and signaling to a marksman who took the firing line and the action was resumed.

Suddenly at the cry of "MARK!" the Senator heard a fierce sound like that of air bursting from a punctured tire and saw a surprised pigeon bouncing some twenty feet into the air above the trap, hanging there for an instant of flurried indecision then taking off on a swift, rising course to the right; and he could see the marksman now, taking his time, his feet precisely placed, swinging smoothly onto and past the rising bird, and at the sound of the shot the bird abruptly folding on its course and as a second shot exploded, bursting apart in the air.

"Onesie, twosie, it's a doosie," a supercilious voice called behind him, but before he could turn to see who it was, the cry of "MARK!" came again and he was watching a pigeon taking off to the left and halting suddenly as though struck by a baseball bat, its feathers flying, as yet another bird shot aloft on a screeching jet of air.

Having dropped his final bird, the smiling marksman stepped back with lowered gun waving as applause and shouts of "Bravo!" erupted from the spectators; and now, as another gunman took the firing line, the action accelerated, moving so swiftly that the Senator had an uneasy feeling that things were getting out of hand. A fateful accuracy marked the match, disturbing him profoundly as the gunners, coming and going in swift rotation, took continued advantage of second shots and made great slaughter on the grass.

Suddenly, as a huge marksman wearing baggy seersucker pants took the line, a small, stooped, stiff-necked man appeared smoking a long cigar. As he came prancing along just inside the ring and waving a sheaf of banknotes about, he yelled, "Heads, gentlemen! I'm taking bets on heads alone!"

Heads, the Senator thought, what does he mean . . . ?

"What! Are you kidding?" another man called.

"Not kidding, sir," the little man said. "I'm betting a thousand that he

leads the next bird so precisely that the pattern alone will take off the head and leave the body untouched."

"You're nuts and you're covered," the second man called; and now as the next pigeon sprang free the Senator watched the huge marksman wave his gun about like a weighted pool cue, wait until the bird had leveled, then cut loose shooting from the hip. And now he could see something fly away from the bird to sail across the ring as its body continued a few feet in headless flight and then collapsed.

There was wild applause and the Senator watched the little man laughing and dancing a jig step as he waved a fistful of money and yelled:

"Heads today and tails tomorrow! Heads! Heads! Heads! Who'll bet three grand that he touched nairy a tail feather, a breast feather, nor nairy a feather in either wing? Speak up!"

"What's the bet?" someone called from the rear.

"No breast! No tail! No wing! And ding-a-ding-ding at three thousand bucks a number seven shot," the little man called.

"Covered!" the voice called, and as the Senator watched the little man scampering around the ring to where an attendant was picking up the headless bird the betting became furious.

Returning with the bird now plucked of its feathers, the little man displayed it proudly, pointing to the unblemished state of its skin and collecting his bets with an air of fierce satisfaction.

"How about you, sir," he called to the Senator, his teeth clamped fiercely upon his long cigar, "you look like a man of quality, a betting man. Clarence has one bird left in the set and I'll bet you ten thousand that he'll turn him over easy, or turn him over slow. He'll hit him high, he'll hit him low—tip, tail, wing or duster—as you please, sir. Just say the word."

"No," the Senator said, "not today or ever."

The little man laughed, revealing a set of wolfish teeth. "Smoked you out, didn't I," he said. "Four little children and a very nowhere wife, is that it?"

But when the Senator started to answer he moved quickly back into the crowd—which was stirring about and roaring so loudly that the Senator quickly lost sight of him.

Out in the ring now the traps were being sprung in no discernible order and the firing becoming so rapid that windrows of ejected cartridge hulls were piling up near the firing line. Rings of sweat showed at the armpits of the gunners' jackets and the Senator could see waves of heat dancing along the vented gun barrels. Things were getting so much out of hand that he felt that the officials should do something to restore order, or at least slow the pace, but none were to be seen. And as fast as one stack of dovecotes was emptied of birds the handlers rushed replacements to the traps.

The Senator's head felt light now, his nose stinging from the acrid gun smoke and he looked skyward with a feeling that the sun had halted just above his head. I must get out of here, he thought, but when he tried to leave the howling spectators pressed in upon him so tightly that he was unable to move.

Turning his back to the ring, he tried to break free to the rear, to make for the shade of the terrace. But now a woman whose luxuriant auburn hair showed beneath a white leghorn hat with aqua ribbon, pressed so closely against him that he could see beads of moisture standing out on the flesh beneath her deep blue eyes. The woman was smiling mysteriously into his face and he could see deep wrinkles breaking through her masklike makeup, revealing a far darker complexion underneath. Then the woman was saying something which he could not understand and as he bent closer to hear he was struck by a blast of disinfectant which was so repulsive that he turned quickly around and backed against the barrier. It's Lysol, he thought, it's Lysol!

Far to the rear of the crowd now he could hear a husky voice keeping score of the kills while a woman's voice repeated the count in a shrill Spanish accent, lisping her words and shouting, "Olé! Olé!" as the firing accelerated in pace.

Closing his eyes against the blazing scene, the Senator plunged the tips of his fingers into his ears, trying to escape the noise. His leg had begun to pain

*again and he remembered the refreshment that he'd seen the waiters serving
back on the terrace. He longed for a cold slice of melon, an iced drink, a bit
of quiet. But now an explosion of shouting caused him to open his eyes to a
crowd that was leaning over the barrier and shaking its fists in anger. Things
had come to a halt; the guns were silent and no birds flying. At first he
thought the object of the spectators' disapproval was an official's ruling, or
some act of unsportsmanlike conduct by a contestant, and discovered instead
that the anger was caused by a single slate-gray pigeon.*

*Out near the rear of the ring the bird was moving over the grass with the
grave, pigeon-toed dignity of a miniature bishop, its head bobbing from side
to side as it ignored the shouting crowd.*

*Close by, a man cupped his hands to his mouth, screaming, "Flush, you
fink! Use your wings!"*

*"You're wasting your time with that one," another man called. "Where's
the official? Get him over here! Does he consider that a sporting bird? Who
the hell bred the characterless fowl? I say who?"*

*"Now wait," the sun-visored official called from within the ring. "These
birds are the very best. Bred for the ring, for hand-launching and for the
trap!"*

"Then make him fly, dammit; make him fly!"

*"It's sportsman's luck," the man in the visor called. "Some fly, some fail.
We put enough air under these birds to launch a rocket, so if one doesn't fly
it's just too bad. The gunner simply calls for another bird."*

"But I want this one," the gunner called, "he owes me a chance!"

*"He's right," a small blond woman called, "make the buzzard fly! Up in
the air . . . you . . . you pretentious pouter. We didn't come here to see you
strut or take a dive. Play the game, you're stalling the match!"*

But the pigeon continued walking.

Behind the Senator the auburn-haired woman was in tears.

*"It's a crime," she called past his ear, "it's a disgrace. It's impotence, it's
perversity, a politics of evasion and calculated defiance. . . ."*

Bewildered by her analysis, the Senator watched a soft-drink bottle land and scud across the grass, just missing, and the pigeon turning aside but still refusing to fly. And now a man with leather patches on the elbows of his fawn-colored jacket aimed an empty cartridge hull at the bird, cursing when it fell far short of the mark.

"Up, sir," he called, "into the air!"

A tall man with the blue eyes and blond hair of a Viking stepped over the barrier and snatched off his yachtsman's cap, rumpling it in his hands as he addressed the crowd in a cavernous voice:

"It's against the rules," he cried passionately, "the bird should fly! Damn his wings, it's his profession, his identifying characteristic. The other two birds in the set took off, so why should he be a dirty third? If he continues this outrageous conduct I say let the officials give the gunner permission to lower his sights and blast the craven-souled varmit off the face of the earth!"

And before the Viking could continue a short-armed fat man whose eyes burned angrily behind yellow shooting lenses bounced into the ring carrying a gun with an exceptional length of barrel and, with cheek pressed tightly against the stock, got off a shot.

The report was like that of a small cannon and the Senator could see grass and bits of earth fly into the air as the blast lifted the pigeon a foot above the ring. But instead of taking wing, the bird landed on its feet and continued forward, limping now and with a small spot of blood showing on its breast.

For a moment the crowd was silent, gazing out across the ring in amazement; then the Senator's ears were blasted by a howl of rage.

Out in the ring the fat man was in tears.

"Now I get it!" he cried. "Listen to me. We've been betrayed! Some anarchist has slipped a cynical gutter rat of a New York pigeon into our dovecotes. That's what has happened. A guttersnipe!"

"A New York pigeon?" someone called. "What do you mean? Tell us!"

"Hell, it's sabotage," the fat man said. "New York pigeons are simply awful! They walk along the subway tracks, hitchhiking on freight trains! They fornicate on the hoods of moving cars and in the air. It's treason!"

Whereupon he snatched off a shoe and sent it arching over the ring where it missed the pigeon and struck a blue-clad handler, who now stood glaring at the crowd.

"Now you watch it, Mac," the handler called. "Respect the working man!"

"Respect?" the fat man called. "You don't need respect, you get paid. And if you were earning your pay you'd give that stupid bird a goose so the match could continue. Instead, you make us speeches about the rights of labor!"

The fat man was speechless, his face red with anger, but as he started out toward the handler a tall distinguished-looking man in a white deerstalker hat grabbed him and pushed him back. Then, raising his arms for quiet, the tall man called out, "My advice is to have the handlers wring the bird's neck and end this impasse! Anyway we look at it, a bird such as that is a disgrace. It's a disgrace to the breed and to the sport. It's a bloody spoilsport, a cringing dog-in-the-manger! A malicious nigger in the woodpile! A vengeful ghost at the wedding! In other words, it makes everything go bad. So I say, let's wring its neck and immediately after the shoot I shall call a meeting of the governing board to see to it that in the future all such birds are blackballed. . . ."

"There's no need to wait," the fat man said, slamming a shell into his weapon. "I'm taking no more crap from this walking . . ." But just as he raised his gun to fire a woman ran forward and knocked him off balance, causing the gun to discharge into the air and sending the fat man back with a bump upon the grass where he sat cursing the woman.

Watching the pigeon's progress, the Senator felt that he was suffocating. He felt responsible for the pigeon's life but was unable to do a thing about it. Flashes of blue-green appeared above the ring now as the crowd began lobbing Coca-Cola bottles at the bird; but still the pigeon refused to flush, and its orange-ringed eyes seemed to look straight at the Senator as skirting both the bottles and the bodies of its fallen fellows it continued with calmly bobbing head toward the barrier. He watched the iridescent play of the light upon its gorget and the slow pulsing of blood from its breast with painful feelings of identification which were interrupted by a sudden silence: The bird had stopped its stroll and was extending its wings.

"Now! At last," the Viking called, "he's found his courage! He's about to take off, so careful, Mr. Marksman, careful!"

Thinking, Oh, no! Not after resisting this far, the Senator strained forward, seeing the pigeon's head come around and the remoteness of its orange-ringed eye as the bird plucked a single feather from its breast and released it with a sharp snap of its head. Then with a series of short, hedge-hopping spurts it covered the remaining distance to the barrier, where it paused, calmly preening itself for a moment, then turning its back to the crowd it dived with set wings below the cliff.

As the bird dropped from sight the Senator seemed to fall within himself and as he struggled to keep his feet he was aware of a sudden darkening of the sun and looked up to see, at the point where the pigeon had disappeared, a huge hatch of flies boiling up from the river and swarming above the ring, where once again the birds were flighting before the guns.

Perhaps for you there's safety in darkness, the Senator thought. Perhaps a few will have a chance. . . .

But already the flies were thinning out, swarming veillike in broader circles, and as they boiled above the ring he heard an explosion of shrill cries and watched the arrival of a virtual aerial circus of small, sharp-winged birds.

Pouring down as from a net released high in the sky, a flock of swallows began swooping and wheeling between the booming patterns of the guns as they attacked the flies, bringing the air alive with graceful motion. Plunging and climbing, banking and whirling, skimming and gliding, the hunting birds filled the air with high-pitched, derisive cries as they executed power dives and Immelmanns, sideslips and barrel rolls, and dazzled the Senator with the cool, audacious miracle of their flight. Not a single swallow was struck by the flying shot and as they swirled above the ring it came to him that the swallows were contemptuous of both the pigeons and the guns, and there, braced between the auburn-haired woman and a man in a wide planter's hat, and feeling the dank, steaming wetness of their bodies against him, he watched the swallows swoop and soar in grace, moving invulnerable among the doomed and falling rock doves. . . .

Suddenly released and moving through the crowd, the Senator had started along the walk leading back to the clubhouse when suddenly something landed a sharp, stabbing blow to his right heel and he whirled to see a small handsome child who looked up at him out of a pair of intense, black, long-lashed eyes.

Why, I'll be damned, the Senator thought, it's a boy! A fine, grand rascal of a little boy!

The little boy, whose hair was cut in a Buster Brown bob, was dressed incongruously in red satin pantaloons and white satin blouse such as were worn by a child in a painting by Goya, a copy of which the Senator had seen long ago in a museum. Even his pompom-topped white satin slippers were from another time, and behind him, attached to a silken cord which the boy held in a chubby fist, there stood a stuffed goldfinch mounted on a small gilded platform equipped with wheels.

He's been gotten up for either a wedding or a masquerade, but in either case he'll steal the show. Dressed to kill, that's the word, the Senator thought, resisting an impulse to sweep the child into his arms as he smiled down, saying,

"Why, hello there! Don't I know you from somewhere? You look awfully familiar. . . ."

But instead of answering, the little boy darted around him, the goldfinch clattering on the walk as the Senator turned to see the child standing in the middle of the path confronting him with an expression of hostility which distorted his tiny face.

"My, but you're fast," the Senator said. "What's your name? Mine's Adam Sunraider. . . ."

Silently the little boy stuck out a small blue tongue, making an angry face, then with his fingers rigidly extended he thumbed his nose.

The Senator laughed, thinking, My, but he's aggressive. Probably a dis-satisfied constituent . . . And yet he had a nagging impression that he knew the child, had seen him before even though he could think of no one with a child so young.

"Look," he said, leaning forward, "I don't know what you've got against me but I'd like to be friends with such a fine young fellow as you. Shall we shake hands?"

His head shaking violently, the boy's hands flew behind his back as he stared up at the Senator out of hot black eyes.

"Very well," the Senator said, "people who can't talk probably can't know very much. I'll bet you can't even say your father and mother's name. . . ."

The boy grinned, his face transformed into that of a malicious adult as he retreated a step and spat at the Senator's feet, and in a flash his tiny hands were at his head, fluttering like the wings of a hummingbird as he stuck out his tiny blue-coated tongue and thumbed his ears.

Thinking, How on earth could he have become so ill-mannered so young?, the Senator chuckled at the incongruity between the child's size and his ag-gressiveness.

"Young man," the Senator began, "I have an idea you're lost. Maybe you'd better try to take me to where you last saw your mother——" and broke off, taken aback as the child went suddenly into a frenzy of action.

Turning his back and jackknifing forward, the boy was looking up from between his short legs and making a horrible face as he patted his backside and made nasty sounds with his vibrating lips. Then straightening, he raised his leg like a dog and with a grave expression on his face he thumbed the seat of his red satin pants.

"Hey!" the Senator cried, "that's enough of that! Cut it out! What do you think you're doing?"

But instead of answering, the boy began to run in circles before him, mov-ing like a demented toy and stopping every few feet to repeat his insulting gestures. Profoundly disturbed and depressed, the Senator looked beyond the child into the crowd, hoping to see a frantic mother emerging to find the boy. A bird was rising above the crowd and all backs were turned, watching the marksman and the flighting target.

This is awful, the Senator thought, this one certainly needs attention. How did he ever get this way so soon? Probably doesn't even know his alphabet, yet he's already expert in the manual-of-arms of vulgar put-down!

His leg was paining again and now as he started around the boy, he saw the child sneering malevolently as he leaned back and pushed out his little satin-clad stomach and began vigorously to thumb the fly of his red satin pantaloons.

It was too much for the Senator but as he reached out the boy leaped backwards, running and making a turn which caused the stuffed bird to disintegrate in an explosion of flying head and whirling feathers as it struck the walk and lay vibrating there as the boy shot silently into the crowd.

For a moment the Senator stood looking blankly at the shattered goldfinch in his path, thinking, He'll be furious, absolutely furious; and his mother will probably blame me, and her with a boy running wild while she devotes herself to shooting matches. . . . It's a crime. . . . And the Senator moved away.

There was a faint odor of smoke around him now and as the Senator came out upon the steps leading from the building his senses were assaulted by the hushed humid heaviness of the late afternoon air. And then, as at a signal, a silence seemed to move before him and grow like a rolling crescendo of suddenly inverted sound. Sometime earlier a shower had left the atmosphere unbearably hot and although the sky had begun to clear he could see drops of moisture still clinging to the leaves of the trees and the walks glistened with the rain.

Surprisingly, the traffic had disappeared and as far as his eyes could see the traffic signals were blobs of red, shimmering against the moist mistiness *of the fading light. Then a movement down at the intersection of the street and the avenue caught his attention and he saw a bent little black-skinned woman moving toward him.*

Wearing a blue bandanna head rag and a faded yellow apron over a red housedress, she made her way along in a pair of black high-topped old lady's shoes which seemed, suddenly, to expand about her ankles and begin creeping up her legs: expanding and contracting violently as they climbed. It was as though they were intent upon engorging her within the bunion-distorted maws of their interiors. Yet she continued painfully forward and as she moved closer the Senator could hear the rhythmical beating of a clanking sound— But then she was no longer there but transported across the avenue where, standing before a building which showed dark against the eerie light of the fading sun, she called out in a senile quaver, "Hey! Heah Ah is, over heah!" *and threatened him with an old-fashioned washing stick that she shook with awkward vigor.*

"Oh, Ah knows you," *she called.* "You old jacklegged, knock-kneed, bow-legged, box-ankled, pigeon-toed, slack-asted piece of peckerwood trash gone to doo-doo! Ah knows you, yas Ah do! Yo' mammy was yo' sister and yo' grandmaw too! Yo' uncle was yo' daddy and yo' brother's cousin! You a coward and a thief and a snake in the grass! You do the dirty bo-bo and you eats bad meat! Oh Ah knows you, yas Ah does, and I means to git you! I means to tell everybody who you is and put yo' nasty business in these white folks' street. . . ."

What on earth is this, the Senator thought; who is this senile old mammy-auntie and what's she doing up here on the Hill? Where did she come from?

"Ah'll tell you what you is," *the old woman called.* "You ain't nothing, that's what you is! You is simply nothing done gone to waste, and if somebody was to plant you in a hill with a rotten piece of fish you wouldn't even raise a measly bush of beans! You think you so high and mighty but you ain't doodly-squat! You ain't no eagle, fox or bear! You ain't a rabbit or a skunk or a wheel-in-a-wheel! You ain't nothing—neither a mourning dove or a*

lily of the field! You ain't a bolt or a nut or a crupper strap. Ah even knows
pimps and creepers who're better'n you. . . ."

Very well, the Senator thought, but you'll have to admit that if I'm not
all that you say I'm at least a walking personification of the negative. . . .

"Shet up! Shet up! You nothing!" the old woman screamed. "SHET UP!
Or Ah'll tell you who you really is!"

Shaking his head, the Senator turned away, amused but filled with a
strange foreboding. Never mind, he thought, I know who I am, and for the
time being at least, I am a senator.

But now for some reason he recalled a church service of a summer's evening
long past, during which in rapid succession a gust of wind had torn a part of
the roof away and a stroke of lightning had plunged the church into dark-
ness. The choir had faltered in its singing and women had begun scream-
ing—when in the noisy confusion and whirling about Hickman had stamped
three times upon the pulpit's hollow floor, shouting, "Sing! Sing!," startling
them and triggering some of the singers into an outburst of ragged, incoher-
ent sound. Frightened by the storm, he himself had been crying, but as the old
church creaked and groaned beneath the lashing of wind and rain and the
screaming continued, the foot-pounded rhythm had come again, this time ac-
companied by Hickman's lining-out of a snatch of a spiritual in hoarse,
authoritative recitative. And suddenly the singers were calmed and the
screamers were silenced and a disciplined quietness had spread beneath
the howling of the storm. Then through a flash of lightning he had seen the
singers straining towards Hickman who, with voice raised in melody, was
stomping out the rhythm on the floor. And as the singers followed his lead
and were joined by the nervous choiring of the congregation, he had heard the
blended voices rise up in firm array against the thunder. Up, up the voices had
climbed until, surrendering themselves to the old familiar words, they were
giving forth so vigorously that before his astonished eyes the pitch-black in-
terior of the church had seemed to brighten and come aglow with a joyful and
unearthly radiance generated by the mighty outpouring of passionate song.

He 'rose . . .

        Heroes!

He 'rose . . .

        Heroes!

He 'rose . . .

        Up from the dead!

He 'rose . . .

        Oh, yes!

He 'rose . . .

        Oh, yes!

Heroes . . .

        Up from the dead!

A comfort, the Senator thought.

   And moving down the steps and into the familiar scene of the street he felt the images of this long-forgotten incident imposing themselves upon the scene, distorting his vision with teasing fragments of memory long rejected. And now he stumbled along the stone walk with inward-searching eyes, expecting the abrupt tolling of bells, a clash of lightning, a choir of girlish voices lifted in vesperal song. . . .

   Across the way the old woman continued to rail, but now he was listening for the baritone timbre and voicelike phrasing of a muted trombone which would proclaim with broadly reverent mockery the lyrics of some ancient hymn; and looking back to the building entrance, he expected to see a crowd rush forth to shout down denunciations upon him, to shower him with stones. . . . But, like the street, the entrance was empty and the door now closed mysteriously upon the brooding quiet. . . .

   Soon, the Senator thought, it will come. They're beginning to stir, so, as the old trainer said, watch their hands. And as old fighters, he warned, watch hands, feet and head. Yes, they're moving out into the open and things are beginning to heave and the backwash is beginning. But Hickman here? Unlikely—though who knows who it was who came? Nine owls have squawked out the rules and the hawks will talk, so soon they'll come marching out of the woodpile and the woodwork—sorehead, sorefoot, right up close, one-butt-shuffling into history but demanding praise and kind treatment for deeds undone, for lessons unlearned. But studying war once more . . .

Reaching the curb now, the Senator prepared to cross the boulevard when, sensing a rush of movement from his left, he spun instinctively and saw the car.

Long, black and underslung, it seemed to straighten the curving course of the street with the force of its momentum, bearing down upon him so relent-lessly that his nerves screamed with tension as his entire body prepared itself for a supreme effort. An effort which, even as his muscles responded to the danger, was already anticipating itself in his reeling mind, projecting a long, curving, backward leaping motion through which his eyes were now recording in vivid detail of stone-steel-asphalt-chrome, damp leaves and whirling architectural stone as he saw himself sailing backwards and yet he was watching, still on his feet, the car approaching with such deliberate speed that now its fenders appeared to rise and fall with the heavy labored motion of some great bird flying and the heaving of its black metallic sides like that of the barrel of a great bull charging. And now two gleaming, long-belled heralds' trumpets which lay along the enginehood ripped the air with a blast of defiant sound and he saw a pair of red-tipped bullhorns appear atop the radiator, knifing toward him—while an American flag, which snapped and rippled like a regimental pinion brought to aggressive life by a headlong cavalry charge, streamed fiercely above. . . .

Only now did his body catch up with his mind, beginning its backward-sailing fling as the car, almost upon him now, veered suddenly and stopped with a night-piercing screaming of brakes. He was on his back then feeling the pain of the impact exploding in his elbows and spine and in the endless, heart-pounding, head-jolting instant the car seemed to leave the roadway and hover above the curb, hanging there like a giant insect; and inside its wide front seat were three men.

Dark-skinned and broad of face behind the murky window, they peered down at him through dark glasses topped by the narrow brims of high-crowned, shaggy-napped white hats, watching him with intense concentration as their mouths stretched wide in expressions of fierce, derisible gaiety. Whereupon the driver reached for a microphone and looking around his companions addressed him through the herald trumpets which lay along either side of the rakish hood.

"Next time you better swing your booty faster, boy," the voice said, "or by God we go' lo' mo' kick your nasty ass!"

Watching them, the Senator was speechless.

"Don't be laying there looking at us," the voice said. "You heard me correctly; we'll blast you and do everybody some service!"

The Senator started up, trying to answer, but now there came a jetlike blast, and seeing the machine leaping into furious motion he rolled, turning completely over as he tried to escape its path—— But instead of crushing him, the machine was braking and surging backwards with a blast of red and white light erupting from its rear. And then thundering with a rapid shifting and reshifting of gears it left the street once more and hung above him like a hovercraft, the black passengers looking down upon him with grim satisfaction, awaiting his next move. . . .

"Hey, Mister Motharider," the voice called down to him, "how's this for a goongauge?"

"Hey, Shep," the man in the middle said, "don't ask he not'ing! Let's show Charley how de car can curb. I don't tink he believes you cawn drive dis bloody t'ing."

"No, I don't believe he does," the driver said. "O.K., Charley boy, watch me snatch the butter from the duck!"

Staring into the grinning faces, the Senator scrambled to his knees, thinking, Who are they? as the machine shot away and shattered the quiet of the street with the flatulent blasts from its dual exhaust. He watched it lunging up the boulevard at a forward slant, seeming to flatten out and become more unreal the farther it receded into the distance. Techniques of intimidation, *that's what they're using,* the Senator thought. *They were waiting for me; they were watching the building for the moment I started across the street so they could intimidate me. So they'll be back and I'd better leave. . . .*

And even as he watched the car floating away he was aware that somehow it was beginning to flow backwards upon its own movement, dividing itself and becoming simultaneously both there in the distance and here before him, where now it throbbed and puttered, a miragelike image of black metal agleam with chrome, and there up the boulevard, where it was resonating street and buildings with the thunder of its power. And it came to the Senator that he was watching no ordinary automobile. This was no Cadillac, no Lincoln, Oldsmobile or Buick—nor any other known make of machine; it was an arbitrary assemblage of chassis, wheels, engine, hood, horns, none of which had ever been part of a single car! It was a junkyard sculpture mechanized! An improvisation, a bastard creation of black bastards—and yet, it was no ordinary hot rod. It was an improvisation of vast arrogance and subversive and malicious defiance which they had designed to outrage and destroy everything in its path, a rolling time bomb launched in the streets. . . .

And now the image of the machine gleamed and quivered and throbbed before him, glowing with flames of luminous red that had been painted along the sides of the threatening, shark-finned fenders which guarded its licenseless rear. Two slender radio antennae affixed to either side of the trunk lazily whipped the air, one flying an enormous and luxuriantly rippling coon's tail and the other displaying in miniature the stars and bars of the Confederacy while across the broad expanse of its trunk he saw the enormous image of an open switchblade knife bearing the words:

> WE HAVE SECEDED FROM THE MOTHER!
> HOORAY FOR US!
> TO HELL WITH CHARLEY!

They have constructed it themselves, the Senator's mind went on, *brought the parts together and gathered in conspiratorial secret like a group of guer-*

rillas assembling the smuggled parts of a machine gun! —And they've made the damn thing run! No single major part goes normally with the rest, yet even in their violation of the rigidities of mechanical tolerances and in their defiance of the laws of physics, property rights, patents—everything— they've forced part after part to mesh and made it run! It's a mammy-made, junkyard construction and yet those clowns have made it work, it runs! . . .

And now the machine roared back, braking with a violent, stiffly sprung rocking of body and a skidding of tires, and again the men were looking out of the open window.

"Listen, Sunrobber," the nearest called, "what the hell was that you just said about our little heap?"

"Hell, mahn," the middle man said, "don't ask he no'ting! I done tole you the bahstard has low-rated our little load! The mahn done low-rated our pride and joy, so don't ask the bahstard not'ing, just show he whadt de joecah kin do!

"And remembah us mah-toe, mahn:

> Down Wid de Coon Cawdge,
> Up WID DE JOE CAH!

"Then, mahn, I say, KICK HIM ASS!"

"Yeah, man; but not so fas'," one of the others said. "Not before we give his butt a little ride . . ."

A blast of heat struck him then, followed by the opening of the door. And as a dark hand reached down, he seemed to hear the sound of Hickman's consoling voice, calling from somewhere above.

NOTES*

Editor's note: From the time of *Invisible Man*'s publication in 1952 until
Ralph Ellison's death in 1994, he wrote down literally thousands of
notes pertaining to all facets of his novel-in-progress. Some he jotted
in haste on magazine subscription cards or scrawled indecipherably
on the back of used envelopes, bills, or any scrap of paper close at
hand. Others he copied carefully into one of the half-dozen note-
books he kept for the purpose. Still others he typed. Some of the
notes carry on for several pages, spilling over into description or dialogue, as if in the act of brooding over a scene or character, the writer
became his own muse. Others are brief, cryptic, or in some cases
even interrupted by another, sometimes unrelated, thought that took

---

* Asterisks indicate notes that supplement those in the first edition of *Juneteenth*.
I am grateful to Nicole Lindenberg, an Ellison scholar at the University of Münster,
who has given excellent advice on the selection of the additional notes. Lindenberg
is presently at work editing a comprehensive collection of the voluminous notes on
the second novel in the Ellison papers at the Library of Congress.

urgent possession of Ellison's mind during the act of writing. After his death, I found the notes every which way in Ellison's papers. As far as I could tell, they had not been arranged in any particular order. What follows is a selection and sequence of notes that I hope will give the reader a sense of Ellison thinking through the characters, scenes, themes, and method of his ambitious, extended saga of America told and hinted at in *Juneteenth*.

---

*Book II can start with shooting and go through Bliss fighting the dwarf, then Hickman recalling visit to Lincoln Memorial and then go into dream sequence of Senator ending with car.

Hickman's purpose has been to have conversation with Senator and he gets a run around. There is a reversal for when he does see the Senator it is during an assassination attempt and he gets to see him in hospital where he is forced (like Brer Rabbit in the briar patch) to go—all this constituting a passion; for here he strives to keep the Senator alive so that he can learn what happened to Bliss, and how his own plans went wrong. Perception must come at end of book which will be Hickman with his recapitulation of the tragic incident which set off entire complex action.

What are the poles on which the action is hung?

They are a lynching, heart attack and illegitimate birth, during which Hickman delivers a baby.

2) The interruption of a tent service by a white woman who
tries to steal baby from Negroes;
3) An attempt by a suicidal gunman to assassinate U.S. senator during a speech in the Senate.

Underneath this there are themes, actions of a little boy who runs away and transforms himself into a different identity, the search of that child for its unknown mother,

2) The search for a group of old religious Negroes for their
   lost child preacher
3) The search by Hickman for his lost adopted child.

---

*Action takes place on the eve of the Rights movement but it fore-
casts the chaos which would come later. This is a reversal of expec-
tations to consider inasmuch as it reaches beyond the frame of the
fiction. This looks forward to the reassertion of the Klan and the
terrible, adolescent me-ism of the '70s.

---

*Plot? Perhaps one could look back after twenty years from the
perspective of the new illusion which the black militants are attempting to put into action.

Remember that "the essence of the story is what goes on in the
minds of the characters on a given occasion." The mind becomes
the real scene of the action. And in the mind scene and motive are
joined. Even the opposing characters are transferred there as images.

The method is naturally antiphonal. Senator and Rev. Hickman,
little Bliss and Daddy Hickman. The antiphonal section, or Emancipation myth, is spun out in hospital where Senator confesses to Hickman under pressure of conscience, memory and Hickman's questions
and it takes form of Bliss's remembered version versus Hickman's
idiomatic accounts.

The thing to remember about the antiphony between Daddy
Hickman and little Bliss is that the two are building a scene within
a scene and it must be on a borderline between the folk poetry and
religious rhetoric. Thing to do is to point it up.

The sermon of Hickman and Bliss which takes place on June-teenth must be related to later speeches made by the Senator while in Washington. . . . The rhythms of all this should feed back one upon the other proving not only perspectives by incongruity, but ironies, and some measure of comedy.

———————

Make Washington function in Hickman's mind as a place of power and mystery, frustration and possibility. It is historical, it is the past, it is slavery, the Emancipation and a continuation of the betrayal of the Reconstruction. He would have to imagine or try to imagine what Bliss knew about the city and its structure of power. He would wonder how, given his early background, Bliss could have gone so far in the gaining and manipulation of power, the juxtapositions of experience and intelligence which allowed him to make his way.

———————

Hickman has staked a great part of his life on the idea that by bringing up the boy with love, sacrifice and kindness he would do something to overcome the viciousness of racial division. He accepted Bliss's mother's most incongruous request in desperation. Hate would not assuage his grief over his brother's lynching and his mother's death so he takes the baby, becomes a minister, brings the boy up as a little minister and then suffers when the boy runs away. Yet does not lose his idea, instead it intensifies his faith. It drives him to keep up with the boy's career, especially when boy becomes a politician, and it takes him to Washington when he learns that he is in danger. He wants to talk to learn what happened, what lead to break and to negative acts toward Negroes after boy became powerful. Was it perversity, or was it that the structure of power *demanded* that anyone acting out the role would do so in essentially the same way?

———————

Hickman is intelligent but untrained in theology. Skilled with words, he reads and mixes his diction as required by his audience. He is also an artist in the deeper sense and has actually been a jazz musician. He has been a ladies' man, but this ceased when he became a preacher. Devout and serious, he is unable to forget his old, profane way of speaking and of thinking of experience. Vernacular terms and phrases bloom in his mind even as he corrects them with more pious formulations. In other words he is of mixed culture and frequently he formulates the sacred in profane terms—at least within his mind. Orally he checks himself.

———————————

Proposition: A great religious leader is a "matter of ecstasy." He evokes emotions that move beyond the rational onto the mystical. A jazz musician does something of the same. By his manipulation of sound and rhythm he releases movements and emotions which allow for the transcendence of everyday reality. As an ex-jazzman minister Hickman combines the two roles, and this is the source of his leadership. He possesses a power which is not directly active—or at least not recognized for what it is in the South's political arena, but it is there.

———————————

*[Hickman] tells Bliss: "Boy, you have a white skin and that's a natural fact, but the truth isn't in the fact, it's in the spirit. There is a world of difference between facts and truth, boy."

———————————

Bliss, [Hickman] said, there are facts and there is truth; don't let the facts ever get in the way of your recognizing and living out the truth. And don't get the truth confused with the law. The law deals with facts, and down here the facts are that we are weak and inferior. But while it looks like we are what the law says we are, don't ever forget that we've been put in this position by force, by power of numbers, and the readiness of those numbers to use brutality to keep us within the law. Ah, but the truth is something else. We are not what the law, yes and custom, says we are and to protect our truth we have to protect ourselves from the definition of the law. Because the law's facts have made us *outlaws*. Yes, that's the truth, but only part of it; for Bliss, boy, we're outlaws in Christ and Christ is the higher truth.

Hickman tells Bliss, "Little boy, we have a covenant, but when you ran away you broke it. You fell down, Bliss; you fell down. But that doesn't change a thing. Not for you, not for me, ever . . . '

Negroes appear to whites to enjoy themselves more because they have so little of that which is material. They appear to whites to suffer grief, heartbreak, and sadness more because they have, apparently, so much to be unhappy about. And the source of that unhappiness is seen as based in their color and social status rather than in their humanity.

Hickman has tried to teach Bliss not to turn himself into a figure based upon the materialization of himself, i.e., into someone whose identity is based upon color alone. He has tried to teach him to see himself and those close to him in terms of their inner spirit, their human quality, their quiet, understated heroism.

---

*Bliss, Hickman said, you have a history and it has to do with your being with us. You can try to ignore it but you'll find that it won't let you alone. It's in you, boy and it won't be denied.

For a little while two people grasped one another and something happened and that something was you, boy. That was history and all the rest was mystery. History was there before it happened and it was there afterwards. So you have to go on living with the mystery just like the rest of us do.

History must resonate in the background, thus counterpointing the subjective action. (make chart of what happened between [Bliss's] birth and his reaching D.C.)

Note: US Grant's determination was needed to end slavery, while his inadequacy as a politician led to the betrayal of the Reconstruction and the Golden Age. Nevertheless, the slaves were freed.

————————

[Hickman] has his own unique way of looking at the U.S. and is much concerned with the *meaning* of history. There is mysticism involved in his hope for the boy, and an attempt to transcend the hopelessness of racism. After the horrors connected with or coincidental with his coming into possession of the child he reverts to religion and in his despair begins to grope toward a plan. This involves bringing up the child in love and dedication in the hope that properly raised and trained the child's color and features, his inner substance and his appearance would make it possible for him to enter the wider affairs of the nation and work toward the betterment of his people and the moral health of the nation.

————————

Bliss symbolizes for Hickman an American solution as well as a religious possibility. Hickman thinks of Negroes as the embodiment of American democratic promises, as the last who are fated to become the first, the downtrodden who shall be exalted.

————————

But he is tested in every way by the little boy—and especially after the boy has run away. These are ideas when grasped at their fullest, and they go to the heart of the American dilemma as far as Negroes are concerned. Hickman is tested of his faith in his own people and in his belief in America. A question of fatherhood in one sense, and in terms of his maturity, his spiritual maturity also. H. affirms ultimately for himself, to save his own sanity and soul. He clings to an idea and urges his people to do the same because he sees in this direction an affirmation of his own humanity. To surrender Bliss, or the hope symbolized by the child, is to accept not only defeat but chaos, human depravity.

---

*Hickman to Bliss after the child has seen a photograph of lynching: "Bliss boy, you are free because you were given a life here among us and the conditions under which you can leave and live among the others. Because the Lord saw to it that you're not simply white or black, you're both and therefore you have a choice that most of our folks don't have. But there's a catch in it, Bliss; because while you might think that having such a freedom of choice is a blessing and an easy matter to deal with, the freedom that lies in the shade of skin and the shape of bones and texture of hair is simple to think about, but if you ever put it to a test in action you're going to find that it's terrible freedom that is based on such things as you see in that picture. Still, you have an advantage that few folks, not even the President, have. And that's because you have seen us from the inside and when you have seen them from inside you can know the truth and choose."

Hickman and the old Negroes have learned charity, hope, and faith under the most difficult conditions.

"Bliss, you can count on this: I'll be there when you finally are forced to remember me!"

"I never want to remember," Bliss had replied.

---

*When told of Negro history Bliss tells Hickman, "I don't like it. I don't want it."

"But it's not something you can reject, Bliss. It's in you, it's all around you."

"But it's mean, and I don't want it."

Hickman knows the true identity of Sunraider through having had friends and members of his church keep an eye on the runaway. This had continued over the years, and he has opposed anyone who thought of exposing Sunraider—even though Sunraider's political position appalls him and he holds his peace out of the compact he made after the third time Bliss ran away and was caught, and out of loyalty to his old dream. He also feels guilty for his role in Sunraider's career of deception and prays that the Senator will change his ways. Hickman despises the man, but loves the boy whom the man had been.

---

*He hates them and he hates us, he thought. And because he'll never be sure that he is legitimately one of them he'll always be vulnerable; and he hates us because he *knows* that he was one of us and that we know who he is or was and what he is beyond any consideration of blood. So he outrages them and savages us to prove that he is superior to both sides. Yes, but without them to hate and us to despise what is he? How did it start and how will it end? If I had known who his father really was would I have taken the child and tried anyway? Run the risk of all that disappointment and the knowledge that I might be fattening another frog for the snakes?

This society is not likely to become free of racism, thus it is necessary for Negroes to free themselves by becoming their idea of what a free people should be.

A novel about the rootless American type—products of our loneliness. Those who reject the self in favor of some illusion, who while proclaiming themselves democrats thirst and hunger for aristocracy.

Who become actors and confidence men, demagogues, swindlers, and spiteful destroyers of the nation.

----

*Bliss: a fallen minister, a manipulator of images, an orator, a player upon American possibilities, a seeker for self, a defier of social structuring or hierarchy, a sometimes rationalist who is also obsessed by his need to reject his given past of class and race but who would extend the sensibility of those he left behind through negative, insulting pressures. He'd reject their love, their humanity while pointing them toward ways of realizing the values for which he deserted them. He'd have it both ways: hate and love, rejection and guidance never realizing how shady his values are in comparison with Hickman's humanity. Progress, nihilism.

Innocence of a vicious American type which despoils, murders, and exploits while claiming the best of intentions.

Bliss rejects Christianity as sapping of energies, Hickman sees it as a director of energies. In this he foreshadows Martin Luther King, while Sunraider repeats the betrayals of the past.

Bliss, the little boy, learns the viciousness of the human condition while missing its grandeur, precisely because he was catapulted into manhood too early.

Bliss has seen fear on faces of Negroes, the white woman has called herself his mother; Hickman and [Sister Bearmasher] have taken redhead to town; Bliss has been taken home by Negro woman and there he raises her gown during night. Next day he is taken to see Hickman, who has been beaten. He feels guilty over beating, believing that it is connected with his being snatched by the white woman and with his having raised the nightgown. On the other hand he is fascinated by the white woman and tries to follow her, is brought back by church member. Later when Hickman is recovering he takes Bliss to see movie and it is here that Bliss begins to have fantasy that his mother is one of the white stars.

———————

Bliss's coffin is a threshold, a point between life and death. Note that after its symbolism of rebirth (Christian) he does indeed find rebirth—but in an ironic reversal he becomes white and anything but the liberator he was being trained to become.

———————

Bliss realizes political and social weakness of Hickman and other Negroes when he's taken from his coffin, and this becomes mixed with his yearning for a mother—whom he now identifies with the redheaded woman who tried to snatch him from his coffin. Which was a symbol of resurrection in drama of redemption that Hickman has structured around it. But he goes seeking for life among whites, using the agency of racism to punish Negroes for being weak, and to achieve power of his own. As with [the] man, [the] politician's politics is a drama in which he plays a role that doesn't necessarily jibe with his own feelings. Nevertheless he feels humiliated by a fate that threw him among Negroes and deprived him of the satisfaction of knowing whether he is a Negro by blood or only by culture and upbringing. He tells himself that he hates Negroes but can't deny his love for Hickman. Resents this too.

He is a man who sees the weakness in the way of social hierarchy has dealt with race and it is through the chink that he enters white society and exploits it.

———————

He is a rootless man, an American who has turned upon his loneliness and twisted it into spite and opportunism. He is full of nameless fears and in seeking to overcome them he bypasses the humanizing influence of that mastery, since this would require that he accept himself and his past, and uses the insight to destroy others. The center does not hold.

> "Things fall apart; the center cannot hold
> Mere anarchy is loosed upon the world.
> The ceremony of innocence is drowned;
> The best lack all conviction, while the worst
> Are full of passionate intensity."

That is, "Let us break bread together," is counterposed by the drowning of innocence, the assassination of character, the destruction of belief.

————————

Bliss, remembering Hickman's talks about R. W. Emerson, refers to his motion-picture camera as a "transparent eyeball." Through which he is able to see possibility in its latent state, his "blue glass" peers into blue scenes and characters but he is unable to see that which he looks upon.

————————

Bliss's purpose (immediate) is got get money to carry him further west. Secondarily and psychologically, it is to manipulate possibility and identities of the townspeople and to take revenge upon his own life. And to play! He is the artist as child in this.

————————

The more Bliss plays with the camera as a means of forgetting, then of denying, and then of distorting, burlesquing, the more he is forced to forget the old identity and to speculate upon what it might have meant and what it might have become. Thus he abandons art. Each adventure is thus no mere enclosure in his coffin, but a plunge into death. But with no Hickman standing over him, and no congregation singing and rejoicing and shouting that he (and they), the spirit, has been once more resurrected. He turns then to more malicious means of denial—he wants to emphasize their otherness of skin, or through their skin—by playing upon their own urge to denial. This is destructive and criminal and anti-human. Hickman knows this, just as Bliss knows this. Humanity *must* reside somewhere else.

———————

The point to stress has to do with what Bliss learns from his scam, and this has to do with the relationship between the movies and politics, and the American's uncertainty as to his identity as an area exploited by the movies and politics alike. . . . He ties this in with his seduction of Severen's mother, which gives him a sense of creative potency. He realizes that he doesn't have to know who his parents were, and that he can create a political identity out of racial prejudice, and that this will not be questioned because it is centered not in biology and class, but in social power.

———————

Bliss is fascinated by moments of blackness between cinematic frames, and his life is hidden here much as his activities before becoming politician are hidden. "Look for me between the frames, in the dark . . ."

Consider possibility that there is an obligatory incident missing from his character.

There is the contradiction that he continued to love the old people but exchanges his obligation to them and to his past for the formal possibilities available to him through betrayal. The imposition of social hierarchy based upon color upon human values.

———————

Bliss's attacks on Negroes are a form of running away. He feels a guilt which he will not admit. His adventures with moving-making ditto. He is fascinated that the secret of film lies in the fact that most of the action which gives a movie movement lies between the frames, in the dark. Thus the viewer is manipulated in the dark and he is the manipulator. This carries into his politics, wherein his motives are hidden behind what appears as simple racial prejudice, but in his twisted way he sees himself as putting pressure on Negroes to become more powerful through political action. One of the implicit themes at work here is Hickman's *refusal* to act politically, his refusal to use politics as an agency for effecting change. And at this point we enter the historical circumstances of the fifties wherein the Negro ministers became overtly political through the agency of passive resistance.

Hickman, are you a minister-man or a minstrel man?

I'm both, I'm afraid—But remember, the Word is tricky!

N.B. For Bliss the riddle of the Sphinx takes the form of his recognizing that Americans are actors, thus his manipulating the camera. But this leads to his further confusing his own basic confusion when he impregnates Severen's mother; which, in a sense, returns him to and compounds the mystery of his own identity.

It is important to remember that Bliss's denial of Hickman is a denial of himself. It is a denial which grants him a certain freedom, but it is a chaotic freedom and leads to an uncertain psychological balance. He becomes compulsive on the subject of race, Negroes and racial mixing. Thus his denial of Severen and his refusal to see him or to accept his role of father. (The old American refusal to recognize its racial diversity.)

If his flight is a night-journey, it is one through blazing lights wherein he remains in part unseen—Except to the Negroes who monitor his activities.

Bliss suffers because, as Hickman tells him, he has tried to be a total individual. In doing so, he runs away from those who have provided him with completion. By becoming "white" he tried to make himself part of a whole which rejects his essence, and in doing this he poisons his spirit. Bliss the Senator, remains incomplete, Hickman and the others are his missing part. He seeks power but he has detached himself from his true source of power and by doing so he has turned himself into a political demon.

When Bliss moves among Northerners he's constantly surprised that he is aware of possibilities of which they seem unconscious—even though he realizes that they cannot *see* his background. Yet knows that this is also a matter of historical consciousness and that they have forgotten or have never known the real issues of American life. This is one reason that he enters politics. This is why he joins the Southerners; he realizes that they never stop playing their knowledge against the ignorance and disinterest of the Northerners. The strategy of the guerrilla fighter transposed to the world of politics.

Account of how Bliss disciplines himself for the use of power. To master his facial expression, to steel himself as to hide any trace of his Negro past, his southernness except when he can use it to confuse. His adaptation of religious rhetoric for political ends. Perhaps this could delineate differences in attitude imposed by race. And draw out cultural traits that make for a shared cultural identity.

*Sunraider is potentiality, a symbol of possibility.

His manipulation of the movies plays upon the townspeople's sense of mystery, their own and that of their section their state and their country.

He symbolizes "the promise" of the ideal democracy which cannot be kept. A symbol of the mystery at work beneath the order imposed by racism.

———————

Sunraider knows that the question of his having Negro blood isn't important, it is the fact that *he* himself can't be sure whether he has or not. Because he knows that many who think they don't, do. It is a matter flowing from the way society has been arranged, the power that flows from that arrangement. There is danger to his position because his own power depends upon the manipulation of race. As does the power of all politicians of any importance. That was the joke of it. The power was not biological or genetic, but man-made and political, economic . . . and immoral as far as the American ideal has a religious component.

———————

Hickman asks Bliss, "Boy, why didn't you stick to religion? You could have hustled people in the name of the Lord who has always been looking at you? But instead *you* go into politics—where people don't ever know who you *are*! They don't even *care*, as long as you tell them the lies they want to dream by. So you went into politics! You dared to trick the people in the one area that is where they *really* want to believe."

———————

*Bliss: But you were trying to shape me in your own image and even if yours is the image of God I still wanted to be myself, to have my own image.

Hickman: So you have acted in your own image? Is that what you've been doing, Bliss? Or is it that throughout all these long years you've been trying to destroy me/my image? The senator was silent, his eyes directed toward the ceiling.

"Perhaps only your image of me," he said.

Bliss, since you *had* to go the way you did, why didn't you pattern after Abraham Lincoln?

That time is dead, he's dead and they whipped him in the end.

But they had to kill him in order to stop him, Bliss. He had heart, boy. *That* was the man for you to follow. He was a big man, who had the mud between his toes. He knew pain and how to hold it and ride it out. He wasn't simple, Bliss. He was one of the most complicated of all the great men. He had been baptized in many streams.

Note: That sacrifice is required to overcome the background of racism, and to transform the effects of American history.

Faith, or indecision in faith, and the blues as a form which gives expression simultaneously to faith and doubt.

If a white child is brought up with Negroes he will fulfill the democratic promise—unless he becomes a racist.

---

*What would have happened if Hickman had found some way of giving Bliss a creative insight into his racial ambiguity?

The Running of the Sun. . . . A summer day's dying. Not long enough. The running of Sunraider is something else.

---

*How arrive at the whiteness of whiteness without dealing with the blackness of blackness? And how arrive at the blackness without dealing with its opposite, the whiteness of whiteness?

Both of these racial extremes lead to false conclusions, for the true direction is Americaness. And it is our "Americaness" which poses the problem and the mystery which transcends race, religion, country of natural origin, and previous condition of servitude.

---

*In this country whenever power and authority is concerned always look for the Negro in it, whether positive or negative. This seems obvious to me, since the basis and division of political power has always turned on the question of race no less than on wealth.

Hickman is "Jim" and Bliss is "Huck" who cut out for the Territory.

The Mississippi is not a "white" river, nor is it a Lady as Mark Twain knew, it is a muddy masculine son-of-a-bitch and marvelous.

C.L.R. James makes the point that it was slavery which helped release the eloquence of Abe Lincoln, which is true. It also released the eloquence of many who believed in the institution—but best of all, it was the source of Negro American art. This is not as paradoxical as it might first appear. Slavery has *always* been an institution which brought out the best as well as the worst in the human. It also produces some of that which was noblest in Northerners.

Nota Bene! This is not what I intended to write when I started. Therefore, there is something else to explore, to remember.

Albert and Anatole's objections to proliferation of dreams misses their function of revelations of psychic states, just as they miss the nature of my characters. Incompletion of form allows the reader to impose his own imagination upon the material with too little control from the author. Thus I don't like to show my work until it is near completion.

AFTERWORD: A NOTE TO SCHOLARS

At his death in 1994 Ralph Ellison left behind notes, typescripts, and computer printouts and disks: most likely, with one exception, everything he had done on the book, however fragmentary, over a forty-year period. That exception is what he called in a December 9, 1967, letter "a section of my work-in-progress" destroyed in the Plainfield, Massachusetts, fire that burned down the Ellisons' summer home ten days earlier. As I tried to discern one coherent, inclusive sequence, I realized slowly, somewhat against my will, that although Ellison had hoped to write one big book, his saga, like William Faulkner's, could not be contained within the pages of a single novel. Aiming, as Ellison had, at one complete volume, I proceeded to arrange his oft-revised, sometimes reconceived scenes and episodes according to their most probable development and progression. While doing so, I felt uneasily procrustean: Here and there limbs of the manuscript needed to be stretched, and elsewhere a protruding foot might be lopped off, if all the episodes were to be edited into a single, coherent, continuous work.

Now, the editor of a posthumously published novel should not use his own words to finish what the author left unfinished or unsaid. The state of the manuscript (or manuscripts) should determine editorial decisions, and, if all things are equal, the latest version of an author's manuscript should carry special authority. Appropriately, the problem of an authentic reader's edition was solved by the latest manuscripts of what Ellison had labeled Book II as early as 1958 or 1959. In it he had written a fiction whose action, characters, and prose show him in the prime of his imaginative, novelistic powers. Of the potential "three volumes" Ellison had referred to in 1970 but not yet finished, Book II had come to constitute an all but complete novel. Except for a very few, very brief passages written in the early 1990s, the novel is not Ellison's most recent effort, but it is the most ambitious and latest, freestanding, compelling, extended fiction in the saga. Moreover, it contains the story and relationship of the two principal characters at the heart of the work Ellison had set his sights on and described over the years.

From this manuscript (and the Prologue to Book I), in 1959 Ellison culled, stitched together, revised, and carefully edited the first published piece from the novel-in-progress, which appeared in Saul Bellow's *The Noble Savage* (1960) under the title "And Hickman Arrives." *Juneteenth,* then, consists of the following: "And Hickman Arrives"; Book II, whose latest manuscript, according to Mrs. Ellison's note, was retyped in 1972 and contains subsequent revisions and corrections made in Ellison's hand up until at least 1986; a thirty-eight-page manuscript referred to as "Bliss's Birth," now Chapter 15; one paragraph from "Cadillac Flambé" (*American Review,* 1973), inserted to give the Senator's speech in Chapter 2 greater continuity with the novel's final scene; and several words and brief passages from later versions of the Lincoln Memorial scene in Chapter 14 inserted to clarify and intensify the action. I should note that in addi-

tion to "And Hickman Arrives," Ellison published three other excerpts from Book II—"The Roof, the Steeple, and the People,"
"Juneteenth," and "Night-Talk." All appeared in the *Quarterly Review
of Literature* in 1960, 1965, and 1969, respectively, and now reappear in their appropriate places in this volume. Unlike "And Hickman Arrives," each is a continuous part of Book II, and Ellison's
photocopies of these three published excerpts contain a few small
corrections or additions in his hand. In cases of variation between
the previously published version of an episode and the manuscript,
I have opted for the former except in those instances when Ellison
has clearly revised *after* publication or when restoration of passages
deleted from the published version serves to heighten the meaning
and continuity of the narrative as a whole.

Ellison's entire manuscript has numerous space breaks, but
within Book II he did not designate chapters as such. As editor, I
have respected Ellison's breaks; in addition, keeping the reader in
mind, I have divided *Juneteenth* into chapters at appropriate points in
the manuscript and the action. At times, divergence between manuscript pagination and certain of Ellison's rather definitive notes in-
dicates that he had not reached a state of certainty about the
sequence of the action. Inevitably, in such matters much depends
upon an editor's taste and sense of the writer's intentions. For my
part, I have arranged Chapters 9 through 11 according to the sequence Ellison mapped out in an undated note outlining the narrative action from the time of the attempted kidnapping of Bliss to the
point when Hickman "takes Bliss to see movie and it is here that
Bliss begins to have fantasy that his mother is one of the movie
stars." Ellison also provided an important clue, this one silent, about
how to end *Juneteenth*. In this instance he added a key passage in different, larger typeface to page 284 of the most recent manuscript of
Book II. In a few words he brings the episode in question to climax

and closure. The passage projects what Ellison called "that aura of a summing up, that pause for contemplation of the moral significance of the history we've been through," and, therefore, it strengthened my impression of this scene as the most logical and emotional place to end the narrative that I think Ellison might have called *Juneteenth*.

Finally, there is the matter of editorial corrections to passages in the manuscripts that are the copy texts for this edition of *Juneteenth*. I have silently corrected matters of accidence, e.g., spelling "deification" for the typescript's "diefication." Occasionally, I have also made silent corrections on matters of substance, such as correcting erroneous quotation ("Full fathom five" for "Four fathom five"). For clarity's sake and to avoid a redundancy I believe Ellison would have addressed before publication, I have slightly pruned several passages in Chapter 2. In Chapter 3 I deleted two brief passages referring to a different speech than the one the Senator gives in Chapter 2. Lastly, I have not included an intriguing but clearly unfinished, unrevised episode Ellison seems tentatively to have tacked on to the end of the typescript of Book II. Because this edition of *Juneteenth* is a reader's edition, I have not encumbered its pages with lists of changes made for reasons of accidence or substance. A subsequent scholar's edition will document my corrections and include sufficient manuscripts and drafts to enable scholars and readers alike to follow Ellison's some forty years of work on his novel-in-progress. Upon publication of the scholarly edition, the notes and manuscripts in the Ellison papers at the Library of Congress will be available to those interested in working with them.

John F. Callahan
February 1999

POSTSCRIPT TO
THE AFTERWORD (2021)

It is fitting to note here that Professor Adam F. Bradley, author of *Ralph Ellison in Progress*, and I fulfilled the pledge I made to follow the first edition of *Juneteenth* with a scholar's edition of the manuscripts from Ellison's forty-plus years of work on his epic, unfinished novel. Bradley and I delivered on that promise in 2010 and 2011 when Penguin Random House published Modern Library hardcover and paperback editions of *Three Days Before the Shooting . . . The Unfinished Second Novel*.

Three Days includes the typescripts of Books I and II: Ellison's novel-length computer sequences, *Hickman in Washington, D.C.* and *Hickman in Georgia and Oklahoma,* as well as "McIntyre at Jessie Rockmore's"; two early drafts of the opening of Book II; eleven variants of the first paragraph of *Juneteenth*; and all eight excerpts from the second novel published by Ellison during his life. There are also two comprehensive introductions from the editors, an editor's note for every separate manuscript, and an important "Chronology of Composition," which is especially useful to readers of this Vintage International edition of *Juneteenth*.

John F. Callahan

February 2021